SHATTERED
STARS

By Hilary Norman

IN LOVE AND FRIENDSHIP
CHATEAU ELLA
SHATTERED STARS

SHATTERED STARS

*

HILARY NORMAN

Delacorte
Press

Published by
Delacorte Press
Bantam Doubleday Dell Publishing Group, Inc.
666 Fifth Avenue
New York, New York 10103

Library of Congress Cataloging in Publication Data

Norman, Hilary.
    Shattered stars / Hilary Norman.
      p.   cm.
    ISBN 0-385-30001-8 (hc) : $20.00
    I. Title.
PR6064.0743S47   1991   90-47855
823'.914—dc20   CIP

Manufactured in the United States of America

May 1991

10 9 8 7 6 5 4 3 2 1

BVG

C 2

For my sister, Helen

Acknowledgments

Numerous people and organizations assisted me during the research and writing of this novel, but I would especially like to thank the following (in alphabetical order):

David Balfour; Howard Barmad; Luigi Bernabò; Carolyn Caughey; Livia Dowland; Jackie Farber; Sara Fisher; Sharon Freedman; Grazia, of American Express, Florence; David Glenister and Jim Greenfield of Dorking; Michael E.J. Hackett, FRCS; Shelagh Harris; John Hawkins; Peter Horwitz; Michael Ingram; Josephine Inzerillo; Brian Levy; Mrs. H. Norman; Philippa Pride; The Saddlery, Salisbury, Connecticut; Susan Sheldon; Anne and Nicholas Shulman; Dr. Jonathan Tarlow; Michael Thomas; Rae White; Wendy Zimbler.

The Palio of Siena of August 1977 was won by Oca, the Noble Goose district, with a horse named Rimini. My account of that race is a fictitious one.

Contents

SHATTERED STARS

Part One
*
CHILDHOOD
*
1951–1959

Lucchesia, Tuscany
August 17, 1951

It always began and ended the same way.

First the wine, lifeblood of their family. Then the passion, loving, tender, and indestructible, his strong, large brown hands taking their fill of her heavy breasts, taking possession of her. His seed, thrust into her, rooting within her, thriving, draining her. The fleeting ecstasy of new life in her arms. And then the bleakness, bottomless and agonizing, the inexplicable, sinful pain that no one understood—for how could they, when she had never understood it herself?

It always began and ended the same way.

Chapter 1

THE SMALL STONE FARMHOUSE stood at the top of the gentle hill, the ruddy, cracked tiles of its roof silvered by the full moon, the terraced *sangiovese* vines rolling down the slope like a black carpet, the olive trees ethereal and ghostly, the tall cypresses marking out the boundaries like dark sentinels.

The Tuscan countryside slept, the land, punished by the grueling August sun, steaming a little even at midnight, drawing breath again beneath the starry sky, the hardworking *contadini* snoring in their beds, renewing themselves for another dawn.

Serafina Cesaretti, at thirty-one, had already borne five children, all of them conceived on nights such as this one, with the air, still hot and sultry, gliding through the open windows, mingling its perfume with the stale smells of her husband's evil-scented *toscano* cigar, the lingering aroma of their dinner, and sweat.

The house was silent. Upstairs, the children slept, all in one room, except for the baby, Giacomo, whose crib stood in his parents' bedroom. Vittorio, the oldest at eleven; Francesca, aged nine; the five-year-old twins, Luciano and Giulietta—all good children. And their father, Giulio, surely slept too, drunk from *vino rosso.*

✶

Serafina sat, alone, staring out of the window. Outside, invisible cicadas droned incessantly and a dog, somewhere nearby, barked, but Serafina did not hear them.

They had danced earlier that evening, a wild tarantella, Giulio dancing with verve, in spite of a bellyful of his favorite *ribollita*, pausing only to refill his wineglass and to plant kisses on Serafina's wide mouth, while the two older children laughed and clapped. Until the dance had become lustier and less controlled, their father perspiring and panting with manifest, crass desire, their mother, too, working herself up, reaching a hysterical crescendo of what seemed to her, suddenly, to be a *danza di morte*—a dance of death.

And Vittorio and Francesca had eyed one another uneasily, and had crept quietly and unnoticed upstairs. And soon after, Giulio had given one final and joyously suggestive thrust of his crotch, and then staggered up the narrow steps to await his wife in their worn-down bed.

And now Serafina sat, alone.

She had been born in the Tremezzina, near the shores of Lake Como, with the blond hair, blue eyes, and slender height of many of the German-descended people in the north of Italy; had grown up with the sweet breath of Switzerland behind her, with no desire to leave, until she had gone, as an eighteen-year-old, on holiday to Florence, and had met the Cesaretti brothers, two men as dissimilar in character, taste, and style as it was possible for siblings to be. Bruno was nearly forty, the older by seven years, proprietor of a jewelry store on the Ponte Vecchio and married into an old and prosperous Florentine family. Giulio was slimmer than his brother, with more hair and darker, more shining eyes; he was less mature for his age—he loved sunshine, the land, wine, freedom, and sex. He had been offered a partnership in his brother's business, but had turned it down, choosing to work his own small piece of Tuscan soil. Serafina fell in love with Giulio on the afternoon of their first meeting, and he with her. The life he brought her to was hard but worthwhile. She wanted babies as much as her husband did, wanted to perfect the earthy happiness of their marriage and thought her life replete when she held Vittorio, their firstborn, in her arms.

Until the despair had begun. "Postpartum depression," it would have been labeled had she been in a city hospital or registered with a good obstetrician. But Vittorio was born in his parents' bed in the Tuscan countryside, on June 11, 1940, the day after Italy entered the war, and there was no expensive doctor, only a busy midwife who cut the cord, washed the infant and placed him to his mother's breast before departing. So there was no diagnosis, no rational explanation for the bottomless black pit into which Serafina felt she had plummeted, and out of which it took all her strength to clamber. And when Francesca was born it was the same again—and with the twins—and with little Giacomo just a year ago.

And now she thought she might be pregnant again, though it was too soon to be certain. And if she was not, then with a man of Giulio's unquenchable libido, she soon would be. Especially after a night like this.

It always began this way.

Serafina rose from her hard chair. In her head, a ghostly tambourine began to jangle the persistent rhythm of the tarantella. Alone and silently, she started to dance again.

The tambourine seemed to urge her on. *But to what?* she asked herself. *And for what?* To go upstairs to Giulio—to spread her legs and open herself to him again, to let him pour himself into her. To sleep, at last, like a dead person, only to wake again to the same toil, the same struggle.

Serafina stopped dancing, stood stock-still in the center of the stone floor.

"*Sono pazza,*" she murmured. "I am insane."

She feared madness more than anything, woke every morning terrified that this might be the day when she would finally snap completely, that she might injure one of the children. Even worse, she was tormented by the idea that she might have passed her insanity on to them. She quailed at the prospect of another pregnancy, another birth. Not the physical suffering, but what would follow—another demanding, screaming mouth greedily grasping at her breasts—more months of that burrowing, mindless agony when no one would comprehend her anguish.

She began to dance again. On and on, faster and faster, panting now, mewing with pain, only just able to stop herself from screaming out loud. She could not stop dancing. Like the victim of the spider's venom, she wanted to dance on and on into oblivion. She kicked off her soft shoes, felt the cool stone beneath her feet. She unbuttoned her blouse, let it slide from her arms—then her skirt, spilling onto the ground. Her twirling, pale reflection in the dark window taunted her. *Una pazza*—dancing alone in her underclothes.

"I am evil," she whispered, still whirling. *"Sinful."* She had not been to mass or confession for more than two years—not even after she tried, in vain, to end her last pregnancy.

The perspiration trickled down her face and body in runnels, sprinkling the floor. Outside, in the night, clouds covered the moon and stars, swiftly propelled by an unseasonable sirocco sweeping up from the south and making the air even more unbearably oppressive. The music in Serafina's head grew louder, a monstrous clamor, so that, still dancing, she thrust her hands up over her ears to try to blot it out.

"I want to die," she heard herself moan. But if she died now, if God in all his mercy struck her down, she would surely go to hell for all eternity, punished for her wickedness.

Unless she could find a way to purify herself before it was too late. If it was not already too late.

Still spinning, breathless, heart pounding, she began to tear off her remaining clothes—her slip, her brassiere, her panties, her fingernails ripping her skin in her urgency. She must be naked to be purged, naked as an innocent, newborn child.

Serafina thought of the embryonic being perhaps already nestling within her, depending utterly upon her, and she clasped her stomach protectively, swept by the sudden absolute conviction that this child must be spared, saved from the agonies of life.

Abruptly, she stopped dancing, stumbling and dizzy, but quite blinded by the clarity of her revelation. *This child must not be born into suffering.* It must go to God untainted by her sins.

✶

Serafina knew what she must do. The ultimate release. The hot, humid night bore down on her, suffocating, unendurable. She could not wait any longer.

Fire. Cleansing, purifying, sanctifying.

She was calm now, no longer hearing the relentless beat of the tambourine. Her movements were smooth and deliberate, her tortured mind suddenly quiescent, lulled by resolve, by the knowledge of imminent salvation. She glided, barefoot, into the small kitchen, opened the door of the larder, took out the metal container of paraffin oil and a box of matches.

On she went, padding through the scullery, unscrewing the top of the container, already pouring some of the *paraffina* onto the palm of her right hand and beginning to spread it over her body, anointing her breasts, her belly, rubbing it into her blond pubic hair and onto her thighs.

And with each footstep the oil splashed down over the floor of the scullery, trailing her as she went out of the door into the tiny backyard, where she laid the matchbox down, carefully, and straightened herself again.

"Santa Maria," she began, and stopped. She was not yet fit to pray, not while she was still too steeped in mortal sin for her prayers to be heard. Only through this ancient ritual, this *purificazione,* might she, or at least her unborn child, be granted absolution.

Serafina did not hesitate. She raised the container high, holding it in both her hands, and poured every last drop of the oil over herself. It drenched her hair, filled her nostrils and trickled into her mouth. The smell was pungent, choking, her eyes streamed with tears, but still she did not falter, longing for this last agony, yearning for the end.

Silently, she put down the empty can and picked up the matchbox. For one moment, she looked up into the sky, seeking just one star, hoping for something she did not quite understand, one tiny, consoling particle, perhaps, of infinity. But there was nothing, only the angry, stormy blackness.

✴

Serafina's sigh was little more than a whisper. With fingers slippery from paraffin, but which scarcely even trembled, she opened the little box and took out a match—

She heard the rasp as she struck it. And then the first gentle, rushing sound as she touched it to her hair. And she saw a mad, kaleidoscopic flash of color sweep past her face. And the flames slithering swiftly down, squeezing and licking at her like icy-cold serpents.

And Serafina looked down, and the last thing she saw was the round white flesh of her breasts melting as the fire began to devour her, and at last, from deep within her, came a long, hideous, dying scream. And in her final conscious moments, she began to whirl again in her *danza di morte,* spinning in a frenzied, flaming human vortex—

And the sirocco gathered force, and blew, like an evil, whistling demon, toward the little Tuscan farmhouse, puffed the snaking wall of fire over the threshold, greedily sucking up the spilled puddles of oil. And caught the faded fabric curtains that Serafina had hung, in optimism, a dozen years before, at the scullery window.

✴   ✴   ✴

Vittorio woke first, stirred from sleep by a strange, dull crackling sound from below.

"*Cosa c'è?*" He sat up, sniffing, instinctively, like a dog. Realization dawned, and he sprang, terrified, from the bed. "*Incendio!*" he shouted, and shook his sister roughly. "Francesca, wake up, for God's sake, the house is on fire!"

She stirred, and was abruptly wide awake. "What's wrong?" Her dark, almost black eyes gazed up at him fearfully. "What's happened!"

Vittorio ran to the door, opened it a crack and slammed it again. "*Dio!*" He stared toward the twins. "Francesca, get them up, quick as you can—try not to scare them."

"What about Mamma and Papa?"

Vittorio dashed over to the basin on the dresser, wet a flannel, and ran back to the door. "Just get them up, and then tear all the sheets into strips and knot them together!"

Francesca, tall for her nine years, began to shake Luciano out of his deep sleep. "What are you doing? Where are you going!"

"I'll be right back. Now get *moving!*" Clamping the wet flannel over his nose and mouth, he opened the door again and slipped swiftly out, closing it securely behind him. The landing was already starting to fill with smoke, and he could see flames at the bottom of the staircase.

"Papa!" he yelled, and opened his parents' bedroom door, choking as the smoke, much thicker inside the room, engulfed him. His father lay supine on the bed, out cold and immovable.

"*Mamma!*" Vittorio screamed, but received no answer. Acting on blind instinct, he turned to where he knew his baby brother lay in his crib, and snatched him up. Giacomo's body lolled limply in his arms, and a shiver of dread prickled down Vittorio's spine, but he forced himself not to think, only to act.

Back in their room, the smoke had begun to filter through, and all the children were coughing badly, despite the open window. The door burned Vittorio's hand as he shut it quickly, but the first of the flames had whipped past him, licking around the walls, seeking nourishment and finding it within seconds in a woven rug on the floor.

The two blond five-year-olds huddled together near the window, Giulietta screaming with terror, Luciano staring wordlessly as their older sister doggedly knotted strips of sheeting, and Vittorio placed Giacomo, tenderly, on his bed.

"Give him to Giulietta," Francesca said, not pausing in her work. "He will occupy her."

"No."

At the starkness of his tone, Francesca looked up, startled, but the grimness in his eyes kept her silent.

"*Dov'è Mamma?*" Luciano's voice was tight and small.

"Outside, safe."

Giulietta stopped screaming. "Why can't we go to her?"

"We will, *piccola,* in a minute." Feeling dizzy, his eyes sore and streaming, Vittorio took one end of the knotted rope, tied it firmly to the foot of Francesca's bed, and dragged it to the window. "You first," he told Francesca.

She stared fearfully at the rope. "I can't!"

He slung the sheeting over the narrow sill into the dark. *"Fa presto,"* he ordered her. "Climb down."

Her lower lip quivered. "The little ones—"

Vittorio seized her hands and placed them on the rope. "I'll lower them down after you, *cara*— you have to be down there to help them."

White-faced and trembling, Francesca clambered onto the sill.

"Go *on!*"

Francesca launched herself out into the night, her eyes screwed tightly shut, her heart pounding to bursting point. The world spun around her, smoke now belching out from the house, smothering her— and then suddenly there was no more sheeting for her feet to twist around, and she was dangling by her hands. She screamed, her wrists wrenching as she hung on for dear life—

"Jump!" Vittorio's hoarse voice bellowed from above. "It's not far! You must *jump*, Francesca!"

She let go, and hit the ground with a great thump.

"Francesca!"

She was too winded to answer, gingerly flexing her limbs.

"Francesca!"

The desperation of the moment penetrated her befuddled brain, and she scrambled to her feet. "I'm all right!" she yelled back. "Hurry up!"

Rapidly, Vittorio hauled the rope back up and tried to loop the end around Giulietta's waist, but she shrieked and struggled so wildly that he turned, in despair, to her twin, praying that the bedroom door would continue to hold back the real force of the fire.

"Forza, Luciano!" he urged encouragingly.

The child clung to his sister. "I can't!"

"Sure you can. Show Giulietta how it's done."

The little boy, trusting his older brother implicitly, relaxed his hold on his twin, and dumbly allowed Vittorio to tie the sheeting under his arms. Swiftly, Vittorio lifted him up onto the window ledge. "Francesca!" he yelled. "Catch Luciano, then untie the rope!"

Behind him, Giulietta's screams trebled piercingly, and Vittorio spun around to see that her nightdress and long blond hair were on fire. Flinging himself onto her, knocking her to the floor, he beat out the flames with his bare hands, feeling no pain, aware only of his little sister's piteous shrieks of agony, which stopped, mercifully, when she fainted.

Snatching her up, Vittorio ran back to the window, coughing and choking. He tested the rope, found it weightless and pulled it back up.

Giulietta lolled in his aching arms, and Vittorio's heart twisted as he saw the raw burns on her shoulders and chest. His lungs strained almost beyond endurance, he tied the sheeting around her waist and raised the unconscious child over the sill—

With a great thundering roar, the door burst open, and all the searing weight and power of the blaze roared into the room. The knotted sheeting, scorched and stretched past breaking point, ripped apart, sending Giulietta plummeting to the ground.

"*Mamma!*" Vittorio screamed, tears of anguish and terror and sheer, unspeakable panic coursing down his cheeks. Dimly he saw Giacomo's tiny body lying still inert on his bed. Grabbing him up, he held him to his chest.

"*Papa!*"

The heat was unbearable. Vittorio flung one leg over the window ledge, saw certain death behind him and a terrifying void before him.

Tightly, he clasped his baby brother in his arms, and closed his eyes. And jumped.

Chapter 2

THEY WERE REALLY the most fortunate of children.

To be sent to Florence. To the Palazzo Speroza, the home of Bruno and Livia Cesaretti, uncle and aunt to the surviving, orphaned children of Giulio and Serafina.

Palazzo Speroza. It sounded so grand, so forbidding—so magnificent. Yet in truth, in a city crowded with exquisite and superb Gothic, Renaissance, and Mannerist palazzi, the only one of those three adjectives suited to Palazzo Speroza was "forbidding."

It had always been a smaller, lesser structure, more of a great, gloomy house than a palace. And then, adding further insult, it had been converted, for financial motives, into apartments. The Cesaretti family inhabited the most spacious, and also the darkest, of these apartments, taking up the ground and first floors, with the advantage of a small inner courtyard, and the disadvantage of a damp, smelly cellar. The Cesarettis owned the largest apartment because Livia was, by birth, a member of the Speroza family, and if she, secretly, might have preferred, as fervently as Bruno, her husband, to live in a sunny, airier villa outside the city, her innate Florentine pride would never allow her to admit it.

"What fortunate children you are," the *principale* of the orphanage in Pisa had told them for the umpteenth time, as he had seen them onto the Florence-bound train, one month after the fire. He had shaken his head, as if in wonder. "Penniless peasants, to be plucked from destitution to luxury."

Vittorio, his right leg heavily plastered, had longed to trip up the callous old man with one of his crutches, but he had looked grimly at Francesca, holding Luciano's hand, and had restrained himself.

"Are we going to see Giulietta today?" asked Luciano, as soon as they were on board.

"Not today, *piccolo*," Vittorio said gently.

"Why not?"

"She's still in the hospital, *caro*," Francesca reminded him.

"Vittorio was in the hospital, but he's with us now," the five-year-old reasoned.

"He wasn't so badly hurt as Giulietta."

Luciano's face crumpled. "Poor Giulietta."

Francesca, her face pale, her long black hair fastened tightly into a plait, sat straight and still, staring unseeing out of the window.

"So when *can* we see her?" Luciano persisted. On the subject of his twin sister, he was rarely to be diverted for long. With the simplicity of his five years, he had been able to accept that his mother, father, and baby brother were dead—or at least, that God had snatched them out of the flames that had consumed their house, and that he would not see them again until it was his turn to go to *paradiso*. After all, he had seen with his own eyes the ruin of their home, and it was better to think of Mamma and Papa and Giacomo in heaven than in that black, charred tomb.

Giulietta, however, was another matter. She had not gone with God —she had emerged from the fire just as he had, except that she had fallen onto the ground, and had been taken away in the *ambulanza* with Vittorio. But he was here, on the train, almost well except for his leg and the bandages on his hands, but of Giulietta there was still no sign.

"I want to see her," he said mutinously.

"Soon, *piccolo*, soon," Francesca soothed him.

"No, now!"

"Shut up," Vittorio said roughly.

They didn't understand. No one could understand the way it was between Luciano and his twin. He adored his older brother and sister, often liked them better than Giulietta, for the twins had quite contrasting personalities, and often fought. But their closeness was of a different kind, at least for Luciano, for he sometimes knew what his twin sister was *thinking*. They were always together—they had never been apart before.

He needed her.

Both Francesca and Vittorio had felt, ever since the fire, that they were tightly held in the grip of a ghastly living nightmare from which they still, despite themselves, prayed they might wake. It was too much to take in. The loss of their parents, of a brother, of their home and possessions—of everything familiar and comforting and *normal*. Too much.

The moment, however, that they stood before the great, dismal, rusticated stone edifice in the Via dei Vecchietti—at that moment, all the dread and horror and grief that had, until now, been held back by a wall of sheer disbelief, smothered them so chokingly that they could hardly breathe.

"What is this?" Luciano's small voice wafted uncertainly up to them as they all climbed, silently, from the big black car in which Guido, their uncle's chauffeur, had driven them from the Stazione Centrale.

"*Questo è Palazzo Speroza,*" the chauffeur told him gently, the shock and dismay of the older children transmitting itself to him.

"But this is not a palace!"

The street in which they stood was a fine Florentine street, and the palazzo, like so many other buildings in Tuscany, based upon Michelozzo's great Medici Palace—a small, mediocre copy of that extraordinary house, in fact—was quite an impressive structure; but to a five-year-old child of the countryside, used to an infinite, natural horizon, his knowledge of the unexplored world gleaned chiefly from fairy tales, this ugly, dark building couldn't possibly be a palace. If anything, it was a dungeon.

Pulling herself together, Francesca took Luciano's hand firmly in hers. "This is a city palace, *piccolo.*" She managed a smile. "Wait until you see inside."

Vittorio still stood motionless, wordless and appalled, leaning heavily on his crutches.

Guido rang a bell at the side of the heavy bronze door.

Several moments passed. The car was parked, snugly, against the wall, and the children stood, in an agony of suspense, on the pavement, so narrow that it was little more than a rim edging the buildings.

The door opened. Francesca, holding Luciano close, felt a wave of temporary relief. Though their uncle had visited Lucchesia periodically, he had only once been accompanied by his wife, and Francesca had a vague, unpleasant recollection of a cold, elegant, withdrawn woman. The girl in the doorway was clearly a servant, dressed in black, but young and pretty.

"*Ciao,* Maria," Guido greeted her.

She stood back to allow them to enter. Guido made the introductions, handed Maria the small plastic suitcase that held their few remaining possessions, and stepped back.

"I must go," he said. "I wish you good fortune." He gave his hand to Vittorio, who shook it as strongly as he could, and then stooped to Francesca. "*Coraggio, signorina,*" he whispered in her ear, ruffled Luciano's hair, and was gone.

Maria closed the door. The sound was solid and final. The children glanced at one another.

"Signora Cesaretti is in the *salotto.*" The girl smiled at them. "I will take you to her."

She wore a creamy linen dress, tight-waisted with an oval skirt, and navy and cream high-heeled shoes. She was supremely elegant, and with her dark brown hair drawn severely back from her pale, fine-boned face, she looked as chilly as Francesca had remembered her.

"*Buon giorno,*" she said. Her voice was low, but not at all mellow.

Vittorio looked at Livia Cesaretti, and knew, immediately, that he hated her. Francesca wished desperately that she could have washed and tidied herself before meeting their aunt. And Luciano began to cry.

"Was your journey tiresome?" She ignored the little boy, pretended not only that he was not weeping, but that he did not exist.

"Not very, thank you," Francesca answered.

The room in which they stood was wide, with a vaulted ceiling, and so long that only now did they notice a couch, at the far end, upon which two older children sat, unmoving. Their cousins.

Livia raised her left hand, palm up and gracious. "Letizia, Fabio—come and meet your cousins, please."

The children rose from the couch and walked unhurriedly toward the newcomers, their faces shrouded in shadows until they stood beside their mother, near an arched, barred window.

"This is your cousin Letizia." For the first time, Livia Cesaretti softened slightly, smiling as she indicated her daughter, dark-haired, brown-eyed and round-faced, like her father.

"*Buon giorno*," Francesca said politely.

"How do you do." The response was stiff, hostile.

"And this is Fabio," continued Livia.

Her son, at thirteen, was far better looking than his sister. With good bone structure and paler, more aristocratic skin than Letizia, Fabio was clearly a Speroza, resembling markedly at least two of the ancestral portraits that hung around the *salotto*.

He nodded, but said nothing.

For the first time since getting out of the car, Vittorio spoke. "Where is our uncle?"

"He will be here shortly," Livia replied. "For luncheon." She glanced down at Luciano, who had stopped crying but was still a picture of misery. "You will want to change, I expect." She moved to a wall and pulled at a tasseled bell-cord. "Maria will show you to your rooms."

They had been allotted two bedrooms close to the kitchen on the ground floor, clearly part of the servants' quarters, though they would soon learn that Maria was the only member of the household staff who

now actually lived there. Before the war, there had been a full comple-
ment of resident servants, but nowadays both the cook, Louisa, and
Guido, who apparently doubled as chauffeur and general aide, reported
for work each morning and went home each night.

Francesca and Luciano were to share one room, with Vittorio alone
in the other.

"Where will Giulietta sleep?" was Luciano's first question when he
saw only three beds.

"They'll put in an extra bed as soon as she's better," Francesca told
him. "Perhaps Aunt Livia will let you both share a room."

Vittorio looked in on them. "She told us to change." He looked
ironically at the little case that contained only underwear, dressing
gowns, and a Bible.

"We'll just wash," Francesca said, yearning for cool water and soap,
for the house, as the rest of the city they'd driven through, was almost
unbearably hot. Their rooms had been dim and gloomy when Maria had
opened the doors, and Vittorio had quickly rolled up the wooden blinds
to let in what light there was, but with the meager sliver of sunshine had
come a great waft of stuffy heat and street noise.

"What did you think of her?" Vittorio asked Francesca.

"Aunt Livia?"

"*Sì.*"

Francesca unplaited her hair and shook it loose around her shoulders.
Her dark eyes were noncommittal. "She's quite beautiful."

"I hate her." Vittorio sat heavily down on Francesca's bed and
winced as his plastered leg struck the floor too hard.

"Why?" asked Luciano, letting Francesca undress him.

"Because she doesn't want us here."

Francesca shot her older brother a warning glance. "That isn't true,
Vittorio. We wouldn't be here if she didn't want us to come."

"We would if Uncle Bruno made her."

"What about our cousins?" Francesca asked.

Vittorio shrugged. "They're all snobs."

"I want to go home!" Luciano was close to tears again.

"Well, you can't," Vittorio said shortly.

"Why *not?*"

"You know why, *stupido.*"

"Don't be mean to him," Francesca said anxiously. "Come on, we'd better get ready. Uncle Bruno will be here in a minute, and we mustn't be late for lunch."

"I'm not hungry," Vittorio said mulishly.

"Of course you are. You're just tired and hot." Francesca went over to the hand basin and turned on the cold tap. There was a rumble from the pipes, and the water came at a slow trickle, tepid and murky. She wanted, suddenly, to cry, but for Luciano's sake, she had to keep up a cheery front.

"Some palazzo," Vittorio scoffed.

"We'll use the bathroom." She took Luciano's hand again. "Us first, *piccolo.*"

"*D'accordo.*" Vittorio's voice was dull.

Tentatively, Francesca bent down and kissed his cheek. She seldom told her older brother what to do—he had always been the leader, but since the fire the terrible anger eating away at him seemed to have dragged him down, so that she was, for the time being, the clearer thinker of the two.

Vittorio looked up at her, sullenness having given way to open, helpless misery. "How can we bear it, Francesca?" he appealed to her.

Decisively, she straightened up, and stood as tall as her four and a half feet would permit her. "We're together, *caro*, aren't we?"

Halfheartedly, Vittorio nodded.

"And soon Giulietta will be here too, right, Luciano?"

The little boy smiled up at her.

"We can bear it, Vittorio. We can bear *anything* so long as we have each other."

Uncle Bruno's entrance into the house, just as the three children emerged nervously from their rooms, was like a breath of fresh air.

"*Benvenuto, benvenuto, bambini!*" He beamed, tossing down his attaché case and opening his arms to them. "I am happy to see you."

Livia stepped into the entrance hall, Fabio and Letizia behind her. *"Buon giorno, Bruno."*

Her husband kissed first her cheek, then his children. "So they've come, the little ones."

Livia smiled. "Indeed." She glanced over at them. "I thought you were going to change your clothes for luncheon."

Francesca flushed. "We don't have any other clothes, Aunt Livia. The fire—"

"Never mind, never mind," Bruno quickly dismissed. "Your aunt will take you all shopping tomorrow."

"Tomorrow is Sunday, Bruno," Livia said stiffly.

Bruno shrugged, still beaming. "So not tomorrow, but soon."

Livia nodded. "Of course."

Luciano extricated himself from Francesca's firm grasp, ran over to his uncle, and, encouraged by his evident warmth, tugged at the hem of his silk jacket. *"Zio* Bruno, have you seen Giulietta?"

"Naturalmente, Luciano."

"Is she better yet?"

Bruno stooped, and looked kindly into the little boy's troubled face. "Not yet, *caro."* He paused. "It will take some time, I'm afraid."

"How much time?"

Maria, the maid, appeared noiselessly in the hall. "Luncheon is served, *signora."* She wore a crisp white apron.

Glad of the diversion, Bruno stood and rubbed his hands together. "Excellent," he said. "I'm hungry, and I'm sure you three must be starving." He patted Vittorio on the shoulder. *"Andiamo.* Let's eat."

Luncheon was strained, but excellent. The dining room, another lofty, vaulted room, was truly magnificent, so that Luciano, more wide-eyed than ever, began to believe that he was, after all, in a genuine palazzo. The furniture and doors were of dark walnut, with polished brass mountings, there was a massive fireplace of smooth gray *pietra serena,* and a richly woven, if very aged, carpet covering most of the stone floor.

Uncle Bruno sat at one end of the heavy oval table, Aunt Livia facing him, Fabio and Letizia between them on one side, and the three newcomers opposite their cousins. The first course, dishes of prosciutto and salami, together with a salad of mushrooms in olive oil, was already set on the immaculate white cloth when they took their seats, and was followed by *pollo alla cacciatore* and rice.

"Do you come home every day for lunch, *Zio Bruno?*" Francesca inquired, as the food and cool mineral water began to revive her spirits.

"Alas, no. Often, I am too occupied with business."

"And we don't eat such a big luncheon each day," Livia pointed out. "Today is Saturday, but once you are in school, you will, in any case, not return till afternoon."

"Except for Luciano," said Vittorio.

For an instant, Livia looked irritated, but then, perhaps because of her husband's presence, she said pleasantly: "Maria will collect Luciano from kindergarten, of course. I am often out during the day, but he will never be alone."

Bruno glanced at his son and daughter. "I am sure you will both help your cousins all you can." He took the wine bottle from the ice bucket beside him, and poured a little more first into Livia's glass, and then his own. "They will need your friendship, as you realize."

Letizia, who had hardly spoken during the meal, cleared her throat, but still said nothing. Fabio, very much the young gentleman, smiled at Bruno. "*Certo,* Papa. Leti and I understand completely."

"*Bene.*"

Dinner that evening, or rather supper, was infinitely less nerve-racking for the children, for their aunt and uncle had theater tickets, and their cousins apparently had plans of their own. Vittorio, Francesca, and Luciano ate a simple *spaghetti al burro* in the kitchen with Maria and Guido, who had returned to the palazzo after driving his employers to the Teatro della Pergola. It was a little cooler tonight, and the kitchen table was stained and old, with tiny splinters that scratched the children's legs, but which, somehow, reminded them of home and·brought great lumps to their throats, so that they did not dare to speak in case they wept, which suited Maria and Guido well, since they had eyes mainly for each other.

Soon after several nearby church bells had struck midnight, while Vittorio lay, unable to sleep, on his hard bed, there was a soft knocking.

Vittorio sat up. *"Avanti."*

His uncle's face peered around the door. "Am I disturbing you? May I come in?"

"Of course."

Bruno shut the door quietly behind him and came over to the bed.

"Sit down, please," Vittorio invited him.

"Can't sleep?"

"No."

"I'm not surprised." Bruno paused. "I'm sorry that we left you tonight, but it was an important premiere. I did not want to disappoint your aunt."

"We didn't mind, *Zio.*"

"Perhaps not, but I did." He searched for the right words. "My wife, Vittorio, is not one for public mourning. She lost both her parents some years ago, and her brother died during the war."

Vittorio was silent.

"She grieved for them deeply, in her way, but she is one of those people who believe that life is for the living." Bruno swallowed. "I suppose she has a point, but . . ." Again he paused. "But I have lost my brother."

"Did Aunt Livia not like my father?" Vittorio asked in a low voice. "She never came when you visited us. Except for that one time."

Bruno shrugged. "She did not understand him, or rather, she did not understand the life he chose to live."

"On the land, you mean?"

"Livia is a true daughter of Florence," Bruno attempted to explain. "The city may be the capital of Tuscany, but the Tuscan people are warm and welcoming, while the Florentines often seem dry and proud, perhaps a little haughty."

Vittorio's mouth twisted involuntarily as he remembered their welcome that morning.

"Above all, proud, Vittorio. To your aunt, the city is everything, even if she recognizes its faults. She could never comprehend why your papa chose a farm above a partnership in my business."

"And you? Did you understand him?"

"Very well." Bruno smiled a little wistfully. "If I had not fallen in love with Livia, I might even have joined him, but— That's life, my boy. It takes many turns." He shifted on the bedcover, and a light from the open window shone on his head, illuminating his round bald patch. "Do you think your sister and brother are sleeping?"

"They were exhausted."

Bruno remembered his leg. "Are you in pain, Vittorio? I can fetch you a tablet, if you like."

"No, thank you, *Zio*. I'm all right."

Bruno eased his bow tie and loosened his stiff collar. "I'm sorry that I did not see you more often in Pisa," he said, a little awkwardly. "There was so much to be done—so many arrangements—the funerals, legal matters, Giulietta's care."

"About Giulietta, *Zio*."

"*Sì?*"

"Why were we not allowed to see her in Pisa?" His bandaged hands played restlessly with the sheet. "Even when I was in the same hospital, no one let me near her."

Bruno looked even more uncomfortable. "They have rules," he began. "They considered it would be too distressing—Giulietta was in a special ward. She was very poorly."

"And now?"

Bruno shook his head. "She is in a critical condition, Vittorio," he said gently. "Her back was injured when she fell, and her legs."

"And the burns," Vittorio added dully.

"Exactly."

"I want to see her."

"And you shall, as soon as the hospital gives permission."

"I want to see her soon. This week."

Bruno reached out to pat the boy's arm kindly. "I will do what I can." He paused. "She doesn't know anything, Vittorio—or anyone. She sleeps all the time, because of the drugs."

"I still want to see her."

"*Naturalmente.*"

They fell silent for a few moments. Then Bruno, remembering, took something from his jacket pocket. "I brought you this."

It was a photograph, old and a little curled at the edges. Vittorio took it and held it up to the faint light at the window.

"Your parents," Bruno said. "Taken on the day they first met, in the Accademia." He paused, thinking back. "In 1938, at the feet of David. The most famous statue in the world."

Vittorio still stared at the photograph.

"I thought," Bruno continued, "that you would want something to remind you of your mamma and papa."

Vittorio looked up at him, and there were tears glinting in his eyes. "Thank you." The words were whispered.

"You have nothing to thank me for." Bruno rose, seeing that the boy was exhausted. "You are my brother's children. *Siamo di famiglia.* We are family." He opened the door, not looking back. "*Buona notte*, Vittorio."

"Good night, *Zio.*"

In their bedroom, Livia was waiting for Bruno, still wearing the Pucci silk dress she had bought only two days earlier especially for tonight's occasion. She was smoking, and clearly irritated.

"You've been with your nephew."

Bruno took off his jacket. "Yes."

"You were a long time."

"He couldn't sleep. I thought we should talk." He opened a wardrobe and took out a hanger. "It will be very hard for them, growing accustomed to Florence."

"I should think it will be hard for all of us."

"They've lost everything, Livia," Bruno reminded her quietly. "Everyone, and everything." He paused. "I gave Vittorio a photograph of Giulio and Serafina. There was nothing left in the house, not even a snapshot."

"I know, I know . . ." Livia took a quick, exasperated puff of her cigarette. "You've told me enough times, Bruno. I know it's a tragedy for them, I *know*." She looked directly at him. "I just don't want you to neglect your own children."

"Neglect them?" Bruno was astonished. "What on earth do you mean?"

"Nothing, yet." She shrugged lightly. "Going to the boy's room, when you might have looked in on Letizia."

"How do you know I didn't?"

"Did you?"

"No." He hung up his trousers and unfastened his cuff links. "But then, I haven't looked in on Letizia or Fabio late at night for some time. Leti complains that I wake her up, and our son considers he's too grown-up for a good-night kiss."

Livia stubbed out her cigarette. "How is the boy?"

"He has a name, *cara.*"

"I asked a question." She looked with mild distaste at her husband. "Must you walk around with your shirt hanging down like that?"

Bruno sighed, took off his shirt, and slipped on a plum silk dressing gown. "He's deeply unhappy, of course. As they all are. I can't begin to imagine what the shock has done to them."

"They're young, Bruno," Livia said, not unkindly. "They'll recover quicker than you expect." She turned her back so that Bruno could unzip her dress. The Pucci silk slid to the carpet, and Livia bent to pick it up, with her husband's admiring gaze on her. For a woman of forty-two years, her body, kept in trim with daily exercise, was more like that of a thirty-year-old.

Bruno, a decade older than his wife, was often woefully aware that, against all the rules, it was Livia, and not he, who was growing more attractive with age. He would have welcomed graying temples, but instead his hair, still a glossy, dark brown, became sparser every year. His only exercise was the walk to and from his jewelry stores on the Via della

Vigna Nuova and on the Ponte Vecchio, and, like most Tuscans, Bruno reveled in good food and wine, while Livia, grittily determined to remain slender, nibbled *insalate* and sipped *acqua minerale* whenever possible.

Bruno sighed. "We shall all have to help the children all we can."

"You sound like a damaged record." Livia sat at her dressing table and dabbed irritably at her cheeks with a tissue and cold cream. "The children and I will do what we can, *caro*, but you cannot expect the civilized world to stand still for three peasant children."

Bruno fought his rising anger. "My brother's children may not be worldly, Livia, but they are *not* peasants. And there are four of them, not three. Have you forgotten Giulietta?"

Livia tossed her tissue into the small embroidered basket at her feet. "How could I possibly forget her?"

She had only just stopped herself from shuddering. She had seen Giulietta once since the fire, and she had, of course, felt pity for the child, but she had been so utterly repelled by her injuries that she had tried to blot her from her mind, certain that it could only be a matter of days before they were told of her death.

Yet three weeks had passed since then, and Giulietta had not died, not yet, at least. And if she did, ultimately, survive, she would be crippled and scarred, like one of the pathetic, ugly derelicts who sat around Santo Spirito, begging for alms. Except that she would never become a beggar, because Bruno would insist on her coming to live in Palazzo Speroza with her sister and brothers. And that, Livia could not, *would* not, tolerate.

". . . Vittorio is anxious to see Giulietta."

Bruno's words stirred Livia from her thoughts. "The hospital won't permit it," she said swiftly, automatically.

"I think he's right. He and Francesca should see their sister. If she should die—"

Livia picked up a silver-handled hairbrush, stamped with the Speroza coat of arms, and began brushing her hair with calm, sweeping movements. The germ of an idea had come into her brain, and she needed time to consider it.

"I think it would disturb them too much to see her as she is now, *caro,"* she said thoughtfully, continuing to brush her hair. "Perhaps if I go again, during the next few days—"

"You?" Bruno was surprised. "But you were so distressed last time—you always hate hospitals."

She shrugged. "Who does not?" She waited an instant. "But maybe I should speak to the child's doctors. I might be able to judge, less emotionally than you, if Vittorio and Francesca should go, or if they should wait."

Bruno laid his palms gently on her firm, smooth shoulders. "I would be grateful, Livia—more than I can say. It's hard for me to travel back and forth, especially at this busy time—and I know it would mean so much to the children."

"Then it's settled." Livia laid down her hairbrush.

Bruno looked past her, meeting her reflected eyes in the antique mirror. "I know this is very difficult for you, *cara mia.* But there was no alternative."

"It's all right, Bruno," Livia said softly.

He went on, grasping the moment of gentleness. "I know they look shabby, and that their speech embarrasses you." His brother's children spoke in the Tuscan manner, substituting an "h" for a hard "c," and Bruno had already observed the barely concealed sneer on Fabio's lips at luncheon when he listened to his cousins. "But they will soon adapt, and they could find no finer teacher than you to educate them in the ways of society."

Over my dead body, Livia thought. She might have agreed to give them a home, to put a roof over their heads and food in their mouths, and since she would never be able to prevent Bruno from introducing them as family, she would have to steer them toward respectability, but there it ended. Fabio and Letizia were the only Cesaretti children who would be acceptable to Florentine society.

She forced a smile. "I'll see about their clothes on Monday."

"Perhaps some of Fabio's and Leti's older things might fit Vittorio and Francesca?" Bruno suggested.

Livia suppressed another shudder. Those beautiful clothes from Neuber and Principe, those pure cottons and silks and velvets draped over those coarse, sunburned *contadini*—

"I'll try to find something," she said smoothly, "but I give most of the children's clothes to charity when they have outgrown them." She would tell Maria to take their measurements, she decided, and to go to UPIM to find them something suitable. They were not possessed of limitless wealth, and with three extra mouths to feed, Bruno would have to understand that Leti and Fabio must come first.

Three extra mouths to feed, she pondered anxiously. And there was still the fourth, hovering between life and death, another cuckoo unconsciously aspiring to nest in Palazzo Speroza.

One had to draw the line somewhere.

Chapter 3

Sнe тоок the Lancia, her own car, choosing a day when, in any case, Bruno needed Guido's services. Not that it was unusual for Livia to drive herself. Though she took pleasure from being chauffeured in the city, she had always thrived on a little adventure, particularly of the most private nature. Livia did not yet know what precise shape this *avventura* would take, but she did know what the outcome would be, and whatever it took to achieve that objective, she was willing to do.

It was not necessary for her to drive right into Pisa, for the hospital was on the outskirts, but there was something so tragic about the city since the war that Livia always felt oddly stimulated by it. The great monuments had more or less escaped the bombings, but the center of the town, especially the boulevards on the Arno, were desperately ravaged. The destruction in her own beloved city had dismayed Livia, of course—seeing every bridge but the Ponte Vecchio disappearing, worst of all, perhaps, the glorious Santa Trinità—but she had never cared much for Pisa in the past. War had lent it, for her at least, excitement.

The *ospedale* choked off her sense of liberty and fun. It was a deeply depressing building, with endless, bleak, identical corridors. Livia wasted no time, going directly to the ward where she had last seen her husband's unhappy niece.

Giulietta's condition seemed, to Livia's recoiling gaze, unchanged. She still lay strapped into immobility, both her legs suspended, the grafted flesh on her shoulders and chest swathed in bandages, a pathetic, living corpse. Although the nursing nun who had brought Livia a chair assured her that the child was not comatose, she was, mercifully, in a deep, drugged sleep. Livia had accepted the chair, quelling her desire to flee. It might be as well to demonstrate her care for the patient.

Livia had, from childhood, always been unnaturally repelled by sickness and any type of disfigurement. Her parents had both died swiftly and naturally, but her only beloved brother had been monstrously wounded in 1941, and Livia remembered, with self-disgust, feeling a true, loathsome flash of relief when he died, releasing them both from a disability that would have led, almost certainly, to her hatred of him.

She sat by Giulietta's bed for what seemed an age, compelling herself to watch the unconscious battle for life, praying that the child would not wake during her visit.

Giulietta did not wake, only lay on the stark hospital bed, either healing herself or dying, Livia could not fathom which. But by the time she judged it right and proper to stand up from the hard wooden chair, Livia had determined, precisely, the next step of her plan, and as she left the ward she knew she was going in search of the collaborator she would need if the plan was, ultimately, to succeed.

In less than ninety minutes, she had found him. It was, of course, a man. It had always been men, throughout Livia's life, who had aided and abetted her, who had done her bidding, willingly or otherwise. Carlo Clemenza was the man of the moment, although when he first laid eyes on Livia Cesaretti, he could never have guessed that her intentions were anything more than carnal.

"I understand, Signora Cesaretti, that you wish to make a donation to our hospital," he said. His voice was very soft for a man, and a little high, but Livia thought it went well with his pointed, foxlike face and slim, well-dressed body.

"Correct." She smiled.

He folded his hands under his chin, in a prayerlike gesture. His fingernails were manicured, Livia observed, and was satisfied with her choice. Carlo Clemenza had expensive tastes, certainly more expensive than his position as hospital administrator could easily accommodate.

"But I understand that you wish to learn more about the hospital."

"Also correct."

"How may I be of assistance to you, *signora?*" he asked. "A tour, perhaps?"

Heaven forbid, Livia thought, suppressing a grimace. "I rather thought we might—talk," she said smoothly, "over luncheon."

Carlo Clemenza's narrow eyes appraised her, taking in the lustrous hair, the impeccably applied makeup, the exquisite suit. It was hot in his office, for his ceiling fan had broken months ago, but Livia Cesaretti looked cool and unruffled. He might be wrong, of course; she might simply, genuinely, wish to know about the cause before bestowing her largesse. But he had met her kind before, and he flattered himself that his instincts were sound. Right now, Carlo wanted, more than anything, to mess that perfectly coiffed hair, to make her perspire—and something in those calm brown eyes told him, clearly, that she was a woman of considerable appetites.

"Luncheon." He nodded, and rose. He had already eaten—a dull grilled fish in the staff *mensa*—but he could force himself. It might, after all, be worthwhile, for him as well as the hospital. "I know just the place."

He had to make do with lunch, that afternoon, at least. For Livia, time was of the essence, but she knew better than to rush an important seduction.

The next meeting was more fruitful. Livia came to Clemenza's office, exhausted and distressed by the short time she had spent at Giulietta's bedside. It was clear that she was a woman in need of comfort. A more private luncheon, Carlo suggested gently, away from prying eyes. Somewhere she could rest for a while, perhaps unburden herself to a friend, relax before the return journey to Florence.

Livia was immensely grateful. She was fortunate, indeed, to have found a man of such sensitivity and understanding. She sat, pale and unhappy, while the fox-faced *amministratore* made the necessary reservation at the Grand Hotel, his eager fingers trembling slightly as he dialed the number.

By three o'clock that same afternoon, they were in each other's arms beneath hotel sheets. Carlo was enthralled, no part of him in the least disappointed by the reality of this magnificent older woman's superbly maintained body. He kissed every inch of her with his hard mouth, messed her hair as he had longed to, tweaked her splendid nipples, then sucked on them, and at last, when he could bear the waiting no longer, thrust himself between her open thighs, frenziedly moaning as he ejaculated deep inside her.

"*Dio*," he murmured, still trembling.

Livia opened her eyes. "I have to leave." She managed to sound regretful. "My husband—"

Clemenza sat up. "I understand," he said, his soft, high voice conspiratorial in the dimness of the hotel room.

Livia thought about the photographs she had seen on his desk. A smiling wife, grown plump, and four children. Naturally he understood. "I will be back in two days," she offered. "If you wish."

Carlo's hard, dry lips brushed her shoulder.

"I wish," he said.

She came late in the day the next time, knowing that it would be harder for him to be with her, knowing, nonetheless, that he would make it possible.

He did.

She kept him there, in the big hotel bed, for more than an hour longer than he had allowed for when making his excuses to his wife.

"Tomorrow?" she said as they rose to dress.

Clemenza's erection returned again. "God, yes."

"But in the early afternoon. That's easier for you, isn't it, Carlo?"

He drew her to him. "Not only beautiful and sensual, but considerate, too," he marveled.

Livia pushed him gently away, a tacit reminder of the family who awaited him.

Just once more, she thought. *Then it will be enough.*

Three days later, they sat in his office again.

"It's time for business," she said.

"Business?"

Livia nodded. "As with all business transactions, Carlo, the benefits must be reciprocal. You, as a man of the world, must realize that."

The vague, foolish expression on Clemenza's face vanished, and the sharp, foxy features Livia had first observed tightened up.

She told him.

In return for a substantial donation to the hospital, and an additional, personal gift for himself, Clemenza was to ensure that Giulietta Cesaretti disappeared, permanently, from Livia's life.

"I want her moved from this hospital." She smoothed the skirt of her Balenciaga suit. "Away from Pisa."

"To Florence?"

"Away from Florence, from Tuscany. As far away as possible."

Clemenza was baffled. "To what end?"

"I haven't finished," Livia said curtly. "The move is to be kept secret. From my husband, from the other children, from the hospital staff."

"That's impossible."

She ignored him. "My husband will learn, within the next few days, that Giulietta is dead."

Clemenza stared, appalled.

"Taking into account her condition, the news will come as no great shock."

Livia continued. Giulietta was removed from her ward several times a week for treatment. She must be diverted. Clemenza was to select two competent individuals to oversee her transfer, and to pay them handsomely for their cooperation and silence. He was to prepare the death certificate—

"You're crazy!" Clemenza interrupted. "I'm not even eligible to sign death certificates."

"Nevertheless, you will sign this one." She went on. "As for the funeral, a coffin, weighted with stones—you can arrange that, too."

"*Never!*"

Livia smiled slightly. "If you do this for me, Carlo," she said softly, "I will give you my word that neither your wife nor your superiors will learn of our affair."

Clemenza's face grew white. "My wife knows I've slept with other women."

"But not, perhaps, that you spend afternoons and evenings at the Grand Hotel—that money which should be for the family is spent on champagne and sex." She went on ruthlessly. "And on the subject of money, how would your employers regard a man who connives to keep a percentage of a charitable donation for himself?"

"They'd never believe it!"

Livia shrugged. "I am well known in Florence, as my mother before me, as a benefactress—I am a pillar of the community. Who will they believe?" She paused. "Carlo, the child will not be harmed. I'm certain that whichever hospital you choose for her, the care will be just as good as at this one."

Clemenza struggled to bring himself under control. "And when—if it is done, what will become of the child?"

"*When* it is done"—Livia rose from her chair—"then Giulietta Cesaretti will have ceased to exist, and another patient, with another identity, will be on her way to a new hospital, and to a new life."

It took eight days. The call came on Friday morning, when Livia was alone in the house except for Maria. She waited for ten minutes, composing herself, and then telephoned her husband at his store on the Via della Vigna Nuova, telling him to come home immediately.

His black suit and tie were laid out on the bed for him when he arrived.

"I'm so sorry, Bruno," she said, going to embrace him as he entered the room.

"*La povera piccola.*" He shook his head, sinking into an armchair. "No life at all, and such a terrible end."

Livia looked at the dark suit. "We have to go right away," she said gently.

"Of course." Bruno stood up wearily. "Have you called the schools?"

"I thought that tonight would be soon enough."

Bruno sighed and nodded. "You're right. It will be terrible for them."

Livia looked at her wristwatch. "Get changed, *caro*. I'll wait for you downstairs."

Fifteen minutes later, he met her in the dark entrance hall. "I'll tell Guido to bring the car."

"I've already told him to go." Livia held up the keys to her Lancia. "I want to drive."

"Whatever for? It's too tiring."

"It's an easy drive," she scoffed gently. "I've grown used to it."

Bruno looked at her with concern. "You've done far too much over the last few weeks. Things I should have done."

"You're busy enough." Livia linked her arm through his, and guided him to the door. "And haven't I always supported you, my dear, in important matters?"

Bruno smiled. "You have." He held out his hand for the car keys. "If you've sent Guido away, I'll drive. It's the least I can do."

Livia kept her hand tightly shut. "You're too tired, and too upset." She kissed his cheek. "Perhaps on the way back."

It was vital that she drove, for Bruno would have gone, naturally, to the hospital, whereas she had a different destination in mind.

As she parked the car Bruno woke up from his doze and looked around him in confusion. "But this is a cemetery—why are we here?"

"For the funeral." Quickly, she covered his hand with her own. "I know what you're thinking, I know. The children should be here."

"Of *course* they should be!" Bruno sat forward angrily. "They should be consulted about the service—they—"

"It's too late now."

"She was their *sister!*" His eyes were wide with shock. "Livia, I don't understand—how could you do such a thing?"

"Because it was necessary." The sudden sharpness in her voice was startling. "She died during the night, Bruno."

"Why didn't they call us immediately?"

"I don't know. Some delay—who can say why?"

"Anyway, what difference does it make *when* she died?" he asked irritably.

Livia lowered her eyes. "They told me she—" She hesitated, biting her lower lip.

"*What?*"

"She deteriorated, Bruno." Livia looked back at him, her eyes filling with tears. "Very quickly—something to do with the kind of injuries, they thought." She cleared her throat. "It was necessary to arrange matters swiftly."

"I see." Bruno sank back against the seat. "You should have telephoned the schools. Vittorio and Francesca should have been told."

Livia took an embroidered handkerchief from her handbag and dabbed at her eyes. "I thought it was too cruel—too much of a nightmare. Too sudden." A tear slid slowly down her cheek. "I thought it would be kinder to arrange a memorial service for them, afterward."

Bruno said nothing.

"I'm sorry." Livia's words were choked.

He turned to her, his face pale and anxious. "I should be sorry, *mia cara.* You've done everything you could."

"I believed I was doing the right thing, Bruno."

It was a long time since he had seen his wife cry, and the sight moved him intensely. "Of course you did. And you were right." He took her right hand and drew it to his lips. "I'm grateful to you, Livia. You've been so strong—I know what these visits must have cost you."

More than you imagine, Livia thought wryly, then pulled gently away. "We must go, my dear. They are waiting for us—the priest, and a man from the hospital."

Walking into the cemetery, Bruno suddenly stopped, looking around. "Giulietta should be buried with her parents, and little Giacomo."

For the first time, Livia felt real fear, but she forced herself to remain calm. "If there had been time, *caro,* of course it would have been best. But under the circumstances, I felt we should take the advice of the hospital."

For another moment, Bruno remained motionless. He seemed dazed. Livia hardly dared to breathe.

And then he sighed, his face ineffably sad. "As you say, Livia, under the circumstances—" He began to walk again, and Livia, weak with relief, slipped her hand into his.

Less than a half hour later, the small, polished casket, packed with its carefully calculated filling of stones and straw, was lowered into the ground.

It was with the warming knowledge of a replete bank account, and the even more satisfying thought that he was, thank the Lord, free of Livia Cesaretti, that Carlo Clemenza returned to his office at the hospital.

And it was with a lighter heart, and a new, if temporary, generosity of spirit, that Livia returned that same afternoon to Palazzo Speroza.

The children were, predictably, desolate.

Luciano, in particular, was inconsolable. It had been small enough comfort to hear that Mamma, Papa, and Giacomo had gone to *paradiso,* and at least he knew that they had gone together, but his beloved, inseparable twin, so much a part of himself, had died alone, and no amount of reassurance from Francesca that Giulietta, too, was in heaven, could convince him that, having made the journey so much later, and unaccompanied, she would be able to find the rest of the family.

Francesca, too, was heartbroken, fighting to suppress her natural desire to weep openly for Luciano's sake. Yet she had expected, somehow, that this would be the outcome, that they would never see Giulietta again. The fact that she had known that, however, did nothing to lessen her grief.

Vittorio, on the other hand, was too bound up in his all-consuming anger and bitterness to grieve properly for his little sister. It was hardly possible to conceive that anyone could have been so cruel, so *savage*, as to separate them from Giulietta for the last, miserable weeks of her life, and he could not, would never, accept it. Vittorio blamed Aunt Livia completely, knew instinctively that though Uncle Bruno was also guilty, it was his wife who controlled her family.

There was nothing he could do for Giulietta, no way he could ever undo the past. But he would never forget, and he would never forgive Livia Cesaretti, and one day, perhaps soon, perhaps far into the future, he would repay her.

It was the beginning of October before they held the service that Livia had promised, and in the end it was little more than a few prayers said by a local priest, and an opportunity for the children to stand at their sister's grave.

"I asked them if they wanted something special," Livia had told her husband. "But it seemed too painful for them to think about. I believe they need simplicity."

Bruno had nodded, certain his wife was right. Since the child's death, he had found it harder to communicate with his nephews and niece, especially Vittorio, who had withdrawn into a cold, hard shell.

And so it was. Absolute simplicity. Bruno, Livia, Fabio, and Letizia standing on one side of the grave. Vittorio, Francesca, and Luciano on the other, with Guido, very somber and awkward, beside them.

A plain white stone had already been erected at the head of the grave, the only one in the row without a commemorative photograph of the deceased. Before they left, the bereaved children laid small bunches of flowers, bought for them that morning in the Santo Spirito market by Maria, and already wilting from the heat, at its base.

Francesca was weeping bitterly. Luciano, chalky-faced and too daunted by the cemetery to associate the occasion with his twin, held tightly to Francesca's hand. Vittorio deposited his lilies of the valley, and stared dry-eyed at the stark lettering on the stone.

GIULIETTA ANNA CESARETTI

9.6.46–19.9.51

Con Gesù Cristo

Chapter 4

IN THE OSPEDALE San Felice di Dio, not far from the Palazzo Madama in Turin, the patient known as Giulietta Volpi, the victim of a road accident in which her parents and brother had been killed, lay waiting, as she did every day and every night, for someone to rescue her from hell.

"We will look after you," the sisters had told her kindly. "We are your family now."

"*Mamma*—" the child had whimpered, weakly.

Gentle hands had touched her forehead. "She cannot come, Giulietta. But we are here to care for you—don't be afraid."

"Luciano—" she had tried again.

"Gone, *piccolina*," the voice told her. "They are all with Our Lord. Try to rest now. Try to forget."

The ward in which she lay was a haze of gray. Everything was unclear, nebulous, confused. There was pain, terrible pain, and there was sleep, deathly and heavy, or light and dizzying. They told her to forget, but even through the mist of medicine and agony, the child remembered a small stone house, and a vineyard and an olive grove—and fragrant air, and green grass, and sweet laughter and warmth—

And a mother and a father, and the companionship of other children.

And Giulietta Volpi lay trapped in her bed, a prisoner of plaster and traction and bandages and drugs, and people who would not listen to her, and who, as the days dragged on, seemed, increasingly, not even to hear her.

And she lay very still, and thought that perhaps, if she was very good, and did exactly as she was told, she might still be saved.

She *had* been loved. She remembered.

She could not believe they would not come.

Chapter 5

Two years passed, and the unhappiness of the three *orfani* in Palazzo Speroza hardly diminished. Rather, in many ways, at least for the two older children, the misery magnified.

The Florence in which they now, unwillingly, lived was not the glowing, romantic city beloved of artists and tourists. It was noisy and overcrowded; its character was private, even taciturn; when it was not suffocatingly hot, it was either unpleasantly cold or exceedingly wet.

Life inside the palazzo was hateful. When their uncle was at home, the situation improved—they sat at the dining table with the family, and Bruno did his best to involve them all in relaxed conversation. But he was seldom home, electing to immerse himself in business rather than spend too much time in the bosom of his difficult family. When he was absent, the *poveri* ate in the kitchen and remained in their rooms—in many ways less of an ordeal for them, since Aunt Livia, grudgingly cordial when Bruno was home, was openly hostile when he was not, resolute as ever that her own children's futures would never be jeopardized by the interlopers.

Fabio and Letizia, unable to accept that their cousins were no threat, were equally antagonistic. They resented every kindness bestowed on them by their father, and at every opportunity they derided Vittorio, made trouble for Francesca, and tormented Luciano.

Luciano had adapted more easily to city life than his brother and sister. Young enough to tolerate change, he had been an eager pupil, first at the *giardino d'infanzia* and, after his sixth birthday, at the *scuola elementare,* and he had an inborn capacity for escaping into daydreams at tense moments.

He had never really come to terms with the loss of Giulietta. His twin was not, of course, beside him physically, but she was seldom out of Luciano's head. She seemed as much rooted in his thoughts—and consequently in his life—as before her death. She figured in most of his daydreams, participated in his mythical adventures. But it was at night that Luciano really suffered, for he was plagued by nightmares—hideous replays of the fire and, worse still, terrible dreams in which Giulietta was in agony, and crying for him to come to her.

"This is not the first time that the bridges of Florence have been destroyed," one of Vittorio's teachers said, referring to the wartime damage to the city. "In the great flood of 1333, for example, they and many buildings were swept away, together with, it is believed, the Martocus, the guardian statue of Florence."

Vittorio wished that it had all been swept away, every last dreary statue and building—*especially* the Palazzo Speroza. He felt constantly bored and morose, longing for fresh air and the freedom of the countryside. He felt isolated, especially at school, and burdened by his awareness that as the oldest, he must also be the strongest. On the rare occasions when Uncle Bruno found time to give them treats, taking them to the Uffizi or into the Boboli Gardens, or for ice cream at Giacosa, Francesca and Luciano appeared to enjoy themselves, but to Vittorio it was all one. It was old, ugly, and dull. He loathed Fabio and Letizia, despised Aunt Livia.

Life was unbearable.

By the late summer of 1953, the atmosphere inside Palazzo Speroza had neared boiling point, the heat itself fraying tempers badly, though Fabio and Letizia were far better off than their cousins since their bedrooms were large and airy, with ceiling fans, and they went daily to swim in the Tennis Club of the Cascine park, a luxury Livia would not consider allowing Vittorio, Francesca, or Luciano.

By siding with the orphans, Bruno did not realize that he was making their lives more difficult. The more kindness and generosity he demonstrated, the more Livia retaliated, frequently by using Francesca as an extra servant.

There was a new reason for Letizia, especially, to despise Francesca. Livia's daughter was now an uncomfortable thirteen, bloated by baby fat and duly self-conscious, particularly when faced with her eleven-year-old cousin, who was developing into a naturally beautiful, leggy, woman-child.

Francesca's eyes were glowing brown, wide and slightly slanted, with remarkable, finely shaped eyebrows that flared, almost winglike, at the outer corners. Her nose was straight, her cheeks high-boned yet soft, and her chin was elfishly pointed beneath a mouth that was not too wide, not too narrow, but just right.

"Common girls often show the greatest promise when they are very young." Livia sought to comfort her daughter, resolving to tempt her ever so slightly greedy child into another diet by bringing home an array of irresistible clothes one size too small. Unkind, but effective.

"Francesca doesn't *look* common," Letizia sulked.

"Not yet, perhaps, Leti, but she will assuredly become a slut, and her looks will quickly fade." Livia wished she could believe her own words, but to her daily displeasure, her husband's niece looked increasingly aristocratic with every passing month, and far more like her handsome son's sister than Letizia ever had.

It was Fabio, fifteen years old and more arrogant than ever, who brought the animosity to a head. A born mischief-maker, he had recently taken to making vulgar remarks to Francesca, alluding to her noticeable adolescent breasts and what he called her "sensual peasant" looks. He knew that by doing this, he goaded Vittorio into fury and prodded Letizia into complaining, more jealously than ever, about Francesca.

✳

On a warm Saturday afternoon in late September, when Luciano was out with Maria, Aunt Livia and Letizia had gone shopping and Uncle Bruno had taken Vittorio to his Ponte Vecchio store, Francesca stood in the palazzo courtyard, carrying out the latest tasks allotted to her by her aunt to keep her in her place. Francesca seldom minded these menial jobs—they kept her occupied, stopped her from thinking too much, and besides, she had always helped out at home, either in the house or in the vineyard and orchard. The courtyard was just a small quadrangle, with a little central fountain and six lemon trees in earthen tubs. It was almost entirely shadowed by the palazzo walls surrounding it, but it was possible to look straight up and see the sky, and though the air trapped in the square was quite stagnant, from time to time a whisper of true, fresh air would filter down.

Francesca swept the paving stones first with a long-handled broom, then attached the hose to the rusty tap in one corner and turned on the water. She liked to give the trees a drink, and to tug out any choking weeds, before washing the ground or cleaning out the fountain. It was the arid, dead quality of Florence in the summer months that she hated most, and even the paltry, spindly weeds that she uprooted and held to her face were enough to remind her of the wonderful, sorely missed smells of soil and grass.

Francesca closed her eyes, and listened to the spray from the hose and the bubble of the water playing in the fountain. In her mind's eye, she was back in Lucchesia, standing near the stream that had meandered through the neighboring farm's apple orchard—

"You'll drown that tree."

Francesca's eyes flew open. Fabio had come silently out into the *cortile* and stood just a yard away from her. He wore white linen trousers, a blue Lacoste cotton sweater, and tennis shoes—he looked cool and graceful and relaxed.

"Allow me." He reached out and took the hose from her.

"You'll get wet," Francesca said carefully. She had learned long ago that any courtesy from Fabio was short-lived.

"A little water never hurt anyone." He directed the spray at the next tub. "What were you thinking about?"

"Nothing."

"Your eyes were shut—you were dreaming."

"Perhaps," she admitted.

"About a boy?"

"Of course not!" Francesca felt her cheeks flush. Something about Fabio's eyes made her uncomfortable. "I'd better finish that."

"Leti thinks about boys all the time," Fabio said.

"Does she?"

"But then she's two years older than you, isn't she?" He reached into the tub, tore off a sliver of weed and tossed it to the ground, fastidiously holding his fingers under the hose to rinse any dirt that might cling to them.

Francesca walked over to the fountain, and looked at the small bronze statue of a naked boy, constantly urinating into the pool surrounding him. She was supposed to check that the aperture through which the water ran was clean and unblocked, but her cousin's presence embarrassed her. She turned away.

"Your mother will be upset if she sees you doing my work."

"It's hard to believe you're just eleven, Francesca." It was as if he hadn't heard her. "You're very attractive." He paused. "Not like a child at all."

"Fabio, let me have the hose." Francesca put out her hand.

"Say please."

Her cheeks blazed. "Please give me the hose."

"You know Leti's jealous of you, don't you?"

"What does she have to be jealous of?"

"Your face, for one thing." Fabio grinned. "Leti's face is like a pudding."

"Don't be horrid."

"And then there's your body."

"Fabio, I must get on with my work—please give me the hose back." Francesca's voice quivered slightly, but she held out her hand resolutely.

"*Ecco*—" Without warning, Fabio made as if to toss the hose at her, and the jet of cold water struck her, soaking her thin white cotton blouse. He clapped a hand to his cheek, feigning remorse. *"Dio mio,* I'm sorry."

Francesca stood still, startled and dripping. "It doesn't matter."

"Of course it does." Fabio dropped the hose to the ground, where it coiled snakelike, hissing water up against a wall. He came closer. "I've ruined your blouse."

She shook her head. "It's just water."

His hand was on her before she could blink. Against her wet blouse, feeling the damp. "Cool," he said softly.

Francesca jumped away.

"Calma," he said, and came toward her, smiling as she backed into the fountain. "Let me—" He put his hand on her again and squeezed. "Ah," he laughed, "a baby breast—"

"Basta!" Francesca slapped at his fingers and tried to dart away, but he grasped at her arm roughly.

"You like it—don't deny you like it."

"Let me go!" she gasped, but he only laughed harder. "Let me *go!"* Wrenching herself out of his grip, Francesca dived for the protection closest to hand. Seizing the hose with both hands, she aimed it straight at him, drenching him thoroughly from head to foot.

"Merda!" Fabio lunged at her, all humor gone. "Give that to me!" Cold water hit him full in the face. "Bitch!" he shrilled in outrage and disbelief.

Francesca dropped the hose and snatched up the broom, thrusting it toward him. "Now will you leave me alone?" she demanded.

"Pazza!" Fabio shouted. "You're crazy, just like your mother!"

"Don't you *dare* talk about my mother!" She lashed out at him with the broom, and a long, sharp twig caught his right cheek, making it bleed. Half triumphant, but half terrified by what she'd done, Francesca let go of the broom, and it clattered on the wet paving stones.

"I'm sorry," she breathed, watching the blood streaking down his face—

And then she ran, as fast as she could, back into the palazzo, her damp sandals sliding on the stone floors, knowing there was nowhere she could escape to but the bedroom she shared with Luciano.

She got into the room, slammed the door, and since there was no lock, she pushed her only chair, a rickety thing, up against the handle.

"Santa Maria," she whispered, and shut her eyes. She hardly ever prayed; neither Mamma nor Papa had especially kept after any of them to say nightly prayers, and they had gone to mass more often since coming to Florence than they had ever done at home—but Francesca knew enough to know that one prayed when one was in trouble, and whether Fabio bothered to follow her now or not, she was certainly in trouble.

When Livia and Letizia returned from the Via Tornabuoni, Fabio was awaiting them, his wet clothes in a pile on the floor and a large sticking plaster on his cheek.

"Fabio? *Cosa c'è?*" Livia looked at the heap of clothes. "What has happened?"

Letizia bent and picked up her brother's crumpled trousers, bought just a month earlier in Milan. "Whatever have you done to these? They're *ruined.*"

"I did nothing," Fabio said ominously.

"What do you mean?" Livia asked irritably, tired out from doing everything possible to make the most of her daughter's unsatisfactory figure. "Pick those things up from the floor immediately, or they'll leave a stain."

Fabio fingered his cheek.

"And what have you done to your face?"

"I was attacked."

"*Prego?*" Livia stared at him. Letizia listened with new interest.

"My cousin," Fabio said darkly.

Livia's eyes narrowed. "Vittorio attacked you?"

Her son shook his head. "Francesca."

Livia looked disbelieving. "*Francesca?*" she echoed.

Letizia giggled. "How did she attack you?"

"First she tried to drown me with a hose—then she slashed my face."

"With what?" Livia had already forgotten her weariness.

"*Una scopa.*"

"With a *broom*?"

Letizia giggled again.

"Another inch, and she might have blinded me," Fabio said with dignity. "I can't see much to laugh at in that."

"Neither can I," his mother agreed, her outrage growing.

"But why did she do it?" Letizia asked mildly. "I mean, it's bad enough she did it at all, of course, but she must have had some reason."

"Certainly," Fabio said.

"What?" Letizia was avid for more.

"She was flirting with me, and I—"

"*Flirting!*" Livia's eyes widened. "She's just a child."

"She often does it, Mamma—she's a born *puttana*, I've told you before." He paused. "She was in the *cortile,* supposedly cleaning. She became overfamiliar—I rejected her, and she lost her temper, like a vixen —a mad person."

"And struck you with the broom?" Livia said grimly.

"As you see."

Letizia stared at her mother eagerly. "What will you do, Mamma?"

"Mamma?" Fabio echoed.

Livia eyed his cheek. "I think we should send for the doctor."

"There's no need."

"It could turn septic."

"It'll be all right." Fabio looked impatient. "Mamma, what are you going to do about Francesca? You will do something, surely?"

Outside the children's room, Livia rapped on the door. "Francesca?" She tried the handle. "Open the door."

A soft, scraping sound came from within as Francesca removed the barricading chair.

Livia went in. Francesca stood in a white cotton shift, her eyes fearful.

"Will you please come with me." Livia held out her hand, and, reluctantly, Francesca took it, her heart pounding.

In silence, Livia drew her down the drab servants' corridor and through the dim back hall toward the rear staircase and to a solid oak door under the stairs.

"Aunt Livia?" Francesca watched as her aunt took a large key from the pocket of her skirt, fitted it into the lock and turned it, still holding fast to her niece's hand. "Where are we going?"

Livia opened the door. There was nothing to be seen through the entrance, but pitch-darkness.

"Inside," Livia said, and tugged at Francesca's wrist.

Francesca held back, rooting herself to the spot.

"*Inside!*" Livia commanded, and thrust her through the doorway.

Francesca stood at the top of what seemed, in the weak light from the hall, to be a long, narrow flight of stone steps leading down into blackness. Her heart contracted with fright. "*Zia* Livia—" she quavered, her eyes even larger than usual, their pupils dilating.

Her aunt folded her arms. "You assaulted my son."

"No!"

"You should be turned out of this house, but the orphanage would never take a *whore.*" Livia almost spat the last word. She stood, righteous and erect, barring the doorway.

"He wouldn't leave me alone." Francesca was breathless. "He *touched* me—"

"*Liar!*" Livia unfolded her arms and grasped the handle of the door. "You are no better than an animal. We took you into our home, and you repay us with violence and lies—"

"No!" Francesca began to weep. "It's not true!"

Livia's eyes seemed to glitter with rage. "They tell me there are rats in the cellar. I can only hope that a little sojourn with vermin may teach you to appreciate charity."

She began to close the door. Francesca clasped at her arm, trying to stop her, but Livia shook her off easily.

"No!" Francesca watched as the heavy door swung to, as the dim light receded and then vanished. "*No!*" she screamed.

She heard the key turning in the lock, heard the firm click of her aunt's heels as she walked away.

"Aunt Livia!" she screamed again, piercingly, but there was no response, no relenting footsteps—nothing at all.

Francesca's heart beat wildly, her face and body grew flame hot while her hands and feet seemed to turn to ice. She could see nothing at all, thrust into sudden, total blindness. Falling to her knees, she lowered her face near to the ground in the hope that a crack of light might show beneath the door, but the base fit snugly, built to preclude drafts or unwelcome visitors from the cellar.

Rats.

She snatched her face from the floor, almost choking with revulsion. They had often had mice in the house at home, coming in from the fields and meadows, and she hadn't minded them at all, but even the mental image of a rat, big and dark and evil, was enough to make her feel physically ill.

Francesca straightened up, staying close to the door, her mind in turmoil. She wanted to batter at the wood, to scream and shout and plead, but something told her that her aunt's heart might just be hardened by a further display of unruly behavior.

Perhaps the best thing to do was to wait, right there by the door, in silence—to close her eyes tightly and to be very brave. Her uncle would be home soon, and Vittorio. *He* would want to know where she was— Vittorio wouldn't let them leave her in here—

Something brushed at her cheek. Francesca gasped and slapped at it, stinging her face. She whimpered, and tears began to fall in earnest. Uncle Bruno had never been unkind, but even he was bound to believe Fabio rather than her—and if he was on Aunt Livia's side, Vittorio wouldn't be able to do anything to help her.

Something crawled onto her left foot, and Francesca gave a shriek of horror. Not a rat, it was too small, smaller even than a mouse, but—

Una blatta.

She clapped her hands over her mouth and stamped her feet. Cockroaches didn't bite, but they were disgusting, revolting, *filthy* creatures—

There was a sound, just to her right. She jerked her head to that side and listened, her terror mounting. A rustle—no, a fluttering noise—

Something flew against her hair. With another small, choking scream, Francesca flailed her arms around her head, but again the phantom grazed first her hair, then her right ear.

Sobbing violently, Francesca abandoned the door, stepped gingerly forward into the inky blackness. The steps—she had to be careful not to fall—if she stumbled and struck her head, she might lie unconscious and her aunt might never tell anyone where she was, and—

The fresh, strange scrabbling sound halted her again on the third step down. The small demonic screech from just below almost unhinged her. Wailing desperately, she turned and flung herself back up to where she'd begun—

It came again, a rasping squeak. Francesca fell onto her knees, scraping them. She scrambled back to her feet and hurled herself forward, hitting the oak door with her shoulder.

And then it bit her.

In her mind, she saw it, massive, furry, beady-eyed, its teeth like needles, dripping with her blood—

Her heart pounded, she could hardly breathe—the icy sensation that had started in her feet and hands spread right through her, making her heavy and leaden and sick—

"*Help me!*" she thought she screamed, but her voice was just a whisper—

And then she fainted.

It was just after six o'clock when Bruno and Vittorio returned to the palazzo. The stores had closed at lunchtime, but Bruno had wanted to check stock and go over some books, and to his pleasure, his nephew had, for once, displayed some interest in the Cesaretti stores. In truth, Vittorio was wholly uninterested, but his uncle, though weak, was a kind and caring man, and however much Vittorio hated Palazzo Speroza and despised the rest of the family, he had no desire to hurt Bruno's feelings.

Letizia was hovering around the entrance hall, aching to spread the news of her cousin's disgrace as swiftly as possible.

"Papa." She greeted her father, warmly kissing him.

"*Ciao*, Leti."

"Vittorio." She nodded at her cousin.

"Did you have a nice day?" Bruno asked her. "Successful shopping?" He knew only too well how troublesome Livia found it to buy clothes for Letizia.

"Wonderful, Papa." She paused, and her expression became grave.

Bruno, about to mount the sweeping, round staircase, eyed her. "What's wrong, Leti?"

"It's Fabio and—" Letizia hesitated. "And Francesca."

"What about Francesca?" Vittorio asked sharply.

"She attacked Fabio."

"Rubbish," Vittorio dismissed rudely.

Bruno, hot and tired, set down his crocodile-skin attaché case. "What are you talking about, Letizia?"

"His sister," she said maliciously, "drenched Fabio with the garden hose—ruined his best clothes—and attacked him with a broom."

"With a broom?" Bruno looked incredulous.

"You should see his face, Papa—she really hurt him. There was blood *everywhere!*"

"You're a liar."

Letizia swung around, to find Vittorio's livid face just an inch from her own. "I'm *not,*" she protested. "Ask Mamma, she'll tell you. She had to lock Francesca up. She was like a she-devil, trying to scratch and kick—"

"She locked her *up?*" Vittorio turned and stormed in the direction of their rooms.

"Not there," Letizia called loudly.

Vittorio stopped. "Where, then?" He stalked back to his cousin. "Where is my sister?" he bellowed.

"*Calma, calma,*" Bruno intervened. "It's all right, my boy—leave this to me."

"But it's a pack of lies," Vittorio exclaimed wildly, pure hatred in his eyes. "And now they've shut her up somewhere, and I want her *out!*"

"Vittorio, be quiet, please." Bruno turned to Letizia. "Where is Francesca?"

"In the cellar."

"*What?*" Vittorio seized his cousin by the arm, making her squeal.

"Stop that immediately!" Bruno's voice was unaccustomedly fierce. "I've told you I'll deal with this."

Vittorio let Letizia go, and stood trembling with rage.

"She's in the wine cellar?" Bruno asked his daughter.

"No." Letizia faltered genuinely for the first time. She looked at her arm, red where Vittorio had grabbed her. "Mamma put her under the stairs."

Bruno looked disbelieving. "She wouldn't do such a thing."

"Why not?" Vittorio demanded. "What's under the stairs?"

Bruno ran his hands through his hair.

"Answer me!"

Letizia took a step back before answering. "There are rats down there," she said.

With a roar, Vittorio rushed to the staircase.

"Not that staircase, *idiota*," Letizia said. "At the back of the house."

In a second, Vittorio was hammering on the locked oak door. "Francesca!" There was no reply. "Where's the key!" he screamed back over his shoulder, and then rattled the door handle. "*Francesca! Are you all right?! Answer me!*"

Bruno came hurrying toward him, Letizia following.

"She doesn't answer!" Vittorio shouted, tears of rage and fear in his dark eyes.

Bruno rapped loudly on the door. "Francesca, *piccola*, can you hear me?"

"Oh, God, where's the *key!*"

Bruno turned to Letizia. "Where's your mother?"

"She went to take a bath."

Bruno started up the stairs, but was overtaken by his nephew. "Vittorio, wait!"

Vittorio was ahead of him at the door of the master bedroom.

"I said *wait!*" Bruno called sharply. "I'll get the key."

He opened the bedroom door. Livia, wearing only a fluffy white towel, lay on the bed, resting, a magazine at her side. *"Ciao, caro."* She smiled at him.

"Where is the key?" Bruno asked.

"Prego?"

"To the cellar door. Where have you put it?"

The door banged open.

"Give it to me!" Vittorio was quivering with rage.

Livia held her towel closer. "Get out of here!"

"Do as she says," Bruno said quietly.

"Not till she gives me the key!"

"Bruno, make him go!"

"Where is it? In her bag?" Vittorio stalked over to one of the armchairs, upon which Livia's soft kid clutch-bag rested.

"Don't you dare touch my handbag!" Livia jumped off the bed. "Bruno, stop him!"

Vittorio forced open the clasp and emptied the contents onto the carpet. "Make her give me the key!"

"How *dare* you!"

"Vai via!" Bruno ordered Vittorio. There was no doubting his anger. "Go downstairs, and I'll bring the key."

"Get out!" Livia screamed.

Vittorio walked back to the door. "If you don't unlock the door in the next five minutes," he said, his voice husky with intensity, "I'll break it down any way I have to."

Livia stared him in the eye. "Try it," she replied coldly, "and I will call the police and have you arrested." She paused. "You *and* your whore of a sister."

When the door opened, and Bruno, holding a flashlight cautiously before him, peered into the darkness, he could hardly contain his horror and shame. Francesca lay huddled just a yard inside the entrance, weeping bitterly, too cowed to move.

"*Dio,*" Bruno murmured. He bent down to pick her up, and saw and smelled that she had vomited and wet herself. Grateful that he had ordered Vittorio to wait in his room, Bruno stroked his niece's damp hair, and whispered to her soothingly as he gathered her into his arms.

"I'm sorry," Francesca whimpered against his shoulder.

He gritted his teeth. "For what, in God's name?"

"For making trouble."

Bruno looked down at her face. Her skin was white as snow, with streaks of grime and tears. "Don't worry," he told her, and hugged her gently closer.

In the dingy corridor outside their rooms, Vittorio was pacing tensely. As Bruno approached, he leapt forward and seized his sister from his uncle's arms.

"*Piccolina*—" For a moment, pity and love banished fury, and, cradling her, he took her into her room and put her tenderly down on her bed.

"Where is Luciano?" Bruno asked quietly, hoping to spare the little boy.

"I asked Maria to keep him in the kitchen."

They both looked silently down at Francesca, who lay on the coverlet, eyes closed and deeply ringed with shadows. Bruno bent and brushed a large dusty cobweb from her long hair and heard Vittorio's shocked hiss.

"What?"

"Her ankle." Vittorio stooped, carefully examining the bruised puncture marks just above Francesca's right foot. There was hardly any sign of bleeding.

"*Uno ratto.*" The rage was back in his eyes.

Bruno's mouth was a hard line. "I'll telephone for the doctor," he said. "Stay with her."

Vittorio's voice was immeasurably bitter. "Do you think I would leave her?"

If the atmosphere in Palazzo Speroza had been unpleasant before that September evening, now it became almost intolerable. Francesca was ill for one week, confined to bed and ordered by the disapproving doctor to be carefully attended. Bruno, knowing as well as his wife that their son was a liar, threatened to beat Fabio if he ever laid a finger on Francesca again, but where Livia herself was concerned, he was at a complete loss. Her callous cruelty had shocked him to the core, and he could hardly bear to sleep in the same room with her.

Bruno blamed himself as much as anyone else. He had failed to keep control over his household, had been too busy working to attend to his responsibilities. Perhaps he had asked too much of Livia; she had, after all, not *wanted* the extra burden of his nephews and niece, and she had lectured him often about the risks of neglecting his own children for the others. Letizia and Fabio were fundamentally selfish and arrogant, convinced of their own superiority over their cousins. It was not wholly their fault—they were a product of their mother's influence and Florentine pride. As Bruno saw the situation, all the pressures were now upon him —difficult as it might be, he resolved from now on, to divide himself into many more segments, giving care, attention, and guidance to the whole family.

It was, of course, an unworkable resolution.

✳

Vittorio felt more like a caged beast with each passing day. He hated school more than ever, and the endless preoccupation of his teachers with their precious city and the stones from which it was built. Stones with different names—*pietra serena, macigno,* marbles from Carrara and Prato—but all of them hard and dead and inhuman.

Though their home life in Lucchesia had often been far from serene, Vittorio had, since the fire, imbued those early years with the rosy tint of selective memory. Florence weighed suffocatingly upon him; the cacophony in the streets, the threatening crowds, the motorcycles and scooters and trucks—often sent him scurrying back into the palazzo for shelter, yet as soon as he was in the dark and gloom, the oppressive quality of his life surged up inside him like sickness, making him long to escape again.

It had never occurred to Vittorio that he *could* escape, until early that autumn, when his class had gone on an excursion to Bellosguardo to see one of the most famous vistas of the city.

The teacher had spoken of beauty, and Vittorio had observed that his fellow pupils were genuinely touched by the glory. But while they had looked down at the gold and ochre stones, Vittorio had stared beyond the city and up into the sky, and had realized that, at that moment, while his contemporaries were fully absorbed, it would be an easy matter for him simply to run away—and the desire to flee had been so vast and all-consuming, he could hardly bear it. Only the knowledge that he could never abandon Francesca or Luciano had kept his feet on the dusty ground, had prevented the rest of his body from following his soul back into the *campagna,* back to where the cypresses grew and the children roamed free and the air was sweet.

It was in late October, after overhearing a small dispute between his aunt and Francesca about a scolding she had given to Luciano, that Vittorio made the decision that would irrevocably alter all their lives.

"You made him cry," Francesca accused Livia. She was very wary of her aunt these days, but the defense of her little brother always lent her extra reserves of courage.

"He cries too easily," Livia dismissed. "He should be discouraged."

"He's only seven."

"Boys must learn not to resort to tears at the slightest thing, even at seven. Fabio was far stronger at that age."

"Luciano is a gentle child."

"Gentleness is for weaklings, Francesca."

"Uncle Bruno is gentle."

"Don't be impudent!"

"I'm not!"

Livia's eyes flashed. "Have you already forgotten the lesson I taught you, Francesca? The lesson I thought you had learned."

Francesca did not dare to answer.

"The cellar is still there, you know," Livia threatened, "if you over-step the mark, young lady—just remember."

Never, Vittorio thought grimly, standing just around the corner, out of sight. *Never again.*

He heard Livia's high heels clacking away on the stone floor, and then he thought he heard his sister's small, suppressed whimper of fear.

He remembered the horizon beyond Florence, felt again the burn-ing, aching desire he experienced every day to run from Palazzo Speroza and to leave Florence forever.

It's time, he thought. *It's too late for Giacomo and Giulietta, but we can still do it.*

And for the first time in months, Vittorio smiled.

Chapter 6

THERE WAS A SMALL children's play area in the grounds of the Ospedale San Felice di Dio, in which, each afternoon, a number of recovering and convalescing youngsters between the ages of about five and twelve could be seen running, skipping, or jumping around. Some of them seemed too fit and healthy to be in a hospital at all; some moved tentatively or with real difficulty, while others merely sat back in their wheelchairs and enjoyed being out in the fresh air.

There was one child, in a corner of the playground, aged seven years and four months—tall for her age and thin, with long, straight blond hair tied back with a scrap of thin blue ribbon—who was one of these onlookers. She leaned back in her chair, gazing in the direction of the participants, yet if one studied her more closely. it was clear that she was only staring into space, not really watching at all.

The visitor, accompanied by a nursing sister, noticed the child almost immediately. There was something about her that drew her attention.

"Who is that?" she asked.

"Giulietta Volpi," the nurse answered. "Full-thickness burns to chest and shoulders, multiple fractures to both legs."

The visitor looked a little more closely. "How long ago? She seems well recovered."

"I believe she's been with us for two years."

The visitor was startled. "Why?"

"Nowhere else to go, for one thing."

"No family?"

The nurse shook her head. "All lost in the car crash that put her in here."

"Why the chair?"

"Giulietta is a deeply withdrawn child," the sister explained. "We've never been able to get through to her. She never really cooperated with her physiotherapists. She had no will."

"Then why is she still here? Why hasn't she been sent to an institution?"

"I understand she's due to go to an orphanage next month. I'm not sure why they've kept her here this long." The nurse paused. "I believe you're lunching with the *direttori*—you could ask them about Giulietta."

"I shall." The visitor looked back at the child. "But I'd like to speak to her first, if I may."

The sister nodded. "By all means."

The blond girl did not look up as the visitor approached, just continued to stare vacantly into space.

"*Buon giorno*, Giulietta."

"*Buon giorno.*"

"*Mi chiamo* Elizabeth Austen." The visitor waited for a moment. "*Sono inglese.*"

Without another word, she sat on the low wall beside her.

Giulietta turned her face to look at the stranger. She was quite old, but pretty, with wavy brown hair and gray eyes. She looked different.

"Are you a doctor?" she asked.

"*Sì.*"

"Oh."

Elizabeth Austen sensed her disappointment. Just another doctor.

"But I'm from England," she said again, as if that might make a difference.

Giulietta remained silent.

"Do you like it here, Giulietta?"

"It's all right." Her voice was flat.

"Do you mind talking to me?" Elizabeth asked gently.

"No."

"Good." She paused. "What's the matter with your legs?"

"They broke."

"But they're mended now, aren't they?"

Giulietta gave a little shrug. "They don't work."

"Don't you like crutches?"

The child shook her head.

"Why not?"

Giulietta made a small, frustrated movement with her hands.

Elizabeth thought for a moment. The little girl's hands and arms were curiously still, especially for an Italian child. She remembered the burns. Giulietta wore a long-sleeved blue dress, so that it was impossible to see her scars.

"Don't your arms work either?" she asked softly.

Again, Giulietta shrugged.

"Can you catch a ball?"

"No."

"Or swim?"

"I don't know."

Elizabeth got off the wall. "Can you shake my hand?" She extended her arm toward the child.

Giulietta raised her right arm a little way, but not high enough to touch Elizabeth's hand.

"*Bene,*" Elizabeth said.

Giulietta frowned. "*Perchè?*"

"It's good because I think I may know how to make your arms work properly."

"*Sì?*"

Elizabeth smiled. "*Sì.*"

It was as if a spark, almost of recognition, passed between them, linking them to each other.

Giulietta Volpi stared into the gray, friendly, *honest* eyes.

And she, too, smiled.

"I want to take her to England," Elizabeth Austen told the *direttore* of the hospital.

"Really?" He sounded surprised.

"As soon as possible."

The dark-suited Italian eyed her quizzically. "You are affected by this child, *Dottoressa.*"

"True." Elizabeth had no objection to the familiarity of his comment. She had visited Giulietta every day since she had first spoken to her ten days earlier, so it was hardly surprising that she had aroused interest.

"May I ask why? She is such an ordinary child."

"No child is ordinary, *signor.*"

"Of course not—and especially not to a pediatrician." He smiled. "But you don't want to take every child to England, *Dottoressa.*"

"No."

"Then why *this* child?"

"Because I think I can help Giulietta," she said. "And because I feel that she is—special."

"To you?"

"Yes."

"You have no children of your own, do you, *Dottoressa?*"

"I have not."

"And would you think of adopting Giulietta?"

"I might," Elizabeth replied steadily, "if it were feasible." She paused. "And if she wanted it."

The *direttore* smiled. "Then Giulietta is a very fortunate child."

"She hasn't had much good fortune until now," Elizabeth said dryly.

"Then it is a lesson to us all, never to give up."

✳

He sat, for a long time, after the Englishwoman had left his office, contemplating the small problem that she had created for him.

The source of the money that had arrived each quarter ever since Giulietta Volpi had come to them had been anonymous. And the only condition of the donation, which was generous—more, by a fair amount, than was needed for the child's care—had been that no attempt must ever be made to locate the donor. Had Giulietta gone, as planned, to the orphanage, the money would, of course, have gone with her for the benefit of that institution. This, however, was a very different situation. Elizabeth Austen was a well-to-do English pediatrician, the widow of an eminent surgeon. She would neither need the money nor would she, he was certain, wish to deprive the *ospedale* of useful sums.

There it was, then. The Volpi child's records were pitifully scanty, with little real information about her past. In a sense, the *direttore* mused, the bleakness of Giulietta's history might assist Dr. Austen, for since there were no relatives to care about her, there would be no one to oppose either her removal to England or her eventual adoption.

✳

Elizabeth was thoroughly aware of the effects of institutionalization on long-stay patients. Two years for an adult could be harmful enough, but for a child in her formative years, any displacement was bound to be traumatic.

She had attempted to explain, simply and clearly, what was going to happen to Giulietta if she agreed. When she had asked the little girl if she wanted to go to England, Giulietta had quickly consented, but Elizabeth knew that for this child, England was nothing more than a small blob on a geography map. It was doubtful that she had ever traveled in anything more complicated than a car, bus, train, or ambulance. There was no way of knowing how she would react to a flight in a BEA Viscount airplane, let alone to an alien language, climate, and people.

"You understand that I want to help you, Giulietta, don't you?"

Elizabeth said to her the morning before they were due to leave the hospital.

Giulietta nodded.

"And you realize that when we get to England you will be going to another hospital?" She had told her as much as possible about what she hoped could be done for her, frankly explaining that there was no way to be sure how much she could be helped to walk and move around more freely until the *specialiste* had examined her.

"There may be some pain," Elizabeth said, aware that in this field, at least, she was talking to a veteran. With burns of the type that Giulietta had suffered in the accident, there must have been a prolonged period of agony, only partially muted by drugs.

"I understand," Giulietta told her, keeping her eyes fixed unwaveringly on the gray, kind eyes that had suddenly, in the past fortnight, become a lifeline to her.

"And you will need to be very patient, and very good."

"*Sì, Dottoressa,*" Giulietta said, almost resignedly.

Elizabeth laughed. "I've told you all this a dozen times already, haven't I, *piccola?*"

"*Sì.*"

"So tomorrow we go."

Giulietta nodded again.

Elizabeth studied her for a moment, thoughtfully. "Tell me, Giulietta, have people treated you kindly here?"

"Yes." The blue eyes were solemn, still glued to hers.

"But you have been unhappy."

First hesitation—then another nod, shyer this time.

Elizabeth, too, felt a strange sense of inarticulateness and of humility. "I think—I hope—that we're going to be great friends, Giulietta."

This whole area was utterly unfamiliar to her. As a doctor, she had spent the last ten years of her career fighting against feelings of attachment to patients, a feat especially hard for a pediatrician. But there was the difference, and a crucial one. Giulietta Volpi was not a patient. She was a child of mystery, a skinny, golden Italian orphan who would certainly be a beauty but for the ugly, disfiguring scars on her body and her disability. Elizabeth would never truly understand what had happened that afternoon in the playground, but it was as if the child, remote as she might have appeared, had waved a sorceress's wand over her, beckoning her to her with her sad eyes and her lovely, unsmiling mouth.

Giulietta had asked no questions of Elizabeth, had simply seemed to accept her at face value. *Had* she asked, Elizabeth would readily have answered anything and everything she wanted to know. She would have told her about her life, about her happy childhood, about her joyous marriage and its grievously premature end. She would have told her that she had never had children of her own, because neither she nor Edward, her husband, had felt the need; she had always had all the children she needed through her work, and Edward had wanted no one but her.

But she had not asked, and so at this moment there existed the strangest and most precious of bonds between them—that of inexplicable, unquestioning trust.

"I feel," Elizabeth said softly, "that you are very special to me. I don't know why that should be, for we hardly know each other, yet it is true."

"Yes," Giulietta agreed gravely.

Elizabeth felt her heart twist. "You feel it too?"

The child did not answer in words. Instead, she lifted her right hand from her lap—her still, expressionless hand—and placed it in Elizabeth's open palm.

Elizabeth wanted to weep—to *sing*—but she held herself under control.

"I must go now," she said steadily. "But I'll be back before bedtime to help with your packing."

"For England." The blue eyes shone with hope.

Elizabeth nodded. "*Sì*, Giulietta."

Chapter 7

VITTORIO had it all worked out.

He had planned it alone, plotted the entire strategy without confiding even in Francesca. She was too fragile these days, too nervous for him to risk burdening her with such a monumental secret too soon.

It had taken him some time and a great deal of work. He had never applied himself with such diligence and energy to anything, but then he had never felt such intense motivation. He was utterly committed. No matter how difficult or dangerous, he would never let his sister be subjected to such horror again. They were born to sunlight and fresh air, and to grass and trees. If they could only get away from the murky waters of the Arno and the dark, sinister streets, they could start to breathe again, to *live*.

His first choice would, of course, have been to return to Lucchesia, perhaps even to the ruins of their old house, but that would be the first place anyone would look for them. No, it had to be far away—*very* far—where nobody would recognize them and they would be safe.

Certain that he would find a way, he began to smuggle books and maps home from school, and took to studying them late at night under his bedclothes with a flashlight, and gradually, painfully, his plan took shape.

They would leave Florence at night, when everyone was sleeping, and would head, by bicycle, out to the west, following the Arno toward

Empoli and Cascina, aiming for the coast, where they would travel south over the Maremma, a wild, swampy plain extending from Livorno almost down to Civitavecchia. Vittorio's books taught that this had been a malaria-infested and taboo part of Tuscany until they had begun a reclamation program, but even though the disease had been eradicated, the photographs were still desolate and unwelcoming.

Perfetto! he thought triumphantly. The Maremma might not appeal to normal visitors, but it had three features that made it ideal for their purposes. There was plentiful hunting—deer, wild boar, sheep, pheasants —and all manner of fishing. There was shelter—crumbling watchtowers along the coast, from which, in olden times, a lookout had been kept for Saracen invaders. And best of all, no one would dream of looking for them there.

The Maremma was, of course, only part of Vittorio's *grande progetto.* They would make their way steadily and stealthily south until they came to Naples. Naples, the country's greatest port and—for Vittorio, Francesca, and Luciano Cesaretti—their gateway to liberty.

The plan would work. He was sure it would work.

He told Francesca.

"But we don't have bicycles."

"We'll find them."

"You mean steal them."

"Perhaps." Vittorio reddened with frustration. "Is that all you can talk about—*bicycles?* I've just told you how we can get out of this bloody place—and all you can say is that we don't have any damn bicycles!"

Francesca hushed him. It was after one in the morning, and she had crept out of her room, careful not to wake their young brother. "Luciano has never ridden a bicycle."

"So we'll teach him." He paused, and seized both her hands. "Francesca, it'll be so *good* for him—for us all!" His eyes gleamed. "There are half-wild horses on the plains—we may be able to ride them—and we'll swim and we'll be *free!*"

"Luciano will be scared."

"We'll look after him."

She still looked doubtful. "He hasn't been nearly as unhappy here as we have, you know. He doesn't seem to mind Florence, and he adores school." She paused. "What *about* school?"

"Who cares about school!" Vittorio scoffed. "I'll be fourteen next June, and then I'll never have to go again anyway!"

"Luciano needs education," Francesca insisted quietly.

"He'll have all the education he needs once we get to America." She stared at him.

"Sure." Vittorio grinned broadly, delighted at her shock. "Where did you think we would go once we reached Naples?"

"I don't know—Sicily?"

"Too close."

Francesca's mind was reeling. "America," she murmured.

"It's full of Italians—I read all about it," Vittorio enthused. "It's where people always try to go to when they're running away—escaping, like us. '*Il paese delle opportunità,*' they call it." His eyes misted over with fantasy and longing.

Francesca gazed at her older brother with wonder.

"Do you really think we can do it?"

"We have to." Vittorio's tone became urgent. "*I* have to, *carissima.* If I don't leave this place soon, I'll *explode!*" He reached for her hands again. "Say yes, Francesca," he implored her. "We can do it, I *swear* it!"

"There's so much to think of," she said distractedly. "The bicycles— teaching Luciano—" Her eyes widened. "*Telling* Luciano."

Vittorio shook his head emphatically. "We can't tell him until the last possible minute—you know he can't keep a secret."

"I still don't know—"

"Francesca—" He stopped her. "Think of the cellar. She's threatened to do it again, and she will." He paused. "Remember it," he said grimly.

Francesca closed her eyes. The rat of her waking nightmare appeared instantly, brown and huge and vivid. Bile rose in her throat, and she shivered.

"*Allora?*" Vittorio pressed softly.

She opened her eyes. "How soon can we leave?"

The biggest problem was teaching Luciano to ride the small machine his brother had stolen from the Boboli Gardens without anyone finding out.

"It's a surprise for Uncle Bruno," Francesca whispered to him. "He's going to buy you a bicycle for Christmas, and think how wonderful it will be if you can ride it straightaway."

"But he doesn't have to buy me one—I've got this one."

"That's only borrowed—and if anyone finds out about it, Vittorio will get into terrible trouble."

"It's ages till Christmas," Luciano pointed out. "I'll learn long before then."

Francesca ruffled his fair hair. "I hope so."

They had to wait until the second weekend of December, though by then they had been ready to leave for a good ten days. Francesca was horribly nervous. Luciano was oblivious. Vittorio was a seething bundle of temperament, restive and dangerously irascible.

"You must be more careful," Francesca warned him one night after a dinner when he'd sat on his uncle's left and squeezed his glass so ferociously that it had snapped at the stem. "You'll give the whole thing away."

Vittorio chewed at the knuckles of his right hand. "I can't help it, *cara*—I can't take much more."

"It's only a few more days," she soothed him.

"A *lifetime*," he whispered sharply, and sprang off his bed to pace the room as he did for much of every night.

They had earmarked that particular weekend because Livia had persuaded Bruno to let Fabio and Letizia accompany them on a visit to

Rome for a jewelry exhibition. It would be a lavish and extravagant few days; they would stay at the Hassler and Livia and the children would, undoubtedly, spend hours on Via Condotti. Maria had been directed to cancel a weekend at her parents' home, but otherwise the place would be deserted.

The three stolen bicycles were hidden in an old shed at school. Under Vittorio's bed was the fishing rod and net he had managed to buy, together with a slightly torn canvas bag, containing the binoculars given to him on his last birthday by his uncle, a compass, two maps, and a knife.

The first hint of disaster struck on the Friday morning.

"*La signora* is ill," Maria told the children at breakfast.

"What's wrong with her?" Vittorio asked brusquely.

"The doctor came during the night—he said she was poisoned."

"Poisoned?" Francesca, already pale, grew whiter.

"By the oysters she ate yesterday in a restaurant."

"What's oysters?" Luciano asked, looking up from his *caffè lungo*.

"Will she be well enough to go to Rome?" Francesca fought to sound casual.

Maria shrugged.

"Oyster poisoning's nothing," Vittorio said vehemently. "A boy at school said his father had it, and was fine next day."

"But they're going *today*," Francesca blurted, unable to keep the panic from her voice.

Maria shrugged again. "Today, tomorrow—who can say?"

"What's oysters?" Luciano asked again.

No one answered him.

Bruno, Fabio, and Letizia left at six o'clock that evening. Aunt Livia, they told the others, was too weak to face the drive, but hoped to follow next morning.

"Do you think she will go?" Francesca asked Vittorio as soon as they were alone. The bicycles had been transferred, earlier, from the school shed to a nearby alley.

"She has to."

"But what if she doesn't?"

Vittorio bit his lip. "It changes nothing," he said decisively.

"How can it change nothing?"

"We'll wait till she's asleep tomorrow night."

"I hope she goes," Francesca said fervently.

"*Gesù,* so do I."

Livia did not go to Rome. Complaining all through the day at her misfortune, she nonetheless told Maria that there was no need for her stay at the palazzo overnight, so long as she came in next morning.

"But Louisa is off until Monday," Maria pointed out. "Who will cook for you, *signora?*"

"I couldn't think of food," Livia groaned.

"But the children."

"Surely my niece is capable of making a little supper. Stop making a fuss and let me rest." Livia, still in bed, laid her head back against a pile of large white pillows.

Maria closed the door softly, a smile on her lips. She had already told her parents not to expect her, and now she and Guido would have the whole night together.

At half past midnight on Saturday night, one hour after the light under Livia's door had been extinguished, Vittorio went down to the kitchen to raid the larder. When he returned, fifteen minutes later, he took one look at his sister and blinked in astonishment. "What have you done to yourself?"

Francesca pointed to a pair of scissors lying on her bed beside a heap of dark hair. "I thought that if they do come looking for us, they won't be looking for three boys."

Vittorio stared at her in some awe. Francesca had transformed herself. He had never considered just how feminine she was—she was just his sister—but now, looking at this stranger with cropped, urchin hair, wearing a pair of his own rolled-up trousers, the difference was dramatic.

"*Uno ragazzo,*" he murmured. "A boy."

"*Sì.*" For an instant, Francesca's eyes, more enormous than ever now that her elfin face was deprived of its frame, pricked with tears, but swiftly she brought herself under control, and helped to unload the pickings from the kitchen larder onto his bed. He'd taken three loaves, two *salami toscano,* a large slab of *pecorino* cheese, a bag of apples and the sweet, fortifying *panforte* that Louisa had baked only last week, and from which just two slices had been extracted.

"Shall we wake Luciano now?"

"Not yet." Vittorio paused. "There's one more thing I have to do first."

"What?"

"Money." He looked her in the eye. "We have to have some money with us. We'll need to buy our passage to America—we can't go anywhere without money."

"No," Francesca begged softly. "No more stealing."

"Just this one last thing."

"No."

"I'm not going to take from Uncle Bruno—I wouldn't," Vittorio said earnestly. "Fabio keeps cash in his bedside table."

"He'll have taken it with him to Rome."

"He never takes it anywhere. He doesn't need to—his mother sees to it that he has more than enough. He showed me once how he turns out his pockets every night and stuffs all his spare lire into the drawer. You know how he and Letizia love to preen and boast before the *poveri,*" he finished bitterly.

Francesca shook her head. "I still don't think we should—"

"Why not?" Vittorio interrupted. "Why *shouldn't* we?"

"Because we're not common thieves, and that's what they'll call us."

"I'll send it back," Vittorio said. "Not for Fabio, but for our uncle. When we're in America and we have money of our own, I'll send it back." He looked at his sister's unhappy face. "Francesca, we have to have it."

Francesca said nothing for a moment, then sighed. "All right." She shrugged. "If we have to, then—"

Vittorio kissed her soundly on the cheek. "I'll be just a few minutes, and then we'll wake Luciano and be on our way."

"I'll pack the food."

"And the hair. They mustn't know that you cut it." Silently, Vittorio opened the door.

"Vittorio," Francesca called quietly after him.

He turned his head. "What?"

"Be careful."

His feet were soundless on the soft carpet outside Fabio's bedroom, but still he thanked providence that his aunt and uncle's suite was on the opposite side of the house.

The handle was cool and turned smoothly. Inside the room, he closed the door and went straight to the bedside table on the right of the bed. There was no need to switch on a lamp—the moon shone through the unshuttered windows, illuminating the polished mahogany furniture.

He tried the drawer. It was locked.

He swore softly.

He had slipped the kitchen knife through his belt at his right hip. Swiftly, he drew it out and, kneeling, inserted it into the narrow gap between the drawer and the frame and jiggled it back and forth. The drawer opened. The cash was there, as he had known it would be, the casually discarded notes of a spoiled and arrogant teenager.

He slid the knife back into his belt and then, with both hands, stuffed the money into his pockets. They felt bulky. For a moment, thinking of the round, kind face of his uncle, he flushed with shame. And then, just as quickly, he thought of Fabio and Letizia and their mother, and the guilt receded.

He turned, and padded back toward the door.

There was a click, and a flash of light, and he stood, rooted to the spot, like an animal frozen in shock.

"A thief."

Livia's voice broke the silence, harsh, censorial, and knowing.

Vittorio could not speak.

"Just a common thief," Livia said. "I warned my husband, but he was too kind."

She wore a white silk peignoir, and her hair was a little disheveled.

"Empty your pockets," she ordered.

"No."

"I said *empty* them." Her outrage was majestic.

Vittorio stood his ground. "No," he said again, his heart pounding furiously.

Livia flushed with anger. "Very well—better, perhaps, that your uncle sees for himself how you've stolen from him."

"Not from him." Defiance masked his rising fear.

Her eyes glittered. "You steal in his home, you steal from him. And you know what happens to thieves, I'm sure. They go to prison."

Vittorio's mind began to work, feverishly. He was as tall as his aunt; he could push past her easily and run, but Francesca and Luciano were not prepared.

"Come with me," Livia said.

He wavered.

"This *instant.*" It was a whiplash command.

Vittorio gave a shrug, insolent and casual. Livia reached forward and grasped his left arm. Her fingernails dug into his flesh.

They began to walk, along the still dark corridor to the main staircase. They descended, in silence, Livia holding the banister rail with her left hand and her captive's arm with her right.

"Are you calling the police?" Vittorio asked, still docile, while his brain burned with hatred and determination.

"Certainly," Livia answered. "When your uncle gets home."

"But that's not until Monday."

She said nothing more, towing him along, her peignoir sweeping behind her, creating a whisper of breeze. They passed out of the main hall, and for a moment Vittorio thought she was taking him to his bedroom—but then he saw the back staircase and the oak door, and he knew what she intended.

"*Un sapore di prigione,*" Livia hissed. "Just a little taste of jail before the real thing."

They stopped before the door. The key was in the lock.

If she gets me down there, Vittorio thought, *it'll all be over.*

Denial, trenchant and enraged, swept through him like a wild, rapid transfusion of strength. He would not allow her to end it, to stop them—

Keeping hold of his arm, Livia turned the key.

He would not let her.

She opened the door.

"There," she said. "A cell for a thief."

He did not fight her. He let her steer him through the doorway, so that the smell of the place, dank and foul, flowed into his nostrils. She stood right behind him, seeming to enjoy the moment.

Vittorio was very still. The blood pumped in his ears, almost deafening him. He was waiting—just a split second more—for Livia's viselike hand to relax its grip on his arm, and then—

"Do you have nothing to say?"

"Nothing."

"*Bene.*"

The instant came. The hand on his arm loosened. He heard the shuffle of her slipper as she took a backward step—

"*No!*"

The single word was a roar as he spun around, every muscle and sinew straining with effort and the joy of release, and grabbed her. His right hand seized her left wrist, his other hand snatched first at her waist, lost its grip and swiftly flew up to clutch at the collar of her robe.

Livia shrieked, kicked out at him with her right leg and missed, her slipper hurtling from her foot and striking the wall.

"No, *Zia* Livia!" Vittorio hissed in her ear. "You won't do to me what you did to my sister!"

"Let me *go!*"

"See how you like it, bitch!" With another immense surge of

strength, he whirled his aunt around so that now it was she who stood just inside the cellar entrance, her back to the stone steps.

Livia's eyes widened. "Don't you *dare!*"

Vittorio stared contemptuously into her face.

"Don't be a fool—think of the *consequences.*"

Vittorio thought—of Livia, locked in damp darkness with rats and cockroaches for company until Maria came in the morning, just a *scrap* of time compared to what she had intended for him—and his blood roared victoriously through his veins, and he threw back his head and laughed.

"You're mad!" Livia's eyes were full of horror.

His laughter stopped. "Not at all." His grip was tighter than ever. "Just getting even."

Her fear was palpable now. "Help me!" she cried, and her face contorted. "Someone *help* me!"

"No one will help you."

Livia was very white. "You *are* mad," she said. "Your mother was insane—"

"Shut up!"

"Does a sane woman burn herself and half her family to death?" she taunted, and then, unexpectedly, kicked at him again, hitting her target this time with her left foot.

Vittorio, caught off balance, gasped with pain. Livia took advantage of the moment and wrenched her right arm free, raking at his face with her red fingernails.

"No!" Vittorio thundered, and desperation was like a mist before his eyes, so that he saw his aunt dimly, as if through a veil of fury. "*No!*"

He thrust out both hands, catching her on the shoulder and stomach, and with one mighty shove, he pushed her away from him—

Livia Speroza Cesaretti screamed.

Her eyes were huge, wrenched open—her mouth gaped in terror—she stumbled, her remaining slipper twisting under her left foot—

And she began to fall.

✶

Vittorio backed into the hall and slammed the door shut. He could not breathe—he could not see—

The key was still in the lock, and mechanically, he turned it.

The scream seemed to go on forever, muffled by the solid oak door, yet jangling deafeningly in his ears.

And then he heard the thud—dull and heavy—

And then there was silence.

Francesca stood in his room, her face agonized with the suspense of waiting. She took one look at the bloody scratches on his cheek, and blanched.

"What happened?"

Vittorio said nothing. His jaw worked, and he moistened his dry lips with his tongue.

"My God, what *happened*, Vittorio?" Francesca put up her hand to touch his face, and stared at her fingers as they came away sticky with blood.

"She—" He swallowed.

Francesca seized his hands. "You're trembling—why are you *trembling?*" Her eyes widened. "Aunt Livia caught you."

The mention of the name brought Vittorio back to his senses, and he wrenched his hands from his sister. "Go and wake Luciano," he said.

"Not till you tell me what happened. Where is she?" She, too, was shaking. "Where is Aunt Livia?"

"In the cellar." His voice was so quiet, Francesca had to strain to hear him.

"What?"

"I locked her in the cellar." Vittorio's eyes were quite black. "She was going to shut me in there till Monday, but I got away."

"And locked her in." Francesca looked at him with a mixture of uncertainty and fear. "You didn't hurt her, did you?"

"Go and wake Luciano," he said again.

"Vittorio, you *didn't* hurt her, did you?"

Vittorio shook his head. "I don't think so."

"You don't *think?*"

Abruptly, he grasped her by the arms. "Francesca, I told you to wake Luciano. Get him dressed and ready to go."

"But we can't just leave her in the cellar!"

"Why not?" He let her go. "She left you for long enough, didn't she? And I told you, she wanted to leave me down there till Uncle Bruno got back." He turned away to hide the fear in his eyes, and pretended to check the contents of the canvas bag. "Anyway, Maria will be here in a few hours—she'll let her out."

Francesca gnawed at her lip. "You really think we should still go?"

He whirled back to face her. "Are you nuts? We have to leave more than ever." He walked back out into the corridor. "Now for the last time, see to Luciano."

"Where are you going?"

"Back to Fabio's room."

"What for?"

"Never mind."

Upstairs, the light still shone in the plush bedroom. Vittorio wasted no time. Taking a handkerchief from his pocket, he wiped the bedside table, turned off the light switch, wiped that, and then, moving swiftly to the window, he wrapped his right hand in the same handkerchief and smashed it. If Aunt Livia was safe, he would, without question, be marked a violent thief—if not, then perhaps, just *perhaps*, Uncle Bruno might believe that a burglar was responsible for—

If not.

Vittorio shuddered violently and drew a feverish hand across his eyes, fighting back sudden tears of delayed panic. The thought that he might, perhaps, have killed his aunt filled him with unspeakable horror. The prospect, on the other hand, that Livia might be able to condemn him was even more terrifying.

✴

Within two hours, they were out of Florence, riding west along the Arno, waterlogged by a tremendous thunderstorm. Young Luciano, utterly confused at having been dragged from his sleep, bundled out of the palazzo, planted on his bicycle, and ordered to pedal as hard and fast as he could, cowered at every lightning flash and begged Vittorio to let them stop.

"I want to go home!" he cried out as another great boom of thunder rolled around them.

"Keep pedaling!" Vittorio shouted back over his shoulder.

"But where are we *going?*"

"To a safe place," Francesca, keeping up the rear, told him.

"But we were safe at home!"

"That wasn't our home, and we weren't safe!" Vittorio blinked away the blinding raindrops as a new flash of lightning illuminated the landscape. "Stop talking, *piccolo,* and save your strength!"

"I'm *cold!*" Luciano complained.

"I know, *caro,*" Francesca sympathized.

"I want to go back!"

Vittorio, his face set against the wind, gritted his teeth. "We can't go back," he said. "Not ever."

Just before half past four in the morning, Vittorio allowed them to take shelter in a thicket not far from the Empoli road.

"I'm hungry," Luciano whimpered, his legs aching from the unaccustomed exercise.

"I'll give you some *panforte.*" Francesca began to feel around in the canvas bag.

"Not yet." Vittorio's voice stopped her.

"But he's hungry."

"If we start eating now, we'll run out of food before we get to the Maremma."

"So when *can* we eat?"

"When we stop for a real rest. We'll have to find a place to hide during the day—we can't risk being seen."

"Why not?" Luciano demanded. "Is it dangerous here?"

"No, darling, it's quite safe."

Luciano began to cry, and Francesca folded him in her arms and stared accusingly at Vittorio. "You're expecting too much of him. He's exhausted and hungry and frightened."

"All right," Vittorio relented grudgingly. "He can have some *panforte*, but just a little."

The ferocity of the storm had abated a little, leaving long periods of unrelieved darkness, and the lack of thunder, too, meant that for the first time since leaving the city, the children could hear the myriad night sounds that the countryside tossed into the air after sunset. Crickets rasped, owls hooted and screeched, the river frothed and raced, gorged by the cloudburst, distant dogs barked, and other anonymous night birds added to the clamor.

"Was it always like this in the country?" Francesca asked Vittorio uneasily. "I don't remember."

"It's been more than two years."

"I suppose we were always asleep by this time."

A new voice interrupted them, a strange, unearthly howling, and Luciano, terrified, dropped the cake he was eating and clutched at Francesca's sleeve.

"What was that?" She could not sound calm, even for Luciano's sake.

"Don't know," Vittorio muttered.

"I want to go *home*," Luciano wailed.

"I told you, we can't," Vittorio said grouchily.

The howling began again.

"It's a dog," Vittorio said.

"Is it?" Francesca murmured uncertainly.

"Is it a wolf?" Luciano wanted to know.

"Of course not."

A screech owl flew overhead, too close for comfort, and all three children jumped. Luciano began to weep again, and Francesca stood up.

"Where are you going?" Vittorio asked.

"Nowhere." She could just make out the outline of her bicycle, and she rummaged in her saddlebag.

"What are you *doing*?"

"*Aspetto.*"

She found what she wanted and, gingerly, she pulled it out and returned to the others. "Switch on the flashlight," she whispered.

"We have to save it."

"Switch it *on.*"

Vittorio clicked on the light, and stared.

"*Gesù!*"

"A gun!" Luciano's wide blue eyes looked uncanny in the bright pool of light. "Is it real, Francesca?"

She nodded.

"Where the hell did you get it?" Vittorio was staggered. "It's Uncle Bruno's, isn't it?"

"I knew where he kept it," she explained, a little shyly. "I've seen him cleaning it, and I thought we might need it for hunting."

"Give it to me."

She handed the black revolver to her older brother with a sense of relief. "I got bullets, too," she said, and produced two handfuls from her trouser pockets.

Vittorio was hunched over the gun. "It's not loaded now, is it?"

"I don't know."

He fumbled for a moment, then discovered how to break the weapon in order to see into the chambers. "No," he said.

"Can I touch it?" Luciano had stopped crying.

"No!" Vittorio said sharply. "It's dangerous—you must never touch it." He glanced up at Francesca with new respect. "You stole something too." He smiled at her.

"I know." She was glad that the darkness hid her flush.

"*Grazie,*" he said softly.

"*Niente.*" She gulped.

Vittorio took the bullets from her, pocketed half and put the rest at the bottom of his saddlebag. Then he switched off the flashlight, and stared into the inky black night.

The possession of the revolver was a genuine asset. It would protect them, if necessary, and it would, as Francesca had suggested, help with the hunting.

It also set off a new and chilling awareness in him. A stolen weapon could only exacerbate their situation. In the space of a few short hours, he had become, at only thirteen, a wanted criminal. There was no possible way of knowing what lay ahead for the three of them.

He only knew that there was no going back.

Maria arrived at Palazzo Speroza at eight o'clock, after an excellent and romantic night with Guido, followed by morning mass. The house was still—even the children, who were usually early risers, seemed still asleep.

Innocenti, she thought benevolently, and wondered at what time Signora Cesaretti would want breakfast. Not before nine, she decided, and put her feet up in the kitchen.

It was ten minutes after nine when, bearing a beautifully laid tray, hoping to put her mistress in a good temper for the morning, Maria found her bed empty.

It was another fifteen minutes before she discovered that Vittorio, Francesca, and Luciano were gone.

And it was just before ten o'clock when she was finally drawn to the cellar door by one of the palazzo cats scratching insatiably at the oak door.

Uno ratto, she mentally dismissed it. But after a minute, seeing the strange wildness of the well-fed animal, she unlocked the door.

It was pitch-dark inside, and Maria cursed Guido for not having come with her this morning, but still, that was men—never there when you needed them.

She went to the kitchen for a flashlight and returned to the open door. The cat had disappeared. Maria stepped tentatively through the entrance, screwing up her face at the dankness. She shone the beam of the flashlight around, wondering what she expected to find except vermin.

"Foolish cat," she muttered.

And then she saw her.

"*Madre mia.*"

Livia Cesaretti lay sprawled at the foot of the steps, like a discarded puppet. Her legs were twisted, her eyes were torn wide and glazed with terror.

And her neck was broken.

Chapter 8

"**Why do you** never cry, Giulietta?"

"I don't know." The blue eyes gave nothing away.

"You are in pain, aren't you, *piccolina?*"

The child shrugged.

"It's fine to be brave, *cara*, but it's all right to cry if you want to."
Elizabeth Austen paused. "They told me, at the *ospedale*, that you used
to cry—in the early days, after you arrived."

"Did I?" She sounded mildly curious.

"So they say."

"I don't remember."

England was damp, cold and gray. The people were pale and composed, and spoke in an incomprehensible language. The food was stodgy
and, to Giulietta's palate, tasteless.

But for the fact that she was, for the moment, still cradled in the
familiar antisepsis of hospitalization, she might as well have been on
another planet.

Yet she thought—and it was only a suspicion, since she could not
recall ever having experienced it before—that she might almost be—
happy.

Stoke Mandeville Hospital, near Aylesbury in the county of Buckinghamshire, was perhaps the most famous hospital in the country, or even in Europe, because it housed the National Spinal Injuries Centre, the unit created and run by a refugee from Nazi Germany, Ludwig Guttmann. Starting its existence in 1944 in a converted Nissen hut, with its only X-ray machine in an overturned cupboard, the unit had revolutionized the future of patients with severe spinal injuries, transforming what would, before Guttmann, have been little more than a lingering death into a positive, useful return to the world.

There were, however, far more parts to Stoke Mandeville than the remarkable center. It was also a busy general hospital with a fine burns unit, and some of the best surgeons and physiotherapists in the land. Elizabeth Austen wanted the best for Giulietta. If asked, she still could not have explained exactly why that was—it just *was*. Her determination to see the little Italian girl planted on the road to a normal life was as steely and single-minded as her ambition, as a twenty-year-old, had been to become a pediatrician. Elizabeth had met many aimless people, with no apparent goals to stimulate them, and she realized what a blessing it was to be able to diagnose a desire, like an ache, and to set about healing that ache with achievement. Marriage to Edward Austen had been that kind of a challenge; she had known, the instant they'd met, that she intended to love him till death.

The feelings she had for Giulietta Volpi were different, yet she had experienced the same, odd sensation of being blessed, at that moment in the playground. And perhaps the greatest miracle of all, and the most alarming, was that the child, who had every justification to be suspicious of life, seemed, absolutely, to trust her.

The recommendations of the experts who had assessed Giulietta's condition were straightforward. Her fully healed scars should not be interfered with, to any great extent, but they could be rearranged to eliminate the contractures that had, as Elizabeth had suspected, effectively tethered her arms to her body. Her spine, mercifully, had not been damaged, but since Giulietta had not walked unaided for years, the way ahead was promising, but long and painful.

"It's down to physio, mostly," Elizabeth told Walter Schuster, her Canadian-born lawyer and old family friend. "Hard work, frustration, and tears."

"Will she go along with it?"

Elizabeth nodded. "I think she will—all except for the tears, as I've told you."

"Perhaps she doesn't feel like crying," Schuster, a burly man with a head of thick white hair, suggested.

"But that's so unnatural. In the past few weeks, that little girl has been snatched from her native land, terrorized by her first airplane ride, prodded and poked with needles—"

"She's had you."

"She's had *pain,* and she hasn't shed a tear."

"Maybe she's accustomed to pain."

Elizabeth looked sad. "Maybe she wept for so long, in vain, that she just gave up." She thought for a moment. "Giulietta's blocked out her past totally—the car accident that killed her family, everything before it —even the time following it."

"Isn't that a natural response?"

"It's probably what pulled her through the years—but now I don't know if we should be trying to unlock her past, or if she should be allowed to scuttle it and start again." She paused. "As it is, we may never know whether she was a happy child before the accident, or if she was desperately miserable."

Schuster shrugged. "Surely it's her future that counts now. It seems a little barbaric to try to force her to look back."

"I'm inclined to agree. I'd prefer to try to make her new life as normal and content as possible—then maybe when she's older, and more secure, she could be encouraged to delve into the past—into her roots."

They spoke about Elizabeth's desire to adopt Giulietta, and the potential legal complexities of the process, but in spite of all the problems, a glow of excitement radiated from Elizabeth.

"I can hardly believe the way I feel," she confided in her friend. "Of course I've always cared deeply for children, but I never longed for babies of my own—there were always so many to look after—"

"But this little *bambina* has changed all that."

"Yes." Elizabeth's voice was soft. "Giulietta has so many problems ahead of her—her scars, for one thing. She may not care about them at seven, but at seventeen she'll look in the mirror, and her body will seem very ugly."

"When will they operate to release her arms?"

"It's a small operation—she'll be out of hospital in time for Christmas. She can have physiotherapy as an outpatient."

"And where will she be living?" Schuster asked gently.

Elizabeth flushed. "She's agreed to come home with me to Dorking." She paused. "She's going to need a great deal of help, Walter."

"She's going to need a mother."

Elizabeth was silent.

Schuster smiled. "She'll never find a better one."

Giulietta Volpi knew nothing about the possibilities of being adopted by Elizabeth Austen, nor about the traumas that might, or might not, face her in the years ahead. She knew nothing about the Englishwoman's heart-searching, nor about her hopes or fears.

She knew that the only life she remembered had been drab, and lonely, and devoid of happiness, and that the *Dottoressa* had come to save her—had rescued her, and had brought her to this strange, alien place, in order to help her, and to transform her life.

She did not need to know anything else.

And she did not need to cry.

Chapter 9

"**Murderer!**" Letizia sobbed for the umpteenth time.

"*Assassino!*" spat Fabio. "A thief and a killer!"

"Stop it, children," Bruno begged, as he had done for the last five days. "There is no proof."

"No proof?" Fabio was distraught. "They've gone, haven't they? Along with half the food in the larder and my money! How much more proof do you need, Father? He killed Mamma, for God's sake, and you *defend* him!"

Bruno was hopelessly torn. However often he pointed to the broken window in Fabio's bedroom and to the possibility that the children had been frightened away by robbers, he knew he was clutching at straws. There had been no break-in, although the investigating *agente di polizia* was polite enough to allow for the hypothesis. The simple, horrific truth was that only food and minimal cash had been stolen, and that Livia, her arms bruised by someone's fierce grip, was dead.

That his wife of more than sixteen years should be abruptly and so violently gone was shocking enough to Bruno, without the accusation against Vittorio. Livia had been difficult to live with—haughty and harsh and, often, spiteful; but she had been strong and loyal, vibrant and sexual, clever—and so much alive.

It must *have been an accident.*

He told himself the same thing over and over again, longing to believe it. Yet Fabio and Letizia, grief-stricken and raging that Vittorio had always had a violent temper, had undeniable truth on their side.

But he could not believe—would never believe—that Vittorio was a murderer. His children pointed to the cellar as proof of their cousin's revenge for Livia's unkindness to Francesca, but Bruno found himself wondering whether, perhaps, his wife had tried to administer the same punishment again, and if Vittorio had turned the tables on the woman he hated.

Her death was an accident, surely. A flash of temper, perhaps. Cold-blooded murder, *never.*

They buried Livia, and attended a special mass in the church of Santissima Annunziata, the most fashionable church in Florence, and Letizia, without her mother to advise her, bought a wildly expensive and unsuitable black dress for the occasion, which made her look even plumper than she was, and magnified her heartbreak, which was, in any case, intense and noisy.

The police had no leads, but were confident that the missing youngsters could not remain undiscovered for long. It was, after all, vital that they be found as quickly as possible for, putting the most generous complexion on the matter, they must at least have important evidence regarding the death of their aunt. Even if they had found shelter somewhere, the children would need food and support. Bulletins had been issued to every *posto di polizia* in the country, with their photographs. Signor Cesaretti must try not to distress himself too much, for they would be found.

"May they rot in prison," Fabio said, and Letizia echoed him with more weeping, but Bruno was more tormented than ever.

I am guilty, he thought.

He had failed everyone he cared about. He had vowed, after Francesca's nightmare in the cellar, that he would take more responsibility for his nephews and niece, would keep an eye on the household and take the pressure off Livia and his own children to try to dampen the potential explosiveness of life in Palazzo Speroza. But he had not done enough. He was as much to blame as anyone.

It was too late for Livia, and in time Fabio and Letizia would recover and continue with their lives, but as the days and sleepless nights passed, one thing became clear to Bruno. If the police succeeded in tracking down Vittorio and the others, their young lives would be destroyed forever. It might well be proved that their older brother had brought that on himself, but whatever Vittorio had done, Francesca and young Luciano were surely innocent.

Bruno had to find his brother's children *before* the police—and to that end he paid a visit, five days before Christmas, to the office in the Oltrarno of an *investigatore privato* named Ludovico Lippi.

"Can you find them?" Bruno asked, after relating the story and background to the surprisingly well-heeled, middle-aged detective.

"I take pride," Lippi said in a husky voice. "If I cannot find three frightened children, alone and without funds, then I am worthless."

"You have to find them before the *polizia*," Bruno reminded him nervously.

"*Naturalmente*," Lippi agreed.

On his way home, Bruno stopped at a church to light a candle for Livia, to go some small way toward salving his guilty conscience.

He lit the first, and then another, and another, until he had lit one for Giulio, his brother, and for Serafina and the baby, and for poor Giulietta—and then he lit three more, for his missing nephews and niece. And then he knelt to pray.

He did not know what else to do.

Chapter 10

UNABLE TO TRAVEL at more than ten kilometers an hour, and feeling it safe to cycle on the roads or near the railway lines only between ten at night and five in the morning, it was not until they had skirted around Livorno in the early hours of Tuesday that Vittorio felt he could allow Francesca and, more especially, Luciano to relax a little.

"*Forza*, lazybones!" he had pressed him regularly, whenever the younger boy had grown weary or afraid. Time enough, he reasoned, to rub Luciano's back and calm his fears when they were off the roads during the day, hiding in barns or outhouses, hardly daring to breathe lest they were reported.

It was the sea that restored them all. Even in the dead of night, with only a watery moon to guide them, the lapping of the waves lulled them, reassured them. It was December, and the sea would be icy cold, its currents lethal, yet the children romanticized its powers of protection; little empty boats bobbed up and down at their moorings—if a policeman leapt out at them from the shadows, they had a means of escape. The idea, foolish as it was, comforted them all, even Vittorio, and from then on they hugged the coast as much as possible.

Luciano had no real understanding of why they had run away, or why they could speak to no one, not even the most ordinary farmer or fisherman, but Vittorio was their leader, and Francesca, his gentle protector, told him that it was better for him *not* to know too much.

"Why?" he had asked her.

"Because if you know nothing, no one will be able to blame you for anything, *caro.*"

Another child might have been frustrated, but Luciano, the dreamer, was also something of a natural fatalist, and in any case, he trusted his brother and sister too completely to challenge their important decisions.

"When are you going to be a girl again?" he asked. The loss of Francesca's beautiful long hair on the night of their flight had been almost as shocking as their departure.

She smiled, and stroked his cheek. "When we get to America," she replied.

"They won't chase us any more in America, will they?"

"No, *piccolo.*"

"And we'll still be together?" A small frown of fear creased his clear forehead. "We'll live in a house again, like normal people?"

Francesca felt a pang of guilt. "We'll always be together, Luciano," she promised.

"*Veramente?*"

She looked at him solemnly. "Cross my heart and hope to die," she said.

They were a long way from America. Between Livorno and Naples lay the Maremma, the stretch of plain which had figured so positively in Vittorio's *grande progetto.* Just as the children had, at first glance, imbued the Mare Ligure with a benevolence it did not possess, so had Vittorio assumed, almost blithely and certainly mistakenly, that the Maremma's desolation would grant them sanctuary.

The truth bore swiftly down on them all, even Luciano. It *was* a plain, and it was, inevitably, broad, flat, and, so it seemed, menacingly infinite.

"I want to go back!" Luciano's querulous voice echoed what the other two thought, but would not admit.

"We can't, *piccolo.*"

"But it's like the desert!"

"It's *nothing* like the desert." Responsibility, like a great weight, had descended on Vittorio, making him irritable. "There's the sea, and there are sheep and horses and cattle and—"

"Where?"

"In a few miles"—Vittorio tried to be gentler—"it will look quite different. There'll be pine forests and lovely beaches—"

"And animals?"

"*Sì, piccolo.* And animals." He raised his binoculars and gazed toward the sea. "We have to find the Via Aurelia and head for Grosseto."

"How far is that?" Francesca asked.

He checked the map again. "About forty kilometers." He managed a smile. "Just a few hours more, and we can throw away all that stale rubbish and have fresh meat."

"From the *macelleria* in Grosseto?" asked Luciano.

"From hunting."

They found a watchtower late that night, a few kilometers south of Alberese, after they had left the Via Aurelia, the ancient road that followed the coast except where it was separated from the sea by the Uccellina hills.

It was pitch-dark, and drizzling, but they could smell the difference in the air. In spite of the winter cold, the plain had smelled somehow musty, but here the vegetation seemed to pump fresh oxygen into the atmosphere.

Vittorio was triumphant. "Now we can rest for a while, and no one will find us." Switching on the flashlight, he found the entrance, and poked his head through into the dark. It smelled dank, like the cellar in the palazzo, and Francesca, following, shivered and withdrew.

"Can't we wait till morning?" She felt uneasy. "I don't think we should climb the steps until it's light."

"But it's raining," Luciano complained.

The drizzle had become harder and more insistent, and the wind whipped up from the sea, slapping their cheeks.

Vittorio shone the light inside. "There's room for us down here, at the foot of the steps. At least we'll be dry."

He woke first, next morning, and climbed cautiously but eagerly to the summit of the tower. The steps were crumbling in places, but held his weight easily.

He emerged at the top, and found that almost half of what must have been an observation platform had long since broken away, the fractured edges smoothed over by the elements. Still, it was possible to stand, in safety, and look out to sea. It was a glorious morning, and what was now, according to his map, the Mare Tirreno lay mirrorlike and blue, small caps of rippling waves glinting in the sunlight. Vittorio raised the binoculars to his eyes and began, slowly, to turn around—

His heart plummeted to his boots. No more than a kilometer away, to the southeast, was a brand-new, gleaming road.

"*Dio!*" His eyes filled with tears. Near the road were two long, broad channels dug into the soil, either for drainage or perhaps for laying pipework. There was, as yet, no sign of life, but it was less than an hour after dawn—it was just a matter of time before the whole area was crawling with laborers.

"It's not *fair!*" In despair and rage, he smashed the binoculars down on the parapet, cracking the left lens.

"What's wrong?"

Francesca's dark, cropped head appeared from the stairwell.

"We have to leave," he said shortly. "Look over there." He handed her the binoculars.

"They're broken."

"Close one eye."

She squinted for a moment.

"You see?" Vittorio was grim and pale.

Francesca lowered the glasses. "I'll wake Luciano."

He shook his head. "We can't go anywhere till tonight, after they've stopped work. It'll be safe to move on then." He sighed heavily. "I'll check the map again—I think the hills broaden out a bit farther south. We'll have to find another place."

Francesca put the binoculars carefully down by her feet, and embraced her brother. "Don't worry, *caro*," she said softly. "It'll be all right."

"I shouldn't have brought you both." His voice was husky, his anguished face hidden against her shoulder. "It's all going wrong." He struggled against his desire to weep.

"No, *caro*," she soothed him.

"We have to waste another day sitting in this stinking, lousy tower, using up our precious food! I thought I could go hunting today—I thought we could rest and I could teach Luciano to fish—" He broke off in despair.

"You'll do all those things." Francesca hoped with all her heart that she sounded more confident than she felt. "What's one more day in a master plan? We'll go on tonight, and we'll find another tower—somewhere lonelier than this, where it's still swampy, where the *zanzare* still buzz and bite."

Somewhere, she thought, but did not say, that three children in their right senses would never dream of venturing. Somewhere no one would look for them.

It was late on Saturday night, one week after they had left the palazzo, that they found what they were searching for.

It was an eleventh-century abbey, abandoned for more than three hundred years, partially ruined and almost wholly concealed by oak trees and bushes in a small valley on the ridge.

Their joy was boundless. It was *perfect*! It was large, and had a splendid tower, and, with work, it would make an ideal temporary home. When Vittorio climbed to the top of the tower and peered, apprehensively, through the binoculars at the surrounding area, he saw no roads, no machinery, no ditches, and the relief was almost overwhelming.

"It's dark," Francesca said cautiously.

"There's a full moon," Vittorio rejoiced. "I could see forever, and there's nothing!" He grasped his sister's hands and whirled her around. "Tomorrow I'll go hunting!"

Tucked into the protective hills, the abbey was less than a half hour's walk from the sea, and the children felt they had found a real oasis in the midst of the Maremma "desert."

With only moldy cheese and a little *panforte* left in their rations, Vittorio knew he could afford to waste no more time, and on Sunday morning, he took his fishing rod and net to the shore, but the shallow water yielded only tiny fish, more bones and scales than flesh.

Next morning, he tried his hand at hunting. Knife sheathed in his belt, loaded revolver in his right hand, he soon realized that the barren, wintry forest was not, as he had hoped, brimming over with food.

"*Morto*," he said aloud, with disgust, after two hours of fruitless scanning of branches and undergrowth, and slouched down onto the thick, wet carpet of decaying leaves.

It was then that he saw the rabbit. Young, succulent, and innocent, evidently as untutored in survival as Vittorio was in the art of stalking, it sat, perfectly still, less than thirty meters away. A thin ray of sun, filtering through the trees, touched its floppy ears, seeming to emphasize its blamelessness. Vittorio stared at it for several seconds, half willing it to see him and flee.

And then his empty stomach rumbled softly. Very carefully, perfectly silently, he raised the gun, the handle firm and cold against his palm. And he pulled the trigger.

"Beginner's luck," he said modestly as he presented the limp little corpse to his sister and brother, but he glowed with triumph.

Francesca planted a kiss on his cheek and then gazed down at the rabbit. "What do we do with it?" she asked.

"Skin it and cook it, of course."

A small sound made them both look up to see that Luciano had turned away, clearly weeping.

"What's wrong with him now?" Vittorio looked impatient.

"*Il coniglio,*" Francesca said quietly, and touched the creature's soft fur. "It's upset him."

"He's eaten meat all his life, for God's sake."

"But it never had ears and a tail."

"Well, he'll have to get used to it now," Vittorio said sharply. "If we don't kill, we won't eat."

The blunt words brought a flush to his cheeks and a swift flash of nausea to his stomach. He was right—he knew he was absolutely right. A hunter, like a farmer, had to be practical. Killing was sometimes necessary.

The dull sickness did not disappear.

It was not the rabbit he was thinking about.

By Tuesday afternoon they were hungry again. Francesca, appointed butcher as well as cook, had quickly learned that she knew nothing about skinning game, and she had wasted almost more meat than she had saved, though the flesh had been delicious when cooked over the fire they'd lit in the mossy *cortile.*

Clearly, the rabbit had been beginner's luck. For two more days all their meals consisted of the unsatisfying little fish that Francesca and Luciano caught while their brother sought more substantial fare, but early on Friday, fortune turned in their favor again, when a deer wandered into view, and Vittorio brought it down with his third shot.

"Meat for a week!" Vittorio declared jubilantly.

"You'll have to help me cut it up," Francesca said, glad that Luciano was on watch duty at the top of the tower, for the sight of the deer's graceful legs and bullet-mangled beauty distressed even her.

"Roast venison!" Vittorio hummed happily as he brandished the knife. "*Delizioso.*"

∗

Yet again, fortune proved fickle. The weather turned unseasonably mild and, with no experience in preservation, the meat began to rot after their second meal. By Monday afternoon, they were irritable and starting to carp at each other.

"Lambs," Francesca muttered disconsolately as they sat, in the hour before sunset, on a half-crumbled low stone wall outside the abbey. "Pheasants."

"What?" Vittorio kicked at a clod of earth.

"The creatures you promised us. Where are they? The cows we were going to milk. This rainwater's upset Luciano's stomach." She paused. "Anyway, it hasn't rained for three days, so we'll probably die of thirst."

"I suppose that's my fault too." Vittorio's dark eyes were bitter. "Along with Luciano's depression and the fact that you can't bear life without a bathtub."

"I couldn't care less about having a bath," Francesca protested. "If you'd remembered to bring soap, I wouldn't complain." They washed each day in a stream not far from the abbey, but the water was far too murky to consider drinking, and Francesca never felt properly clean.

"So why didn't *you* think of soap?" Vittorio demanded, not unreasonably.

"Because it was your precious plan!"

Luciano was, indisputably, depressed. Vittorio could not see why a seven-year-old boy should not be thriving on adventure, especially since most of the pressures were on his shoulders, but Francesca did not find it hard to understand what was wrong with her younger brother. He missed the security of the palazzo, he missed school and the books that he had grown to love, he missed civilization—and he was, above all, *hungry*.

Two days later, the weather changed dramatically. It became bitterly cold, with a raw northerly wind, and the three children were forced to stay inside.

Late that night, Francesca woke to see Luciano standing, staring out of one of the cracked, arched windows. His breath misted in the cold air, and he was hugging himself against the chill and, when she touched him gently on the shoulder, he turned, and she saw that he had been weeping.

"What's wrong, *caro*? Are you ill?"

His blue eyes were very round, the black pupils huge. "Giulietta," he whispered.

"One of your dreams?" Sympathetically, Francesca put an arm about him. Luciano had never ceased to dream about his twin, and he generally woke distressed.

He shook his head. "It didn't feel like a dream. It was real."

"Dreams often seem that way."

"This was different." He sounded positive.

"How?"

"I'm not sure." He hesitated. "It was—funny. I felt I was inside her—I saw things, I felt things—but it wasn't me—"

Francesca was fascinated. "What kind of things?"

"I saw a lady," he said, "and a funny-looking house—and it was snowing." His eyes glistened. "Most times, when I dream about Giulietta, it's sad, you know—"

"I know."

"But this time . . ." He paused, trying to find the words to explain his feelings. "It felt good. I felt happy, inside—but it wasn't *me*—it was her."

"It was a lovely dream," Francesca said softly.

Luciano's face grew somber again. "But it wasn't real, was it?"

"No, darling." Francesca tried to draw him close, but he moved out of her reach. "I'm sorry."

"It's all right," he said, but his voice was choked.

"No." She felt her own throat tighten with tears. "No, it isn't all right."

At noon next day, she made an effort to shake off the apathy afflicting them all.

"Do you realize it's Christmas Eve?"

Vittorio didn't move, and Luciano merely shifted his position.

"Come on, you two! Didn't you hear what I said?"

Vittorio shrugged. "It's Christmas Eve. So what?"

"So we should celebrate."

Luciano stirred with something approaching interest. "How?" he asked.

"What do we have to celebrate?" Vittorio said sourly.

"Freedom," Francesca replied. "Being together." She paused. "Anyway, if it's Christmas, we should do something."

"Like what?"

Luciano looked from his brother to his sister, waiting for words of wisdom. He had never felt so tired, so lethargic. He knew he was hungry, but it didn't seem to matter anymore—nothing seemed to matter very much.

"We should at least eat," Francesca suggested.

"It's too cold to go hunting," Vittorio said tersely. "And anyway, there's nothing to kill."

"We never eat meat at Christmas," Francesca pointed out. "So we can go fishing."

"I'm sick of fish." Vittorio scowled.

"So am I," echoed Luciano.

"Well, we have to eat it tonight," their sister insisted. "It's tradition, and I'm not going to let this family starve to death at Christmas." She looked around for her jacket. "If you won't come with me, I'll go alone."

"You can't," Vittorio said sulkily. "You won't catch enough."

Francesca picked up the rod and net and put one hand on her hip. "Well then?"

Fate seemed utterly bent on cowing them. They fished for three hours, unable to venture in too far because of the icy water, and returned to the abbey with a miserable handful of scaly creatures that would scarcely have provided a decent first course for a single person. As soon as they lit a fire, the heavens opened and doused the flames, and finally even Francesca was forced to admit defeat.

"*Merda!*" she swore, in desperation, and burst into tears.

"I want to go home!" Luciano joined in.

"You haven't *got* a home!" Vittorio snarled, distressed by Francesca's weeping, but not knowing what to do to help.

"Then I want to go to America!" Luciano retorted, rubbing his red, wet nose with his sleeve.

"We *can't!*" his brother shouted. "Not yet."

"Why not?"

"Because we'll be arrested! Why don't you ever listen, idiot?"

Luciano threw himself down on the mossy ground and began to sob as though his heart would break. Vittorio looked at him and at Francesca, who, for once, just stood motionless, not attempting to comfort the younger boy, her own eyes still flooded with tears.

"*Cara?*" he ventured, in despair.

She didn't respond.

Vittorio remembered, a few minutes later, what he had tucked into his saddlebag two weeks before. *Two weeks,* he thought, shaking his head. How had he imagined, even in his wildest dreams, that they could hide out here for months? It had been madness—sheer madness.

The bicycles stood, side by side, leaning against a wall on the other side of the abbey. Leaving the others without a word, Vittorio unfastened the strap of his saddlebag.

It was there, safe at the bottom. He drew it out, using both hands. A glass bottle, almost full of golden liquid. *Haig,* the label read. *Scotch whisky.*

Vittorio had never tasted whisky, but he had observed his uncle drinking it, usually when he was tired or in one of his rare bad moods, and it had always seemed to cheer him swiftly. "First aid," he had joked. If anyone needed first aid, Vittorio thought wanly, he did this evening.

Glancing furtively around, he opened the bottle, raised it to his lips, took a gulp and almost choked—

"*Gesù!*" he gasped as his throat burned—yet almost within seconds, the miracle began to work, filling him with a delicious reviving warmth.

He lifted the bottle again.

✻

Half an hour later, he had made the decision.

"We're going to leave. Move on."

The other two stared at him.

"If there's no food, we'll die." He shrugged. "Maybe this isn't such a great place after all. I think we should pack up, and start cycling south." It was the right solution—the whisky had given him new courage and vision.

"To Naples?" Francesca asked, taken aback.

Vittorio nodded. "Now."

"Tonight?" Francesca frowned. "In the dark?"

"We always travel at night, don't we? That way no one can see us." Vittorio felt happier already, almost invincible.

"Let's go now!" Luciano jumped up, suddenly animated.

"I don't know." Francesca was still doubtful. "It took so long to find this place."

"And it was fine, but now it's time to move on." Vittorio's eyes challenged his sister. "Trust me."

Back on their bicycles and away from the abbey, their spirits rose, and Vittorio's new optimism infected the other two. An hour later, they found a beach. Broad, long, and white in the moonlight that now streaked through the breaking cloud cover, it was one of the loveliest spots they had found since their journey had begun. Discovering that their wheels made slick, elegant tracks in the damp sand, the three children wove back and forth, splashing into the waves, not minding their iciness now, or the empty grumbling of their stomachs.

"Let's race!" Vittorio's blood surged through his veins.

"I bet you can't catch me!" Already a good twenty-five meters farther up the beach, Luciano began to pedal furiously away from them toward the dark pine forest bordering the beach.

"Be careful!" Francesca warned, but Luciano took no notice. "Vittorio, stop him!"

"Luciano, don't be an idiot!" Vittorio shouted as they gave chase, but he had already disappeared into the blackness of the trees.

"You'll get lost!" Francesca yelled.

The forest halted them, dark, forbidding, and damp.

"Where *is* he?"

The air was torn by a terrified, high-pitched scream.

"*Dio.*" Francesca clutched at Vittorio's arm.

"Where are you, *caro?*" he shouted.

"Over there!" Francesca still held on to his arm. "Let's leave the bikes."

They crashed blindly through the undergrowth, calling frantically. Bracken scratched them, branches tripped them up, flapping sounds unnerved them—

"*Help me!*" Luciano's voice was shrill.

"We're coming, *piccolo!*" Vittorio ripped the knife from his belt and slashed at some low-hanging branches.

"There!" Francesca pointed. Dimly, they saw him, arms flailing, down in a steep dip.

"I fell off my bike—I'm stuck!" Luciano began to sob.

"Don't cry," Vittorio called. "We'll get you out."

"It's *pulling* at me!"

"Oh, God, it's the swamp!" Francesca gasped.

Vittorio moved tentatively to the edge of what seemed to be a large, murky hole, filled with black, sludgy water.

"I can't reach him from here—I'll have to go down."

"Be careful," Francesca warned him.

He pointed to a low, scrubby bush. "If you hold on to that, I'll try to hang on to you while I climb down."

"I'm sinking deeper!" Luciano cried piteously.

"No, you're not—it's only mud."

"Be brave, *piccolo!*"

Francesca experimented with the bush, first sitting, then lying flat. "You'll have to hold my feet."

"Hurry *up!*" Luciano begged.

Grasping Francesca's ankles firmly, Vittorio slithered over the edge legs first. His boots broke the slimy surface with a small splash.

"Are you in?" Francesca asked, unable to see.

"I'll have to stretch out all the way." He slid farther, increasing the pull on Francesca's ankles. "Am I hurting you?"

"No," she lied. "Go on."

"Right—I'm going to let go with my left hand. Hang on tight—"

He let go. The extra weight tore at Francesca, making her cry out in pain, but still she held on, gritting her teeth—and then the handful of branches in her right hand snapped from the roots.

"It's broken!" she shrieked, and then shrieked again as Vittorio's grasp on her ankle vanished and he dropped the rest of the way into the swamphole with a yell of alarm that cut off with a gurgle as his head went under.

"Vittorio!" Francesca screamed, twisting around and staring over the brink. "*Vittorio!*"

He came up, spluttering and spitting furiously, desperate to expel the foul, deep brown water from his mouth and nose.

"Are you all right?" Francesca shouted.

Vittorio could only cough. He felt sick, and furious with himself.

"You fell."

He looked coldly at his younger brother's chalky face. "Yes," he said, and spat again.

"Now we'll never get out, will we?"

"Sure we will."

"How?"

Vittorio had no answer. He tried shifting his feet, but like Luciano's, his boots seemed firmly rooted in the thick mud at the bottom. "Anyway," he said as cheerfully as he could, "we're not sinking."

They both looked up. Francesca's face, pale and scared, hovered over the hole.

"I don't know what to do," she whispered.

"We need a rope," Vittorio said.

"We don't have one."

"So what are you going to do?"

A gust of cold wind blew through the forest, and the trees creaked and rustled, sending shivers up Francesca's spine. There was no choice. She took a deep breath and lay flat on her stomach.

"What are you doing?" Vittorio hissed.

"Maybe if I can reach your hand—"

"Don't be stupid," he snapped. "You could never pull me out."

"There's no other way—you have to try to reach my hand." She began to stretch herself out as far over the edge as seemed safe. "And then I'll try—"

"*Stop!*"

—She thought, at first, that Vittorio had shouted at her, but then she looked down and saw his expression, and realized that he was as startled as she was.

"*Keep still!*"

The voice, loud and clear and male, came closer. "Keep absolutely still!"

"*Gesù.*" In the hole, Vittorio blanched.

A twig snapped loudly. Dazzling light blinded them all.

"*Allora, bambino*—" Hoarse and deep, the voice came from directly over Francesca's head, and a large, rough hand seized her left arm. "Get up, boy—you're safe now."

Back on her feet, Francesca shielded her eyes, trying to see. Down below, Vittorio and Luciano were too shocked to speak.

The light diverted from Francesca's face, and pointed down at the two boys. She blinked. A large, swarthy man with black hair, a long, straight nose and a bandanna handkerchief tied around his neck stood beside her.

She tried to speak, but her throat felt constricted.

"Don't be afraid, boy," the man said to her, still staring down into the swamphole. "We'll get them out."

Francesca found her voice. "I'm not a boy."

The light swung back to her face, and a second voice spoke: "She's not." It was younger, lighter than the first.

"*Andiamo,*" the older man said. "Let's go to work before they freeze."

"Who are you?" For the first time, Vittorio spoke.

"Are you policemen?" Luciano asked.

"God forbid." The man laughed. He had already whipped a thin, ropelike belt from around his waist. "Yours too," he said to the younger one.

Francesca watched in awe as the two strangers—the second one was a boy, no older than Vittorio—knotted their two long belts together and made a large noose.

"You," the older man called roughly to Vittorio. "Loop this under the little one's arms!" He tossed the rope down and Vittorio caught it, holding tightly with numbed fingers.

"Quickly," the younger one urged impatiently, hands on hips while Vittorio secured the noose. Father and son, Francesca thought—they looked alike, though even in the dark she could see that the son had a paler skin and was more handsome than his father.

"Ready!" Vittorio called.

They made a human chain, the man anchoring himself to a tree trunk by hooking his legs around it and holding fast to the boy's legs, while the boy twisted the rope twice around his right wrist and hand.

"When we pull," the man shouted to Luciano, "try to help—come with the rope!"

After four tugs, Luciano's feet were free, and a moment later, he lay on the ground beside Francesca.

"Warm him," the younger stranger said, releasing the noose from Luciano's chest and unknotting the bandanna from his own neck. "Use this to dry his face and hair." His eyes, dark as his father's, were kind.

"Thank you," she whispered, and knelt down beside Luciano, who flopped limply against her, eyes closed. She began to mop his sodden hair, watching all the time as the strangers went back to work, to rescue Vittorio.

It was a strange, silent procession that retrod the path back through the forest, collecting their abandoned bicycles on the way. On the beach, the moon was high and unhampered by clouds. The older man, who'd carried Luciano in his arms, set him down on the sand.

"Now," he said quietly, addressing them all, "you have a choice to make. You may take your bicycles and go on your way."

"Or?" Vittorio's tone was hostile.

"Or you may come with us to our camp, where you will be given food and a warm bed for the night."

Francesca stared at Vittorio, willing him to choose the second option.

"Camp?" Vittorio asked suspiciously.

The man smiled. "*Siamo zingari*," he said. "We are Gypsies."

"Gypsies?" Luciano gazed up at the man in awe. "Truly?"

"Truly." He paused. "My name is Emilio Dante, and this"—he indicated the boy—"is my brother, Niccolo."

"I thought you were his father," Francesca blurted, and flushed.

"Understandable." Emilio Dante's face was weather-beaten and friendly. "I thought you were a boy."

Francesca's blush heightened, as she remembered her awful hair which, as it had begun to grow again, stood out spikily and untidily from her head, making her look like a hedgehog.

"What are your names?" The boy, Niccolo, looked at her.

"I'm Francesca," she said, and then glanced furtively at Vittorio, thinking perhaps he might have wanted her to keep silent.

"I'm Luciano." The filthy child was recovering rapidly, cheered by the prospect of an adult taking charge.

Niccolo Dante turned to Vittorio, but receiving no response, he looked back at Francesca. "Where have you come from?"

"Naples," Vittorio answered swiftly. "And my name is Vittorio."

Emilio Dante extended his hand. "*Molto lieto*, Vittorio."

Vittorio shook it briefly, suddenly conscious that he felt queasy, and that the stagnant water had left him smelling worse than a pigsty.

"So what have you decided?" Emilio asked. "To continue your journey immediately, or to stay as our guests."

"Just for tonight?"

"Unless you choose to rest a little longer."

Vittorio looked at Francesca and Luciano. Their expressions were intent and appealing. He glanced at the bicycles on the sand, and thought of their empty stomachs. One night could do no harm.

"Thank you," he said. "We will come."

The camp was little more than a kilometer away, on the other side of the hills, in a sheltered valley, with a clear, cold stream running close by.

None of the Cesaretti children had ever seen anything like it. They had seen a few Gypsies before, in Florence, but they had been ragged youngsters, begging in the Oltrarno; this was an entirely different matter —this was a revelation.

There must have been at least fifty caravans, some of them quite drab, with splintered wood and flaking paint, others vastly superior, ornately carved and decorated. Gazing about with wide, astonished eyes, their exhaustion temporarily forgotten, the newcomers registered an intriguing bustle of unusual-looking men, women, and children, dogs, cats, and horses. The whole camp was bright with tidy, blazing fires, each surrounded by what seemed to be a large family group. There were old men with straggling white beards and long hair, old women with head scarves tied over their gray hair and large hooped earrings framing their wrinkled faces. There were younger people, their clothes colorful and outlandish, high boots, tight trousers, and all manner of jackets from velvet to threadbare cloth for the men, long, flowing skirts and brilliant shawls for the women. And then there were those who looked much like ordinary city folk, wearing up-to-date dresses and suits, a few men even, incongruously, wearing ties.

"What do you think?" Niccolo Dante asked Francesca.

"It's—*wonderful*," she murmured, feeling as if they had entered another world. The air was filled with scents—woodsmoke from the fires, different smoke from cigarettes and pipes, and food—mouth-watering aromas filtering from the great iron pots that hung over many of the fires. There was an atmosphere of happiness and excitement. Children of all ages played and laughed all around, and from somewhere, though she could not tell from where exactly, came the haunting sounds of a violin.

"Is it always like this?" she asked Niccolo. "It feels like some kind of celebration."

The Gypsy boy smiled, and she saw that his eyes were a rich, dark brown. "It's Christmas Eve," he reminded her. *"La vigilia di Natale."*

She remembered, abruptly, the earlier part of the evening, the abortive fishing expedition and the hideous episode in the forest, and for a moment she felt quite ill.

"Francesca?" Vittorio said sharply.

"Breathe deeply," Niccolo Dante told her quietly, and put a gentle, supportive hand on her arm. "You must come to our *tsara.*" He saw the question in her heavy eyes. "That means caravan in our language."

"But you speak Italian," Vittorio said, keeping a watchful eye on Luciano, who had wandered closer to one of the fires to have a better look.

"We all speak two languages," Niccolo said. "The language of our country, and Romany, our own tongue." He paused. "Now you should come—Emilio is speaking to our grandparents, telling them that you are here."

Francesca noticed suddenly that the people nearest to them were staring at her and Vittorio.

"It's because you're *Gadje.*" Niccolo observed her discomfort. "Strangers. All outsiders, anyone who is not a Gypsy, is a *Gadja.*"

"Isn't it exciting!" Luciano came running.

"He looks almost like one of us with all that mud." Niccolo grinned.

"Of course he doesn't." Vittorio defensively drew his brother close. Gypsies had a bad name; everyone always said that most of them were thieves, and that they even sold their children as pickpockets.

Emilio Dante returned. "Papo and Mami say that you should come now. Antonia is heating water so that you can wash yourselves, and you can eat as soon as you wish."

"Most of us won't eat dinner till much later, after mass," Niccolo added.

"You go to mass?" Francesca asked, astonished.

"On Christmas Eve, of course." Emilio was amused. "You imagine we're heathens, Francesca? Our family are Christians—we have our own traditions and ceremonies, but we're also Catholic."

"Where will you go to mass?" If there was a church in easy reach, then they were much nearer to civilization than Vittorio had thought. The idea alarmed him.

"There is a church in Talamone, a few kilometers to the south," Emilio replied. "It's just a fishing village."

"But known because of Barbarossa and Garibaldi," Niccolo added.

Emilio laughed. "My brother the scholar. Always reading or listening to stories."

"Luciano's the same," Francesca said.

"How will you get to Talamone?" Vittorio wanted to know.

"We'll ride."

"On horses?" Luciano was enthralled.

"Sure." Emilio ruffled the boy's golden hair. "But not for an hour or two." He glanced at Francesca, who was beginning to wilt again. "*Andiamo,*" he said. "Let's get you to Antonia."

"Who's that?" Luciano asked.

"My wife."

They might have been in heaven. Antonia Dante, a strikingly good-looking young woman with flowing black hair, looked after them with great care and kindness. Their caravan was one of the more handsome in the camp, painted royal blue with stylish gilded carvings. All the Cesaretti children were especially fascinated by the wood-paneled interior, which gleamed so lustrously that it might have compared favorably with some of the furniture in Palazzo Speroza. Once they had finished bathing, in an iron tub placed discreetly behind the caravan, they were shepherded by Antonia to the fire, and given bowls of steaming and excellent fish stew.

While they ate they became aware of two pairs of dark eyes solemnly regarding them from a safe distance.

"Our *bambini,*" Antonia explained. "They find you very interesting."

"Because we're *Gadje?*" Francesca queried, remembering what Niccolo had told her.

"You learn swiftly."

Luciano wiped a slice of bread around the sides of his dish. "I'm glad I fell in the swamp."

Francesca shuddered. "I'm not."

"But if I hadn't, and if Vittorio hadn't fallen in too, we'd never have come here, and we would have starved to death."

"I don't think your brother would have allowed you to starve," Antonia said mildly, then added enigmatically: "In any case, you would probably have come here in time."

"No, we wouldn't," Luciano argued. "We would have been on our way—"

"Finish your stew," Vittorio interrupted, cutting him off.

The Gypsy woman smiled.

Once they had finished eating, all three of the visitors felt almost too sleepy to talk, let alone move, and Antonia took them into the *tsara* and showed them where they could sleep.

"But aren't these your beds?" Francesca asked.

"Don't worry about us—we won't be going to sleep for many hours yet."

"Are you going to Talamone now?" Vittorio asked wearily. There was little risk of the Dantes bringing the police to the camp, he'd decided—after all, Gypsies were always on the wrong side of the law, weren't they, and he was simply too exhausted to worry about it anymore. . . .

He woke, about four hours later, with a start, and it was several moments before he remembered where he was. His head ached, and he could hear music again, an accordion this time, and other sounds—clapping and laughter. He sat up. The other two were sound asleep. Quietly, he climbed off the wooden bunk and looked around for his clothes, but Emilio's wife had taken them to be washed. He reached for a blanket and, wrapping it about him, he crept out of the caravan.

About thirty people sat around the Dante fire, talking and drinking companionably while, farther away, other groups laughed and sang and danced. Emilio and Antonia saw him, and immediately Emilio rose and came toward him.

"All right?"

Vittorio nodded. "I want to thank you," he began, awkwardly, then stopped.

"It's nothing." The big, strong-looking man had an unusual gentleness about him. "We are glad to help. We, of all people, know what it means to be persecuted—" He paused. "Or hunted."

Vittorio looked up, alarmed.

"Don't be afraid," Emilio reassured him. "I know nothing of your circumstances, and unless you wish to share your burden, I will ask no more questions." He gestured with the unlit pipe he was holding. "It was obvious to us that you were in hiding at the abbey—"

"You *saw* us there?" Vittorio was aghast.

Emilio nodded. "We saw the smoke from your fires, and we heard your pistol shots."

Vittorio shut his eyes.

"We had no wish to intrude, but we knew how difficult it was for you, so we kept a watch—"

"You spied on us?"

Emilio shrugged. "We were concerned for your safety."

"You followed us when we left the abbey?"

"We kept watch," the Gypsy said simply. "We have lived here for some time. We know the area, and the forest, very well."

"And the swamp," Vittorio said bitterly.

"Naturally." Emilio looked sympathetic. "I have spoken to my grandparents and to our *baro manush*—our leader—and we would like to invite you to stay with us for a time." Vittorio began to speak, but Emilio raised his hand. "If you feel you must continue on your journey, so be it, but since you are an intelligent boy, you must know it will always be a terrible struggle for you all."

"We'd manage."

"Perhaps you would. But if you chose to stay at the camp for a little while, perhaps we could share some of our centuries of experience with you, and you would certainly leave us better equipped for survival."

"Why would you do that for us?"

"For *Gadje*, you mean?" Emilio shrugged again. "Because you're children—or Luciano is."

Vittorio, gratified by the implication that he was grown up, remained silent.

"Because you're courageous," Emilio went on. "But most of all, because you are in need of our help." He tapped his pipe. "Niccolo has been to the abbey this evening."

"Why?"

"To remove all signs that you were there. You left without enough preparation—you were careless."

Vittorio flushed.

"Niccolo has cleared everything, buried the ashes of your fires and the remains of the animals and fish you caught. He also covered many of your bicycle tracks along your route." He paused. "Your first lesson. If you fear discovery by an enemy, never permit yourself to be careless, for any reason." Again he smiled his warm, crooked smile, showing several gold-capped teeth. "You have no need to worry, Vittorio. No one has followed you since you came to the Maremma."

"How do you know?" Vittorio stared at him.

"We know." Emilio Dante's breath steamed in the cold Christmas night air. "Have no fear, *amico mio*. Whatever you have done, whoever is looking for you, you are safe while you stay with us."

Chapter 11

GIULIETTA CAME HOME to Dorking with Elizabeth six days before Christmas. Although she spent much of her time in her two-room flat in Wimpole Street, conveniently placed two doors from her consulting rooms, Elizabeth never regarded the London flat as anything more than comfortable and utilitarian. Without it, her life would be difficult, since she was often too weary after a long day to contemplate the drive south into Surrey, only to have to rise brutally early to return the next morning. It would create havoc if she were ever compelled to give up the flat, but it would not break her heart. Her house, on the other hand, in many ways *was* her heart.

She and Edward had bought Kaikoura, their beautiful half-timbered, whitewashed home, three months after the end of the war. Its first owner, and creator, an elderly and imaginative native New Zealander, had only enjoyed nine years in his dream house, and, tragically, Edward had only lived in Kaikoura for four years before his death in 1949. Elizabeth might easily have turned against the house, but the years in Dorking had been the happiest of her life, and she had grown to love every inch of Kaikoura's handsome interior and wonderful gardens.

"What do you think?"

Elizabeth watched Giulietta's face anxiously as she sat silently beside her on the brown leather seat of Edward's old Rover 16, another possession Elizabeth refused to part with, even though time and miles were beginning to take their toll.

"Giulietta?" she nudged gently.

The child turned her wide blue astonished eyes to her. "This is your house?"

Elizabeth nodded. "It is." She paused, seeing Giulietta staring at the smooth front lawn and at the splendid spruce and Scots fir trees that sheltered it from the public gaze. "This is Kaikoura, my home." She felt her heartbeat increase its pace. "And yours, if you want it to be."

A tiny frown puckered Giulietta's smooth forehead. "Is it a hospital?"

"No," Elizabeth said firmly. "I told you, this is a normal house, a home."

"But it's so big."

Elizabeth smiled. "Not so very big, *cara*, not once you get to know it." Kaikoura was by no means one of the grandest houses in Deepdene, the peaceful and rather select part of Dorking she lived in, just five bedrooms and two reception rooms, but it was spectacular at first glimpse even in winter, because of its setting at the top of a steep, gloriously landscaped slope.

Very slowly, Giulietta shook her head, just once, a small, expressive movement that spelled out her disbelief more articulately than any words could have.

"Shall we go inside?" Elizabeth's hands rested on the steering wheel. They looked calm, she observed wryly, the hands of a sensible, unruffled doctor who took life in her stride, not of a foolish, unnerved woman whose pulses galloped wildly and whose stomach lurched with anxiety.

Fighting to maintain her air of outward tranquility, she put the big, heavy car back into gear and drove up the circular driveway, stopping right outside the front door. "Sit tight," she said reassuringly. "I'll come round to help you."

Inside the trunk lay a brand-new suitcase and a pair of wooden crutches. Elizabeth had purchased the leather case for Giulietta in Harrods a week earlier, telling herself that she was not trying to buy the child's gratitude with expensive gifts, but that she simply wanted her, upon leaving the hospital, to own at least one item that was of high quality and tangibly hers. In any event, the little girl had not even noticed, had been far too enveloped and overwhelmed by the adventure of leaving Stoke Mandeville to care if her scanty possessions were packed into a suitcase or a paper bag.

The crutches were of far greater importance. It was very early days, much too soon for Giulietta to regard them with anything except loathing, since they had replaced her wheelchair and caused her nothing but pain. The operation on her contractures, however, had successfully released her arms, so that it was now physically possible for her to use the sticks, and Giulietta had made it clear both to Elizabeth and to her physiotherapist at the hospital that she was ready to cooperate, however much agony it cost her.

"*Dottoressa?*"

Elizabeth stirred herself. The voice was tremulous but impatient.

"I'm coming," Elizabeth called. She looked again at the crutches, a small nag of fear holding her back. What if Giulietta fell while entering the house? There were two steps to negotiate before the front door—if she stumbled and hurt herself, she might hate Kaikoura before she even made it inside. Perhaps she should get someone to help—Mrs. Loom was out today, but maybe the gardener was somewhere at the back—

"What's wrong, *Dottoressa?*"

"Nothing." Elizabeth shook her head angrily. *Don't you be neurotic,* she scolded herself, and determinedly plucked the crutches out of the trunk. "All right," she said brightly, opening the passenger door. "Take it slowly. Turn yourself around—legs first, then let me help you out."

Giulietta's hand was surprisingly firm on her coat sleeve. "*Non aver paura,*" she said softly. "Don't be afraid."

Elizabeth's cheeks grew hot, and tears pricked startlingly at her eyes. "Aren't you afraid?" she asked.

Giulietta smiled. "Not when I'm with you."

✷

By Christmas Eve, Giulietta thought she was in paradise. Kaikoura was the most beautiful place she had ever seen, its walls either oak-paneled or painted white, its floors gleaming parquet, Elizabeth having, for the moment, removed most of her Persian rugs, because the rubber tips of Giulietta's crutches found a more secure grip on the wood. There were two large rooms downstairs, a long lounge and an imposing oak-beamed dining room. The lounge had leaded-glass windows to the front and side of the house, with small, diamond-shaped panes of glass, and French windows that opened directly onto the back garden; sunny all day, it was chilly in the evenings, despite the well-lined curtains and two blazing fireplaces. Kaikoura's creator had disdained central heating, and neither of the Austens had ever found the time to bother with installation, but now, watching Giulietta hugging herself and blowing, regularly, though without complaint, onto her cold fingers, Elizabeth made a mental note to contact her plumber directly after Christmas.

They spent most of their time in the kitchen, a big, bright room with a china-laden pine dresser and a solid matching table made friendly by numerous marks, grooves, and burns; but without a doubt, the room that Giulietta gloried in above all others was her own. Elizabeth had had two spare bedrooms to choose from—the third having become an invaluable junk-room, since the attic was both full and hard to reach—and though one had been far larger than the other, she had selected the smaller, because it was right next to her own. Elizabeth anticipated nightmares and nocturnal visits, so the closer she could be the better. In fact, the knowledge that the *Dottoressa* was next door, together with the joy Giulietta felt every time she looked around the cozy little bedroom with its slanting ceiling, the white wardrobe, almost empty but her own, and pretty chintz curtains, gave the child a greater sense of security than she had ever known before. Besides, even if she had been afraid or in pain, years of being a long-stay patient in a hospital where the attention of night staff was necessarily directed toward the newer, needier patients had taught Giulietta a type of self-discipline that few seven-year-olds possessed; and even on the second night, while Elizabeth slept peacefully and a gale blew violently through The Glory Wood, which backed onto Kaikoura's gardens, Giulietta lay still and silent in bed, watching the eerie shadows thrown onto the ceiling by the moving branches, and waiting, hopefully, for dawn.

The afternoon before Christmas Eve, it began to snow, steadily and silently, with no signs of stopping. Giulietta, who had seen snow before in Turin, but could not remember having seen a real country snowfall, sat glued to the windows, staring out into the garden, her eyes huge with delight.

"May I go out, *Dottoressa?*" she asked Elizabeth. It was the first time she had felt any desire to leave Kaikoura, with its beautiful Christmas tree and its solid security, but suddenly she longed to be outside.

Elizabeth was doubtful. "It's very slippery," she pointed out. "And you're still quite a beginner on your crutches."

"I won't fall," Giulietta tried to reassure her. "And the snow is soft, isn't it?"

She gazed with yearning at the transformed world. Yesterday, Kaikoura's garden had been majestic but, aside from its evergreen trees and holly bushes, barren. Now, every dark, naked branch was cloaked in brilliant white, the lawn a tempting expanse of virgin sleekness.

Elizabeth gave in. And watching the child an hour later, screaming with joy as she slipped for the third time onto her bottom on the soft lawn, and then reached, almost effortlessly, to scoop a handful of snow from the top of a heaped rhododendron bush, she knew that everything —all the time, trouble, and heartache that, inevitably, lay ahead—would be worthwhile.

The most significant differences between an Italian and an English Christmas were that in Italy dinner on the Eve had to be of fish instead of meat, and presents were opened after coming home from midnight mass. Elizabeth habitually attended services at St. Martin's, but this year, she had decided, they would go to St. Joseph's Catholic church.

On finding, however, that fifteen icy steps separated the road from the entrance, they were forced to sit in the Rover, with the heater blowing and the windows open, listening as well as they could to the sounds of choir and congregation filtering out to them.

"Why don't you go inside, *Dottoressa*?" Giulietta suggested. "I can wait for you."

"The point of coming here," Elizabeth said, "was for us to be together." She smiled. "Though maybe, for the time being, it might be simpler if we went to my church—just until steps get easier for you."

"Isn't this your church?" Giulietta looked puzzled.

"Mine is Anglican, not Catholic."

"Don't they have steps there?"

"No." Elizabeth thought. "I don't think so."

"Don't you pray to Our Lord and the Blessed Virgin?"

"We believe in Jesus Christ. It's just a little different."

Giulietta nodded. "*Voglio andare alla sua chiesa*," she said decisively. "I want to go to your church." She looked earnestly at Elizabeth. "Please."

Elizabeth took Giulietta's gloved hand in hers, and squeezed it gently. "We'll go there tomorrow."

Giulietta was satisfied. She did not care what church they went to, or even if they went at all, except perhaps to thank the Blessed Virgin for sending her Elizabeth. She felt as if her life had only just begun, as if she had been in *purgatorio* all these years, until Elizabeth had released her.

She did not need to go to church anymore. Kaikoura was Elizabeth's house—and the English doctor was her savior.

It was freezing cold when they got home, both fires in the lounge having gone out, but in spite of the lateness of the hour, Elizabeth set about lighting them, telling Giulietta to keep her coat on until the room warmed a little.

"You wait here, *piccolina*—I'll be right back."

When she returned, with a pile of brightly wrapped parcels, Giulietta sat in silence, suddenly stiff, her face miserable.

"*Che cosa c'è?*" Elizabeth asked softly, kneeling beside her. "Why do you look so unhappy?"

Giulietta bit her lip.

"Tell me, *cara,* please."

The little girl flushed. "I have no present for you."

Elizabeth felt a pang of guilt. She had thought so long and hard about the right things to give to a seven-year-old who had virtually nothing, but she had not considered Giulietta's own pride.

"It doesn't matter," she tried to reassure her. "How could you have anything when you haven't been to a shop since you came to England?" She paused. "Besides, you have given me the most wonderful present."

"I have?"

"Of course, *tesoro,*" Elizabeth said gently. "You're here, aren't you? With me."

It was still cold in the lounge, but Giulietta felt a great warmth flowing through her.

She opened her gifts: a small dollhouse, a blue lamb's-wool pullover that matched her eyes, an Italian-English dictionary, a *Beano Annual,* and a teddy bear. She could hardly take them in—she had no words to explain how she felt—

It was the bear, with its gleaming button eyes and kind, stitched smile, that drew the greatest squeal of pleasure, and the most fervent hug for Elizabeth.

"I have one more thing—something we must talk about." Extricating herself from Giulietta's arms, Elizabeth rose from the settee and went to the mahogany secretaire in the far corner of the room. Rolling back the top, she took an envelope from a drawer within and returned to the settee.

"Giulietta," she said. The child was playing with the dollhouse, opening and closing the tiny hinged windows and front door.

"*Sì?*"

"Come and sit here for a minute."

Obediently, Giulietta pulled herself up with one crutch.

Elizabeth felt her stomach tauten with tension. "Giulietta, I know you've only been here for a few days—"

"Six days," the girl said eagerly.

"Yes." Elizabeth hesitated. "I have felt that, on the whole, you like it here at Kaikoura—"

"I love it, *Dottoressa*."

Elizabeth smiled. "I'm glad." She paused again, and licked her dry lips. "I realize you can't possibly know whether you'll still feel as happy when you've been here for a few months—"

"Why not?" Giulietta asked simply.

"Because life won't always be like this. It won't always be Christmas —and we won't always be at Kaikoura."

"Why not?" Anxiety clouded Giulietta's face.

"Because I'm a doctor, and because most of my patients are in London. You remember I told you about my flat—"

"In Wimpole Street," Giulietta said. She remembered everything that Elizabeth told her.

"That's right. I have to go there every week, for a few days. Sometimes, if my patients are very ill, I have to stay in London all the time."

"Can't I come with you?"

"Yes, sometimes—of course you can." Elizabeth spoke carefully. "But if you do stay here—in England—you'll go to school, and you'll be having your physiotherapy, and there will be times when we can't be together."

Giulietta looked grave. "Will I stay here alone?"

"Certainly not. Mrs. Loom will be here to look after you."

"I like Signora Loom."

"Good." Elizabeth had seen Hilda Loom, her housekeeper, playing with Giulietta, and had marveled at the way they had managed to communicate without a word of common language.

"*Dottoressa?*" Giulietta's voice was very intense.

"Yes, Giulietta?"

"Will you let me stay here?"

Elizabeth was surprised. "Of course I will."

"But you said—you must talk to me. I thought—"

"That I didn't want you?" Elizabeth drew her closer. "I want you very, very much, *tesoro*."

Giulietta relaxed a little. "What is that?" She pointed to the envelope in Elizabeth's left hand.

"This is a letter from my solicitor." Elizabeth took a deep breath. "Do you know what 'adoption' means, Giulietta?"

Giulietta frowned. "I'm not sure."

"It means that a person becomes, by law, a parent to a child who has no mother or father."

Giulietta was silent.

Elizabeth felt herself trembling. "Giulietta, I would very much like to adopt you. I would like to become your mother."

There was a pause.

"Because my parents are dead?" Giulietta's voice was small.

"Because of that, yes—but more because I—" Elizabeth took the child's hand and held it tightly. "Because I care for you very much, Giulietta—and I would like to make you my daughter."

Two spots of color rose in Giulietta's cheeks.

"If you do decide," Elizabeth went on, fighting to sound calm, "that you want me to become your mother, there will be many complications. You are from another country, and so you belong, by law, to the Italian government, and I have no husband to become your father—"

"I don't mind," Giulietta said hastily.

"You might, in time."

"Never!"

"Even so, the people who make the laws have to decide what is the best thing for you—whether you should stay in England, or whether you should live in Italy—"

"I don't *want* to go back to Italy!" Giulietta burst out.

"Not to the life you had, of course not, *cara*. But if you were to be adopted by people in your country, people who speak your language and who understand—"

"*You* speak Italian!" Giulietta was on the verge of tears.

"Of course I do, *tesoro*," Elizabeth soothed her, "and besides, you'll learn English in no time. You just have to understand that we have to get permission."

They both fell silent for a few moments, then Giulietta, a brand-new excitement in her eyes, looked at Elizabeth.

"If you can—adopt me, will you really be my mother?"

Elizabeth nodded. "I will."

"And I could call you Mother, instead of *Dottoressa*?"

"Of course."

Giulietta thought for another moment. "How long will it take?"

"I don't know," Elizabeth answered honestly. "Perhaps quite a long time."

Giulietta looked back down at her presents. "I never had anything like these before, *Dottoressa*," she said softly.

The grandfather clock in the hall struck two o'clock, and Elizabeth stirred herself. "We must go to bed—it's very late."

Giulietta glanced toward the stuffed bear. "May I take him with me?"

"Of course you may." Elizabeth smiled. "What will you call him?"

Giulietta considered. "Luciano."

"That's a handsome name for a teddy bear." Elizabeth smiled. "Why did you choose it?"

Giulietta closed her eyes. There was something at the back of her mind—very faint, and far, far back—but it was too big an effort to capture it.

She opened her eyes again.

"I don't know," she said.

Chapter 12

FEBRUARY WAS COLD and damp in Florence, and the atmosphere in Palazzo Speroza unhappy and hostile. Fabio and Letizia nagged their father persistently to lash the police into more effective action, but though Bruno did telephone the *commissario* weekly, there was no progress to report. The young fugitives, the senior policeman said, must have found shelter, but sooner or later they would have to show themselves. It was still just a matter of time.

"It's disgraceful," Fabio fumed. "Three children, with clear descriptions—wherever they are, they must stand out a mile. You haven't done enough, Father—you just accept whatever the police tell you."

"I think they let them leave the country," Letizia said direly. She had lost weight in the first month after her mother's death, but had soon begun to eat for comfort and now, without Livia's controlling influence, Letizia shopped incessantly and more unsuitably than ever, and looked increasingly plain.

"The *commissario* assures me they are still in Italy," Bruno told them for the hundredth time. "They were watching all the ports from the first day, and in any case, they have no money."

"They're thieves—they could easily have stolen again," Fabio pointed out, not unjustifiably.

Bruno sighed.

✱

Ludovico Lippi, Bruno's private detective, had had no more success than the police, but whereas Bruno was aware that the official investigation had lost its impetus, Lippi seemed keener with each passing week to track down the runaways.

"*Poveri bambini,*" he said, shaking his head. "Let's hope they have found help."

"You've heard nothing from your agents?" Bruno asked. "Not a single sighting?"

"Nothing that led to anything. I would have told you."

"Of course." Bruno looked depressed. "If I only knew they were safe, and that the police wouldn't find them—"

Lippi lit a cigar. "You didn't like your wife too much, did you, Signor Cesaretti?"

"I loved my wife." Bruno was not offended. He'd grown to respect the rasping-voiced detective over the last two months, and he accepted his brusque honesty. "I admired her, too." He gave a small shrug. "But no, I didn't like her."

Lippi blew a cloud of smoke over his desk. "It happens."

"So," Bruno returned to the matter in hand, "do you think you'll have better luck than the police?"

"Sure I will—because I'll never give up, unless you tell me to." Lippi swung his chair around and pointed at the map of Italy hanging on the wall behind him. "From what you told me about Vittorio, he won't give up either, and since his freedom is clearly crucial to him, he won't want to be cooped up any longer than he has to. So they will—if they can—try to make it out of the country."

"The police say they're watching all the ports."

"I'm sure they are—with their eyes half shut. They probably have the children's descriptions pinned up on notice boards in the port authority offices." Lippi grinned. "I have agents in Genoa, Civitavecchia, Naples"—his pointing finger thrust across the map—"Ancona and Pescara. They are there almost all the time, *really* watching, because I'm paying them to watch, and because, if they find them, they'll get a fat bonus."

Bruno leaned forward. "I don't want them scared. If they are spotted, I want you to tell me immediately."

"Of course." Lippi turned back to face his client. "How long will you look for them?" he asked curiously. "It's a costly business."

Bruno's round face was somber. "The lives of three children—my brother's children—are at stake, Signor Lippi." He thought of Letizia and Fabio, and of their unbridled fury if they ever learned of this wasting of their inheritance, and he was conscious, as usual, that his whole being was still riddled with guilt.

He looked back at Lippi.

"We'll look until we find them."

Chapter 13

FRANCESCA THOUGHT that Niccolo Dante was the most beautiful boy she had ever seen. His hair, long and even darker than her own, gleamed like the manes of the most handsome Maremmana horses; his eyes were dark as bitter chocolate, his body tall for his age and slender, lean, yet well muscled from physical work. Niccolo was strong and courageous, but quiet and gentle, and his wonderful, exuberant laughter that rang frequently through the camp belied the impression he might otherwise have given of being overly serious.

Having lived with the Dantes and their extended family for more than two months, Francesca, Vittorio, and Luciano were learning about a world they had never dreamed existed.

Once Vittorio had confided in Emilio and Niccolo, Antonia had been instructed to see that the outsiders blended in, as well as possible, with the Gypsy children. Francesca's hair had been cut again, in a ragged, boyish cut, her budding breasts concealed under baggy overshirts, and the skin of all three Cesarettis was darkened with vegetable dye. Every day brought new lessons, taught mostly by Niccolo; all the skills they lacked, but needed if they were to fend for themselves—hunting and fishing successfully, covering their tracks, and, most glorious of all, riding the semiwild Maremmana horses that Vittorio had read about in Florence. Niccolo, who had a special gift for communicating with the solidly built animals, showed them how to gain their trust, how to mount them without bridle, saddle, or stirrups, and, most important, how to stay on and ride bareback, wetting the inside of their trouser legs to give them a better grip on the horses' flanks.

"How long have you been riding?" Francesca watched in admiration as Niccolo sprang up onto his own horse's back.

"Since before I could walk." He caressed the big chestnut mare's mane. "Horses are my *grande passione*—I'd give anything to work with them all the time."

"Perhaps you will," Francesca ventured softly.

Niccolo shrugged. "Perhaps. Many Gypsies keep racehorses or trade them."

"How do you make a living?"

"We are true travelers," Niccolo said. "Sometimes we work in fairgrounds, sometimes we make pots and pans to sell." He glanced at his wristwatch. "Time to go back. I want you to show me if you can skin a rabbit properly yet."

Francesca winced. "I hate doing it."

"I know." Niccolo smiled. "Much easier to be a *Gadja* and go to a butcher's shop." His tone was wry, but his eyes were gentle.

"Much," Francesca agreed, and heard Niccolo's chuckle as he turned his horse back toward the camp.

Niccolo was different from the others, Francesca had come to realize. She'd felt, almost from the first, a special empathy with him, had felt less alien with him than with the other Gypsies, but she hadn't truly understood it until he'd told her, late one evening, the story of the Dante family. It was the saddest, most glorious, most *romantic* story she had ever heard.

Emilio, it transpired, was Niccolo's half brother. Their father, Giuseppe, had married his first wife, Maria, in a traditional Gypsy ceremony in 1919, and Emilio had been born a year later. Just three months after his birth, Maria had died after a fall, and Giuseppe had been heartbroken. It had taken him twenty years to fall in love again, but this time it was with a girl from Siena, a *Gadja*. The wrath of both Giuseppe's family and the Sienese girl's came crashing down on the lovers with full force; marriage to a non-Gypsy often resulted in the sinner's being banished from the tribe, and the girl, Andrea, came from a family steeped in the traditions of their ancient Tuscan city. Love and obstinacy won the day, and Giuseppe and Andrea were, on the whole, happier than anyone could have imagined. Niccolo was born in 1940 on a soft bed in a Sienese house—Andrea's single concession to her parents had been to promise that she would come home for the birth of any children—and somehow, that unusual beginning was to mark Niccolo out as different from other children in his tribe.

"A baby born to Gypsy parents," Niccolo had explained to Francesca, "is swept into ritual as soon as the umbilical cord has been severed. A red cap should be put on his head, red wool tied round his arms, and an amulet given to him, all for good luck. I had none of these things, so my father's family feared for my future."

Andrea had been determined to respect her husband's customs, but the marriage was, inevitably, volatile. Giuseppe Dante was a broadminded man, but he was still a Gypsy—Andrea an impulsive, emotional, loving woman, but a *Gadja* nevertheless. She traveled with Giuseppe, Emilio, and Niccolo willingly, but their caravan always contained tangible reminders of her past, and her unspoken desires. Books, in particular, were her most cherished possessions, for Andrea had been a promising student at school, and now she led a vicarious, private existence through the pages of novels she had brought with her from Siena, or which she collected at every opportunity.

"She taught me to read and write, and about the value of education," Niccolo told Francesca. "And about possessions—she used to whisper to me, when no one else could hear, about the things she'd left behind that she missed—"

"What sort of things?" Francesca asked.

"Her parents' house, more than anything—their backyard, the paintings and photographs on their walls—the gramophone, the books she couldn't carry—"

"And her family, surely?"

"She loved my father more," Niccolo said simply.

Andrea *had* been happy with her new family, but she had been unable to stop herself from sowing seeds of dissatisfaction in her son, and from encouraging him to learn to follow his heart and yet to be practical, too, when he grew up.

"I want things," Niccolo said, and his eyes burned quite black.

"Horses?" Francesca guessed.

"More than just horses. I want a house, and a garden—and I want—" He searched for the word. *"Indipendenza."* He shook his head. "But I can't have it. I won't have any of those things."

"Why not?" Francesca asked, distressed.

Niccolo shrugged. "Because I am what I am."

Andrea Dante had died of typhoid fever in the summer of 1950, and Giuseppe had succumbed less than a week later in an epidemic that had wiped out more than sixty Gypsies in their community. Some of the older and most superstitious survivors claimed that the Dante union, having produced only one child, had been *marime,* or unclean, and had, finally, brought bad luck on them all, but Emilio and his young wife, Antonia, poured healthy scorn on the rumors, before ten-year-old Niccolo's grief was magnified by ignorance.

The tears had trickled unchecked down Francesca's cheeks as Niccolo had finished his story. "Are you very unhappy?"

"Not anymore." Niccolo smiled at her. "It was terrible when Mamma and Papa died, but I still had Emilio—and I know how to look after myself."

He certainly did, Francesca thought. And it was strange to hear him say that he would never have the *indipendenza* he yearned for, because Niccolo Dante was the most independent boy she had ever met.

It was then that she had begun to wonder if he might consider coming to America with them when the time came, and the feeling of sheer misery that swept over her when she thought, for the first time, of saying good-bye to Niccolo made her wonder, too, if perhaps she was a little in love with him.

There was a mirror on the wall in Emilio's *tsara,* and sometimes, when no one was looking, Francesca would stare at her reflection, at her cropped hair and her sunburned face and boyish clothes, and she would close her eyes and think about Niccolo, and she would wish, more than anything, that she could look like a girl again.

Every year, near the end of May, Gypsies from all over the world traveled to the south of France to a village named Saintes Maries de la Mer for the festival in celebration of Black Sarah, their patron saint. This year, for the Dante's commune, would be no exception. They would begin their journey at the beginning of the month, in order to arrive at their destination in time for the start of the festivities on May 24.

It was time for the Cesaretti children to decide.

"We've always known," Emilio told them in early April, "that we would, eventually, have to go our separate ways, but the decision must be yours."

Vittorio stared at the ground. He had known, of course, as Emilio said, that this time would come, and he had never deviated from his original plan to get to Naples, and out of Italy, but the moment of truth still struck a bitter blow. They had all been so content with their new friends. They had eaten well, slept peacefully, learned, in just three months, more useful rules of life than years of school could ever have taught them—and they had known that they were with human beings they could trust.

The three children were silent.

"I think the best thing to do," Emilio said gently, "is to reexamine your strategy, Vittorio. We know that it began badly for you, but that was because you had no experience. Now you have." He sucked on his pipe. "Is it still a good plan for you to go to America? And do you have any real alternative?"

"They could stay with us," Niccolo said.

"Yes, they could," Emilio agreed. "But they are not Gypsies, Niccolo —they have their own destinies, different from ours." He looked back at the Cesaretti children. "Talk it over, all three of you—and if you decide that it is still a good plan, then we have friends in Naples who will help you."

Vittorio nodded, still silent. He realized that ever since Christmas

Eve, he had been able to relinquish his role as leader, had been a boy again, with people older, wiser, or simply more experienced to call upon. Now the burden of responsibility had been thrust back on his shoulders, and he balked at it.

"Couldn't we stay with them, at least a while longer?" Francesca could hardly bear to think about leaving Niccolo.

"Yes, couldn't we?" Luciano urged. The change in him had been profound. The rather pale, nervy child who had tagged unhappily behind his brother and sister from Florence to the swamphole had been replaced by a sparkling-eyed, sunburned boy, more confident than he'd ever been. The prospect of being back on the road, however, without the protection of the Gypsies, still alarmed him.

"Emilio's right," Vittorio said reluctantly. "We're not the same as them, and we never will be. We don't belong."

"Do we belong in America?" Francesca asked quietly.

"I don't know, *cara*. But at least if we make it there, we'll have a chance. I told you, I read about it—they're good to immigrants, many Italians live there." Vittorio looked sad. "If we stay with the Gypsies, we *will* be like them in one way—we'll never have a home."

✳

Late that night, when the others slept, Emilio told Vittorio what he had learned some weeks before—that Livia Cesaretti was dead, and that the Florence police had been hunting for them since December.

Vittorio was ashen beneath his tan.

"Have you considered going back?"

"To Florence?" Vittorio was appalled. "Impossible."

Emilio took out his pipe. "Your uncle sounds like a fair man. He might forgive you, if you gave him the chance."

Vittorio shook his head vehemently. "No man could be that forgiving." He remembered Bruno's kindness and generosity, and the way he'd allowed him to come into his jewelry stores, against Livia's wishes, and his eyes shone with unshed tears. "I gave up my rights to my uncle's protection the night I—" He stopped, unable to go on.

There was a long pause.

"What about the others?"

"What about them?"

Emilio looked uncomfortable. "They could go back. At least Luciano would never be accused of having anything to do with your aunt's death—"

"*Never!*" Vittorio snapped. "I will never let anyone or anything separate the three of us. We're family."

"I understand." Emilio smiled and patted his shoulder. "I would say the same thing. Family is everything to the Gypsies."

Plans were laid within a week. They were, at present, camped just south of Tarquinia, on the coast, where the commune would remain until May 7, the day after St. George's Day, an occasion celebrated by all Gypsies everywhere. A few days before that, Emilio and Niccolo would escort the Cesaretti children safely around Rome and through the Campagna to Anzio.

There, while Emilio went on to Naples to arrange their ocean passage with a contact who owed him a large debt, Niccolo would take them on the ferry to Ponza, and from there, they would take a small boat to Palmarola, an island where they would be able to stay, without fear of discovery, until it was time for them to board their ship in Naples—the *Vulcania,* a passenger ship of the Italia Line, sailing to Boston in the middle of May.

"Have you heard of the Palio?"

The Cesaretti children shook their heads.

Niccolo Dante's eyes were distant. "It is my ambition," he said.

They had been on Palmarola, their sanctuary island, for seven days, and would remain there for another six. It was a wild, magical place, with strangely shaped coves and deserted caves where they slept at night, and could take shelter if a stray tourist came too close for comfort.

All the tensions and fears that had reawoken in them when they had realized it was time to move on had evaporated again in the warm, sunny, peaceful air. The scenery was spectacular, the fishing excellent, the seabirds flamboyant and exuberant. The children swam and lay, naked and unselfconscious, to dry in the sun, and Niccolo entertained them with stories of his life. He had a special affinity with Siena, the city of his birth, and a place he had returned to only three times in the ten years before Andrea, his mother, had died.

"The best time was in the days of the Palio."

"What *is* the Palio?" Luciano was intrigued.

"It's a unique race, run twice each year in the city, a fantastic, wild bareback horse race, surrounded by celebrations and ritual. Believe me, none of you has ever seen anything to compare with it." His dark eyes glittered. "Though I am, of course, a Gypsy, I am also Sienese for life, and one day I will go back again, if possible, to ride in the Palio."

"I'd love to see it." Francesca's expression was rapt.

"But you will be in America." Niccolo's soft, wry tone brought her abruptly back to reality.

She glanced at Vittorio, who was lying on his back, eyes shut, perhaps asleep, perhaps listening. "I don't want to go to America," she said, very quietly.

"What do you want?"

To stay here with you, she thought. *To grow up with you, and to watch you ride in the Palio.* But they were only thoughts, and she said nothing at all.

Six more halcyon days, and it was over. Their mood grew bleak, and they became irritable with one another. As they journeyed on south, Vittorio was increasingly morose, Luciano was more fretful than he had been for many months, and Francesca had a frequent desire to weep. Even Niccolo was somber and quiet.

Francesca knew that they were all afraid.

✳

Naples was a shock to their senses. However noisy Florence had seemed after the peace of Lucchesia, it had never been as clamorous as this. The streets were crammed with vehicles and people, some rushing about their business, some idling away the time, standing in shop door-ways chattering, shouting, and even singing.

Within an hour of their arrival, Niccolo had met with Emilio's con-tact, only to be told that it would not be possible for Vittorio, Francesca, and Luciano to board the *Vulcania* until three hours before the official embarkation began next morning. That left the evening and night to stay clear of danger, but Niccolo had visited Naples before, and knew that they could spend the whole night in Piazza Garibaldi, without at-tracting special attention.

"It's always packed with derelicts and street kids."

Luciano looked admiring. "You know everything."

Niccolo shrugged. "I've been here before, that's all."

"You've been *everywhere*," Luciano said.

"Not to America," Niccolo said softly, and Francesca thought she saw a flicker of envy in his eyes.

They had felt confident that they were, for the moment at least, alone and unobserved.

They were not.

The detective had recognized Vittorio and Luciano near the Sta-zione Centrale. A few minutes later, following them, he had noticed that one of the two boys with them was not a boy at all. He studied her behind—that tiny swaying motion—not much, but enough to betray her.

Francesca Cesaretti. He had them all.

At the first opportunity, while the children, sharing a single bottle of Coca-Cola, rested in Piazza del Mercato, the detective made a telephone call to Florence.

★

Less than fifteen minutes later, Bruno Cesaretti was called to the telephone in his store on the Via della Vigna Nuova.

"*Pronto.*"

"This is Lippi. They are in Naples. We have them under surveillance."

"*Dio.*" Bruno took a large silk handkerchief from his breast pocket and mopped his brow. "At last."

"We should leave immediately."

Bruno's mind worked rapidly. "I'll call the airport—"

"And waste time driving to Pisa? We should hire a private plane and fly direct from here."

"I'll arrange it." Bruno spoke quietly into the mouthpiece. "Signor Lippi, they must not be approached until we are there—they must not be frightened away." He hesitated. "You're sure that your people are right—it is them?"

"Almost certainly." Lippi's shrug was clear even through the telephone. "Until you see them for yourself, there's no way of being one hundred percent sure."

The children had passed a restless, uncomfortable night. Just after eight in the morning, munching hungrily on slices of pizza bought from one of the *bancarelle,* they emerged from Piazza Garibaldi, their limbs stiff, their eyes bleary. The pizza was good—and helped, a little, to dull the churning apprehension in their stomachs. They were all jittery, but Vittorio was strung taut.

"Soon," Niccolo said, trying to calm him, "you'll be on board the *Vulcania.* And in a few more hours, you'll be on your way to America."

Vittorio shook his head. "I won't relax until we've left Genoa." The *Vulcania* would sail first to Genoa, then Barcelona, Lisbon, and the Azores, before moving out into the Atlantic. "Maybe not until we're really *in* America."

"The trouble with you, Vittorio," Niccolo said, gently, "is that you don't really know how to relax."

"Yes, he does," Francesca defended her brother. "He did on the island."

"But that," Niccolo said, "was *paradiso*. It wasn't real." He looked at his watch. "*Andiamo*," he said. "It's time to go to the dock."

There was a café near the corner of the broad Corso Umberto, where people, mostly tourists, sipped their first coffee of the day and enjoyed the gentle, early sunshine.

At a table near the edge of the pavement, Ludovico Lippi watched Bruno's face.

"It is them, isn't it?"

Bruno, unshaven, his throat tight with conflicting emotions, nodded. "It is." He paused. "They look—different."

"Older."

"Much." Bruno sat forward. "And more—alive—than they were at home."

"It wasn't their home," Lippi said. He drank down his black coffee. "Do you recognize the other one?"

Bruno shook his head. "You think they're going to the docks?"

"I'm sure of it."

"Let's go." Bruno rose.

"Wait—" Lippi pulled him back down. "They'll see you."

✶

"That man," Niccolo said. "He's staring at you."

"What man?" asked Vittorio.

"The café—that table near the street."

They all looked.

"It's Uncle Bruno!" Luciano cried.

"It is!" Francesca gasped.

"*Merda!*" Vittorio was stunned.

"Come on," Niccolo said, fighting to stay calm. "Let's start walking —slowly."

The Cesaretti children did not move.

"Come *on*," Niccolo urged.

"They've seen you," Lippi said, and swore.

Bruno stood up again. He opened his mouth, and yelled, his voice carrying over the rush-hour cacophony—

"*Vittorio!*"

"No!" Vittorio was panic-stricken. "*No!*"

Yanking at Luciano's hand, still in his own, he turned and began to run. "Follow me!" he shouted back over his shoulder to the others.

"Vittorio, slow down!" Niccolo tried to halt him.

"Come on," Lippi said to Bruno, "or we'll lose them for sure!" He threw some notes onto the table. "For God's sake, man, let's *go!*"

They ran out into the street, Bruno cursing his overweight, unathletic body.

"Stop!" he shouted, at the top of his voice. "Vittorio, for the love of God, *stop!*"

—From just around the corner on Corso Umberto, two *carabinieri*, alerted by Bruno's cries and seeing two middle-aged, respectable gentlemen chasing a group of children down Corso Garibaldi, presumed a gang of thieving *lazzaroni* and joined in the pursuit.

"The police!" Luciano shrieked.

"We've had it." Niccolo, skidding to a halt for an instant, looked around for an escape route but saw none.

"What can we *do?*" Francesca pleaded.

Vittorio, hearing the whistles of the policemen and the shouts of the crowd, had never known such fear. Everything came flooding back—the fire, Giulietta, the palazzo and the screams of Aunt Livia, the woman he had murdered—

In prison, his terror-crazed mind told him, he would die. He could not bear it.

"I won't let them!" he bellowed, running faster and away from the others. "I won't *let* them!"

Niccolo, seeing the danger, yelled after him. "Not in the street, Vittorio! Be *careful!*"

If he heard, he was unable to pay any heed. Vittorio was off the pavement, running for his life, fleeing for survival, mindless of any danger other than those men in uniform and the cell doors that would surely close on him if he stopped.

He didn't look to right or left. He didn't see the girl on the motorcycle, swerving to avoid him, nor the Fiat forced out of its lane—nor the heavy lorry with a picture of two car tires painted on its side, skidding out of control toward him, its driver pounding on his horn furiously—

Francesca screamed with all her might.

The lorry hit Vittorio from the left, sending him flying through the air and crashing down on the warm tarmac—

"*Gesù Cristo*, no!" Bruno, panting desperately, stared in horror and disbelief.

Ludovico Lippi, accustomed to witnessing tragedy, stopped where he was, his own guilt sticking in his throat.

The two *carabinieri*, like dogs with the scent of blood in their nostrils, thundered on.

Francesca, hysterical, crouched at Vittorio's side. "Get up," she begged him. "We have to get to the ship!"

He lay, heavy and still and moaning softly, and she saw that blood oozed endlessly from the left side of his head, and trickled from his ear.

"Please try to stand up," she whispered to him, great tears flooding her eyes and pouring down her cheeks. "We need you—we can't go without you—*please*, Vittorio—"

Behind her, Niccolo, holding on to Luciano with all his strength, ignoring all his pleas, touched Francesca's shoulder. "We have to go on," he hissed, his own face ashen with horror. "The police—"

"I won't go without him." Francesca turned her face up to Niccolo, and her voice was almost a snarl. "I won't leave him!"

But he's dying, Niccolo thought, but couldn't tell her.

Cradled in her arms, Vittorio was trying, with his last strength, to speak, but his voice was gone—

"What, *tesoro?*" Francesca put her ear close to his mouth. "What did you say?"

She heard him then. Just one word. And she pretended that she had heard nothing, and so Vittorio said it once more.

"*Go.*"

His face didn't alter, his eyes still stared at her, but she felt him sag a little, against her, and the small sound in his throat told her what she could not believe.

"*E morto,*" Niccolo said, longing to be gentle, but knowing there was no time. Hanging on to Luciano with his left hand, he seized Francesca's arm and dragged her to her feet.

"*No!*" she screamed.

"For Vittorio." His voice shook.

She stared down at her brother's body, and something inside her snapped, went wild—

"All right."

They began to run again, and the hunters, who had stopped to try to help Vittorio, looked up, startled, and renewed their chase, blowing their whistles.

"I can't!" Luciano sobbed.

"Not far now." Niccolo urged him on.

And then Luciano tripped, blinded by tears, and fell, and Niccolo stopped to help him up—and in those few wasted seconds, the *carabinieri* were on them—

And Francesca, quite mad with grief and shock, paused only for a fraction of a second. She didn't really hear Luciano's shrieks, or her uncle's pleading cries, nor did she see Niccolo's grim, stony face.

All she saw was Vittorio's face, dying—dead.

All she heard was his last word. His command.

"Go."

Chapter 14

O N   T H E   F I F T E E N T H day of June that same year, 1954, the complicated
legal process to transform an Italian orphan into the daughter of an
English pediatrician was completed. And on that same day, Giulietta
Volpi took the name that she had longed for since Christmas Eve—
Juliet Austen.

She felt as if she had been newly born.

"Where shall we go to celebrate?" Elizabeth asked her after breakfast that morning.

"Stay here, please." Giulietta was making great strides with her private English coaching, and even when Elizabeth spoke to her in Italian,
she tried to make an effort.

"We must go somewhere, darling."

"Why must we?"

"Because this is a very special occasion." Elizabeth persevered.
"Wouldn't you like to go to London? We could lunch somewhere wonderful—anywhere you like." She hugged her new daughter. "Darling, I
really want to take you out."

"Okay." Giulietta went over to the kitchen window, and gazed out
at Kaikoura's glorious rhododendrons. The entire Deepdene area had
been awash with lush, vibrant color since early May. "Can we have a
picnic, please?"

"*Another* picnic?" Elizabeth sighed. "But wouldn't you rather go to a restaurant?"

Giulietta turned back, and her blue eyes opened wide with appeal. "Please?" She paused. ". . . Mother."

Giulietta hated leaving the house for any reason. Since she was determined to rid herself of her despised crutches at the earliest opportunity, she cooperated with the physiotherapists at the London hospital where she attended as an outpatient, and she had grown used to the Wimpole Street flat, comforted by the fact that Elizabeth was nearby—but she was only truly happy in, and close to, Kaikoura.

When September came, she knew that she would have to start school, and that she would often be separated from Elizabeth for five days each week—Mrs. Loom was going to live at Kaikoura from Mondays to Fridays during term time. Giulietta knew that all those things would come to pass, no matter how much she feared and dreaded them, but she also knew that she would do anything and everything that Elizabeth asked of her, for her sake.

Elizabeth—her mother.

The very thought made her glow with pride.

She was in her bedroom, when she heard Elizabeth calling from the foot of the staircase.

"Giulietta, do you want to go to the Nower or Forewents Pond?"

Giulietta did not reply. Silently, she limped out on bare feet to the top of the stairs.

"Giulietta!"

Still she said nothing, waiting, biting her lip.

Down below, Elizabeth, catching a glimpse of movement, felt momentarily puzzled—Giulietta was always a most willing and obedient child.

And then she understood her mistake. This might well be one of the most precious days of her own life, but for an eight-year-old, traumatized girl who had blotted out from her memory most of her existence, it was surely little less than sacred.

Elizabeth felt a great surge of love.

"Juliet," she said, clearly and steadily.

The child who came, still painfully, down the staircase wore a broad smile of exultation.

"Coming, Mother," she said.

Chapter 15

BRUNO HAD OVERRIDDEN his children's fury and disgust, and had brought Luciano back home to Florence. Vittorio was beyond their retribution, and Francesca had disappeared. Surely even Fabio and Letizia did not believe that this young, unhappy boy could have played any part in Livia's death. Whether or not they agreed, he would entertain no arguments.

He had arrived at two major decisions. First, for their own good, and if Bruno was not to end up actually despising his own children, they would have to be sent away. Letizia would go to school in Switzerland, where he felt sure she would thrive, no matter how much she protested, and Fabio would attend a military school, prior to conscription.

Bruno's second decision was to sell their apartments in Palazzo Speroza. He had never really personally cared for the property, but had accepted it for Livia's sake, and while he knew that his children would condemn him for selling their birthright, he was certain, in his own mind, that a move would be best for them all.

Fabio and Letizia would be injured by these decisions, and this knowledge did not permit Bruno any peace of mind. But there was another child to consider now—a young boy, lonely and vulnerable and confused. Luciano had wept almost constantly for a week after their return from Naples, but had stood dry-eyed and white-faced when Vittorio had been laid to rest beside his twin sister. He had never cried openly since that day.

"Can't you try to guess where Francesca might have gone?" Bruno asked the boy almost every day, in as many different, gentle ways as his imagination allowed, but Luciano always shook his head and compressed his lips, and refused to answer, for though he missed Francesca with every ounce of his being, and longed desperately to see her again, he had heard his cousins' threats against her, and he was sure that if they found her, she would be locked up in prison.

At least this way, he could imagine her in Boston, waiting for him to come to her as soon as he was old enough. Luciano was sure that Francesca must have managed to board the *Vulcania*, for if she were still in Italy, she would have found a way to fetch him from Palazzo Speroza— yet still, just in case, he waited up every night, sitting on a chair by the window of his new bedroom, fighting off sleep for as long as possible so that he would not miss her if she did come.

It was mid-August before Luciano, caught off guard, let slip that Vittorio's plan had been for them to go to America.

Bruno was swamped by a mixture of relief and panic. Lippi had told him that a ship had sailed from Naples to America that day in May, though Francesca's name had not appeared on the passenger list of that or any other ship. What in the name of God had happened to the child? Could she perhaps, somehow, have got on board—and if so, where was she now?

Having ascertained from Lippi that the *Vulcania* had docked in both Boston and New York, Bruno began to place weekly advertisements, in Italian, in the personal columns of the New York *Daily News* and the *Boston Globe*, praying that Francesca would, by some miracle, see or hear about the advertisements, and get in touch. Lippi, morosely, told him that without some other lead, even the most tenacious private detective would not find her, and after all Francesca had been through, Bruno was loath to inform the American police. The one remaining person who might be able to help to trace Francesca was the young stranger, still in custody in Naples.

The boy, captured on Corso Garibaldi, had refused to identify himself and, having no papers on his person, had been charged with resisting arrest, assaulting a police officer, and aiding and abetting a suspect in a murder investigation.

Bruno tackled Luciano again.

"This boy helped you, didn't he?"

Luciano nodded.

"And now he's in jail. Wouldn't you like him to be free again?"

"Of course."

"Then won't you please just tell me his name?"

Luciano didn't speak.

"If you don't tell me, I cannot help him."

The boy gave way. "Niccolo," he said. "Niccolo Dante."

Bruno smiled. "A fine name."

"He's a Gypsy."

Bruno nodded. "Is he indeed?"

It was clear to Bruno that the young Gypsy deserved a reward rather than a prison sentence. He now knew that Niccolo and his older brother had saved Luciano and Vittorio, and that the Dantes had protected and cared for the three Cesaretti children for almost five months. Bruno tried, in vain, to persuade the police to release Niccolo, but they alleged that he was a delinquent, who showed no trace of remorse or cooperation.

In the first week of September, he flew down to Naples to visit Niccolo. The boy was thin, but striking. Bruno hardly knew where to begin. He realized now that he owed the Dante family a great debt of thanks, and that Niccolo was being unjustly punished. There was, alas, nothing to be done for him legally, but if there was anything else—

"Such as?" Niccolo's voice was quiet.

"Would you like me to contact your brother? I would very much like to meet the man who saved the lives of my niece and nephews."

"That was nothing."

"Hardly." Bruno hesitated. "May I seek out your brother?"

Niccolo shook his head. "I don't think that he would wish to be found, Signor Cesaretti. And neither he nor any of my family requires thanks."

Bruno felt dismissed. The boy was so self-possessed and dignified.

"I have to ask you another question."

"Of course."

"Do you know where Francesca is?"

"No." The answer was swift and definite.

"Do you know where she might be?"

"No, *signor.*"

"I mean her no harm," Bruno persisted. "I'm afraid for her—I care for her." He paused. "I know she may be in Boston, but without more information there's no chance I'll ever trace her." He watched the boy's dark, impenetrable eyes. "I could give her description to the Boston police, but I don't want her deported as if she were a criminal."

"She's had enough trouble," Niccolo said, softly.

A flicker of hope rose in Bruno. "So you'll help her?"

"I only wish I could."

"You *could,*" Bruno said urgently, "if you'd just tell me whatever you know."

Niccolo Dante stared at him long and hard, before answering. "I don't know anything," he said at last. "I'm sorry."

Bruno sighed. "Not as sorry as I am."

The Gypsy gave a small, taut smile. "I wouldn't count on that."

Bruno rose from his hard chair. "Are you sure," he asked again, "that I can do nothing to help you? Surely you must need something?"

Niccolo felt sorry for the man. "Thank you," he said, and there was a spark of warmth in his voice. "But there's nothing I need from you."

Deeply depressed about Francesca, and at a loss to know what else to do for the unjustly imprisoned young man, Bruno visited the main Naples branch of his bank, and opened a deposit account in the name of

Niccolo Dante, into which he transferred the sum of one million lire from his personal account in Florence. Explaining the unusual circumstances, he instructed the manager to forward all statements and correspondence to the *direttore* of the prison, until Dante's release.

"This is most irregular." The manager was courteous, but transparently disapproving.

"Surely not," Bruno said dryly. "New accounts must be opened every day."

The bank manager shrugged, grateful that Signor Cesaretti lived in Florence, and that the vast majority of his clients were, to the best of his knowledge, not convicts.

"One more thing," Bruno said, rising. "On his release, if Signor Dante does visit you, I trust I can depend upon you to give him as much of your excellent professional advice as he will accept."

Or tolerate, he thought as he stepped back out onto the hot pavement. For all he knew, Niccolo Dante might be too proud to accept the money. Bruno hoped not. Luciano and the other two children had obviously liked and trusted the Gypsy boy.

He understood why.

Chapter 16

IN THE HOURS that had passed after she felt Vittorio dying in her arms, and after she had seen Luciano and Niccolo captured by the *carabinieri*, Francesca had, literally, lost her mind.

"*Go*," Vittorio had commanded her, and she had responded, half mechanically, half mad. She had gone, as they had planned, as Niccolo had told them they would, to the docks, and had found, as arranged, Emilio's contact at the pier, waiting for them—waiting for three children, and receiving just one.

"You want to go alone?" he had asked her, not caring, for one was less trouble than three, and he had been paid in advance. Francesca, unable to speak coherently, had nodded, Vittorio's last word reverberating, over and over again, in her head.

The *Vulcania* was an impressive ship, and the passengers who queued to board her three hours after Francesca had been smuggled past the uniformed authorities were eager with anticipation of a delightful voyage.

Francesca, meanwhile, sat hunched over in the crawl space that was to be her home for almost three weeks. She had no natural light—just a small flashlight handed to her by the nervous sailor who would be her only human contact for the duration of the journey, a man named Fredo

Lombardi—but she did not care. She sat in the pitch-darkness, without bothering to switch on the flashlight, not minding that there was scarcely enough air for her to breathe, nor that the only sanitary provision in the crawl space was a bucket. For those first few hours on board the *Vulcania,* she felt nothing at all.

One day out to sea, of course, and that had altered, for now Francesca's initial, deadening shock had subsided, and in its place was horror and grief, and an intense desire to die as soon as possible.

She did not die, not the first day, nor the second, nor the third, nor any other day of the voyage. Fredo Lombardi brought her scraps of leftover food and water to drink and wash with, and every two days, he brought a little disinfectant to clean the foul bucket, yet Francesca hardly registered her discomfort. She did not dare to contemplate her aloneness or her desolation either. Her losses, when added up, were so great, so vast and unbearable, and her daily struggle, in spite of herself, for survival, both physical and emotional, was so painful, that she erected an imaginary, impregnable wall against all memory or introspection or feeling.

"Where are we?" she whispered, whenever Lombardi paid his daily visit.

She knew when they were in port, for the rolling of the ship stopped almost completely, and during the first stage of the journey, the sailor would answer: "Genoa"—"Barcelona"—or "Lisbon today." But then the ship began to pitch and toss badly, and when she asked Lombardi where they were, between miserable bouts of retching emptily, he would simply shrug his shoulders, and tell her they were on their way.

When the day finally came for her to leave her crawl space, when the sailor came to her, his face and voice taut with nerves, and told her to come out, Francesca was too stiff and weak to move.

"You have to," Lombardi insisted. "This is Boston—I have one hour to get you on shore."

But Francesca could not walk, and Lombardi, cursing under his breath, was forced to carry her off the *Vulcania* in his arms, praying to all the saints that they would not be spotted. He and his family owed an old debt to Emilio Dante, and he had been well paid, but he did not care to lose his job and liberty for a scrawny, flea-bitten girl.

✱

Francesca remembered little of her first days in America. The sailor took her to Salem Street in the area of Boston known as the North End, to the overcrowded apartment rented by his cousin Anthony.

"Are you *crazy?*" Anthony and his wife, Maria, stared at Francesca, who sat limp and trembling on a chair near the front door. "Why bring her to us?"

"What should I do? Dump her on the street? Besides—" Fredo beckoned Anthony into the small kitchen that smelled strongly of onions and garlic, and took the wad of bank notes from his pocket. "Eighty thousand lire."

"*Gesù.*" Anthony looked suspicious. "Where d'you get it?"

"Emilio Dante."

"Dante?" Anthony was startled. "Why the fuck would that Gypsy bastard give you eighty thousand lire?"

Emilio had, in fact, given Fredo one hundred thousand, but the sailor had already peeled off a cut for himself.

"There were supposed to be three kids," he told Anthony, "but the others got left behind. Dante wanted them to have a start over here." He shrugged. "But since there's only one—"

"You reckon she won't need all of it." Anthony scratched his stubbly chin. "Dante wouldn't be happy if he found out."

"Who's gonna tell him? The kid doesn't know about the cash."

"Okay." Anthony held out his hand. "So hand it over."

Fredo looked suspicious. "How do I know you'll give it to her?"

"Sure I will—after expenses." Anthony glanced back into the hall. "She looks half starved."

"She probably is—she's hardly eaten anything for three weeks."

"Maria's going to love having another mouth to feed," Anthony said sarcastically. "For a mother of five, she's a little short on maternal instincts."

Fredo dumped the lire into his cousin's outstretched hand. "Just make sure she does feed her—none of us needs a corpse on our hands."

Though Maria Lombardi would happily have seen Francesca tossed into Boston Harbor and put out of her misery, she knew she was going to have to get the girl up on her feet before she could hope to see the back of her.

"It's disgusting," she complained to her husband on the first evening. "The girl has lice."

"So give her a bath."

"Soap don't kill lice."

"What does?"

"*Disinfettante*."

"So use that, and get off my back."

"We don't have any."

Anthony covered his face with the newspaper he'd been reading. "So go buy some."

"I need money."

"You got plenty of money."

"For *my* kids, I got money—you want me to look after someone else's kid, you gotta give me more." Maria stood her ground, arms folded. "You want your children to catch lice?" She got no response. "*You* want to catch lice?"

Anthony gave her five dollars. "You go buy disinfectant and whatever else you need for her—food, medicine, whatever you need. Just leave me alone and don't tell me any more about goddamned lice."

"I'm gonna need more than this," Maria said.

Her husband covered his face again. "In a pig's ass," he said sourly.

For two days Francesca could keep nothing down, but then Maria, knowing she had no choice but to make a real effort if the girl was not to die, made broth and bought fresh fish, and very slowly, little by little, Francesca began to sip and to nibble, and her distraught, confused stomach began to calm, and by the fifth day, she was eating and walking around the cramped apartment, and—wretchedly—she was also beginning to think and to remember.

"Where are we?" she asked Maria Lombardi.

"You know where—Boston." The answer was impatient.

Knowing what city she was in did not mean that Francesca understood it. Perhaps if she had not spent the voyage in a black, stinking hole, perhaps if she had seen the Atlantic Ocean in all its vastness, and had stood on the deck of the *Vulcania* when American landfall was sighted, she might not feel quite so lost and disoriented, but—

"Do you have a map I could see?" she ventured timidly.

"What the hell would I be doing with a map?" Maria snapped, doubly irritated because her youngest had kept her up all night. "And why would you want one?"

"To learn the city."

"You'll learn the city same way as I did—by using your feet." The woman relented a little. "You're in Boston, which a lot of people seem to think is a great place, but which, as far as I'm concerned, is a dump. And you're in Salem Street, in the North End, which is where a lot of Italians live, and which is also a dump. That's all you need to know until you go out through that front door—" Maria jerked her head in that direction. "Which I hope is soon."

"*Grazie,*" Francesca said faintly, as another great surge of panic and despair swept through her. Though their home was bliss compared to the crawl space, the Lombardis were callous and hateful—but the prospect of being outside, in the absolute unknown, without Vittorio or Luciano or Niccolo was something too terrifying to contemplate.

Anthony Lombardi was determined to get rid of Francesca as swiftly and, with luck, as profitably, as possible.

"Start getting her ready," he told his wife on the eighth day of Francesca's stay. "I got her an interview for a job."

"What kind of job?"

"Why should you care? You want her out of your hair, don't you?"

Maria shrugged. "Sure."

"Get her something to wear—a dress, tight, and a set of underwear —brassiere, stockings, garter belt, whatever."

"She's just a kid."

"She has tits, which makes her a broad." Lombardi thought for a moment. "And get her hair into shape—I never saw such a mess—and find her a lipstick."

Two days later, Francesca stood on the top of the porch steps of the Lombardis' apartment house, clutching a shiny red handbag into which Maria had placed a lipstick, change for bus fare, a small street map of the city, and a pocket-sized Italian-English dictionary.

"Okay," Anthony Lombardi said briskly. "This is a note for your boss—if he likes you—" He put a sealed envelope into her hand. "The address is on the front—can you read it?"

Francesca looked at it and nodded. "Scollay Square?"

"That's right."

She raised bewildered eyes to him. "But how will I find it?"

He nudged her down the steps and pointed. "Start walking that way —and check the map. If you get lost, ask someone the way."

"Will they speak Italian?"

Lombardi shrugged. "Maybe, maybe not." He pointed to the handbag. "That's what the book is for." He pinched her cheek, thinking how sexy she looked. She'd cleaned up pretty good, and somehow her fear enhanced her looks, made her great big eyes even bigger. "Listen, kid, you found Boston all the way from Italy—you'll find Scollay Square, no sweat."

Francesca swallowed nervously. "If I don't, can I come back here?"

"No way." Lombardi shook his head emphatically. "You're on your own from now on, kid. You find the place, you land the job—they'll look after you, even give you somewhere to live."

"And if I don't get the job?" Francesca had tried, over and over again, to discover what this job was, but Anthony and Maria had both been evasive.

Lombardi glared at her. "You *get* it, kid. Don't get cute, don't get fussy—just do as you're told and you'll get the goddamned job."

"But—"

Lombardi was already walking back up the steps and opening the front door. "And if you do screw up"—his tone was almost menacing— "don't bother coming back here, because we won't let you in. From this moment on, *ragazzina*, we never heard of you here." He paused. "You knock on our door, it stays shut. Anyone asks about you, you don't exist."

The door slammed.

Francesca had known more real fear in the last three years of her life than most children experienced in nightmares, but she had never been entirely alone. Even in her worst moments—even down in the cellar in the palazzo—she had known that Vittorio would, in the end, come to save her; even in the crawl space on the ship, she had known that Fredo Lombardi, a stranger, but still a human contact, would come to her. But now, standing on narrow Salem Street, there was no one.

Knowing she had no choice, she began to walk in the direction in which Lombardi had pointed. Her steps were slow and awkward, her toes pinched by her new, high-heeled red shoes, her thighs and knees trapped by the tight skirt of her flimsy dress.

It was a bright, warm June morning, and Francesca could hear birds singing—American birds—but there was no joy in the sound for her. She did not think she would ever experience happiness or pleasure again. Either she would be arrested or murdered at any moment, or she would get lost and wander through Boston until she starved to death. The only thought that gave her a bizarre measure of relief was that Luciano was not with her—for her little brother was surely far safer with Uncle Bruno than with her in this alien land.

Tottering painfully down the street, passing an Italian *panetteria*, she tried to make sense of the map. Left—she had to turn left into Prince Street, and then—she squinted in the sunlight—and then, right into Hanover Street. Getting the dictionary out of her handbag, she looked up the word "street." *Strada, via,* it said—at least that was simple enough.

About to turn into Hanover Street, Francesca noticed, on the opposite side of the road, a man in a dark blue uniform. *Polizia!* Her heart pounding with terror, she turned and fled, as quickly as her shoes and skirt would allow, up a side street, certain that she was still being hunted and that, at any minute, she might be snatched off the street, just as Luciano and Niccolo had been in Naples.

An hour later, soaked in perspiration, her face tear-stained, she arrived at her destination. Having taken one wrong turning, she had stumbled helplessly around in a large circle, tripping on cobblestones, avoiding the stares of the people she passed, all kinds of people, some shabby, many elegant—city people, yet somehow indefinably different from those in Florence and Naples. She heard some Italian voices, which made her feel, fleetingly, less lost, but the mass spoke English—she couldn't imagine *ever* being able to understand, let alone speak, such a strange, impenetrable language.

The city was full of contradictions—one minute, she was in a narrow, steeply sloping road, with painted shutters on the windows and tufts of moss spiking up between cobbles, the next she was in a busy main street, with shops and red-brick houses and huge cars and buses—but Francesca was oblivious to everything except getting to Scollay Square without having to resort to asking for help.

Keep away from people, Vittorio had said repeatedly, while they were in the Maremma. *Strangers are dangerous.*

A great sob escaped her lips, and total wretchedness engulfed her for the thousandth time—and then she saw the name on the sign. *Scollay Square.*

The building she entered was old and dilapidated, with a narrow, slanting staircase and three closed doors on every story, bearing strange-sounding names on rusting metal plates. On the fourth floor, peering at the door to the right of the stairs, Francesca recognized the name on the envelope given to her by Anthony Lombardi.

Ruby & de Santi
Artists' agents

Gathering all her courage, and praying that Signor de Santi, whoever he was, was a kind man, Francesca knocked at the door. Receiving no response, she tried again, and when that failed, very tentatively she opened the door.

The room she entered was crowded with people of all ages, colors, and shapes—a gaggle of men, women, and children all talking at once and incomprehensibly, except for a few morose-looking individuals who sat on benches around the walls, staring into space.

Curbing her desire to run, knowing that there was nowhere for her to run *to*, Francesca approached a thin, sharp-nosed man who sat behind a desk at the rear of the room, reading a newspaper and ignoring everyone.

"*Mi scusi, signor*," she said softly.

He turned over a page, and stared at some cartoons.

"*Signor?*" Louder this time.

"What?" He didn't look up.

"*Ho una lettera per* Signor de Santi." She put the letter down on the desk.

"Speak English," the man said irritably.

"*Non capisco.*" Francesca said desperately, and pointed to the letter. "*Dov'è* Signor de Santi, *per favore? Ho gia un appuntamento.*"

At last the man glanced up at her. "English," he said again, tiredly.

Francesca remembered the dictionary, and pulled it out of the red handbag, dropping the street map on the floor in her confusion. Frantically, she searched for a word she could use, something that would make this unpleasant man realize she had a right to be there.

"App-oint-ment," she said, with a degree of triumph. "*Con* Signor de Santi."

"Oh yeah?"

Francesca scrambled for another word. "Letter," she said, and stabbed at the envelope again.

"Okay, okay." He picked up the letter, slit it open with a paper knife, and scanned the contents. "Wait here," he said.

Francesca looked blank.

He pointed to her dictionary. "Wait," he repeated.

An hour and a half later, he nudged her shoulder. "Come on." He led her out into the hallway, and through one of the other doorways on the same floor.

"Take a seat."

"*Prego?*"

There were two chairs and two standard lamps in the otherwise empty room. He pushed Francesca toward one of the chairs. "Sit," he said.

Another fifteen minutes passed before the door opened, and a man and a woman entered. Francesca rose nervously.

"Signor de Santi?"

"No."

The man, dark hair slicked down, wore an open-necked, patterned shirt and sunglasses, though the light in the room was poor; the woman, olive-complexioned, looked cool in a short-sleeved gray dress with a tie belt, her face harshened by severe spectacles.

"Walk," the man said.

"*Scusi?*" Francesca saw that the woman held Lombardi's letter in her hand. Her heart thumped. "*Parla italiano, per favore?*"

"*Un poco,*" the woman said. Relief flooded Francesca.

"Tell her to walk," the man said. The woman translated.

"*Dove?*" Francesca asked.

"Nowhere." The woman made a circle with her hand. "Just walk around."

A half hour later, Francesca was no less bewildered. She had been stared at, had bright lights shone in her eyes, had been ordered to pull up her skirt and show her legs, had her still-short hair rumpled, and had been photographed by the man, his sunglasses pushed up onto his forehead. Any questions she had dared to ask had been ignored and, finally, a pretty blond girl, in a skirt even tighter than Francesca's, had been summoned to take her away.

"I'm Suzy." The blonde pointed at herself.

"*Parla italiano?*" Francesca ventured hopefully.

"Shit, no."

They were back out on the street, in the lunchtime hubbub of Scollay Square.

"Come on, we'll take the bus—my feet are killing me."

The bus jerked, the blond girl chewed gum, and Francesca sat, looking down at her own body—at the dress that was not hers, and at the red handbag and then down to the floor at the shoes. She felt as if her mind was the only part of her real self that remained, as if her head had been glued onto another body—and feeling the unfamiliar stickiness of the lipstick on her mouth, she wondered if even her face was no longer her own.

She felt queasy.

"Nearly there," Suzy said.

Francesca came to life. Quickly, urgently, she took the dictionary from the bag and flicked through the pages. Then, taking a deep breath, she said: "What—is—job?"

"Didn't they tell you?"

Francesca looked helpless.

Suzy smiled. "You're going to be a movie star." She waited for a reaction and, receiving none, repeated—"Movie star."

Francesca went back to the book. After a few moments, she looked up again, and her eyes were full of disbelief. "*Una stella di cinema?*"

"If that's what the book says, that's what you're gonna be." The blonde patted Francesca lightly on the cheek. "C'mon, kid—we're there."

It was a derelict warehouse near Long Wharf. Suzy pushed open a heavy door. Two men, heavyset and sullen, stood just inside, but let them pass. Francesca hung back.

"What's up?"

It was pitch-dark. Francesca bit her lip.

"Come on." Taking her hand, Suzy drew Francesca on into the damp, desolate building. They rounded a corner, and suddenly, some way ahead of them, was a pool of light. They heard voices.

"Quiet." Suzy signaled with her finger on her lips. "You wait here while I go find someone." She pointed forcefully at the stone floor. "Wait *here*."

Francesca waited. It was cold. She thought about running away again; she thought, as she had thought countless times, how mad she had been to leave Italy, alone. She thought about going back—if only she knew how—and she thought about Letizia and Fabio, and how much they must hate her—and she thought about Luciano, and about Niccolo and about—

"*Avanti.*"

It was the Italian-speaking woman with spectacles who had been at the office in Scollay Square. Without another word, she took Francesca's arm and steered her away from the light, toward another section of the warehouse.

"Are they really making a film?" Francesca asked.

"Yes," the woman said. "They're making a film."

In a corner, a man waited for them. He wore a black, turtleneck sweater and black trousers, his hair red, his face pale in the light from a single bulb above.

"Take off your dress," the woman instructed.

"Why?" Francesca's skin prickled.

"Because I tell you to." The order was sharp and cold.

Francesca felt as if she were being sucked down into a great, bottomless hole. Real life had ended. She felt bloodless. Mutely, she unbuttoned her dress, and stood, shivering, in her new underclothes. The unaccustomed brassiere felt uncomfortably tight, yet she was, fleetingly, thankful to Maria Lombardi for making her wear it, now that the pale-faced man was scrutinizing her so intently.

"Sit down."

The man's voice was little more than a whisper. Francesca's terror of the unknown magnified.

"Sit." Quite gently, he pushed her down onto a chair, and draped a thin fabric cape around her shoulders.

"Okay, honey, let's see what we need." The man pulled up a stool and sat facing her.

"What are you doing?" Francesca turned her head to try to see the woman, but she had disappeared. "What are you *doing?*" Fresh panic surged through her.

"Take it easy," the man whispered soothingly. His movements deft and unthreatening, he fastened Francesca's hair away from her forehead with a grip, and switched on a lamp to illuminate her face. "I'm going to make up your face, honey."

Francesca blinked as his fingers touched her cheeks. *"Non capisco,"* she said tremulously.

"I'm sorry—I don't speak Italian." The man picked up a case from the floor and laid it on the table. "Okay," he said, and opened the case, taking out a small sponge. "Let's go to work."

For about fifteen minutes, he dabbed at her face and neck with an array of brushes and sponges, and with his fingers, and gradually the worst of Francesca's fears receded. She felt numb —even more curiously detached from the real world than before. It was as if this man looked upon her as a canvas to be painted, and for all the time his hands were gently stroking her skin, she did not have to think, did not have to worry about what would happen when he had finished.

"You want to see?"

His voice brought her back to earth, and as he held up a hand mirror for her to survey his work, Francesca looked into the glass and saw not herself, but a bizarre child-woman. Brand-new horror engulfed her.

"You don't like it." The man sighed. "Of course you don't."

Kindly, vaguely tenderly, he drew her to her feet, unfastened the cape from around her neck, and took a garment from the clothes rail on which the woman had hung her dress. "They want you to wear this," he said, and put the cold wire hanger into her hand. "And nothing else."

Francesca stared at the high-necked, frilly white nightgown and began to tremble. She looked at the man, and he nodded. She knew that she had no choice.

"You'd better take your shoes off, honey." He pointed to her feet and, understanding, Francesca kicked off the terrible shoes with a relief that was more than just a release from discomfort; all day, she had been a prisoner of those damnable shoes—now, if she wanted to, if she really needed to, she could *run.*

The makeup man brushed her short hair and sprayed it with lacquer. "Okay—we're all ready." Reassuringly, he smiled at her. "You look great, honey." He paused. "You—look—very—good." He gave her a thumbs-up. "Now let's get going."

It was hot in the brightly lit area, even behind the lights where Francesca waited behind a screen.

The makeup man had gone. She was all alone.

She heard moaning.

The soft hair on the back of Francesca's neck stood up. She moved, silently, to the edge of the screen. The floor felt icy cold beneath her bare feet. For a moment, the light dazzled her, but then, she saw a cluster of activity. One man held a large camera, another adjusted a spotlight—a third man, his voice harsh, gave orders.

Francesca looked past the lights—stared at the big, round bed with black satin sheets. Suzy lay on the bed.

The remaining blood drained from Francesca's face.

Suzy was naked, her body white against the sheets. And a man, enormous, dark-haired, sunburned, and glistening with sweat, crouched over her.

Francesca could not breathe.

The man with the camera moved in closer. Francesca wanted to look away, but could not. The couple on the bed were moving rapidly—Suzy's breasts were heaving, she was writhing against the black pillows as the man buried his face between her plump, carelessly spread thighs—

The director called a new command, and obediently Suzy turned over. The man knelt behind her, positioning himself, and then tore savagely into her—

Suzy screamed.

Francesca closed her eyes and struggled for breath. Her heart pounded violently, perspiration ran down her back—

And then a hand touched her arm.

She jerked away, wildly, arms flailing.

"It's okay, it's okay." The young man who'd adjusted the spotlight stood beside her, watching her intently. "They're ready for you," he said softly.

She stared back at the bed. Suzy and the man lay, apart now, resting. The makeup man wiped them down with a towel, and powdered Suzy's face. Francesca's legs shook, and great waves of nausea swept through her.

"Where *is* she, for fuck's sake!" a voice yelled.

"Go on." The young man pushed her out into the fierce, blazing light, and her right hand shot up automatically to shield her eyes.

"Get on the bed, sweetheart!"

She did not move.

"She doesn't speak English," Suzy called.

"Well, someone show her then, for chrissake!"

A hand, flat and hard against her back, propelled her toward the huge, intimidating bed, toward Suzy and the dark-haired man.

He patted the black sheets, and smiled at her. His teeth were strong and white. His eyes, blue and clear, glittered like icicles.

Suzy lifted her right arm, beckoning to her. "C'mon, baby—don't be scared."

And everything went black.

✳

"Jesus H. Christ, what's going on?"

"Camera's dead too."

"Didn't anyone bring a fucking flashlight?"

"I did!" There was a thud, then a muttered curse, and then, about twelve yards away, a narrow beam of light appeared. Instantly, shadowy figures moved toward it.

Francesca, still trembling violently, peered at the bed, and saw that Suzy and the man had vanished.

For another moment, she remained motionless, and then her brain began to function again. This, she knew with certainty, was her last chance to escape. Even if there was nowhere to run to, even the streets —even the risk of arrest had to be better than this nightmare!

Fighting her natural inclination to run, she moved slowly and silently off the set, trying to memorize the way back to where she had left her clothes. Striking her shin against something sharp, she stifled a cry—oh, sweet Lord, where was the clothes rail?

There.

The table, chair, and stool were still there, but there was no sign of the whispering makeup man. Hands shaking, praying that no one would miss her, Francesca tugged the nightgown over her head and pulled her dress off its hanger—

She was fumbling frantically with the buttons, when another light touch, on her left shoulder, made her yelp with fresh terror. She spun around—the young electrician from the set was beside her, holding a finger up to his lips to silence her.

Neither of them spoke, yet she knew, instinctively, that he had come to help her. Motioning with his hands, he indicated to her to pick up her shoes and bag and to follow him. Skirting around the activity still focused on the blacked-out set, they slipped quietly through the darkness, damp and cool and cavernous, until suddenly, the young man pushed at an iron bar, and a door opened.

The sunlight dazzled them both, and for a few seconds, they stood in the afternoon warmth, not moving.

The air was fresh and salty from the ocean, but Francesca still felt sick with fear, sure that at any second they would hear footsteps, that the door would open and she would be savagely hauled back—

Wordlessly, she stared up at her rescuer—slim as a whippet, dark-haired, with soft, narrow, warm eyes and a keen, long nose. He looked nothing like him, yet there was something about him that reminded Francesca of Niccolo.

Hands still trembling, she took out the little dictionary, and sought a word. Two words in English.

"Thank you," she said, and her voice quivered.

He nodded and smiled. His lips, like the rest of him, were narrow, but his smile was gentle and understanding.

"Where will you go?" he asked, and then, realizing that his words meant nothing to her, he took the book from her and tried to translate. *"Dove—?"* he began, and gave up. He tucked the book back into her bag and extended his hand.

"Trust me," he said softly.

They walked, as swiftly as the red shoes allowed, away from the wharf, back across the hurlyburly of town, into the quieter area known as Beacon Hill.

"I live on Revere Street," he said, slowly, and when they came to the steep hill bearing that name, he pointed first to the street sign and then to himself. "My home," he said, and taking her dictionary from her again, he looked it up. *"La mia casa."*

Francesca felt a confusion of emotions rising to choke her. The day had begun frighteningly, and had climbed, erratically, to even greater heights of terror as it had gone on. Now here was another man, another stranger, who had undoubtedly saved her from a fate she could hardly imagine—but suddenly they were at the front door of his house, and how could she know what lay within?

It was a lovely street, cobbled, with gas lamps and charming, neatly built brown-brick houses with shutters.

Strangers are dangerous, Vittorio had warned them—but what choice did she have? There were the unknown streets, there were terrible people, like the unseen Signor de Santi, there were policemen, there was a language she did not speak—

And there was the young man with the narrow, kind face.

He still had the dictionary.

"*Il mio nome*," he said, and pointed to himself again. ". . . Johnny Chase." He had heard her name in the warehouse. "You are Francesca?"

She nodded.

"Johnny," he repeated.

He took a small bunch of keys from the pocket of his jeans, and stuck one in the lock of his black-painted front door.

"Please trust me," he said gently.

Slowly, he pushed open the door and stepped inside, aware of her fear, not wanting her to feel cornered in any way.

Francesca craned her head to look inside. The air from the house felt cool and smelled of wax polish.

It smelled safe.

She went inside.

Less than half an hour after Johnny Chase had let Francesca into his own apartment, two bright, airy rooms with small kitchen and perfectly clean bathroom on the top floor of the house, his wife, Della, arrived home.

That was the precise moment when the nightmare started to recede, and when Francesca's new life in America really began.

Della Chase was a high school teacher. Her speciality was in European languages. She spoke fluent Italian.

The Lombardis could have communicated with Francesca without any difficulty, but they had not an ounce of interest in her. From the first instant Della saw Francesca, sitting bolt upright on a cane chair in her monstrous streetwalker's dress, her beautiful child's face smudged with grotesque makeup, her slightly slanted, glowing brown eyes still fearful beneath their winged brows, she cared.

The first thing she did was to take Francesca into the bedroom, to give her a terry cloth robe to wear, in place of the dress, and a pair of clean white socks in place of the red shoes. The next thing was to lead her into the bathroom and, very carefully, to wipe away every trace of foundation, and rouge, and mascara and lipstick. And the third thing was to go into the kitchen and to heat up a pot of chowder.

"Very good soup," she assured Francesca, who had become suddenly aware, with the aroma emanating from the stove, that she was very hungry. "A specialty of New England, made of fish, milk, onions, and potatoes." She had dispatched Johnny to the local delicatessen to pick up bread, milk, eggs, and anything that caught his fancy.

Francesca stared up at Della from the sofa, where they had insisted she make herself comfortable. The young woman had bright red curly hair with a lightly tanned, freckled face and gray-green eyes. "You are so kind," she said softly as Della set down a tray on a small, low table beside her. "I don't know what to say."

Della smiled. "You don't have to say anything, unless you want to. And even if you do want to, you're not allowed to until you've finished your soup."

Francesca plunged her spoon into the steaming soup and drank some down. *"Deliziosa,"* she breathed, and continued eating ravenously.

"He helped me," she told Della, when the bowl was empty. "Johnny saved me."

"He told me what happened."

"It was a miracle—the lights went out."

Della shook her head. "That was no miracle," she said. "That was Johnny Chase. He blew the fuses."

"By accident?"

"No."

Francesca's eyes widened. "But won't he lose his job?"

Della shrugged. "It was only a little part-time work. He'd never done it before—" She grimaced. "And he won't be doing it again." She glanced at the framed black-and-white photographs that hung on the walls. "Johnny's a photographer." There was no mistaking the pride in her face.

"That is his *job*?" Francesca asked incredulously. "To take pictures?"

"That's right." Della picked up the tray. "Could you manage another bowl of chowder?"

Francesca was still hungry, but she managed to restrain her eagerness. "Do you have enough?"

"More than enough."

There was the sound of a key in the lock, and Johnny returned, a big brown paper bag tucked under his left arm. "How're you doing?"

The glow in Francesca's eyes answered him.

"She was half starved," Della said.

"Has she told you anything yet?"

"There's no hurry, Johnny."

He put milk, butter, and cheese into the refrigerator and slammed the door. "She has no place to go, has she?"

"I don't think so."

Johnny put his arms around her from behind. "So?"

"So what?"

"Can she stay here?"

Della turned around, still in his arms. They both looked around the doorway to see that Francesca, her dark head lolling against one of their soft sofa cushions, had fallen asleep from absolute exhaustion.

"Poor baby," Della murmured. "Poor baby."

"You should have seen her. She was so scared."

"I'm glad I didn't. Those bastards—I'd have given them a piece of my mind."

"I'm sure you would." Johnny ruffled her red curls. "So can she stay? At least for a while."

Della leaned back and looked into his face. "Do you think I'd let her back on the streets?"

Johnny Chase, a textile worker's son from Lowell, Massachusetts, had come to Boston six years earlier, to study at the New England School of Photography, working nights in bars and restaurants to make ends meet. After leaving college, he'd found a job cleaning up after and generally assisting an established portrait specialist, until he'd met Della, who had encouraged him to go it alone. He'd been struggling to make a living ever since, sometimes forced to supplement their joint incomes with jobs like the one at the warehouse today. After his little act of sabotage, however, he would not be going back, and neither, he and Della stressed, did Francesca have to. She could stay with them in Revere Street for as long as she wanted, and no one would trouble her.

"But I can't just take from you," Francesca protested. It was almost impossible to believe her good fortune after so much agony and fear, but after she told them the story of the past three years of her life, Della and Johnny had determined that this should truly be the end of her suffering.

"You can help Johnny in the studio," Della told her. He often took photographs in the apartment or up on the roof of the building, but he rented another room from the tenant on the floor below, which he had divided into part studio, part darkroom.

"Sure she can," Johnny agreed. "Tell her she can do all kinds of stuff for us, in the studio *and* in the apartment—if she doesn't mind."

Della put the proposition to Francesca, who almost wept with pleasure.

"She doesn't mind." Della grinned.

They had already decided that Della would teach the Italian girl English and, as time progressed, as many other essential subjects as possible. They realized, of course, that a twelve-year-old of obvious high intelligence ought, morally and by law, to be receiving a proper education, but Johnny and Della also knew that if the authorities learned about Francesca at this stage, she would most probably be taken into care or deported.

Francesca earned her keep. Fascinated by Johnny's profession, she avidly watched his every move, tidying up after him, keeping the studio and darkroom free of dust, and learning how to clean his cameras and lenses with fine brushes; she cleaned the apartment too, had dinner on the table for them each evening and, once it became clear that no one was searching for her, she began to run small errands for them.

Here, once again against their better judgment, Johnny and Della decided that it would be wise to capitalize on Francesca's mature physical appearance. Beacon Hill was a respectable part of Boston, and a child seen regularly out-of-doors, instead of at school, was bound to arouse comment.

No one would notice a sixteen-year-old.

"Can you make me look sixteen?" Francesca asked Della with some awe.

"I hate doing it," Della said, "but I think I can." She sat Francesca down at her dressing table, and stared at the pots and containers on the surface.

"Are you going to make me up?"

Della picked up a mascara brush. "Just the teensiest bit—nothing more than a nice teenager would use." She paused. "It's more a case of your clothes, Francesca. You're already much more mature than any twelve-year-old I've ever met, because of your experiences." She stood back to take a better look. "And Lord knows you have a beautiful figure."

"Do I have to wear a brassiere again?" Francesca looked dubious.

"Not if it's uncomfortable for you." Della found a pale lipstick. "And don't forget, this is just for when you're outside the apartment. At home with us, you're twelve again—you're the real you."

"The real Francesca Cesaretti." She giggled.

Della nodded. "The one and only." She applied the lipstick, and nodded again, satisfied, then watched thoughtfully as Francesca pulled faces in the mirror. "I know it's early days, sweetheart," she said carefully, "but have you any idea what you want to do about your brother? In the long term?"

Francesca grew instantly somber. "I don't know," she said. "I haven't really thought."

It was true that she did not know, but not that she had not given it thought. She thought about Luciano, and about Vittorio and Niccolo—about everything that had happened—every single day. But it was too painful to contemplate for long, for she knew that, for the moment at least, there was nothing she *could* do.

"One day," she said to Della, her face still grave, "I'm going to go back to Florence to fetch Luciano and bring him to Boston." She shook her head. "But I can't do that for a long time, can I?"

Della's eyes pricked with tears. She was right—Francesca was mature, terribly so, for her age, and it made her want to weep with outrage.

"No, sweetheart," she agreed, picking up a hairbrush to try a new style on Francesca's now swiftly growing hair. "Not for a long time."

"But I will, one day." Francesca's expression was suddenly fierce. "I swear I will."

On Vittorio's grave, she added silently.

Chapter 17

FIVE YEARS PASSED. A new decade beckoned. The lives of the three Cesaretti children, cast adrift, slowly settled and became, increasingly, normal.

In the autumn of 1955, in the bar of the Excelsior Hotel on Piazza Ognissanti, Bruno Cesaretti had seen a pretty, fair-haired woman in her forties spill the contents of her handbag onto the floor. As he moved swiftly to help her, their heads had collided sharply, and for a minute they had swayed, seeing stars and clutching each other for support until they had recovered and straightened, and Bruno had offered her a drink. By the end of the day, they knew that they had fallen in love. By the end of the week, they knew that it was even better—they liked and respected each other too.

They married the following spring. Kate, Bruno's new wife, was a wealthy American divorcée, petite, with short, wavy hair, frank blue eyes, a vivacious personality, and a kind heart. Both she and Bruno were seeking fresh beginnings, both were willing, even eager, to uproot themselves and set up home in a different environment. Kate had, until her marriage, lived in Philadelphia, but had traveled extensively in Europe and had a particular love for the Côte d'Azur.

They honeymooned in Antibes and Monte Carlo and, within six

months of their marriage, Bruno sold his Florence apartment; he had never found the will to go villa-hunting after moving out of the palazzo and had settled for a modern, fashionable seven-room apartment that he did not really care for. Kate had a strong influence over him, not in the dominant style of Livia—Kate simply understood Bruno, and encouraged him to follow his own instincts and desires. Once he had found Kate, Bruno's instincts and desires were to buy a handsome *appartamento* for Fabio and Letizia, now eighteen and sixteen, to sell the store on the Ponte Vecchio and write the other, on the Via della Vigna Nuova, over to his children, and, finally, to move, with Kate and Luciano, to an idyllic, sun-soaked villa near Eze on the French Riviera.

"Fabio and Letizia will never forgive me," he had told Kate, in one of his fits of self-recrimination. "And their mother, if she's able, will curse me from her grave."

"Your children will have everything they want," Kate said frankly, for she had swiftly come to understand Letizia and Fabio as well as Bruno. "And if they ever learn to love their father more than money, there's room enough in the villa." She kissed him. "As for their mother," she went on dryly, "if Livia wants to haunt our home, she'll have me to reckon with."

There were no doubts so far as Luciano's feelings were concerned. He had never happily resettled into Florentine life without Francesca, though, as the months had passed without word from her, he had gradually stopped waiting for her to come, and had returned to the secure urban routine he'd often hankered after in times of danger, but which now seemed dull and plodding compared with Gypsy life and the glories of Palmarola.

Uncle Bruno, however, had proved himself a true and caring friend and ally. Each morning in Florence, he took Luciano to school; each afternoon, abandoning his business, he collected him. Aware of the boy's aptitude for language and reading, he encouraged him as much as possible, and knowing that some of Luciano's happiest memories were of carefree days outside the city and on the tiny Pontine island, Bruno took him regularly to the seaside at Viareggio, and into the countryside for picnics.

Luciano adored France from the first, and Le Rocher, their villa, from the instant he set eyes on its perfectly proportioned creamy exterior. His one fear had been that Francesca would be unable to find him if they moved, but Uncle Bruno had assured him that instructions had been left with the apartment's new occupants. Le Rocher was everything Palazzo Speroza had never been. It was unabashedly pretty, yet still elegant; it was bright and airy, cool in summer and snug in winter; it had a charming swimming pool, set above the rocks that gave the house its name; it had a sweeping terrace and balconies at every bedroom, and a garden planted with mimosa, jasmine, rosebushes, and bougainvillaea—and, above all, it was a comfortable, easygoing home for a boy to play in and dream in.

As the years went by, Luciano became more conscious of his strangely mixed fortunes. Five ordinary, happy years—then four of tragedy, misery, and finally, resignation—and the last four of quite remarkable harmony and pleasure. Aunt Kate was a warm, relaxed, undemanding person, and Uncle Bruno treated him like a son. His grief over Vittorio and Francesca had faded into a misty filter through which he now regarded much of his past, including the extraordinary months with Niccolo Dante and the Gypsies. He wondered, sometimes, as he lay daydreaming in the warm sunshine, an *orange pressé* and an open book beside him, pages rustling in the breeze, if all those things had really happened or if, perhaps, they belonged in part to the constant stream of fantasy that drifted through his mind.

He could hardly remember, sometimes, what Giulietta had looked like, and yet she still came to him frequently in his dreams, and then it would seem to him as if he had crawled into her head—he was aware of feeling *her* emotions, as he had that night in the abbey, just as if they were his own. The dreams made Giulietta seem real again, and strangely alive—and even the knowledge that she had lain in her grave for years did not alter that remarkable sense of reality.

All dead, except Francesca. Francesca, who had always looked after him, always protected him and understood him. He knew that she was not gone forever—he prayed every night for her to come back; intense, earnest pleas—and yet, in spite of everything, he was happy. It startled him, often, to think how happy he was.

Scholastically, he was not fulfilling his early promise. Perhaps, Bruno suggested, to excuse him, it was due to the many disruptions in his schooling, but Kate, always realistic, knew it was largely because of his lack of concentration.

"Languages and fiction are all that interest him," she told Bruno. "When a subject bores him, he tunes out of maths or chemistry or whatever, and tunes into one of his stories or daydreams."

"Does it matter?" Bruno asked his wife. "Should I be tougher with him?"

"A little stricter, perhaps, sometimes," Kate said, but then she smiled. "I read one of his essays yesterday, and for a thirteen-year-old, it was quite wonderful."

"You think he may become a writer?"

Kate rubbed Ambre Solaire into her husband's back. "I hope so. It's what he was born for."

Luciano was never happier than when he was sitting on his bedroom balcony, scribbling short stories. He wrote on all manner of topics, about all kinds of people and, sometimes, animals—but quite regularly, he wrote odd, highly imaginative, bittersweet tales about enigmatic, anonymous children, in nebulous, faraway places. Kate, intrigued, would ask him periodically about the origin or explanation of these stories, but Luciano would be unable to answer.

"Surely," Kate pressed him, "you must have some notion where they spring from?"

And Luciano would smile, and shake his head. "I don't know, Aunt Kate," he would say. "They just come."

In 1959, in England, thirteen-year-old Juliet Austen was also showing clear signs that she might have a future in writing, though her talents lay more in fact than in fiction, and her work was far more tightly structured and articulate than that of the twin brother she had long ago obliterated from her memory.

Not much remained of Giulietta Volpi. Spiritually reborn, she had ceased almost entirely to think about her life prior to adoption, reminded only by the faintest of limps when she felt tired, and the ugly scarring that marred her shoulders and left breast. These she had grown accustomed to, chiefly by training herself to ignore them. She kept herself covered at all times, even with Elizabeth—even when she was alone. When she bathed, she kept her eyes averted from her body; when she dressed, she never looked in a mirror until she was finished; when she had to change into or out of gym clothes at school, she took her things into the lavatory. Though swimming had been a valuable part of her physiotherapy, she refused, point-blank, to be seen by her fellow pupils in a swimsuit.

Elizabeth's worries about her daughter's early days at school had been justified, for Juliet's first term at the local school in Dorking had been very difficult. The other girls had frightened her, and Juliet had defended herself with an air of superiority, when in truth, she felt miserably inferior and, worst of all, *different*, that most heinous of all sins among children. Many things conspired to make her feel different, but early on, Juliet logged her six top deficiencies:

Being adopted. No father. Mother hardly ever able to collect me after school, she wrote in a secret journal. *My accent*, she continued. *Limp. And scars*.

Juliet had concentrated harder than ever, after that, on eliminating the only two problems over which she had any control. Every morning and evening, she had completed the full program of exercises prescribed by her physiotherapist, determined that she would, ultimately, walk as naturally as any other girl.

And then there was her accent—her *foreignness*. She was already having private elocution lessons at Kaikoura, but now she began to read aloud to herself at night—everything she could lay her hands on, from comics to Enid Blyton and the Chalet School books, to her copies of the Bible and English dictionary.

In 1957, Juliet had passed an entrance examination to Queen's College School in London, the school Elizabeth most wanted her to attend, partly because she, too, had been educated there, and partly because of its location in Harley Street, just around the corner from the flat and her consulting rooms in Wimpole Street.

Queen's College had been the first college for the higher education of women in Britain, and had a fine reputation. Many of the pupils bemoaned the fact that the headmistress, Miss Kynaston, was a stickler for discipline, and the sportier girls envied other, less urban, schools their tennis courts and more lavish facilities.

Such things did not matter to Juliet, who was thrilled to be so close to Elizabeth, and who felt she was at school only to learn and to succeed, for her mother's sake. By the end of her second year, she walked almost totally evenly and had eradicated her accent; with her blond hair and blue eyes, she defied anyone to query her Englishness, though Queen's was well known for its ready welcome to girls of all nationalities. Having learned how to be the "same" as everyone else, Juliet now realized that her new ambition was to be *better* than the others.

The need to earn Elizabeth's pride ruled Juliet's life. The most grievous sin she could commit, in her own eyes, was to disappoint her mother in any way, and so it became of paramount importance for Juliet to do well at her studies, and to be a popular member of her class.

She was too serious to be popular, and as other girls split off into small coteries and formed close friendships, Juliet remained aloof and alone. No one understood that her introversion stemmed from vulnerability and a deep distrust of people that even she did not fully comprehend. With her mother, Juliet was soft, gentle, and confident. Out in the world, despite her unquestionable good looks and intelligence, she was still, secretly, afraid. She did not want Elizabeth to know that she had no friends, so she told lies.

"My friends," she said, when Elizabeth suggested inviting classmates back to the flat for tea, "live too far away. They have to go straight home."

"It's not done," she invented, when Elizabeth asked her if she'd like

to have a birthday party, "to have parties anymore. Parties are for babies."

From time to time, she even went home to change out of uniform,
and went out again, telling her mother that she'd been invited to tea.
Elizabeth, on call to her patients, would put Juliet into a taxi, and then
Juliet would ask to be set down at Regent's Park, where she would walk
for two hours, before going back to Wimpole Street, reporting that she'd
had a good time, but not much of a tea.

So far as schoolwork was concerned, Juliet, like most people, had
weak spots. She excelled at English and enjoyed all language studies, but
she disliked science, was afraid of the chemistry laboratory with its Bun-
sen burners and pungent smells, and she had no natural gift for mathe-
matics. When, at the close of the summer term of 1958, her school
report had reflected poor results in those subjects, Juliet thought she read
sadness in Elizabeth's eyes, and her face had burned with shame.

She began to cheat. The important thing, she realized, was not to
get caught out at it; another girl in her class had given herself away
because she had successfully copied her neighbor's work all through
term, and had then abysmally failed the end-of-year examinations. That
would not happen to Juliet—she would rather die than have Elizabeth
find out the truth. And Juliet wasn't cheating in order to shirk work—
she *wanted* to study hard, to improve. If she copied another student's
work, she strove to analyze what the other girl had done to arrive at that
solution.

She came close to disaster just once, when the equations she'd
cribbed from her neighbor during algebra proved to be wrong.

Summoned after class, both girls were challenged by the teacher.
"One of you has clearly copied the other."

Hot denial sprang from the other girl—Juliet remained calm and
controlled.

"I will swear an oath," she said, in a low, intense voice, "on the
Bible." She fixed her eyes firmly on the teacher's face. "I have done
nothing wrong."

Nothing could be proved. The next term, Juliet changed her place in the classroom, and began copying from a girl who *never* made mistakes.

If anyone had accused Juliet of being a liar and a cheat, she could not have denied it. But her passionate love for her mother, and her unquenchable hunger for Elizabeth's approval, seemed to Juliet to justify any measures, however drastic. No matter what it took, Juliet was determined to make her mark. She would work, she would struggle, and if necessary she would cheat and she would lie—*anything* to make Elizabeth the proudest mother in the whole of Britain.

✳   ✳   ✳

Francesca, at seventeen, had two ambitions: to become a fine and successful photographer and, above everything, to make enough money to put her into the position, legally as well as financially, to bring Luciano to America.

From her earliest days in the Chases' apartment, she had written her brother letters, carefully omitting any detail that might betray her whereabouts, and waiting until Johnny met someone traveling to another part of the United States, so that they could post the latest letter from as far away as possible. Her self-imposed restrictions made her notes frustratingly uninformative, but all that mattered was letting Luciano know that she still loved him and thought about him every single day—and that the time *would* come when she would be free to go back to Italy to fetch him —and that Vittorio had been right, that America *was* a wonderful country, and that she longed to share it with him.

Johnny and Della had given her what she had thought she might never know—stability. Johnny had taught her, willingly and generously, all he could about the craft of photography, while Della had done everything possible to gentle her into young womanhood.

It had not been easy. Francesca had, publicly, been living as a sixteen-year-old for a whole year before she had even begun her periods. She had been fending off men's advances for four years before experiencing the first sexual stirrings in her own body. She had never had the opportunity to participate in the normal social activities of teenage girls, and it was Della Chase who, on Francesca's real sixteenth birthday, had struggled to bring her into line with her true age.

"I know it's hard to believe it's such a big deal, when you've been that age for four years already," Della had told her, "but you'll just have to take my word for it. Sixteen *is* a big deal—sixteen is where a lot of kid's stuff ends and a lot of grown-up stuff starts."

It had been on that auspicious occasion that Johnny had taken a series of photographs of Francesca, and the resulting pictures, taken with love and care and an understanding of her rare natural beauty, had been praised as a stunning image of innocent sensuality when, early in 1959, Johnny had exhibited some of his work at a Back Bay gallery.

Afterward, he had received numerous inquiries regarding Francesca's identity from other photographers and from one or two model agencies, but the memories of her first days in Boston were too vividly etched on Francesca's mind for her to consider ever sitting for anyone but Johnny.

"I'm staying on *this* side of the camera," she declared, squinting into the viewfinder of the Leica that Johnny had lent her for her own use.

"Why?" Johnny asked. "There are a hundred other things you could do, and most of them will bring in more money, unless you're terrific *and* lucky."

"It's not just because of Johnny, is it?" Della, always wary of being too strong an influence, wanted to know.

"No, I don't think so." Francesca polished a wide-angle lens thoughtfully. "Of course, I might never have known it was what I wanted if it hadn't been for Johnny—and it's because he's so good and so exciting that I know how hard I'll have to work, but—"

"But?"

"But I believe that photographs are important—vital even." Her dark eyes were sparkling. "To capture people, their thoughts, their actions and moods—or a tree or a garden, or a wonderful landscape—or an event, or a tragedy or something joyful—and perhaps to be able to do it truthfully and *well*—" She looked at them both. "I think that must be a wonderful thing to do."

"Yes." Della's expression was tender. "It is."

Francesca had not finished. "I have no photographs of my mother or father, or of my sister or my baby brother." She paused. "Or of Niccolo."

"But you carry them inside you," Johnny said gently.

"In a way, yes, or at least their"—Francesca struggled for the right word—"*essenza.*"

"Their essence." Della nodded.

"But it would be different if I could look at them, as I can with Vittorio and Luciano, simply because Uncle Bruno took pictures of us at Christmas one year." She realized she had been squeezing the lens, and carefully put it down.

"It is important."

She had become, by that time, a valued assistant to Johnny, particularly in the commercial side of his work, which consisted mainly of photographing actors for casting directories. And now that she could be trusted with some of his precious equipment, she planned to get out around the city and into the countryside. Boston, she had learned over the years, was a vibrant, exciting city, and Cambridge, the home of Harvard University, just across the Charles River, was the most vital place she had ever experienced, filled with youth and wisdom and knowledge.

But though she knew that she might learn most about her new craft by moving among people, it was the New England countryside that attracted her most of all. October was just weeks away, when the fall would sweep down and across New York State into Massachusetts, and maple, ash, elm, willow, beech, cherry, and oak trees would strike up their overwhelming, glorious orchestra of colors; and Francesca would stand openmouthed, her eyes full of tears, thanking God that she was here, safe in America, and wishing, more than anything, that Vittorio and her other loved ones could be there beside her to share its brilliance.

✳

It was September of 1959.

In three different countries, the three surviving children of Giulio and Serafina Cesaretti were living separate, totally disparate lives, growing up and away from their roots—and from each other.

Part Two

∗

SEPARATION

∗

1967–1974

Chapter 18

ON A COOL AFTERNOON in May of 1967, in the reading room of the library at the University of Sussex, Juliet Austen, less than one month away from her twenty-first birthday, fell in love for the first time.

She had, for the last hour and a half, been reading *Women in Love*, and had been so utterly absorbed by it that it was not until she had finished Lawrence's description of Rupert and Gerald wrestling nude on the carpet at Shortlands that she had lifted her eyes from the pages, hardly conscious that her heart beat more rapidly than usual or that her cheeks were flushed—and had seen him through a mist of repressed erotic desire.

Perhaps he had been there all the time, coiled into his chair, his dark, shiny hair falling over his forehead, his long lashes casting shadows onto his cheeks, his mouth twisted slightly in concentration, but Juliet was certain that she had never set eyes on him before.

I would never have forgotten him, she thought, and stared back down at her own book in startled confusion, troubled by the intensity of her feelings and anxious in case he saw her looking at him.

With fumbling fingers, she gathered up her belongings and stood up, trying to find an exit route that did not mean brushing past him, but there was no other way. *Please don't look up,* she thought desperately, beginning the interminable walk to the door.

She glanced down, hastily, as she passed. The book at the top of the stack on his table was titled *Mind, Self, and Society*—the book he was reading was *From Russia with Love.* In spite of herself, Juliet smiled.

He looked up, stretched like a cat—and winked at her.

Juliet ran.

✶

Despite sharing a house in Woodingdean with four other girls, Juliet was still very much a loner. After taking her A levels at Queen's College, she had hoped to continue her studies in London in order to stay on at the Wimpole Street flat, but Elizabeth had pushed her gently, but firmly, toward Sussex.

"You need to spend more time with young people, darling," she had said. "Sussex will be important and good for you—and we'll never be very far apart, whether I'm at Kaikoura or in town."

Juliet had not wanted to go, but it had been what Elizabeth wanted for her, and Juliet still placed her mother's pride in her as paramount, and so she had agreed.

She had known it would be painful for her. She had not realized quite *how* painful.

The parties were worst of all, the unending, relentless high jinks enjoyed by her peers. Juliet had, by the end of her first year, managed to convince Felicity, Cathy, Rachel, and Marina, the girls with whom she lived, that she was truly uninterested in men, that she genuinely liked studying in her spare time—and that she really, wholeheartedly, detested parties.

Today, however, was Cathy's twenty-first birthday, and the house was being prepared for an onslaught of students, and friends from Cathy's hometown. This was one party even Juliet could not wriggle out of, and she was dreading it.

"Why haven't you changed?" Felicity, with flowers in her red hair and wearing a floaty midi dress, demanded.

"I have." Juliet continued cutting cheddar into cubes.

"A black polo-neck sweater?" Felicity was incredulous.

"Why not?"

"It's a party, not a wake. Apart from anything else, you'll boil."

"No, I won't." Juliet had been relieved when the weather had cooled at the start of the week. She still wore her blond hair long and straight, with bangs, and always wore rollnecks or high-collared blouses so that no one would see her scarred shoulders.

"Why not swap the jeans for a mini—you've got such great legs."

"I'm happy as I am, Fliss."

"But you look so *wintry.*" Felicity shook her head. "At least borrow my leather skirt—that way you'll look sexy."

"This is fine, Fliss."

"Rot."

Felicity had her way. Within fifteen minutes, Juliet's legs were encased in sheer tights, her pullover was brightened with fake gold chains rifled from Marina's dressing table, and she wore hoop earrings and pale pink lipstick.

"You need false lashes."

Juliet shook her head.

"Come on, they'll look fabulous."

Juliet fixed Felicity with her clear blue eyes. "Fliss, please pay attention. No false eyelashes."

"I've got these really short ones—"

"*No.*"

The party had been under way for two hours before she saw him coming through the front door, bearing a bottle of wine and a gift-wrapped package. Her heart began to race.

She was sitting halfway up the staircase, clutching a glass of punch, and her first thought was to run. But there was nowhere to run to, nowhere to be alone.

He saw her almost immediately, and smiled. "Hello."

Juliet nodded, unable to speak.

"Where's Cathy? I want to give her this."

Juliet tried not to stare. His voice was liltingly Irish, and he was even better looking than she'd first thought, with dark blue eyes that crinkled at the corners.

"I'll take it if you like." Her voice sounded breathless. "Put it with the others."

"Great." He handed her the package. "Thanks."

Juliet stood up. Her long legs felt naked beneath Felicity's mini. "Is it tagged? Will she know who it's from?"

"Sorry, no—I didn't think."

"Shall I mark it?"

"Please." He looked around.

Juliet felt self-conscious. "What shall I write?"

He glanced back up at her. "Sorry?"

"What name?"

"Ray." He grinned. "Ray Donnelly."

"Right." She started up the stairs, her cheeks burning.

"And yours?"

She stopped and looked around. He was staring up at her.

"*Your* name."

"Juliet."

Again, he smiled. "Perfect."

And again, Juliet ran.

By the time she had summoned up the courage to come back downstairs, Ray Donnelly had vanished. When she next saw him, he was talking to another girl. Or rather, he was holding her hand and gazing into her eyes. She was short and dark, with curly hair and round dimpled cheeks. The antithesis of herself. Juliet yearned to become invisible.

"Having fun?" Rachel danced past, glamorous in a white knitted tube dress with a chain-link belt.

"Fantastic." Juliet managed to sound lighthearted.

She would have liked to get drunk, but she didn't enjoy the effect of alcohol. She disliked anything that made her lose control. Maybe it was another relic of her years in the hospital, but Juliet needed to be in perfect command of herself all the time; it was a vital part of her plan to succeed.

Out of the corner of her eye, she saw Ray Donnelly and his girlfriend strolling out into the tiny overgrown garden. In spite of herself, she imagined them embracing, kissing, sinking down onto the long grass—

Quickly, she climbed back up the staircase, stepping over couples welded together in various positions. The air on the landing was smoky and pungent with the scent of marijuana and tobacco. Juliet opened her bedroom door, seeking refuge, and stopped dead in her tracks. A naked couple, oblivious of her, lay on her bed, wholly occupied in joyful, thrashing intercourse.

Her immediate anger died on her lips, and defeated, she shut the door again. Unspeakable misery swamped her. She glanced at her watch and saw that it was only just after eleven—the end was nowhere in sight.

And then she heard the man's voice, coming from the bedroom opposite. Rachel's room.

"Laura, what the hell are you doing?"

"Let's spend the night together!" pounded the Rolling Stones from below.

"For Christ's *sake,* Laura!"

The back of Juliet's neck prickled. The voice was not just urgent or angry—it was terrified. For a moment, she hesitated, and then she knocked on the door. No one answered. She heard a scuffling sound, and then a stifled gasp—

As she opened the door, the girl was already poised on the windowsill. She was naked, except for a red ribbon around her neck, and her eyes were glazed. She was more than stoned—she was out of her mind.

"Oh, God." The young man, also nude, stood three feet away, his expression panic-stricken. His voice had died to a whisper, and he no longer dared to move, for the window was fully open.

Juliet's heart began to pound. She stared at the girl.

"Please," she said softly. "Get down."

The girl's eyes changed, as if whatever vision she saw had become suddenly beautiful, and her mouth curved into an almost beatific smile.

"Yes," she said, but did not move.

"Laura!" New fear resharpened the boy's voice.

Slowly, very slowly, she began to turn, her impeccably manicured toes gripping the painted sill, until she was facing the black night outside, her buttocks gleaming in the candlelight.

"Oh, *yes*," she breathed, suddenly ecstatic.

Juliet looked, in desperation, at the young man, still as motionless as a statue.

"For God's sake," she hissed frantically. "Grab her!"

She saw the expression on his face change from panic to horror, to disbelief and, finally, to anguish. She saw the girl bend her knees, like an athlete, saw her body launch itself away from the sill, into the void, unfolding into a perfect dive, legs straightening, feet pointing—

"God only knows," chorused the Beach Boys.

And for just an instant, Juliet felt that she, too, was plunging down into oblivion.

Juliet could not understand her composure during the hours that followed. She knew that she must be in shock, yet it was she who called the ambulance, who attempted to console the agonized young man, who spoke clearly and concisely to the police when they arrived.

She went with them to Brighton General Hospital, where Laura was pronounced dead on arrival, and she remained there for the grim procedures. She knew that she was free to leave, yet she stayed, observing the police officers, gentle still, in spite of the near-certain knowledge that LSD had caused the incident, watching and listening as the dead girl's distraught, bewildered parents arrived.

It was only much later, after she had returned to the now-quiet house in Woodingdean, to her bedroom, emptied of coats and lovers, though not of the clinging, sickening smell of marijuana, that Juliet suddenly understood what had been pricking at her mind for hours, what had made her remain at the hospital with what had seemed almost ghoulish fascination. It was, she realized abruptly, the very thing that separated journalists from other writers—what had divided her, tonight, from those around her.

All her fatigue and depression disappeared, wiped away by this flash of absolute clarity. She had stayed because she had sensed, somehow, that there was a job for her to do. She was going to write an account of the tragedy, she was going to report the events, not simply with factual clarity, but in such a way that a reader would comprehend the folly, the wickedness, and the utter waste of the girl's death.

She wrote until dawn, sitting at the open window, oblivious of the night chill, and then she slept for two hours before picking up her pen again. She missed her first two lectures that day—she who *never* skipped the most tedious of seminars or talks—and when she was finished, she read the piece over with as much critical acuteness as she could muster.

It's good, she thought, *but is it good enough?*

She read it again. The facts had been presented clearly, with an effective and moving blend of compassion and condemnation. *I* think *it's fine.*

She read it one more time.

Although the dead girl had not been a student, Juliet's article was accepted for publication by the *Wine Press,* one of the two university newspapers. No undergraduate at Sussex had ever run up against the law in the matter of drugs, and the vast majority of students were opposed to anything stronger than cannabis. When the *Brighton Evening Argus* reprinted her piece, Juliet was ecstatic. Her ambition, till now, had stretched no further than a first-class degree, but suddenly all the fuzziness about her future dispersed.

At Kaikoura, Elizabeth pasted her daughter's debut article onto the first page of a leather-bound album, and picked up the telephone.

"Isn't it wonderful?" Juliet's voice was vibrant.

"It's the most beautiful thing I've ever seen." Elizabeth smiled.

"I know." Juliet paused. "What do you really think of it? Is it good?"

Elizabeth did not hesitate. "It's clear, it's forceful, it's forthright, and it isn't sensational." She scanned the page for the hundredth time. "I'd have hated it if you'd written anything to magnify that poor family's pain."

"That was the one aspect that troubled me," Juliet said anxiously. "There was such an icy streak in me that night—I felt that I was watching the end of someone's world, and absorbing it for my own use. Doesn't that make me callous?"

"Not if you're aware of it. Not if you remain decent."

Juliet relaxed, allowing the warmth to wash over her again. "I'm going to do it, Mother. I really *am* going to be a journalist." She paused. "Are you proud of me?"

"Always."

"I mean especially proud."

Elizabeth was touched by the need in her daughter's voice. "I didn't think it was possible to feel prouder of you than I always have, my darling. But I am."

When Juliet put down the receiver, she was glowing, and filled with ideas for the future.

She had forgotten all about Ray Donnelly.

One month after the party, Juliet was sitting, alone, in the Mocca Coffee House in Hove, when she saw him come through the door.

Looking for a seat, he spotted her immediately, and smiled. Juliet, toying with her cappuccino, felt herself blush.

"Great—a friendly face." He sat down opposite her. "Do you mind?"

"Of course not." She spoke tightly.

He settled down comfortably, and ordered coffee. "You do remember me, don't you?"

"Ray Donnelly," she said. "Reading sociology and James Bond." She blushed again.

"You got the order wrong." Fishing around in the case he'd brought in with him, he plucked out a paperback and showed it to her.

"*Goldfinger.*" She smiled.

"Speaking of which, would you come with me to the cinema?"

"When?" she asked, startled.

"Now. I'm on my way to see the René Clair film."

"*Les Belles de Nuit.*"

"That's the one." He bent toward her. "Will you come?"

Her heart pounded. "As a matter of fact, I was going anyway."

"Grand." He drank down his coffee, and stood up. "Come on then."

Juliet stared up at him. "Do you remember my name?" she asked, abruptly.

"Everyone knows your name." His dark blue eyes twinkled.

"What do you mean?"

"Your byline," he said. "Juliet Austen—" He sketched an imaginary line in the air. "Looks good."

She laughed, with pleasure, and stood up too.

"You don't often do that, do you?"

"What?" She followed him out into Bedford Place.

"Laugh."

"How would you know?" Juliet was taken aback. "You've only ever seen me twice."

"Not so," Ray corrected. "I've seen you dozens of times on campus."

It was true. He'd noticed her on numerous occasions, had noted, with admiration, her long, swinging hair, her lovely oval face and shapely legs. He had also noted her closed, grave expression, and the fact that she was, almost always, alone. Which was what had kept him at a distance until today, for Ray was too gregarious and popular to bother wasting time and energy on the very difficult.

Suddenly, however, at closer quarters with the awkward beauty, he thought it might just be worth the trouble. Or, at the very least, the price of two cinema seats.

Juliet had believed that romance would never happen to her, that it only happened to girls like Rachel or Fliss or Cathy—not to her.

How wrong she had been—how *gloriously* mistaken!

Ray was everything she could have dreamed of in a man, if she had permitted herself to dream. He was handsome—no, not just handsome, he was *beautiful*— he was intelligent, he was good-natured, popular, and generous—and he cared about her.

He had taken her out four times so far, twice to the cinema and twice to supper, and he'd insisted on paying on every occasion, even though his digs were on the gloomy lower ground floor of a paint-peeling Kemp Town house, and his finances were always stretched to the limit.

Heavens, she was happy—or at least, she *would* have been deliriously happy if the end of term had not been so close. In less than a fortnight, Ray would go home to County Wicklow, and Juliet would return to Kaikoura. It was almost impossible for her to believe that anything, or anyone, could make her feel reluctant to go back to her beloved home.

On the evening of their fifth date, Ray arrived at the Woodingdean house with a large, flat cardboard box under his arm.

"What's that?" Juliet asked.

"Later." Ray kept a hold on the box.

At the restaurant, over a bottle of wine, he invited her to accompany him to the summer ball.

"Me?" Juliet was pink with excitement. "Really?"

"Why not you?" Ray shook his head. "Why are you always so surprised that I want to be with you?"

"I'm not—it's just—"

"What?"

"Nothing."

"So you'll come?"

"I'd love to."

Ray remembered the box, on the floor beside his chair. "You'd better have this now." He placed it on the table.

Juliet gazed at it.

"Go on—it won't bite," he urged.

With nervous fingers, she eased off the lid and found a smooth layer of tissue paper. "What is it?"

"Only one way to find out."

She lifted the paper, and gave a small gasp. The most glorious fabric rested beneath her fingers—silky and very fine, like gossamer, printed with clouds of blues and mauves and rosy pinks—

"It's a dress for the ball," Ray said. "It's midi-length, with a halter neck, and you'll look a dream in it."

Juliet put the lid back on the box. She felt sick. "Can we go, please?"

"What's the matter?"

"I have to go. I don't feel well—" She stood up jerkily.

"Hold on while I pay." He looked around for their waitress, and then back up at Juliet. She was white. "You look awful."

"I'm sorry." Her legs were trembling. "I'll wait for you outside."

By the time he joined her on the pavement, she'd managed to compose herself.

Ray took her arm. "What happened?"

Juliet faced him. "I can't go to the ball, Ray."

"But you just said—"

"I'm sorry." She fought against overwhelming misery. "The dress is wonderful—I'm sure they'll take it back." She averted her eyes again. "You can say it didn't fit me."

"But we won't know that till you try it on." Ray was abruptly aware that the dress held the key to whatever ailed this lovely, strange girl.

"There's no point."

"Oh, yes, there is." He grasped her wrist firmly. "Come on."

"Where to?"

"My place. To try on the bloody dress."

"It's not bloody, it's beautiful," she protested.

"The beautiful, bloody dress then."

In the damp-scented privacy of his flat, he sat her down on the cracked leather sofa and opened a bottle of red wine.

"I don't want any more," Juliet said.

"You've hardly had any." He handed her a glass, and sat down beside her, not too close, sensing that he would get nowhere with her if she felt crowded. "It was the dress that upset you, wasn't it?"

Juliet said nothing.

"Don't you trust me?"

"Of *course* I trust you," she protested.

He moved a little closer. "Then tell me what's wrong." He hesitated. "Why are you so hung up about your body?"

Juliet flinched, startled. "What do you mean?"

"Your clothes," he answered simply. "You're always covered up, even when it's hot."

"I feel the cold," she said defensively.

"I see." For a few moments, he remained silent, and then, slowly and very gently, he put out his right hand and touched her cheek. "I'm your friend, Juliet—let me help."

She looked at him, saw his marvelous face, and his kind, concerned eyes, and knew, suddenly, that she would tell him—that there was no future for them if she did not.

"All right," she said.

"You poor kid," he said.

"Not anymore." She felt so much lighter, so incredibly relieved. He'd understand, now that he knew, why she couldn't wear his dress, or anything else that exposed her ugliness.

"How bad is it?" Ray asked quietly.

"What?"

"The scarring."

"Pretty bad." She shrugged. "Hideous."

For another moment, Ray sat still, and then he stood up and walked over to where the cardboard box had been abandoned. "A suggestion," he said. "Why don't you go into the bathroom, and try the dress on—"

"No!" Juliet looked shocked. "I've just explained—surely you see now that I can't."

"The bathroom has the best mirror," he went on, as if she hadn't spoken. "Take all the time you need—and if you decide you don't want me to see you in it, then I'll respect that." He picked up the box and handed it to her. "Do it for me, Juliet." He saw the indecision in her eyes. "And if you can't do it for me, do it for yourself."

✳

It was almost thirty minutes before the door opened, just a crack.

Ray jumped up from the sofa. "Well?" He waited. "How does it look?"

"The dress is lovely, Ray." Her voice was soft and breathy.

"Does it fit?"

"As if they'd made it for me."

"Am I allowed to see?"

She didn't answer.

"I'd love to see you in it, sweetheart."

"I thought—"

"Yes?"

"I thought, perhaps if I bought a shawl, it might not look too bad." She sounded timid and hopeful. "What do you think?"

"It sounds a grand idea." He paused. "But I can't really tell without looking, can I?"

There was another pause. "Okay."

The door opened, and Juliet emerged, shyly, her shoulders encased in a faded blue Turkish towel.

Ray smiled. "The shawl substitute."

She nodded.

"Let me see." Gently, he approached her and put one hand on her right arm. "You know you're magnifying the problem a hundred times over by acting this way."

"Perhaps." Biting her lip, Juliet allowed him to draw away the towel and drop it to the floor. "Well?" Her voice was taut.

He stepped back and looked at her appraisingly.

"*Well?*" Juliet wanted to run back into the bathroom.

"It suits you." He paused, staring hard at her. "You look very romantic." He smiled again. "And very beautiful."

"But what about the *scars?*"

Ray shook his head. "They're just scars." He came closer again. "Juliet, darlin', will you believe what I tell you, if I swear it's God's truth?"

"I suppose so."

He reached out and touched her left shoulder. "This side's much worse than the right, obviously." He removed his fingers. "Do they hurt?"

"No."

"They're just scars," he said again. "They tell me that you were once very badly burned—and that you're damned lucky to be alive. But that's all." He backed away again. "I'm trying to look at you with a critical eye, Juliet, which is bloody hard for me, since I think you're one of the prettiest girls I've ever known."

"Do you?"

"You know I do." He shrugged. "Those scars spoil your shoulders, of course they do. But they're such a small, negligible part of you that they make no real difference." He continued to stare. "If they were on your face, then I'd feel sorry for you—and even then I hope I'd be able to see through them, but I can't be sure." He paused. "I'm being honest, darlin'."

Juliet's knees were trembling, her whole body quivering, and tears filled her eyes. "Thank you." She could hardly speak.

"For telling you the truth? I just wish I'd met you years ago, so that I could have talked some sense into you before."

"I don't know *how* to thank you," she whispered.

Ray smiled. "Two ways. First, you'll come to the ball—" He raised a hand to silence her. "We'll find the perfect shawl, if you feel you need it —whatever you want." He took her hand. "Will you come?"

She looked down at herself, at the dress—and then back up at him. "Yes," she said.

"Thank Christ for that!" He led her back to the sofa. "Now for the second way you can thank me." He sat her down. "You can let me kiss you."

Juliet gazed into his eyes. At that moment, cloudy with love and gratitude and wine, she felt that she would trust Ray Donnelly with her life. And there was nothing she wanted more than for him to kiss her, so she closed her eyes and moved her face close to his. And the *kiss*! The kiss was more wonderful than anything she had ever imagined—and when she felt the strong, sweet moistness of his tongue, and the firmness of his lips, she felt her limbs liquefying, and knew that if he didn't stop soon, there was nothing on earth that would make her call a halt . . .

He did stop, but still she felt bewitched by the kiss and his care and by the floating fabric of the magical dress—and when he turned on his record player and Frank Sinatra crooned "In the still of the night," she moved, joyously, into Ray's open arms, and there, in the dimly lit shabbiness of the Kemp Town flat, Juliet had the first totally romantic dance of her life.

When he collected her on the evening of the ball, Juliet was nervous but glowing, aware, in spite of her fears, that she had never looked lovelier, and also conscious that there would be envious eyes on her that night, simply because she was with Ray. Within an hour, the shawl that she had bought in a new boutique in The Lanes lay draped, discarded and forgotten, over her chair, and Juliet was dancing with increasing joy and release, enjoying the rhythm and beat of the faster music, but loving infinitely more the ballads, when Ray wrapped her snugly against his chest, and she found herself unwittingly weaving fantasies about the future—*their* future—in which all her ambitions seemed almost to have dissolved, and the only things that mattered were bringing Ray to meet Elizabeth at Kaikoura . . . getting engaged . . . and, in time, their white wedding at St. Martin's in Dorking. . . .

It seemed only fitting, later, when it was all over, that she should go back to Kemp Town with him—that the first night of complete, adult happiness she had ever known should culminate in their lovemaking. She wasn't nervous—there was nothing in the world to be scared of, so long as Ray loved her. And it had been so obvious, at the ball, that he loved her just as much as she did him. And as he took her hand, and led her into his bedroom, Juliet found herself seeking, as she usually did at crucial moments, her mother's blessing—but it was only a fleeting need, for she knew that Elizabeth would understand better than anyone, for hadn't she loved Edward so passionately that no one else had ever been good enough to take his place. . . .

Ray's hands were firm and strong about her waist, and she waited for him to lift her in his arms and lay her down on the narrow bed.

"Are you sure?" His face was intent, the Irish lilt huskier and more intense than usual.

"I am," Juliet whispered.

"I want you to be quite, quite certain."

Of *course* she was sure, surer than anything that she wanted what she had read about, in Lawrence and, more sweetly, in Waugh and in Bates—she wanted his hands on her breasts and between her thighs, she wanted him *inside* her, she wanted to be loved by him. But, at the same time, his restraint seemed to spell out that love, and so now she reached up, in reply, and took his face in her hands and kissed his mouth.

"Let's not waste another second," she murmured.

The dress—the magical dress—was fastened by a tiny fabric-covered button where the halter neck lay at the back of her neck. With one hand, Ray undid the button, and the dress, like a willing collaborator, tumbled to the floor, leaving Juliet standing quivering in the strapless brassiere that cut into her flesh and the lacy briefs that she had bought that very afternoon.

Ray's right hand moved directly to the panties, following the curve of her buttocks and tracing a taunting, pulsating line toward what, she supposed, was the target—

He removed his hand and stepped away.

"What's wrong?" Her distress was clear in her voice.

"Nothing." He took off his shoes and walked over to the door. "I thought I'd turn out the light." He hesitated, trying to gauge her feelings.

Her heart swelled with gratitude. "Please," she said.

For a moment or two, the darkness was so complete that he could hardly find her, and Juliet wished, in a way, that he had not been so considerate, for she had almost—almost, not quite, of course—forgotten her scars. But then he brushed against her, and desire leapt back into life, like a great, singeing flame, and she heard the sound of fabric, and felt the warmth from his body as he tossed away his shirt.

"Will you help me?" he asked, and Juliet didn't understand, until he found her hand and guided it to the waistband of his trousers, and she realized he wanted her to undress him, and a new shiver shot through her, for she could feel his heat through the material, and knew that he was straining for release, and she could hardly bear to wait another instant before holding him in her hand, feeling the power and the throbbing—

"Christ," Ray said softly, and his breathing quickened. "Are you sure you haven't done this before?"

Juliet gave a small cry of indignation.

"I'm only teasing—that's wonderful."

With sudden urgency, he scooped her up in his arms, just as she'd dreamed he would, and spilled her down onto his eiderdown. Her eyes growing accustomed to the dim light from the unsatisfactory window, she watched him shedding his briefs and then lowering himself onto her. The warm pressure, the abrupt, delicious shock of his naked body on her own, made her gasp and instinctively buck her hips toward his.

"Steady, darlin'," Ray whispered. "Let's not rush it."

For the first time, he touched her breasts, and for just a moment, Juliet tensed, for though it was dark, she knew how very different and strange her scarred flesh felt compared with normal skin. But if he noticed, he gave no sign, except perhaps that, after the first caress, he seemed to favor her right breast, and Juliet didn't mind, for she knew—he had told her often enough—that there was more than enough of her that was beautiful and perfect. And now, as if to emphasize that, he began to kiss her, everywhere—her nose, her closed eyelids, her mouth, her neck, and then down to her navel and her stomach and her soft triangle of blond furry pubic hair—and Juliet, spurred on, began to touch and kiss him in return, feeling as if she'd always known about this, aware that this was one side of life that needed no prompting, no qualifications and little tuition. . . .

Once his fingers had traveled just a little farther down, probing, seeking, inquisitive and acquisitive, Juliet knew that she could bear it no longer.

"Please," she pleaded. "Inside me—I want you *in* me!"

Ray laughed, a gasping, trembling laugh of pleasure and lust, and spreading her thighs apart with one knee, he found her, wet and hot as himself, and, with one strong, steady lunge, he penetrated her—

Juliet cried out, but not with pain—yes, it hurt, it was as if he had speared her, but she knew all about pain, *real,* unbearable pain, and this —this was a million sensations rolled into one, as if her whole body had been transformed into a single, shuddering, overpowering nerve end—

"Oh, God," she cried, hardly knowing her own voice, for it was as transformed as she was, "I *love* you, Ray!"

And he responded not with words, but with an even greater thrust, deep inside her, and as they both bucked and plunged and spent themselves in orgasms, the little narrow bed rocked and squeaked and groaned and, at last, came to rest.

"If I hadn't felt you tearing," Ray murmured, some time later, as they lay together, still entwined, "I'd never have believed you were a virgin."

"I was," she whispered.

"I know." He kissed her hair. "But you were made for it—it's very rare." He paused, and added: "I think."

She sighed, with happiness and love.

"Just think," he went on, "what you've been missing."

She shook her head. "I wouldn't have wanted to do it with anyone else." She ran the palm of her hand over his chest. "It was only because of you."

Ray rolled over, and sat up. "Bathroom," he said, his voice still husky.

"Don't go."

He chuckled. "I'll be right back."

The bedsprings twanged as he stood up.

And then he turned the light on.

Juliet blinked and, for an instant, shielded her eyes. When she could see again, she looked across to the doorway, and saw that he was standing, motionless, like a carved, beautiful statue, staring at her.

She lay, looking as wanton as she felt, sprawling languidly, legs apart, and for a second, her mouth curved into a smile. And then, in a flash, the happiness was gone.

It was the first time he had seen her completely naked in clear light. The first time he had seen her breasts. The moment was infinitesimal, but undeniable. Ray looked at her—at her left breast, at its disfiguring, hated scar tissue—and there was no mistaking the expression in his eyes.

A flicker, nothing more, but unequivocal.

Revulsion.

She had known, long before morning came, long before they sat again, on the cracked sofa, drinking instant coffee, that it was over. Ray seemed the same—kind, considerate, warm—yet Juliet knew the truth, and she marveled at herself for being able to act and speak calmly.

"Home tomorrow," he said, looking at her with regret. But she knew that he was relieved, that he thought the long vacation would ease him out of a relationship he could not bear.

"I'll miss you," he said.

Juliet stared into her coffee cup, and felt nauseous.

"Won't you miss me?" Ray asked, reaching for her hand.

"Of course," she replied, and knew, dully, that only one of them meant it.

It was only when she was back home, at Kaikoura, that the uncertainty, the foolish, lovesick doubts, began to nibble at her gray acceptance. Perhaps she had imagined that look—perhaps it had been her hypersensitivity. Maybe Ray had meant what he said—maybe he would miss her.

Hope tentatively restored, Juliet started, as she had promised, to write to him in County Wicklow, carefully keeping the tone of her letters light and happy, and praying for a reply.

He did write back, once, on a postcard from Dublin:

> *Hope you're enjoying yourself.*
> *Don't forget to dance!*
>
> *Love, Ray*

She tried, hard, to read more into the words, fought to find care and feeling in the hasty scrawl, but all she really saw was a meaningless and cool attempt at duty—a postcard, bought in a flash, written in a couple of seconds, posted in even less.

"Anything from Ray?" Elizabeth asked one Friday evening in early September.

"Nothing since the card," Juliet replied easily. "But he says he hates writing letters, so I don't mind."

Elizabeth eyed her. "Why don't you phone him? You've got his number, haven't you?"

"He may not be there."

"Then you'll phone again, or leave a message." She smiled. "Oh, go on and try—I know you're longing to talk to him, and he's bound to be pleased."

He was not at home, so Juliet did leave her name with a soft-voiced woman.

"Will I ask him to give you a call?"

"Please," Juliet said. "If he has the time."

He did not find the time.

The hatred only began in earnest on the last day of September, with the start of the Autumn term.

She saw him, in Falmer House, on the very first morning. On impulse, she ran over to him, smiling. "How are you?"

His embarrassment was patent, though he tried to conceal it. "Grand, and you? How's your mother?"

"Very well, thank you." Juliet waited, in mute agony, for more.

He looked at his watch. "I have to go," he said furtively. "To a lecture." He tucked a ring-file under one arm, and picked up some books. "Take care of yourself."

And he was gone.

Juliet could not work, could not concentrate, could not read or eat or sleep. *It's just the brush-off,* she tried to tell herself, as if the commonplaceness of it might make her feel better. But it only made her feel worse, for it only seemed to accentuate the one, unforgivable truth: their relationship, their night of love, their times together, were meaningless to Ray. She meant nothing to him.

But Juliet had only ever had one boyfriend, had only loved one man, had only made love to one man. Had only shown herself to one man.

She never would again.

It preyed on her mind. She'd thought she could trust him, but now that she knew better, who was to say that Ray wasn't telling all his friends about her? About her naïveté, about her eagerness to give herself to him—about her mangled breast.

Night after night, she lay in bed, her fingers digging into her pillows or gouging into the mattress, trying to expunge the hatred, aware that it was more damaging to her than to him, but it was no good. Every morning, when she rose, groggy from too short a sleep, it was still with her, sour in her mouth. Her stupidity. His betrayal.

Three weeks into the term, she saw him with a pretty history student named Ann Walker. Their arms were linked, they were intent on each other. Juliet's loathing reached its crescendo.

Ray glanced up, saw Juliet staring, and gave a small, awkward smile. Then he looked back at the girl, red-haired and pale-skinned, and said something to her. They both laughed.

That was it. The moment of decision for Juliet. He was going to pay for what he had done to her.

She had wished, since the first day back, that Ray would disappear, would simply be gone so that she could concentrate on her work again, think about her writing and forget that he had ever existed. If only he would leave, or, better still, commit so grievous a sin as to be sent down, so that disgrace might shatter his complacent aura—but Ray Donnelly was too bright, too astute, to put a foot wrong.

Unless his downfall could be arranged.

It was not difficult to plan. There was a shop, in The Lanes, in Brighton, popular with tourists and students, that sold anything from maps, printed rock, and trinkets, to silk scarves and even simple gold jewelry. The better-quality items—the heavier identification bracelets, lockets, and watches—were locked in a glass cabinet; the lesser, lighter chains and earrings were hung over or clipped onto velvet boards, making them easy to try on. Or to steal.

Ray often visited the shop, sometimes to browse, but more frequently to buy gifts. He was well liked for his generosity, despite his slender means. He'd bought a silver horseshoe keyring there, for Juliet, one afternoon in June. It was only a matter of time before he went there again, probably to buy a present for his new girlfriend. Rachel had told Juliet that Ray and Ann were going skiing together in Scotland at Christmas.

Juliet's humiliation knew no bounds. She lay in bed at night, still unable to sleep, fantasizing about the redhead, cradled in Ray's arms while he stroked and kissed her pale, perfect breasts.

God, how she hated him.

She began to trail him like a spy. She forgot everything else, studying, lectures, even eating—surviving on a snatched cup of coffee here, a slice of toast or slab of chocolate there.

A fortnight later, he played right into her hands when Juliet saw him on his way to Ann's flat in Ovingdean carrying a gift-wrapped parcel. He stayed until two o'clock in the morning. Ten minutes after he had left, the girl, in her dressing gown, emerged briefly from her front door and stuffed a bag of rubbish into the bin outside. Within another ten minutes, the light inside her bedroom went out.

Juliet waited until she was certain there was no one to observe her, and then she crept to the bin, lifted the lid, removed the plastic bag, and went home. Safe in her room, she spread newspaper on the floor and tipped out the rubbish. The wrapping paper was there, crumpled but clean, with its handwritten gift tag still attached. *To Annie, with love from Ray.*

If it had been hers, she would never have thrown it away.

Ten days later, on a Saturday afternoon, Ray returned to the shop. It was the busiest day of the week, the ideal time for a shoplifter.

Watching closely, and feeling strangely calm, Juliet waited for Ray to come out before she strolled in. It was a cool, damp afternoon, and her raincoat had large, deep pockets. All the assistants were serving, and the manager was intent on trying to sell a gold watch to an elderly couple, while several others waited for service. Two browsing hippies attracted occasional glances from one of the older assistants. No one seemed to notice Juliet.

Within minutes, she was back out in the bustling lane, a fine gold chain and a little, golden initial "A" tucked in her raincoat pocket.

Back home, she carefully wrapped the items in tissue, and then made a small, neat parcel using Ray's discarded and ironed paper and gift tag. Anticipation making her suddenly hungry, she took a packet of biscuits from the kitchen larder, and settled down to wait.

He left his flat at a quarter to eight that evening, and set off toward the bus stop. Juliet waited fifteen minutes.

The bathroom window, as always, was open. She went straight to the bedroom, opened the bottom drawer of his dresser, and hid the little package among his heaviest sweaters.

It was only as she turned to leave, and saw the narrow bed, and was assailed, suddenly, by the familiar mixture of smells—Ray's cologne, stale cooking, damp walls—that she wavered for an instant. But then she saw the photograph of Ann on his bedside table, and the loathing and determination returned with full force.

A few minutes later, from the telephone booth at the corner of his road, she called the police.

Late on Monday afternoon, when Ray arrived home, two police officers and the owner of the shop were waiting for him. No matter what he said, however strenuously he protested, no one believed him.

The evidence spoke for itself.

Juliet's article reported the sad downfall of a perfect, popular student, a brilliant future destroyed. Writing again without sentiment, but with accuracy and compassion, she turned a sordid, minor incident into an exposure of the financial and emotional pressures on many university students and, together with two photographs—one of Ray, jubilant and smiling after winning a squash competition in the Sports Pavilion, the other head down, going into the courthouse—she submitted her piece to the *Sussex Outlook*, the *Wine Press*, and the *Evening Argus*.

At Kaikoura, Elizabeth filled another three pages of the leather cuttings album, her heart swelling with pride because her daughter had been able to put her personal emotions aside in order to write an admirably professional article, devoid of bitterness.

Juliet stood on the platform, watching as Ray heaved his two trunks up into the London train, for the first leg of his journey back to County Wicklow. Ann, red hair flowing in the strong wind, embraced him and then, clearly overcome, turned to go, without looking back.

Ray shut the door and stared after her until she was out of sight. Then, about to find a seat, his eyes lit upon Juliet. He looked startled.

She, too, stared. She took in, once more, the glossy dark hair, the straight nose, the sensuous mouth. The blue eyes that had driven her mad.

And, raising her right hand very slowly from her side, she waved him off, out of the station, out of Brighton, out of her life.

That night, as she climbed, exhausted, into bed, she began for the first time in many weeks to weep. She cried for almost an hour, deep, wrenching sobs that shook her whole body and made her throat raw.

And then she slept, like a baby.

Chapter 19

BOSTON HAD BEEN KIND to Francesca. With Johnny's ongoing tuition and sponsorship, and with her own developing flair for photography, she had gradually built up a clientele of her own, enabling her to pay her way more realistically in the chaotic Chase household; early in 1960, Della had given birth to a son, named Billy, and Francesca had become anxious about draining their resources as well as taking up precious space.

It was not until Thanksgiving of 1967 that she calculated that, at long last, she had managed to put aside enough cash to employ an immigration lawyer.

Robert Stern was thirty-eight years old, stocky, fair-haired, and twice divorced, with three children. He was a top-notch attorney who had, in the course of his career, helped all manner of people who aspired to become Americans, but he had never been as personally moved by any client as by the twenty-five-year-old Francesca Cesaretti.

"Why did you choose me?" he asked her before they began.

"I'm told that you're the best there is." She looked at him frankly. "The problem is, that may mean that I can't afford you."

"The policy of this practice," Stern said, "is not to accept payment for preliminary consultations with personal clients, unless we feel we can be of help." He smiled at her. "Tell me your troubles," he said in his warm, friendly voice, "and I'll give you my on-the-spot recommendations."

✷

By the time she'd finished her story, Robert Stern was more than moved. He was head over heels, stupidly, *idiotically*, in love.

His expression did not betray him. "How much money do you have, Miss Cesaretti?"

Francesca frowned.

"I need to know," he assured her, "or I wouldn't ask."

She nodded. "Just under five thousand dollars." Her pointed chin inched up proudly. "I know it isn't much, but it's been a long struggle saving even that much."

"It's remarkable that you've saved anything under the circumstances."

"If it weren't for Mr. and Mrs. Chase, I couldn't have." She paused. "But then, if it hadn't been for them, I'd probably have been tossed out of America years ago."

"Yes," he said, and fell silent.

"Can you help me?" Francesca asked, after a moment.

He looked at her. "I'm considering." Slowly, he swiveled his chair so that he faced his wall of bookshelves and did not have the impossible distraction of those wide, slanted, sparkling eyes or that sheet of gleaming hair or the calm, sexy mouth—Stern shut his eyes. The solution had struck him immediately—but it would entail him acting in an uncharacteristically rash manner. What he had in mind was not only against his principles and unprofessional; it signified to Robert Stern that, in the space of a single half hour, he had been bewitched and was, therefore, unbalanced.

I have flipped, he thought, and opened his eyes.

His partners would be furious if they found out—and his ex-wives would form a lynching party.

Think of your responsibilities, he told himself.

But when he spun around again, and faced her, he knew that he was lost.

Principles be damned! He was not only going to sort out her residency—he was also going to do everything in his power to make her fall in love with him.

✳

It took a week to persuade her that his proposition was, so far as he was concerned, a genuine business investment, and quite ethical.

"But you *can't* lend me five thousand dollars!"

"Why not? I'd be charging you interest, as a bank would—only I can afford to offer a slightly more flexible arrangement."

"But wouldn't that make us partners?"

"Not necessarily."

"But I don't—" Francesca floundered. "I don't know anything about you."

Stern grinned. "What do you want to know? Do you require references?" He paused. "It's simple, Miss Cesaretti. You have five thousand dollars in savings. If I loan you a further five thousand to invest in a photographic studio, your immigration status can almost certainly be sorted out very swiftly." He paused again, watching her face. "You're questioning my motives."

She grew pink. "I suppose I am." She bit her lip. "I'm sorry."

"Don't be. You're right to." He thought for a moment. "How about if I come over to Mr. Chase's studio, so that I can learn something about the business, and check out your work, too—if you're both in agreement."

"What if you hate my work?" Francesca was suddenly nervous. "If you think I have no talent?"

Robert Stern ran an apparently careless hand through his wavy fair hair, and his gray-green eyes twinkled. "Then I guess you may have shot yourself in the foot."

✳

He'd loved her work, as he'd known he would, and he admired the way she and Johnny managed their existing cramped studio on the floor below their apartment. He'd liked the Chases, too, and had been especially charmed by their son, Billy, who was an extraordinarily good-looking child, having inherited his father's narrow brown eyes and dark hair, together with Della's pert nose and pale, freckled face.

"What a nice man," Johnny commented to Francesca after Robert had left. "And obviously impressed by your work."

"He's nuts about her," Della pointed out. "He'd have thought she was another Cartier-Bresson if she'd taken an upside-down, out-of-focus Brownie snapshot!"

"Thank you," Francesca said wryly.

"Which is not to say he *isn't* a man of impeccable taste—he obviously is, since he's so crazy about you."

Francesca looked even more troubled than before Robert's visit. "That's why I don't think I can accept his offer."

"Why not?" Billy asked. At seven, Billy was seldom excluded from adult conversations, having the ability to listen quietly, and often to contribute usefully and rationally.

"Two reasons, Billy," Francesca said. "If Robert Stern *is* in love with me, then I'd be taking unfair advantage of him. And secondly, it's not wise to mix business with emotional involvement." Hastily, she added: "Not that I'm involved with *him*, if you know what I mean."

"Sure," Billy said.

"As I understand it," Della said slowly, "he just wants to lend you money, to help you out."

"But if he went around lending all his clients money, he'd be bankrupt and certified before six months were up!"

"But he doesn't want to give that kind of help to *all* his clients," Johnny pointed out. "He wants to give it to you." He paused. "And to be honest, I think you'd be crazy to turn him down."

"Do you really?"

"I just said so."

Della looked first at her husband, and then back at her friend. "You know what I feel about Johnny's advice, don't you?"

"You think he's Moses, Abraham Lincoln, and the Oracle of Delphi all rolled into one." Francesca took a breath. "You both think I should accept."

Johnny shook his head. "We think you should do what you think best. You have sound instincts. What do they tell you?"

For a moment, she gnawed at her lower lip. "That if I turn down Robert Stern's offer, I'll be losing not only a real chance at my own studio, but also my best shot at getting a proper legal status."

Billy stared at Francesca. "If you turn down this guy's money," he said, "could they make you leave America?" His face was shocked. "I don't *want* you to leave."

"*Is* it your only shot?" Della asked. "There's no other way?"

"No other way as clear-cut, or with as much chance of success. Robert says that he could file this application at the Department of Labor, and have clearance in a few months, perhaps even less." She shook her head. "The trouble is, there's no other way of finding the cash."

"You want to know what I think?" Billy asked Francesca.

"Sure I do."

"I think you should take the money, buy a big studio for you and Dad, and stay in America forever." He paused. "But I'm just a kid."

"Some kid." Della ruffled her son's hair.

Francesca was staring into space.

"Well?" Johnny nudged.

"I was thinking about Vittorio." Her eyes were wistful. "He was so proud and so mistrustful of people. But even he knew when to accept help."

"Is that what you're going to do?" Della asked softly.

Francesca's smile was tremulous. "I think so."

It took Robert Stern several more meetings to complete the persuasion, and he was happy that Francesca did not seem to mind if the meetings were held in Locke-Ober's, or over a lobster lunch from Sanborn's, or on a bench in Boston Public Garden, but though he learned more about her on every occasion, she gave not the slightest indication that she could ever regard him as anything more than her lawyer and friend.

"Any word from your brother?" he asked her a few weeks after she had finally agreed, and the application had been filed. It had shocked Robert deeply to learn that though Francesca had regularly written to her brother, she had never felt secure enough to send him her address, since she could not be sure how great their cousins' hatred might still be. They might have made more trouble for her and Luciano—perhaps even for Johnny and Della.

Robert had suggested that she use the address of his law firm when she next wrote to Luciano, but by January, she had heard nothing from Italy, and her wish to travel to Florence was more urgent than ever.

"How much longer will it take, do you think?" she pressed Robert anxiously.

"Not too long. Have you found premises yet?"

She nodded. "An apartment on Joy Street. Two bedrooms and a terrific, long living room with windows both ends."

"Mind if I look at it?"

"I wouldn't consider it if you didn't."

"Nice bedroom?"

"The second would make a fine darkroom."

"I didn't ask about the darkroom." He looked steadily at her. Although he'd swear on a stack of Bibles that he'd never let it affect his work as her lawyer, Robert had no qualms about letting Francesca know how he felt about her as a woman. Any concealment of his wholehearted desire for her would, he decided, be hypocritical, even fraudulent.

Francesca's mind, alas, was on higher matters. "Who cares about the bedroom?" she dismissed lightly. "I can sleep anywhere, can't you?"

So Robert remained silent.

Francesca's life with the Chases, so close-knit and private, had, to some extent, kept her from forming too many close relationships with members of the opposite sex. She had had no high school or college boyfriends—and most of the clients who came to the studio were actors, many attractive, some gay, most otherwise attached, though that had seldom stopped them trying to seduce Francesca. She knew that she was good-looking, but she did not understand that she was *beautiful*—and sexy. Her earliest encounter with sex—the horrors in the Boston warehouse—had not scarred her, but had done little for her confidence, and at twenty-five years of age, she was still, remarkably, a virgin.

Johnny and Della teased her gently, told her she was just an old-fashioned Italian girl, that virgins in the "swinging sixties" were as rare as unicorns, not to mention—referring to Robert Stern—handsome, kind, and eligible Jewish lawyers, but Francesca was not to be swayed. She would know, she said, when the time and, more important, the man was right, and as yet, even if it did make her an anachronism, that had not come to pass.

Robert Stern believed in breaking down walls. One day, in early March, he took her firmly by the hand and whisked her from his office to The Bell in Hand tavern. Buying them both a beer, he took her outside and told her to look across the street.

"Scollay Square," he said.

"Not anymore."

"Precisely." Scollay Square, as it had been when Francesca had arrived in Boston, with its strip joints, brothels, and tattoo parlors, had all but vanished under demolition, and Government Center was rising in its place.

"What's your point?" Francesca asked.

Robert looked at her. When Francesca wore high heels, he found himself looking up at her, something that might, under other circumstances, have disturbed him, but not with Francesca—with Francesca, *everything* was different. Christ, he wanted her, but the truly disconcerting fact was that she was so goddamned nice that he liked her even more.

"Fourteen years," he said, raising his voice a little to be heard above the traffic. "Time to take all the bad old memories and stamp them underfoot—bulldoze them, the way they bulldozed Scollay Square, and rebuild."

Francesca smiled at him. "I'm getting there—slowly."

Robert's gaze was steady. "Any day now, you'll be a permanent resident of the United States of America. In a few years, if you want to commit yourself, you can become a citizen."

"Thanks to you."

He went on, seriously. "I'm not saying you can never be hurt, or even scared again, Francesca. But that bad old past—the people who caused you so much pain—won't be able to touch you." He reached for her hand, gently. "You're safe."

She'd been tempted at that moment, charmed and moved by the caring, confident lawyer, aware that at the slightest sign from her, the lavish lunches, civilized teas, and casual drinks would become romantic dinners at the best restaurants in town—and that after that, of course, *anything* could happen. . . . Yet still something held her back—fear, caution, or perhaps just that desire for something that would feel completely right.

Finally, however, his sensitivity won her over. On the fifth of April, Francesca attained the legal status she'd waited so long for, and Robert surprised her by taking her to a noisy little trattoria in the Italian district, rather than any one of the grander, more glamorous places he might have chosen.

"I thought you might need reassurance," he said, after they had drunk numerous toasts in red Chianti.

"Of what?"

"Of the certainty that whatever your future as an American may bring, your true self, your fundamental identity can never be lost."

He looked so handsome, so impressive somehow, retaining his attorney's demeanor in spite of the casual white polo-neck sweater he wore instead of his customary suit and tie—and yet he was so honest about his feelings for her, so *vulnerable*, that Francesca found herself watching him, for the first time, with a stirring of real desire. What would it be like, she wondered, to go to bed with such a man, to give in, to feel his skin against her own?

"Do you want dessert?" Robert asked softly.

She kept her voice light. "I'm tempted by the ricotta cheesecake, though I know it's pure greed."

Robert signaled their waiter. "Tonight is for indulgence," he told her, and a large slice of cake was placed before her. "Just an espresso for me, please."

"Share this with me."

"I have other appetites," he said, softly.

"I know."

His eyes darted to meet hers. "Do you?"

✳

Outside, on the sidewalk, they stood for a moment, enjoying the freshness of the night air, a heady combination of ocean smells, garlic, and traffic.

"I've taken a liberty," Robert said suddenly.

"Really?" Francesca smiled.

"Really." He took something from his jacket pocket and showed it to her.

"A key?"

A strange expression passed over Robert's face, strained, almost shy. "It's a key to a suite at the Ritz-Carlton." His voice became hasty, tension-filled. "We don't have to use it—I just thought—" Even in the street lighting, his cheeks were clearly hot. "My kids are staying at the apartment this week, and I thought we might want to be alone—just to talk, if that's what you want—" He broke off, and plunged the key back into his pocket. "Christ, what an ass I am!"

"Why do you say that?" Francesca couldn't be certain if it was the wine, or the occasion, or the sight of the hotel key, or the remarkable confusion of the normally confident attorney—but she couldn't remember feeling as touched and enthralled, and deliciously *tempted*—

✳

By the time they stood in the elevator at the Ritz-Carlton, with the discreet, uniformed operator, Robert had, at least superficially, regained his equilibrium, but Francesca's legs were trembling.

In the living room, spacious and fragrant with flowers, they kissed for the first time, and Robert's lips were firm and eager, yet Francesca was aware that he was still holding himself in check, anxious not to push her into anything she might afterward regret.

But how could she regret a night spent in the arms of a man as romantic and thoughtful and caring as Robert? He was as adept and considerate in his lovemaking as he was in every other respect; he treated every inch of her with tenderness and awe and passion, caressing and kissing and loving her full, pointed breasts, her remarkable, elegant neck, her waist so slender that he could hold it within his two outspread hands.

He had stopped before sweeping the heavy bedspread back off the king-size bed, to ask her again if she was sure—and he had forced himself to halt again, when, kneeling over her, his erection undeniable and commanding, he stared down at her glorious, flushed elfin face and saw the slanted eyes half closed, lashes fluttering, and was suddenly terrified that she might be scared of what was to come.

"Are you quite sure?" he had whispered, his hands abruptly stilled, his heart pounding, his breath shallow.

"*Certo,*" Francesca had answered with absolute conviction, drawing him back down to her, and opening her thighs to him, for her whole body seemed to have come to sparking, blossoming life that night, and though her heart and mind might be virginal, her flesh knew exactly what to do and what it wanted Robert to do to her. . . .

"All right?" he asked later, for the third time, and his eyes, more green than gray now, reflected his continuing anxiety lest he might say too much, and send this precious girl scurrying away.

"I promise you I'm fine." Francesca smiled, knowing she spoke the truth, for she felt wonderfully well and composed, and even if there had been no pealing of bells or flashing of skyrockets, no woman in her right senses would choose those things over a man as fine and kind as Robert Stern.

They got out of bed at five in the morning, regretful that they could not share breakfast, but Robert felt obliged to be home before his children woke, and Francesca wanted to leave the hotel, as she'd come, on Robert's arm.

"I have something for you," he told her, almost as an afterthought, when they both had showered and dressed. He reached into his jacket and withdrew a long white envelope from an inside pocket.

"What is it?"

"A gift."

Francesca's brow creased. "Haven't you given me enough?"

"This is different. It's for us both."

Intrigued, she tore it open, and stared at the covers of two airline tickets. "What are these?"

"Take a look."

Her fingers quivering, she opened one ticket. "Boston—New York—Rome—Pisa," she read, her voice growing more incredulous with every word. "*Pisa?*" Her heart began to pound, and she waved the tickets agitatedly. "Are you crazy?"

"I thought you wanted to go as soon as you could," Robert said mildly.

Francesca took another look. "April twelfth." Her eyes grew huge. "The *twelfth*? That's next week!"

"Enough time to do a little shopping—and you'll need a passport."

Her legs suddenly weak, she flopped into the nearest armchair. "There's no way, Robert."

"No way to what?"

"No way I can accept this from you." Francesca swallowed. "You're one of the kindest, most generous people I've ever met, and I thank you with all my heart, but I can't—" She shook her head. "I just can't."

Robert sat on the arm of the chair. "You do still want to go to Florence, don't you?"

"Of course, but—"

"But you're scared. Of going back. Of facing your uncle and your cousins."

Tentatively, Francesca looked at the second ticket. "You want to come with me?"

"I said it was a gift for both of us." Robert paused. "It's your birthday next month."

"I can't possibly—it's too much." Again, she shook her head. "Much too much."

Gently, Robert covered her right hand with his left. "Too much money, or too much involvement?"

Francesca hesitated. "Both," she replied honestly.

"Okay." Robert tried to mask his disappointment. "What about someone else—Della?"

"She has a job, Robert—not to mention a family." Francesca looked up at him, hating to hurt him but needing to be truthful. "And I've always planned on making this trip alone."

Robert knew there was no point arguing. "If I cancel my reservation, will you accept your ticket as my birthday gift?"

She glanced back down. "This is first class."

"I like to travel in comfort."

"Well, I don't need it." Francesca grinned shakily. "Anything has to be more comfortable than my journey over here." She paused. "Make this second class—"

"Economy," he corrected.

"Whatever. And add it to what I already owe you—then I'll go."

"But this is a gift, not a loan."

"I told you, Robert, it's too generous." She paused. "Either it's a loan, or you cancel both tickets."

"Could you afford to pay your own fare now?"

"No, not quite." Francesca tilted her chin. "But that's my problem. When I came to your office, I was looking for legal advice, not a free ride."

"Do you think I don't know that? This is a gift, not an insult."

Hastily, Francesca scrambled up off the chair into his arms. "I know that, of *course* I know that—only please, *please* let's do it my way, because otherwise it may be months before I can go to Italy, and Luciano and I have waited long enough!"

Robert sighed, and took the tickets out of her hand. "No trip for me —economy for you—" He shrugged. "And I'll add it to your bill."

Gratefully, she kissed him. "I don't deserve you." Her eyes glittered with sudden tears. "I can't believe it."

"Believe it." He paused. "There's one condition."

"Anything!" She drew back, wary again. "What is it?"

"Can I at least take you to the airport?"

Chapter 20

IT WAS HARD to express the pleasure—the unadulterated deliciousness —of finding out that something that had given one months of purest fun had suddenly turned out to be the basis of a seriously profitable career.

"I still can't believe it—it's too fantastic!" Luciano exulted down the telephone line to Victor Pillement, his literary agent in Paris.

"Not so very fantastic," Victor said. "Lord knows they've rejected enough of your work. If Laurent-Fournay are astute enough to recognize that our friend Holt is just too good to turn down, you may as well believe it."

Luciano laughed, accustomed to the candor of the man who, despite the many publishers' rejections since they had first come together as agent and author, had stuck staunchly to his belief that Luciano would, when he had exhausted all his nonstarters and blind alleys, find his way to success.

"What now?" Luciano wanted to know.

"It's up to you, *mon ami*. Do you feel like getting straight back to work, or coming up to Paris for lunch?"

"No contest." Luciano looked at his watch. "It's too late."

"Oysters," Victor dangled. "Prunier."

Luciano was deeply regretful. It was unprecedented for Victor to be such a bad influence, and he hated to pass up the opportunity. "I'd adore nothing more," he said sincerely, "but it's after ten."

"Air-Inter can probably get you here in time. Or maybe your uncle or aunt can fix you a ride on an unscheduled flight. Either way, we'll wait for you."

"We?"

"François Poiret is anxious to meet you as soon as possible." Victor paused. "Your editor-to-be."

The blood rose to Luciano's cheeks. This was really happening—his fantasies were coming true. *"Fly to Paris immediately!"—"Get over to New York* now!" As he began, feverishly, to dial Nice airport, his brain raced wildly ahead. Next stop, Hollywood!

And then he stopped, and smiled. In the fantasy world, the publishers and film magnates sent first-class tickets. In the real world, Victor Pillement was merely encouraging him to spend his *own* francs.

He made a reservation and called a taxi.

After all, what was money for if not to enable one to down the occasional oyster at Maison Prunier?

In the years since *baccalauréat,* Luciano had concentrated on the one thing he knew he really wanted to do with his life—to write fiction. It had not all been rejection; he'd had enough short stories published in sundry magazines and journals to keep his morale afloat if not high. He had also found a bread-and-butter niche as a translator—Kate had taught him perfect English, and being trilingual had its uses. But he was a very fortunate young man, and he knew it. He did not need to earn money, for he was blissfully happy living at Le Rocher, and his uncle and aunt, fortunately, still enjoyed having him around.

It was just as well, for apart from the publishable short stories, Luciano was in danger of becoming like one of those dilettantish young prewar artists in Paris, churning out useless canvases simply because they yearned to be artists and because no one told them that they were no good. Luciano knew that he *was* a writer—even that he *had* to write— but he was thrashing around desperately in his search for the right material. He tried his hand at tragedy, at comedy—at horror, at satire, and even at a political novel—but nothing worked.

Until he hit on Zachary Holt.

Zachary was a rumpled young American detective, resident in contemporary Paris, a carefree, sexy man with a heart of gold and a nose for trouble.

Once Luciano hit on his new protagonist, it was like finding a friend. For the first time in his writing life, he was having *fun*. And it showed.

✱

"We want to change the title." François Poiret, a round-faced, jovial man who clearly enjoyed eating in the *grand tradition* of his countrymen, swallowed his eleventh oyster. "We think that *Zachary Holt* is excellent."

"Thank you," Luciano said happily, for the umpteenth time.

"I meant as the title."

"Oh." Luciano drank some more Meursault, and shrugged. "All right, if you think so—I didn't care much for the other anyway."

Poiret nodded. "It's vigorous and intriguing—and besides, since we hope that Holt will feature in many more books, it forms the right introduction to a series."

Luciano's elation reached yet another peak. *"Dieu."*

They began to discuss more pressing, practical matters.

"As we've already agreed," Poiret said, "the book needs a quite substantial rewrite—that is to say, a healthy pruning. How available are you for editorial meetings?"

"Completely."

"Bon." Poiret fixed Luciano with a suddenly steely look. "And are you a cheetah or a tortoise? I mean, do you write swiftly or slowly?"

"It varies." Luciano pulled a self-deprecating face. "Sometimes I can muster quite a moderate gallop—other times I'm not even a tortoise, more of a snail."

"Then you must learn discipline." Poiret leaned forward to press home his point. "Snails, *mon ami*, get eaten."

Victor Pillement, thoroughly enjoying himself, sat back and watched the first step in Luciano's return to earth.

Luciano, still far too happy to let anything spoil his mood, could not help but give a wry thought for his most troublesome flaw. His old tendency to daydream still slowed him down, often disturbing his creative process badly enough to stop him altogether. Actually, he realized now, they had never really been ordinary daydreams. More accurately described, they were an intermittent seeping of ideas, strange, disconnected thoughts and feelings, trickling, or sometimes even flooding, through his brain, unwanted and apparently unrelated to his work, yet forceful enough to compel him to leave Zachary Holt in order to note them down as well as he could. Obviously, he comforted himself, they were part and parcel of his existence as a writer; the thoughts might signify nothing useful *now*, but he had a strong sense that nothing, however vague or trivial, must be wasted.

Over coffee and cognac, François Poiret rolled the tip of his cigar around the ashtray. "Laurent-Fournay hope you will allow the company to control and participate in the U.K. and American rights to the book—"

"Subject to a mutually acceptable percentage," Pillement interrupted.

"*Naturellement.*" Poiret had not taken his eyes off Luciano. "The idea is agreeable to you, in principle?"

Luciano remembered his manners. "I must be advised by my agent, of course—" He glanced at Victor, who gave a tiny, almost imperceptible nod. "But yes, thank you, in principle I find it a wonderful idea."

He returned to Eze to find that Bruno and Kate had organized an instant celebration for him, inviting a dozen of their mutual close friends for an informal dinner party.

Le Rocher had never felt more perfect to Luciano. Although it was mid-October, the weather was still unusually warm, and the great folding table that was used for all parties and barbecues throughout the summer months was once again installed out on the terrace.

Almost miraculously, with so little notice, Kate had overseen the creation of a sublime bouillabaisse, and by ten o'clock, all the guests, including Luciano's current girlfriend, Amélie, were blissfully absorbing tastes and aromas, while lively, contented conversations rippled up and down the table.

Between the cheese and dessert, Bruno, balder but fitter and happier at sixty-eight than he had ever been in his life, stood up to make a brief but heartfelt mention of his great pride in Luciano's success.

"It would be tempting," Bruno said, "to claim a little credit for having produced the handsome, delightful young man who has now proved, after years of hard work, how very talented he is."

Amélie squeezed Luciano's hand.

"Neither Kate nor I, however, has that right, for although Luciano is as precious as a son to us both, that particular credit belongs to my late brother and sister-in-law." Bruno raised his glass. "I should like to drink a toast to their memory." His voice quavered slightly with emotion. "To Giulio and Serafina, Luciano's father and mother, who could have been no prouder of their son than we are."

When Luciano was sufficiently composed to reply, he, too, rose to his feet.

"I don't make speeches," he said huskily. "But I just have to tell you all that right here and now, I know that I'm luckier than any man on earth has the right to be." He looked at his aunt and uncle. "Kate and Bruno may not have brought me into this world—but they brought me *here*, and to this moment, with their love and care and friendship. And that's, surely, what it's all about, isn't it? True friends, and family."

There was a low murmur of assent.

Luciano was not quite finished. "There were five of us when we started out, in Lucchesia—I had two brothers and two sisters. Now I have one sister left, and I don't know where she is." There were tears in his eyes. "I miss them all, in spite of my happiness—but I feel Francesca's loss the most, because she is alive, somewhere—and I know, wherever she is, she misses me too."

The only sound on the terrace was of the Mediterranean waves splashing onto the rocks below. No one at the table moved, no one spoke.

Luciano smiled. "I didn't mean to make anyone sad, tonight of all nights." He looked at the faces of those gathered. "Don't be sad, for there's no need." He lifted his glass. "Because I'm going to find Francesca, through my new and valued friend, Zachary Holt." He paused. "Let's drink to him."

Celebrations over, Luciano set to work with an energy and self-discipline he had never known before. Abandoning the short stories that had been in the pipeline, encouraged by Bruno and Kate to cut himself off from them and his friends in order to complete the rewrite, he lived and breathed Zachary Holt until Christmas, when he was able to deliver the finished manuscript to a delighted François Poiret.

In March, the galley proofs arrived at Le Rocher. In his room, his heart beating furiously, Luciano stared at the unbound printed pages—at his own words, crisp and clean and black on the white sheets—and though the room was always bright, the proofs seemed to attract extra sunlight to his desk.

If he felt this way now, how would it be when he held the finished, bound book in his hands? Or was anticipation, itself, almost as fine?

Nothing could be as momentous as this.

Except, of course, the sight of *Zachary Holt* on the tables and shelves of the bookstores of Nice and Paris.

And, in time, of London and New York.

It was more than pure ambition—though that swelled inside him, intense and undeniable—that made him yearn longingly for publication in America. It was the possibility, the unshakable hope, that one day, in some bookstore or library, or perhaps even in someone's home, his sister's glance would fall idly upon a translated copy of *Zachary Holt,* and she would see his name and, hardly daring to believe, would pick it up and open it.

And that she would see, on the third page facing her, his dedication:

For Francesca, wherever you are, with love.

Chapter 21

Entering Florence again, driving herself in a small hired Fiat, was the strangest experience of Francesca's life. She felt like an entirely different person—she could not connect with the past. She was a grown woman now, with a highly developed eye for beauty, and the city she had loathed as a child, and in which she and her brothers had suffered such misery, now looked and felt utterly different. The sun shone vigorously, but without the ferocity she remembered; but then, in honesty, her memories had always focused either on the monstrously hot summers or the chilly, damp winters—if they'd experienced April days like this one, she had scarcely noted them.

Having disposed of her car and unpacked her case at her charming *pensione* near the Piazza della Signoria, Francesca ventured back out with her beloved Leica. She was weary from the journey, but as she had decided not to go to the palazzo until the following morning, this might be her only chance to look upon Florence as a newcomer. It was, by now, late afternoon, the sun was setting, and a gentle atmosphere pervaded the streets, for most working people had reached their homes, and those who still strolled around were there because they wished to be.

She dined that night at Antico Fattore on Via Lambertesca, sitting at a communal table and eating traditional *bistecca*, before falling onto her bed and sleeping dreamlessly until eight o'clock the next morning, when she was woken by the old, familiar din of Vespas, Lambrettas, noisy delivery trucks and even noisier human beings. She sat up, head thumping, realized that in Boston it was still the middle of the night, and groaned.

An hour later, after a breakfast she had been unable to eat, Francesca left the *pensione* and began to walk, on legs suddenly shaky, toward the Via dei Vecchietti.

Palazzo Speroza was as dismal as she had remembered it, its ancient rusticated stone walls as unwelcoming and daunting as they had been when she, Vittorio, and Luciano had first come upon it seventeen years before.

She approached the great door, rang the bell, and waited.

In one sense, Francesca had been relieved to learn that the Cesaretti family no longer lived in the palazzo, for at least it spared her the discomfort of having to set foot inside. But her visit had brought her no closer to Luciano, for the uniformed maid who had opened the door had no forwarding address for Bruno or her brother, and her employers, who might have been able to help, were, ironically, traveling in America.

Her next step, to look at the telephone directory in the main post office in Via Pietrapiana, gave her no more joy, for the only familiar entry under the name of Cesaretti was Fabio. Still hoping for a change of fortune, Francesca walked to the Ponte Vecchio, but her uncle's store had vanished, taken over by another firm of jewelers. Apart from calling on her detestable cousin, there was only one remaining chance.

Bruno's second store, on the Via della Vigna Nuova, was still intact, though modernized, and with a change of name that filled Francesca with foreboding. The old, gilded sign, bearing the proprietor's name, *B. Cesaretti*, had gone, and instead, inscribed in gold script on the wide, armored glass window, was simply *Fabio*. Stomach churning, but knowing she had no choice, Francesca pushed the buzzer, waited for the click, and opened the heavy door.

She recognized him immediately, for the arrogant, disdainful thrust of his features was almost unchanged despite the fourteen years that had passed since she had last seen him.

"*Signora?*"

The low, discreet voice startled her. A woman, brown-haired and expensively dressed, smiled politely. Francesca, unnerved, glanced toward her cousin, attending to a customer with all the smoothness and charm he had already been capable of in his teens.

"I wish to speak to Signor Cesaretti," Francesca told the assistant quietly, and saw Fabio's eyes swivel from the diamond-and-emerald necklace he was showing, to her face. She knew the precise instant of recognition, for the courtesy in his eyes turned to pure ice.

Francesca sat and waited, legs neatly crossed, hands calm in her lap, while the battle against intimidation and old fears raged inside her. Every ounce of pleasure from the previous evening had evaporated as soon as she looked at him; every trace of genuine self-confidence had shattered when he looked back at her. She was grateful that Robert had insisted on buying her the beautifully cut Cacharel suit she wore this morning, aware that any hint of bad taste in this enclave of elegance would have stacked the odds even more menacingly against her.

The necklace was lovingly fingered once more, the stones examined one last time, before it was removed, ceremoniously, for polishing and casing. A check was written, the customer obviously well known to Fabio, hands were shaken, smiles of admiration, deference, and delight were exchanged, and, finally, the door was opened and closed behind them.

And locked.

"*Vada mangiare,* Tina," Fabio directed the saleswoman. Without argument, she disappeared into the back of the store, leaving her employer and his visitor alone.

"My horoscope mentioned surprises," he said at last.

"I never thought of you as superstitious."

"Have you thought of me, then?"

"As seldom as possible."

Fabio drew up a second chair and sat down, facing her. "Why have you come?"

"To find my brother."

"He is not here."

"But you know where he is."

He said nothing, continuing to stare at her until, abruptly, he rose and went to a telephone behind the glass counter. "I must tell Letizia that you are here."

"There's no need to trouble her," Francesca said. "I've come only for Luciano's address."

"Leti would never forgive me if she missed you—she has waited a long time."

He dialed a number and spoke, quickly and so softly that Francesca could not hear his words, before returning to his chair. "She asks you to wait, if you please."

"I am rather pressed for time." Francesca's mouth was dry. "If you'd just give me my brother's address, or a number where I may reach him—"

"Letizia has the details."

They waited, with hardly another word, for thirty-five minutes. Francesca's heart beat faster, her palms grew moist, and she wished, more than anything, that she had accepted Robert's offer of company—she was a fool, an unutterably stubborn *fool*, to have turned him down. But it was too late. If she ever wanted to see Luciano again—and she knew that, in spite of everything, she was closer to that goal than she had been for fourteen years—she would just have to sit here and wait.

When Fabio finally opened the door, and the woman entered, Francesca thought for a moment that this must be another client, for she was slender, and exquisitely chic in silk, with an alluring, perfectly angled, wide-brimmed hat.

Letizia nodded. "Francesca."

Francesca rose, finding it hard not to stare. Where was the plump, overdressed, awkward teenager she remembered?

"How are you, Letizia?" She noticed a wedding band and a large marquise diamond, and was, for just a brief instant, glad for her. "It was good of you to come."

"Goodness had nothing to do with it." It was still there, glittering bitterly from within, the old harshness, the bitchiness, and, more chillingly, the old envy.

Letizia strolled, languidly, back to the door, and opened it. *"Avanti, signori, per favore."*

The two *carabinieri* gleamed in their black uniforms.

Francesca's eyes widened, and she took an involuntary step backward. Memories came hurtling into her mind—the *carabinieri* chasing them in Naples—Vittorio's terror—the moment when the lorry smashed into him—when the policemen had seized Luciano and Niccolo—

"You are Francesca Cesaretti?"

"I am."

"You will accompany us, please."

Francesca stared at Letizia and her brother. Fabio looked faintly embarrassed, as if he longed for the unpleasantness to be gone from his store.

Letizia was smiling.

It began with incredulity, continued with anger, mounted to rage, burst into frustration—and culminated in fear.

"Why are you holding me?" she asked over and over again at the police station on Borgo Ognissanti. "You cannot simply arrest an innocent person for no reason. *Are* you arresting me? On what charge?"

No one paid her any heed. All she was told was that she was required to assist the authorities in their inquiries into a crime.

"What crime?" she demanded, though she already knew.

"Un omicidio."

They transferred her to the Santa Verdiana, the women's jail near San Ambrogio market, and locked her up. She demanded her rights—explained that she was a resident of the United States of America, insisted that she be allowed to call her lawyer in Boston. They pointed out, tersely, that according to her passport, which had been handed in at her *pensione,* she was an Italian citizen and, consequently, subject to Italian law.

"Even so, I'm entitled to speak to my lawyer."

"Do you have a lawyer in Florence?"

"No, but—"

"One will be provided for you."

"Please—right away."

"As soon as possible." The man was bored with her.

"*Subito, per favore!*"

She was in a small cell with a bed, a handbasin, and a bucket. The small, barred window high above her was the only ventilation, and as the day wore on and afternoon stretched into evening, Francesca watched the sunlight fading and refused to allow herself to consider the moment when the single naked overhead bulb would be extinguished.

If she thought about the dark, she would remember her crawl space on the *Vulcania,* would remember the fleas and the stench and the grief and fear—

And the cellar in the palazzo, and the cockroaches and the rat and—

She began to yell for someone to come. She shouted until her throat was sore. She demanded, she threatened, she pleaded, but the only person who came brought her a supper she could not eat. She beseeched them to find her brother or her uncle, or to contact the American consulate. She pounded on the door, and was ordered to stop. Drained and exhausted, she obeyed.

Then the lights went out.

The *avvocato* came before breakfast.

"What took you so *long?*" Francesca's eyes were raw from weeping. "I've been here nearly twenty-four hours!"

"How can I help you?"

"By telephoning my lawyer in Boston. His name is Robert Stern, and his number is—" She stared at the man, who seemed hardly to be listening. "Please, write it down."

"It's the middle of the night in Boston, *signorina*."

"This is his home number—he won't mind—please!"

He took down the number. "It is expensive to telephone America, *signorina*."

"I'll pay, for God's sake." She shook her head. "Never mind—say it's from me and call him collect."

"Is this all you want of me?" the *avvocato* inquired.

"No, it isn't!"

"What else?"

"Get me *out* of here!"

She was questioned, at last. Asked about the night of their flight from the palazzo, she told the truth, so far as she knew it; that Livia Cesaretti had tried to lock Vittorio in the cellar where she, a few months earlier, had been cruelly shut in, and that Vittorio, struggling to get away, had pushed his aunt.

"Down the cellar steps?"

"He just pushed her to get away from her—he didn't want her to fall down the steps."

"And you were not present?"

Francesca shook her head. It all seemed so unreal, so pointless. "I was packing the food we had taken—"

"Stolen."

She nodded.

"Please answer."

"Yes," she said, wearily. "Stolen." She remembered. "A slab of cheese, three loaves, some salami—and *panforte*." She paused. "That lasted a long time."

"Why did Signora Cesaretti wish to lock your brother into the cellar?"

"Because she caught him in her son's bedroom."

"What was he doing there?"

She felt numb. "He was—borrowing money."

"Stealing."

Her eyes burned. "Borrowing. He would have sent it back."

"And you did not know, when you left the palazzo, that your aunt was dead?"

Francesca shook her head. "None of us knew. Not until the following spring."

"How did you discover it?"

"A friend told us."

"Niccolo Dante?"

She gazed straight ahead, at the wall. "His brother."

She asked, when they were finished, if she might leave. They replied, cordially, that certain facts required checking and, therefore, she must stay a few hours longer.

Francesca no longer cared.

Robert arrived next morning. He looked, as he always did in his State Street office, fresh-shaven and immaculate. Almost forty-eight hours had elapsed since Francesca had been arrested.

"Robert—"

She had dreamed of this moment, had been sure she would fly into his arms and weep with relief and joy, yet now she could hardly speak, felt too drained even to move from the hard bed where she sat.

He sat down beside her, and put one arm about her shoulders. "Let's get you out of here," he said gently.

"I can't go."

"Sure you can."

She shook her head. "Letizia."

"She's had her jollies," Robert said wryly. "It's over."

Francesca's mouth trembled. "Truly?"

"Would you prefer to stay?" He took her hand. "The bed's awfully narrow."

"I must look terrible."

"Like hell."

✳

Having retrieved her belongings from the *pensione*, Robert took her to the Villa Medici in Via Il Prato near the Cascine park. The facade was that of an eighteenth-century villa, but the hotel was modern, built in the last decade.

"This place didn't exist when you lived here," Robert said as he steered her to her *appartamento.* "It's a little masculine, with all this dark wood, but it's safe and clean—great bathrooms." He opened her door. "You can soak in bubbles for hours, and sleep and order from room service."

Francesca walked through the doorway, then turned around. "Aren't you coming in?"

"I thought you might need your own room. I'm just along the hall." He showed her his suite number. "You only have to pick up the phone, and I'll be here." He paused. "Was I wrong? Would you prefer me to stay?"

Francesca looked at him, knowing she would never again meet a man like Robert Stern—solid, straight, dependable and willing to do anything for her. And yet every bone in her body ached, and she knew he was right, that she did need to be alone for a while.

"So long as I know you're close by," she said softly.

"You bet."

✳

Her first desire was to crumple up the Cacharel suit into the wastebasket, but a grain of common sense lingered, and she called the valet service instead. After that, following Robert's advice, she took a hot, cleansing shower, scrubbing every available millimeter of herself, before lying back in a more therapeutic, foam-filled bath. Externally purified and a little more relaxed, she realized, for the first time, that she was ravenous.

After ordering from room service, she called Robert.

"Are you okay?" He sounded anxious.

"Getting there. I ordered lunch. I must be more American than I thought—I have a huge craving for prime rib."

"Can they do it?"

"It's on its way." She paused. "Robert, I'd ask you to join me, but I'm not really fit for company."

His hesitation was infinitesimal. "I understand."

"Do you?"

"I can't deny I want to be with you," he said ruefully, "but after what you've been through, you need to let yourself off the hook for a while. If you need peace and quiet, you've got it."

"Robert?"

"What?"

"Thank you."

"You're welcome."

She'd been about to say that she loved him, but she'd stopped herself in time. She *did* love him, of course—how could she not, after all he'd done for her? But she didn't *love* him, and Robert Stern was one man who deserved honesty.

By the time lunch arrived, she was trembling with hunger and, left alone, she devoured everything on her exquisitely laid table, eating like a small, voracious animal before brushing her teeth, making sure that the *Non Disturbare* sign was outside the door, drawing the bedroom curtains against the afternoon sunlight and crawling into the beautiful, clean, soft bed.

She slept for eight hours, and when she awoke, briefly, it was very dark, and she heard voices outside her door, and thought vaguely, for a moment, that one of the voices was Robert's—but then her eyes closed again, and she drifted back down into unconsciousness.

She waited until eight-thirty in the morning to telephone Robert's suite.

"Hallelujah," he said. "I thought you'd never wake up."

"I've been up for over an hour," Francesca said airily. "I ordered breakfast, and had another shower, and I feel completely restored."

"That's good." Robert paused. "Are you up for visitors?"

"Only the loving kind," she said fervently.

"That's the only kind you're getting."

✷

The first buzz at the door was from a bellboy, bringing in a vase of long-stemmed red roses.

She called him again. "They're glorious, thank you. When are you coming?"

"Christ, you're impatient."

"Get *down* here."

"Right away."

This time, he got the hug he deserved.

"You smell wonderful," he murmured, nuzzling her ear for a moment, before shutting the door and drawing her into the sitting room. "Sit down."

They sat, close together, on the sofa, and Robert watched her, thinking that she had never looked more stunningly lovely than now, her freshly shampooed hair like ebony against her white terry cloth robe.

"How do you feel?"

"Reborn."

Robert took her hand. "I found your brother's address."

"You did!" Francesca sat bolt upright. "Where *is* he?"

"He's been living in France since 1956. It seems your uncle remarried—an American divorcée—and they moved, with Luciano, to a villa in the south—"

"*Where?*" Francesca was back on her feet.

"A place called Eze—it's beautiful. Will you sit down?"

"Of course I can't sit down!" Her eyes were ablaze with excitement. "Where's the number? We can call him!"

"I already did—he isn't there."

"Where is he?"

"On a trip with your uncle."

Francesca moaned with disappointment and sank back onto the sofa. "For how long?"

"That depends."

"On what?"

Robert didn't answer. Instead, he rose from the armchair and walked across the sitting room to the far wall.

"On what, Robert?" Francesca repeated. "Is it a business trip?"

Robert rapped on the wall.

"What are you doing?" Francesca was frustrated. "Robert, please tell me what you know. How *is* he? What is he doing? Is he a student?" She stood up again. "*Tell* me!"

There was a door in the wall that Francesca had not noticed before, a discreet, communicating door, and Robert, inexplicably, had a key and was unlocking it.

"Robert, what are you *doing*?"

And then she knew, even before she heard the answering click from the other side—before the handle moved, and the door opened—

And she saw the young man.

The joy was almost unbearable.

Francesca shut her eyes, then, instantly, tore them open again, staring at him.

"Luciano?" Her voice was a whisper. She did not move.

"*Sì.*" He, too, was staring. His eyes were very blue, and swimming with unshed tears.

Still, Francesca could not move.

Luciano smiled, his mouth trembling. "You look the same."

She swallowed. "You don't."

They began to walk, toward each other, and then they were just a foot apart—and as they embraced, their tears erupted in great sobs of happiness, and they held on tightly, brother and sister, unable to speak—

Knowing that he did not belong there, Robert left the room, very quietly.

✳

They were strangers, and yet they were not.

The days that followed were almost dreamlike for both of them—and for Bruno, who, summoned by Robert, had flown to Florence with Luciano to ensure Francesca's swift release, and to bring down the final curtain on the old tragedy that Letizia had sought to prolong.

It was a time of reintroduction, most dramatically, perhaps, for Francesca, since even as a twelve-year-old, she had been, in many ways, the "grown-up" of the family, whereas Luciano had been the most undeveloped, the child led by his older brother and sister.

And now he was a man, handsome and confident.

"Tell me!" was Francesca's most frequent demand. She felt robbed, constantly aware that they had been cheated out of fourteen years' shared experiences; like a starving person, she devoured every morsel of Luciano's information as greedily as she had her first meal after her release. Kate, she agreed, sounded wonderful—the antithesis of Aunt Livia, just as Le Rocher sounded like the perfect contrast to Palazzo Speroza.

The news of his success as a novelist brought her the most joy. Again and again, she gazed at the bound galley proofs of *Zachary Holt,* frustrated by her inability to read much of the French version, but marveling at her baby brother's talent and skill, and deeply moved by the dedication that Luciano had hoped would reunite them.

"But it won't be released in America for six months," she said. "Imagine if I had never seen it—never picked it up—"

"Don't," Luciano said quickly for, like Francesca, their being together still seemed miraculous and terrifyingly fragile. Her many letters, they had learned, through Robert's persistence, had been intercepted by Letizia, and never forwarded to Luciano. It seemed to them an act of savage cruelty—and yet, if they were honest, Letizia and Fabio had suffered, too, had lost the mother they had undoubtedly loved.

"Tell me again about the voyage—about the *Vulcania.*" Luciano was endlessly fascinated by all Francesca's stories; the more she told him of the horrors of her enforced isolation, and of her terrors, and of the crawl space, and of the Lombardis and her first, terrible days in Boston, the more riveted he became, for while he understood how she must have suffered, her tales were the stuff of adventure novels, and fiction was what, more and more, ruled his life.

"And the filmmakers, and Johnny Chase," he nudged her, wide-eyed, reminding her of the child she had adored.

"I've told you," Francesca said again. "Johnny rescued me—gave me a fresh start—"

"Like Emilio and Niccolo," Luciano interrupted.

"In many ways, yes."

"And your career!" He was enchanted by the way Francesca seldom moved without her Leica, the way she constantly focused her lens upon him, capturing precious moments, just as he nagged at her for stories, both of them on edge, almost feverish, as if they were afraid that at any moment they might be forced apart again.

It was Bruno who calmed them down, who realized that the atmosphere of the hotel was too unreal, too temporary for their emotional needs.

"Come back to Le Rocher," he urged. "Kate was going to fly over, but it would be so much more sensible for us all to go home . . ." He hesitated, aware that Francesca's home was now thousands of miles away. "For as long as you want, *cara*," he told her gently, before turning to Robert, who for days had stood undemandingly on the sidelines, simply happy for Francesca. "And you, too, must come to stay with us—there's plenty of room, and my wife would love to meet you."

In the end, Robert elected to fly back to Boston alone, though he accompanied the Cesarettis when they drove, somberly, to Pisa, so that Francesca could see where Vittorio had been laid to rest, and put flowers on his grave.

"He would be happy for us," Luciano said softly. "And proud, I think."

They stood silently for a while, remembering, allowing their minds to float freely in the tranquil spring air.

"Time plays strange tricks on us," Francesca murmured. "I thought this the most terrible, and bleakest place on earth when we came for Giulietta's memorial service—yet now it feels quite serene, and—" She broke off, unable to voice what she felt.

"It's more alive than I remember it," Luciano said. "The flowers, the cypress trees—so many birds singing." He shrugged. "It's not such a bad place to be."

Giulietta's headstone still tore at them, disturbed them more deeply than Vittorio's, perhaps because of the lonely nature of her death.

"When she died, I didn't understand what loneliness meant," Francesca said. "We always had each other, until Naples." She looked at Luciano. "I wish they were all together—Mamma and Papa, and Giacomo too. It's so sad this way. And wrong."

"But unalterable, no matter what we feel."

They looked back to the path, and saw Bruno and Robert, standing quietly and companionably, waiting.

"Why isn't Robert coming to France?" Luciano asked softly. "We'd love to have him there."

"He thinks we should have some time alone."

"He's a remarkable man."

Francesca nodded. "He's made all this possible."

"He loves you."

"I know."

"And you?"

She smiled. "I think we'll have plenty of time to talk when we get to Le Rocher."

They turned back to the graves.

"I wonder when we'll be here again," Francesca mused. "I had decided, after Robert had me released, that I would never set foot in Florence again as long as I lived—that it was poison for me."

"This isn't Florence," Luciano said. "It isn't even Pisa. It's something entirely separate."

"Yes," she agreed. "It is."

✴

They shared one glorious month together on the Côte d'Azur. Francesca realized that she could not have truly understood the man that Luciano had become if she had not seen Le Rocher, nor met Kate, and experienced the warmth and strength that the vivacious, petite American woman had brought to this new branch of the Cesaretti family.

Luciano, inevitably, had hoped that Francesca would come to live with them in France, but she had known, almost straightaway, that she would refuse. It had given her unimaginable joy and inner peace to find her brother and to taste his near-idyllic existence—but she realized, now, how much she owed to America. She would always, of course, be essentially a European, she tried to explain, but she had an adopted country and family, too, in the Chases.

"And there's my studio—I can hardly wait to get that off the ground —you'll love it when you see it," she told Luciano, glowing with anticipation. "And as perfect as Le Rocher and this coast is for you, my life is for me."

They made plans, wrote dates into their diaries—Luciano would come to America for a New England Thanksgiving; Francesca would return to Eze for Christmas; Luciano would have to be in New York when the time came to publish *Zachary Holt* in America. They needed the tangibility of arrangements so that they would both have something to hold on to after they had parted again, so that their reunion would not seem like some abstract impossibility.

"Thank God for my camera," Francesca said at Nice airport, as the family sat, quietly, around a Formica table, having one last calvados together before her flight. She looked at Bruno's kind, round face, the top of his head sunburned in spite of his wife's fond nagging to wear a hat, and at Kate, so easygoing and wise, and so right for Bruno—and at Luciano, who reminded her again, vividly, of the boy she remembered, for she knew from his overbright eyes that he was close to tears.

"I'll send you the best photographs," she said softly, and squeezed his hand.

Outside passport control, having said her farewells to Bruno and Kate, Francesca and Luciano stared at each other.

"I used to get angry with myself," he said, "because I knew I had so much, and yet though I was content, I could never feel completely happy —for how *could* I be, when I didn't even know where you were?"

"You'll always know from now on," Francesca promised him, her own tears now spilling unchecked onto her cheeks. "We'll speak every week—more often if we need to. And we'll share everything, good and bad, and—" She broke off, her voice cracking, unable to continue.

Luciano, too, could not speak, so they embraced again, stood close and tight and warm, and then Francesca drew away, and blew a kiss to her uncle and Kate.

"I'll call you when I arrive," she whispered.

"Whatever the time."

She turned away.

Luciano sat, late that night, in his bedroom at Le Rocher, thinking of the importance of photographs to his sister, and looking at the framed photographs that stood about the room, to which he'd added a poor Polaroid snap of Francesca in Antibes, and which he would exchange for one of the better shots Bruno had taken of them together, with her camera.

The past had, unconsciously perhaps, been separated from the present. On the left, on a shelf, stood two pictures; one, the photograph of their mother and father carried by Vittorio till his death, and the other of Vittorio, taken by Uncle Bruno one Christmas at the palazzo. On the dresser, to the right, were pictures of himself, Bruno and Kate, and now, of Francesca.

The dead divided from the living. And yet there were no pictures of either Giacomo or Giulietta. His twin, and he could hardly remember her, except for a vague remembrance of golden hair and clear blue eyes—

The telephone jangled, startling in the quiet house. *Francesca,* he thought, and smiled.

And returned to the living.

Chapter 22

There's no room for fiction in journalism.

That golden rule, one of many handed down to Juliet during her first months of apprenticeship in the real world of newspapers, was the one she had begun to lament most, however much she respected it.

Being a trainee reporter on a provincial paper, when one aspired to being a prizewinning feature writer, was unbearably frustrating. Juliet was well aware that she was retreading a path well worn by thousands of journalists before her, but she couldn't help dreaming, like most of the others, of the hot scoop that would thrust her into the spotlight.

How long could she wait? How long *should* she wait? If she didn't land a strong, original story soon, and land it *first*, she might just have to start thinking about creating one, whatever the consequences.

After all, she owed it to herself to be the best. She owed it to Elizabeth.

After graduating from Sussex, she had landed an apprenticeship with the Bournemouth *Daily Record*. It had seemed perfect; she'd grown accustomed to the south coast and understood what made an English seaside town tick, and they were willing to train her. A year or so, Juliet smiled to herself, and she'd be where she belonged—in London, in Fleet Street.

It was not to prove so simple. If Brighton had been a mild-mannered town, it had been a positive hotbed of drama and scandal compared to Bournemouth, where, Juliet rapidly came to believe, nothing worth reporting ever happened. Its residents lived happily and peaceably, its tourists enjoyed themselves in a stylish, orderly way, and, in any event, if something momentous did happen, Juliet was not trusted with it. It was her fate to be sent to flower shows and local institutes, to attend weddings, funerals, and christenings, and to report from the local magistrate's court on unpaid parking fines, or unlit bicycles.

In the spring of 1969, the *Daily Record* sent Juliet on an eight-week journalism course at Highbury College in Portsmouth. *This,* she thought, would make the difference—the more she learned, the more qualified she became, the greater would be her share of the reporting pie. Returning to Bournemouth, she wondered why she'd bothered. Allowed, on one occasion, to report on the tragic drowning of a toddler, every ounce of personal thought and comment she'd painstakingly threaded through the bare facts was deleted by the news editor.

"It's *ruined,*" she wailed to a colleague. "There were lessons to be learned, yet I was completely sympathetic. He's turned it back into an ordinary story. It's so *stark*!"

"That's what it's meant to be," the colleague said. "It's not a feature, Juliet—it's news. The facts say it all. The boy's parents are under sedation—their child is dead and buried at two years old. What more is there to say?"

Juliet tried harder to fit in, to suppress what she began to see might seem like arrogance to her associates. This was just the beginning of her career, after all—she must not expect too much too soon. But she was continually making mistakes. All through her first full year at the *Record,* and on into her second job at the *Edinburgh Star,* Juliet seemed to come up against all the Golden Rules.

"You exaggerate, you gild, you don't get *names*"— one of the Rules was that names, especially in a local publication, sold papers—"your interview technique stinks, and you've missed three bloody deadlines!"

Juliet stared miserably at Archie McCullough, her tall, florid editor, and waited for the ax to fall. How could she go home to Dorking if she was sacked? How could she face her mother?

Not only was she not fired, but McCullough took her out to lunch, to try to boost her morale and get her back on track.

"You have to learn to make people feel comfortable around you," he told her over coffee and cognac at the George Hotel. "If they get the impression, however mistakenly, that you feel superior in some way, they'll clam up, and you'll never get a decent quote, much less a good interview." McCullough finished his cognac and ordered another for them both. "What newspapers are you reading, Juliet?"

Her cheeks were hot. She felt like a schoolgirl again, embarrassed and humiliated. "I read *The Scotsman*—and *The Times*—"

"While you're up here, you should read every Scottish publication— the *Edinburgh Evening News,* of course—and make sure you read John Gibson—there's not much he can't teach you about feature writing. That's what you aspire to, isn't it, lassie?"

She nodded.

"How much do you want it?"

"More than anything in the world."

"How would you feel if you lost your job?"

Juliet's apprehensive eyes darted to meet his. "I'd feel shattered."

"And what would you do?" His eyes were keen, despite the red wine and cognac. "Give up?"

Juliet stared at him. "I gave up once," she said quietly, "when I was a child. I'll never give up anything important again—not without a fight."

She thought Edinburgh the most handsome and noble city she'd ever seen, but she missed Elizabeth more than ever, and she had never felt so *cold.* Her flat had no central heating, and the electric fan heaters that she had installed at strategic points could not seem to remove the underlying damp chill, with the result that Juliet had caught one cold after another since her arrival, and was consequently less able than she might otherwise have been to cope with the demands of her job.

On an icy March morning that year, 1970, Walter Schuster, Elizabeth's old friend and lawyer, telephoned Juliet.

"Your mother's in the London Clinic."

"Oh, my God."

"Don't panic, honey," Walter said, in his gentle Canadian voice. "She's just there for some tests and a bit of a rest."

"Tests for what? Why didn't she tell me?"

"She's been under par for a few weeks—nothing specific, just flu-type symptoms—"

"She didn't say *anything*!" Juliet couldn't believe her ears. "We speak twice a week—sometimes more—and she's said nothing."

"You know Elizabeth—she didn't want to worry you."

"She's in hospital, and she doesn't want me to *worry*—" Juliet's voice lifted hysterically. "I'm coming down tomorrow."

"It'll upset her."

"I'm coming anyway."

Walter paused, briefly. "I think you should."

If she had been alarmed already, now she was terrified.

"Acute leukemia," she said numbly, when she called Archie McCullough from London a week later. "She's having chemotherapy."

"You'll be needing a job down there then." The editor didn't wait for her response. "I may be able to help you there—a word or two in someone's ear."

"Thank you, Archie." She knew she ought to say more, to sound more grateful, but since she had learned of her mother's illness, everything else had ceased to matter. She was back in London, away from the chill northern climate, but now the ice was in her bones, and in her heart.

✶

Archie was as good as his word. Within a fortnight, Juliet had the promise of a job at the *Daily Post,* starting in three weeks time.

"They're going to be running a weekly feature article called 'The *Post* Explains,' " Juliet told Elizabeth, weak from her treatment, but eager nevertheless to hear the news. "It sounds a bit dry—mostly research, really—but at least I'm in."

It was dreary work much of the time. The *Post* wanted her to explain to their readers the ins and outs of anything from philately to greyhound racing, to transplant surgery and the life of a test pilot, back down to life insurance and heraldry. A great deal of Juliet's existence was spent at library tables, up to her elbows in textbooks—but at least, she reminded herself, she was in Fleet Street.

She would have been happy. But her mother was dying.

By early summer, Elizabeth was in remission, and Juliet was almost euphoric, for the improvement in her mother's health had coincided with the career boost she had longed for—a job on the paper's diary page. But within two months her spirits had crashed again. She was little more than a dogsbody, a diary drudge, most of her life spent on the phone, checking facts and tip-offs, occasionally permitted to stand around at Heathrow Airport to see if anyone important was coming in to or going out of the country.

"I was doing more worthwhile stuff than this when I was at Sussex," she complained to Hilda Loom at Kaikoura in the first week of September. "I'm just an odd-job woman."

"A bit like me." Hilda smiled. "Chief cook and bottle washer." Her smile faded. "We all want to do more than we can, dear. Life can be very frustrating."

They both knew what she meant. Elizabeth was ill again, and the fact that she had not been hospitalized—except for two days to receive a blood transfusion—only filled them with even greater foreboding.

It had also increased Juliet's sense of desperation. Her mother—the most precious person in her life—was going to die, and suddenly her will to succeed began to take on almost obsessive proportions. She *had* to achieve one real coup while she still had Elizabeth.

She began to drive herself day and night. So long as she fulfilled the demands of her job on the diary, no one could take her to task for fighting to improve her position. She tried every approach she could think of: doggedness, patience, and tenaciousness. She hounded members of the public in search of a story, hung around the law courts, police stations, and fire departments; she eavesdropped on colleagues' conversations in the hope of stealing a tip-off; she tried to bribe staff at the plushest London hotels—*anything* to find an exclusive story. She found nothing.

In early October, Elizabeth returned to the London Clinic, and Juliet plummeted into new depression. Fear gnawed away at her, fear of losing Elizabeth—of failing Elizabeth. She had almost no self-confidence left—she was close to giving up, when, two days later, she came closer than she'd ever been to a genuine, bona fide exclusive—her very own hot scoop for the diary.

She had been dispatched, together with a staff photographer, to cover the arrival at Heathrow Airport of an American film actress. Since every other paper knew her time of arrival, there was no hope of an exclusive for the *Post.*

It was a quirk of fate that made Juliet turn her head momentarily away from the gathering crowd of journalists, so that she caught a glimpse of Brian Brayfield, the Member of Parliament for Claybury North, awkwardly planting a swift kiss on the cheek of a young dark-haired woman.

Juliet watched avidly. Whoever she was, the brunette was not Brayfield's wife, for everyone who read the tabloid press or women's magazines knew that Margaret Brayfield was a tall, thin-faced blonde.

Brian Brayfield, everyone agreed, was a backbencher with a future. Before turning to politics, he had been a popular actor in a long-running television drama serial, and when he'd announced his plans to quit the acting profession and stand for election, his sex appeal had played an undeniable role in his success. Only a year ago, he had married into the aristocracy with great ballyhoo. Watching Brayfield now, engaged in earnest conversation with the brunette, and clearly anxious to escape from the public arena, Juliet was aware, for the first time in her career, of what a real, full-blooded hunch felt like.

"Here she is!"

Reporters and photographers surged toward the actress. A hundred yards to Juliet's right, Brian Brayfield picked up his companion's suitcase.

Now or never, she thought. This was her story—she felt it in her bones. This was *it.*

Without a backward glance to the *Post* photographer, Juliet followed Brayfield out of the terminal building to the taxi rank, hailed the next one in line, and told her driver to follow the M.P.'s cab.

In the backseat, her mind worked swiftly. If this was an innocent encounter, Brayfield would go either east to Westminster, west to his house near Maidenhead, or north to his constituency. Not knowing exactly what she hoped for, she crossed her fingers.

At Chiswick roundabout, Brayfield's taxi turned south.

"How far are we going, miss?" her driver asked as they drove past Richmond. "I mean, is this kosher?"

"Strictly," Juliet assured him, and pushed a ten-pound note through the partition window.

He began whistling.

"They're stopping," the driver told Juliet, just off the main road between Cheam and Epsom. "What do you want me to do?"

"Wait a moment, please."

It was a clinic, its sign neat and discreet. Juliet watched Brian Brayfield help the brunette out of their taxi, pay the driver, pick up the suitcase again, and walk through the front door of the large Georgian house.

"Now what?"

There was a small hotel on the opposite side of the A24.
"I'll get out," she said.

The hunch was paying off, she was sure of it. After ten minutes on
the telephone, she'd ascertained that the clinic specialized in private
abortions.

She kept watch from a bay window in the hotel lounge. The bored
receptionist had responded warmly to Juliet's generous tip, had dispatched a porter to Epsom to buy her a camera, zoom lens, and two rolls
of film, and had supplied her with coffee and sandwiches. There was no
way of telling whether the brunette would stay overnight, or if she was a
day patient—or whether Brayfield would stay with her, or leave.

Juliet waited for six hours. Brayfield and the woman emerged just
after five o'clock. The brunette looked ashen, and clung to the Member
of Parliament's arm as if she might faint.

From the hotel parking lot, Juliet took a dozen photographs,
watched them drive away in a dark blue saloon car, then crossed the A24
to go into the clinic.

She knew, as she handed her story over to the news editor, that she'd
made a terrible mistake. The clinic had already called the paper to report
her attempt at bribery.

"Are you out of your mind, or just bloody stupid?" the editor wanted
to know, after he'd read her pages. "We were told, when the paper took
you on, that you were *trained*!" He ripped the paper to shreds and threw
them into his wastebasket. "You didn't seriously believe we'd print this,
did you?"

"The photographs," Juliet faltered. "They're still being developed."

"I don't care if they're being *framed*! You're not paid to take pictures
—ever heard of unions?" The editor tore at his hair. "The thing that
gets me is that you really had a scoop—you had a fabulous, dirty story,
and you blew it for the paper."

Juliet stared at him, white-faced.

"You know bloody well we never print anything we can't substantiate." His enraged, frustrated eyes flayed her. "Why did you *do* it?"

She took a long, shaky breath. "I needed a story—my own story," she said at last.

"You had a story. You were sent to the airport, to report on the arrival of a big star. You were given a job, and you not only walked out on it, but you behaved in an irresponsible, *lunatic* manner which could have landed your paper with a massive lawsuit!"

"I was trying to use my own initiative—" Juliet's voice was small. "There wasn't time—"

For the last time, the news editor rounded on her. "I'm not sure, at this moment, young lady, whether you're a nutcase, or whether you're just stupid. Either way, the *Daily Post* doesn't want you. We just can't afford you."

She lay on her bed in Elizabeth's flat that night, thinking about her mother, slowly dying. She thought about her own failure, and about her sacking—her self-respect squandered together with her last opportunity to give Elizabeth some final pleasure.

She thought about Brian Brayfield, and the sad, dark-haired woman, and about the fetus, massacred. And she thought again about what the politician had cost her—and about how much she hated him.

And then, at last, she wept, turning her face into the pillow, even though there was no one to hear her. And gradually, the weeping grew wilder, and her grief was consumed by her rage, and she beat the pillow with her fists, and tore at the linen with her fingernails, and imagined that it was Brian Brayfield's face at which she tore—

Finally, just before dawn, she slept.

She knew, as she drank her first cup of coffee a few hours later, what she was going to do. Elizabeth was still alive, and that, after all, was all that mattered—that, and earning her pride.

"It's up to you to make things happen."

Those words, from the past, had come to her as she had woken. They had been spoken by one of her physiotherapists, years before, when she had been at a particularly low ebb.

The words reverberated in her mind. That was how she had got her story about Ray Donnelly at Sussex—she'd *made* the news happen. Perhaps that was the only way she could ever succeed.

Brian Brayfield had cost her her job and her reputation, and somehow, inadvertently, he was going to pay his debt to her. She was going to make news happen again, and when it did, she would be the only journalist on the spot to report it.

It was all a question of working it out—of creating a plot, almost as if it were fiction. It was immoral, she was aware, and unethical.

But it was for Elizabeth.

For more than a week, Juliet led a double life. Half her time was spent with her mother at the clinic—the other half, spying on Brian Brayfield.

She tailed him—from his Westminster flat to the House of Commons, from there to lunches at his club or at Simpsons-in-the-Strand, to dinners at the Savoy or Rules, or at A l'Ecu de France. On the two consecutive Friday evenings that Juliet watched and followed him, he dined in London before driving, in his burgundy-red Jaguar, toward his Claybury constituency on the first Friday, and toward his house near Marlow on the second. She saw Margaret, his wife, on his arm, but she never saw the brunette—discarded, she supposed, along with the tiny human millstone, somewhere near Epsom. She observed that Brayfield was, on the whole, a predictable man, keeping consistent hours, favoring a limited but choice selection of restaurants, nightclubs, and wine bars, attending to business, eating and drinking heartily, enjoying—with the actor's capacity for pleasure that Juliet guessed he must still possess—a full and charmed life.

He never put a foot wrong, so far as Juliet could tell. He led, now that the abortion clinic was an awkward memory, an overindulgent but otherwise apparently blameless life.

She might almost have overlooked her one remaining chance, and given up, had she not, by chance, seen a young woman in the King's Road being stopped by the police, presumably for speeding.

Juliet's mind went into overdrive.

It had been quite a gamble trying to predict what Brian Brayfield's appetite would dictate on the third Friday evening, so Juliet had made reservations at six restaurants to be sure of finding a table in the place of his choice.

It was a little after eight o'clock when she parked her rented Mini in Maiden Lane twenty yards or so behind the red Jaguar—he had left his car on a yellow line, while she had slipped neatly into a meter bay just vacated—and followed the politician into Rules.

The next two hours dragged by painfully, as Juliet picked at her grilled sole and sipped mineral water, while Brayfield and his male dinner companion, after two gin and tonics, ate their way through soup and roast beef, accompanied by a bottle of claret.

Juliet settled her bill and began to make her way out of the restaurant, pausing, out of sight of Brayfield's table, to speak to the maître d'hotel. In a moment or two, it was agreed, the Dom Pérignon paid for by Juliet would be presented, as an anonymous gift, to the M.P. and his guest. *A little insurance,* Juliet thought, with satisfaction.

Back behind the wheel of the Mini, she continued to wait.

When Brayfield emerged from Rules, said farewell to his companion, and strode toward the Jaguar, it was with the placid, slightly overconfident air of a man who had dined and, without doubt, more than slaked his thirst.

✳

He was heading, it was clear, toward Marlow. As Juliet tailed the more powerful car along Western Avenue, her foot was jammed down hard on the gas pedal, and all her nerve ends were tingling with anticipation.

The moment came at Hanger Lane.

As the traffic slowed, Juliet easily outmaneuvered the Jaguar, changing lanes twice and slipping neatly in front of Brayfield. She looked around—this was always a busy junction, a good spot for maximum attention.

The traffic ahead of her began to move. Juliet waited an instant, accelerated away, checked in the mirror to make sure he was following her—and slammed on her brakes. Brayfield's car struck the Mini hard, and a third car smashed into the rear of the Jaguar.

"Are you hurt?" Brian Brayfield, white-faced, stooped to look through her window, while Juliet, exhilarated, sat still, feigning shock.

"What the hell *happened*?" The third driver strode toward them.

Slowly, deliberately, Juliet wound down her window.

"Why in God's name did you stop?" Brayfield demanded.

"Why were you so close?" she countered. "And you were obviously going much too fast." She opened her door, and got out to peer at the damage, before turning back to face the irate-looking M.P. "You've been drinking," she said loudly.

"Rubbish." Brayfield's cheeks turned from white to red. "Don't try and shift the blame, young lady—you caused this fiasco, and you know it."

"He's drunk." Juliet spoke to the other man. "I think we should get the police."

Brayfield, his Jaguar trapped between the other cars, could not escape, for the second driver was growing more self-righteous by the minute.

When the police arrived, Juliet told them calmly that a cat had run in front of her, causing her to brake, and that the driver behind her had clearly been in no fit state to stop in time.

The Breathalyzer was produced. Juliet reached into the crumpled Mini for her camera, and took a series of pictures as the politician, appalled, blew into the small balloon.

"What the hell is she *doing*?" he snarled, as soon as he could speak. Juliet looked at him, unsmiling. "They're for my mother," she said.

It took four telephone calls for Juliet to sell her "exclusive." The article seemed almost to write itself, it came so easily. When she had delivered it, with the roll of film, to the offices of the Sunday newspaper, she went to the London Clinic. They had given Elizabeth another transfusion, and she was very tired.

"You look exhausted, darling," Elizabeth murmured, taking in the shadows beneath her daughter's eyes. "You shouldn't work so hard."

Juliet kissed her, and stroked her hair. "It's been worth it, Mother," she said softly. "With a bit of luck, I should have something special to show you tomorrow."

She slept peacefully that night for the first time in weeks, having set her alarm clock so that she could be at the newsagent's in Marylebone Lane in plenty of time to buy at least a dozen copies of the paper.

The piece looked superb. Juliet's byline was clear and proud, the photograph chosen by the editor capturing Brayfield's shame and anger, the article itself cut, but her words still incisive yet analytical, first reporting the damning facts, then, briefly, pointing out the pressures that drove a man as successful and privileged as Brian Brayfield to break the law and risk his whole future.

No one but she, and the editor at the *Post*, would read the malice hidden between the lines, but Juliet felt no guilt. It was her very first national headline—and her very special gift for Elizabeth.

She arrived at the London Clinic clutching a sheaf of newspapers and a bunch of sweet peas, her mother's favorite flowers.

She was halted, just after emerging from the lift, by the floor sister, her face compassionate.

"I'm so sorry," she said.

Elizabeth had died, suddenly but peacefully, an hour earlier. They had been trying, in vain, to telephone Juliet.

She had known it would happen, but she knew now that she had never truly believed it.

Most mourners grieved partly because the prospect of life without their loved one was unimaginable. Juliet, however, still remembered what her life had been before Elizabeth. She had known pain, and isolation, and fear—but for seventeen years, her mother had almost persuaded her that the bad times were gone forever.

Juliet knew now that they had not gone.

They had been there, all the time, waiting for her.

Chapter 23

On a hot, humid afternoon in August the following year, 1971, a tall, dark-haired man was browsing through the Newbury Street gallery, in Boston, where Johnny Chase's latest one-man exhibit was on show, when he came upon one of Johnny's old studies of Francesca.

For a long time, the man stared at the photograph, as if mesmerized, until the manager of the gallery, who generally allowed visitors to gaze undisturbed for as long as they wished, felt compelled to ask if help was needed.

The stranger stirred, as if from a dream. "I'm sorry." He sounded vague, distant.

"It's I who should apologize, sir, for interrupting you. Are you familiar with Chase's work, sir?"

"Not at all." The man looked again at the photograph. "The girl," he said, and now there was avid intensity in his voice. "Do you happen to know who she is?"

The manager smiled. "As a matter of fact, I do." He walked over to his antique mahogany desk, picked up a catalogue and turned to the third page. "Number twenty-seven," he said, and handed the catalogue to the stranger.

The eyes, a deep, dark brown, seemed almost to ignite. "*Francesca*," he read aloud.

"Yes, sir. Francesca Cesaretti, the photographer, taken in 1959."

The hands, burned dark by the sun, trembled slightly, so that the pages of the catalogue quivered.

"Do you know her?" the manager asked, curiously.

The stranger nodded, slowly.

"I knew her," he said, "a long time ago."

"He looked, for a moment, as if he was going to weep," the gallery manager told Francesca, when she came in later, with Robert, her fiancé of three weeks. "He was a remarkable-looking man, but a little strange."

"And who was he?"

"He left a note for you." The manager rummaged in a drawer. "He wanted your address, but naturally I didn't give it to him. Here it is."

Francesca stared down at the piece of white gallery paper. The handwriting on it was sloping and steady, the loops generous but not flourished.

Her heart turned over in her chest.

> *If you want to see me, and are able, come to*
> *Sonora Farm, Route 41, three miles north of*
> *Salisbury, Connecticut, at around noon any day*
> *this week. I'll be waiting.*
>
> *Niccolo Dante.*

"Tell me again how he looked."

"I already told you five times!"

"I know, but tell me again, please. You said he wore a suit, and that he was well dressed." Francesca's cheeks were hot, and she was quivering with excitement.

"He was extremely well dressed." The gallery manager sighed. "Which was why I noticed his hands—they were working hands, callused and suntanned."

"And his hair was almost black?"

Robert broke in. "Give the guy a break, darling—he's told you all he can."

"What's the story, Francesca?" The manager was intrigued. "You're obviously just as affected by hearing about him as he was by Johnny's photograph. When did you last see this man?"

Francesca could hardly speak. Her eyes had abruptly filled with tears.

Robert answered for her. "In 1954, on a May morning. In Naples."

"He had a slight accent," the manager said. "Did I tell you he had an accent?"

"Yes." Francesca smiled. "You told us."

"When will you go?" Robert asked, as they strolled hand in hand in the Public Garden, close to where the old swan boats sailed serenely on the pond.

"Tomorrow." Francesca felt electrically charged. She wondered if her agitation was transmitting itself to Robert, and she thought of taking her hand out of his, but thought he might misinterpret the action. He was such a sensitive man, so alive to her feelings, so easily hurt in spite of the phlegmatic exterior he showed the world.

"Want me to come?"

Francesca did not answer.

"Actually, tomorrow's a heavy day for me," Robert said quickly. "My calendar's marked up right through to four o'clock—you'll want to leave in the morning."

Francesca squeezed his hand. He always knew when she needed to be alone—one of the many, many reasons she'd finally agreed to marry him, more than a year after he had first proposed to her. She'd refused him then, afraid of saying yes for the wrong reasons. Robert had, in a sense, done too much for her; Francesca had felt obligated to him in a way she thought might be incompatible with a healthy marriage. But when he had asked her again, a few weeks before, on the night she'd moved into her new apartment on Mount Vernon Street—just around the corner from the Joy Street studio—she had realized that she would never find a better, kinder, more wonderful man, and she had accepted, with joy.

"I'll need a car," she said, as they walked out of the garden onto Boylston Street. Her mind was racing feverishly—she, too, had a busy schedule the next day, which she would need to rearrange as soon as she got back to the studio.

"You can have the Cadillac," Robert offered.

She shook her head. "You might need it. Anyway, you know I hate borrowing your car—I'm always scared I'll scratch a fender or something. I'll rent a car."

Robert looked at his watch. "You'd better get home. You'll have things to do, I imagine."

Francesca nodded. She had to call people, cancel sessions, wash her hair, decide what to wear—and most of all, she had to sit down, by herself, and think about Niccolo.

"Will you call Luciano?"

"I think I'll wait," she said, "till after I've seen Niccolo—he might not even be there."

"He'll be there," Robert said quietly, and then he put one hand under her chin and tilted her face toward his. "Are you sure you want to go alone?" He smiled wryly. "I know how you are about the past—but I can't help remembering what happened when you went back to Florence alone."

"This is very different."

"Whatever you want," he said, and flagged down a cab for her. "Just remember I love you."

"I love you too." She kissed him, and climbed into the backseat.

It was only a few minutes later that she remembered the reason she and Robert had come to Newbury Street that afternoon had been because they had finally agreed to make time to buy an engagement ring.

She set off early next morning, her nerves crackling with a mixture of anticipation, pleasure, and apprehension. The humidity of the past few days had cleared, and it was a fine summer's morning for a drive. Taking the Massachusetts Turnpike into the Berkshires, she turned south to Great Barrington, and then headed on down into Connecticut on Route 41, toward the town of Salisbury.

Francesca hardly noticed anything—not the lovely, winding roads, nor the high, stately banks of corn, nor the wooded expanse of mountainside near Becket. She barely saw the cattle and horses in the fields, or the deer that strayed close to the highway, or paused to appreciate the neat charm of the villages or small towns through which she passed. She kept her eyes fixed on the road ahead, and her mind on her driving, trying to keep the memories at bay—

If it is *Niccolo,* she told herself over and over again, *he won't be the same. People change with time. Nothing stays the same.*

It was Salisbury, most of all, that made her feel that she must be on a fool's errand. It was such an extraordinarily pretty town—the archetypal, storybook New England town, so clean and white, with touches of gray wood, and perfect grass verges—that it seemed too absurd to imagine that she could hope to find Niccolo within a few miles. He was a Gypsy, a traveler and, essentially, an Italian—how could he *possibly* be in America at all, let alone in this old, established Yankee stronghold?

And then Francesca smiled, a small, wry pull of her lips, for almost the same, of course, could be said of her.

She saw the sign just in time, directing her off Route 41: *Sonora Farm.* Slowing right down, she turned onto a narrower, but still smooth, asphalt road, flanked on both sides by endless, sprawling fields. Far over to the right, perhaps as far as a mile away—it was hard to measure distance in the shimmering heat haze that hovered over the lush expanse of grass—a solitary horse and rider galloped in the same direction as her car, the horse's hooves sending up a dust cloud into the air.

Francesca drove on, passing through several miles of dairy land, followed by a series of cornfields, but there was no sign of any central core to the farm, no houses or people. Until the road curved westward, and suddenly she had to brake sharply to make way for a large Jeep coming toward her.

She flashed her lights and waved at the driver, who pulled to a halt, his brown, weathered face creased in question.

Francesca rolled down her window. "I'm looking for Niccolo Dante. I think he may be working here."

"Nick? Sure, Nick's here." The tanned face grew friendlier.

"Where might I find him?"

The man jerked his thumb in the direction from which he'd come. "Just keep on going till you get to the fork, then hang a right and drive till you see horses—"

"Horses?"

"You see horses, Nick Dante won't be far away."

All Francesca's doubts vanished.

Approaching the fork and bearing right, as directed, she caught her breath with pleasure—for suddenly she could see forever, over great rolling fields and meadows, down into a valley that seemed almost blue, and up again into misty, exquisite hills—

And then she saw horses.

On the horizon, just coming into view, three horses were galloping over the crest of a hill, wild and free, tossing their manes and flicking their tails. Francesca accelerated, her heart beginning to pound, her eyes trained on that hill.

Paddocks—white picket fences—more lush grass— And more horses, at least thirty more, all of the same breed as the forerunners, elegant, sturdy, muscular, some of them bay or chestnut, some dark brown, others black. They roamed in a large, wide meadow, some cropping at the turf, others simply standing quietly in the sun.

Francesca braked, and sat straight up in her seat.

There was a man, on the far side of the field, one foot up on the fence. He wore a red-checked work shirt and denim jeans, and his hair was black.

And as he turned away from the fence, and approached one of the horses, a brush in his right hand, he noticed her car, and saw the door open, and watched her climb out—and his arm fell to his side.

Francesca began to walk. The man stood still.

Uncertain for just an instant, she hesitated at the picket fence—but then she looked ahead, and saw him still standing motionless, and easily she clambered over it. He was less than two hundred yards away. He was tall and slim, and his hair was sleek, and still he did not move.

She came to within a dozen feet of him—and stopped. And now she saw his face. It was very dark from the sun, and lean, and his nose was straight, and his mouth was sensuous—and he was staring at her, and his eyes were like burning coal, seeing through her.

She did not realize that she was already weeping.

"Francesca," he said, and his voice was still sonorous, but strange to her ears.

"*Sì*, Niccolo," she responded, softly.

A world of pure emotion, of a feeling so intense, it was akin to pain, passed between them in that first, long look. It was a look of absolute joy, of astonishment, of empathy, of vast relief—of coming home.

"I can't believe it," she whispered.

"Nor I."

They could not speak, they were beyond words. And still wordless, they closed the remaining space between them, and they embraced, gently at first, then more tightly, as wave after wave of feeling swept over them. It was a second reunion, for Francesca, with the past, with a loved one, and her thoughts went out, momentarily, to Luciano, as she realized how happy this would make him too. Yet this was so very different, for with her younger brother, Francesca had always felt protective, responsible—and Niccolo had, from the first, been *her* protector, her adored hero—

They drew apart, and began to study one another, eyes taking in every change, struggling to absorb and understand the natural development of seventeen years. Francesca had cherished her memories of Niccolo, the Gypsy boy, long-haired and free, the most romantic person she had ever known—and now here was this fully formed, astonishing, remarkable-looking adult.

"I think I'd have known you anywhere," she murmured at last, unable to wrest her eyes from his face, half afraid that he was a mirage thrown up by the heat haze, and that he might, at any moment, disappear again. "And yet the thought terrifies me that I might have walked past you on a street somewhere, and *not* have recognized you—"

"And you—" He shook his head, marveling, and his eyes, still with their molten intensity, were smiling into hers. "You look as I knew you would—it was so clear, even when you were just twelve, how beautiful you would become."

"Even with my urchin hair." She was crying again. "I looked like a boy—you thought I was a boy—"

"Only for an instant."

The dark brown gelding he had been about to groom sidled up to him and nudged at his right hand, still holding a dandy brush.

"Later, *bellezza*," he said gently, his gaze never leaving Francesca's face. The horse whinnied softly. "Later, for sure—now leave us alone." The animal trotted away.

"He understands you, Niccolo."

He shrugged. "Didn't they always?"

They began to walk, and to talk, mostly in Italian, and Niccolo wanted to know everything that had happened to her, from the moment of separation in Naples to the present day—and each time Francesca paused, and tried to press him, longing to know about him, Niccolo shook his head and drove her on, like a man thirsting for news, until, at last, she was finished, and he knew almost everything there was to know.

"Now you," she said, her voice husky from talking. They were sitting in a deserted meadow, in the shade of a big oak tree, and she was hugging her knees, drained by her own reminiscing, but avid to hear his. "How did you ever get to this place? I want to know it all, every bit of it."

"Where do I begin?"

"As I did—in Naples." Francesca paused. "I know, from my uncle, that they treated you like a criminal. He told me he longed to help you, but there was no way. He felt useless, he said, and terribly guilty."

"Did he tell you about the money?"

"No." She looked curious.

Niccolo smiled. "Your uncle's a remarkable man."

It was the money, of course—so much more money than he had dreamed of—that had changed his life. He had been full of pride and anger, still, on his release from prison, but when the *direttore,* as directed by Bruno, had presented him with the details of his bank account, a core of common sense in him had told Niccolo not to reject the gift out of hand, and instead, he had withdrawn it, and gone in search of his brother and family.

It was Emilio, wise and understanding, who had listened to Niccolo, had heard his rage and resentment, and had understood the changes that his time with the Cesaretti children, and then in prison, had wrought in him. He had been right to accept the money, Emilio told him. It could make a difference, could alter the course of his life, totally reshape the destiny of Niccolo Dante.

"It depends on what you want," Emilio had said. *"Really* want, more than anything."

What Niccolo wanted, he told his brother, was to be free of a law, of a system, that could imprison him for having been a friend to three helpless children. He loved his family deeply, but he had always felt different, had always yearned, as he had told Francesca, for *indipendenza.* He had dreamed, in his cell, of becoming someone apart, a man who could rise above the prejudice that still stalked all Gypsies, and be free in a way he would never truly be if he remained one member of a large, extended family group.

And there was more to Niccolo's ambition. The money, though undeniably left for him by Bruno Cesaretti, was not really his. There was a task he had been forced to leave unfinished, and he intended to do his utmost to put things right, to follow Francesca to America, to locate her and be sure she was safe and well—and to give her the money that he felt was, rightfully, hers.

"I bought a ticket to America," he told Francesca. "On the *Vulcania*. I had a cabin, I sat at a table in the dining room. I had bought a suit in Salerno—Emilio and Antonia helped me to choose it—and I listened to the orchestra, and watched the people dancing every night. You see?" His face was grim. "You see why I felt so guilty, why my good fortune seemed so wrong? There I was, snug and comfortable, while you—"

"You couldn't have known about my crossing."

"Of course I knew—stowaways don't get warm cabins, and I knew that the Lombardis were not kindhearted people. I knew it would be hard for you."

Francesca shook her head impatiently. "Tell me what happened next."

The sea voyage had been crucial to Niccolo, for it was on the crossing that he had learned that he possessed a talent for gambling. There was no casino on board the *Vulcania*—the only game of chance was an innocent race played with numbered wooden horses on which passengers could place bets—but Niccolo had made the acquaintance of some card players, and every night they'd played poker secretly in various cabins. By the time they reached Boston, Niccolo had won back the price of his fare.

He'd visited Anthony and Maria Lombardi, but, dismissive and glib, Lombardi had told him nothing of any use, and though Niccolo had done what he could to trace Francesca, in a city of many hundreds of thousands, it was impossible, especially since, as he now knew, it was the period when Francesca had been living, in anonymity, with Johnny and Della Chase.

He had tried, hard, to get work, moving from Boston to Providence and then down to New York City, and he had found jobs, but he'd never kept them for long, for he frequently lost his temper with the people who took advantage of his illegal work status and rarely troubled to conceal their disdain for him.

"So what did you do?" Francesca was deeply curious.

Niccolo shrugged. "I played cards."

"You're a gambler?"

"Not anymore. But everywhere I went, especially in Manhattan, there were people who wanted to play—so I did. That's when I became Nick Dante, because it was easier to get accepted as one of the boys."

Watching him now, in his jeans and work shirt, windswept and healthily sunburned, Francesca found it hard to reconcile the picture he was painting of a hard-bitten gambler with this contented-looking outdoorsman.

"Gambling was only a means to an end," Niccolo said. "I wanted, as you did, to get enough money to prove I could support myself indefinitely, so that I could get my permanent residence and work with horses."

"That was always what you wanted most." Francesca looked at him with wonder. "How long have you worked here?"

"I don't really work here," he said. "I've lived for a number of years on a ranch in California, and I'm overseeing the transfer of some stock to this farm."

"Are you a manager?" She was even more impressed.

Niccolo stood up. "The horses you saw were Morgans—ever heard of them?" Francesca shook her head. "The breed goes right back to the eighteenth century—a Welsh schoolteacher living in New England named Justin Morgan received a little dark stallion called Figure in payment of a debt. The horse was small, but strong and docile and intelligent—and a fine trotter."

"And Figure was the start of a whole breed?"

He nodded. "More or less. Anyway, the horses I've brought across from California are Arabians—we're planning to crossbreed."

"Has it been done before?"

"With great success. They call the new breed the Morab—they're the stuff dreams are made of." His eyes were gleaming.

"You always had your dreams." Francesca smiled. "Like the Palio of Siena. Do you still dream of going back there?"

"I still dream," Niccolo said. "Of course."

"How long will you be here?" She asked the question lightly, but she was already aghast at the idea of thousands of miles springing up between them when they'd only just found each other again.

His eyes were warm. "I'm flying back in a day or two—but I'll be back and forth on a regular basis from now on."

They drove, in her rented car, to an inn near Salisbury for a late lunch, and Francesca felt suddenly awkward and oddly shy. She was grateful that he had taken the wheel, because she would have found it difficult to concentrate on the road. She had always known that their reunion, if it happened, would be momentous, but now she found it had shaken her to the core.

She had loved Niccolo so passionately as a child, and even then she had recognized it as a different kind of love from that which she felt for her brothers. But this was entirely different again, for from the instant she had seen him in the meadow, Francesca had been conscious of an unsettling, explosive sensation that she had never experienced before.

I want *him,* she thought, sitting motionless on the vinyl car seat, and hot color rose in her cheeks. He was not her beloved Niccolo anymore— he was a grown, potent, *exciting* man—a stranger named Nick Dante.

"*Va bene?*" He was glancing at her sideways.

She could not speak, too buffeted by emotions, as reality began to gnaw at her mind, competing with desire. There was no substance to their relationship except their precious childhood memories and her own, long-cherished infatuation—and yet the moment of their meeting had felt, to Francesca, more like a reunion of long-lost lovers than of dear friends.

For the first time, she forced herself to think of Robert. Dear, kind, loving Robert. Her fiancé. Guilt stabbed at her fiercely. She felt so confused—she didn't understand her own emotions—didn't understand what was *happening* to her. She loved Robert. She was going to marry him, and be happy, and make him happy. And yet—

Instinct warned her to be cautious. The person sitting beside her now was no longer the boy with whom she had shared Palmarola. He *was* a stranger, about whom she knew hardly anything, and after today they would be separated again by the vastness of America.

✳

In the dining room of the inn, however, the force of Nick Dante's personality rapidly overwhelmed her again, driving out all her doubts. She had remembered his charisma as a kind of rare, magical quality, but now, as she studied him, Francesca realized that she had not remembered exactly how vividly he had stood out from the others in the Gypsy camp.

The influence of Andrea, his mother, both physically and emotionally, had set him apart from birth. His half brother, Emilio, had, like many of his comrades, been a swarthy man, while Niccolo had shared the darkness of hair and eyes, but with softer, paler skin. And there were all the other intrinsic aspects of his character that had intrigued Francesca as a young girl—his love of books and of learning, his pleasure with the small possessions he had struggled to collect through the years, his desire for independence.

"Tell me about your home in California," she urged him.

"It's not really my home," he replied, and Francesca thought that a little of the brightness of his eyes was momentarily dulled, but then he said, quickly: "I want to hear more about Luciano," and the mood lifted again.

"He'll be overjoyed when I tell him—he'll probably want to fly over to see you."

"Is he an impulsive man, then?" Nick asked. "He was quite timid as a boy."

"You made him bolder." Francesca smiled. "He thought the time we spent with you the most thrilling of his life, and yet you and your family made him feel secure—he'd been so frightened before we met you."

"You were all frightened, with good cause." Nick paused. "Vittorio most of all."

"He felt responsible." Francesca shook her head. "I wish I didn't always feel so terribly sad when I think of him. I wish I could remember him when he was happy."

Nick's expression had grown suddenly somber. "It was because of Vittorio that I wondered if you might not want to see me again."

"Why should you think that?" She was startled.

"Because I brought you all to Naples. At that stage, *I* was responsible —and I failed you."

"But it wasn't your fault!" Francesca said fervently. "It wasn't anyone's fault. If Vittorio had stopped to listen to you—if he hadn't run—" She was unable to continue. She had never found it possible to talk about Vittorio's death without breaking down, and she did not want to weep now, in this lovely Connecticut inn—not when she felt so happy—

All through lunch, solid American fare of rare beef, baked potatoes and string beans, washed down with a California red wine, they spoke of their Italian past, about those they had loved, tales and anecdotes spilling out, old sorrows and joys linking them—but above it all, hovering over them like a tantalizing, taunting nimbus, overpowering everything else, was desire—intense, erotic, and mutual.

Back outside, in the late afternoon sunlight, with the sound of crickets raucous in the air, and the traffic growing busier on the highway, the harshness of reality, and of parting, drove a wedge between them.

"Are you sure I can't drive you back?" Francesca asked quietly.

Nick shook his head regretfully. "I've a few things to deal with in Salisbury—I'll get a ride back."

Their farewell embrace was tense. They felt deflated—all the joy and ease had left them.

Francesca opened the door of her car. "I don't know what to say." She felt shaky—she wanted to weep again.

"I know." His smile was forced.

"It seems crazy, parting again—"

Nick Dante's eyes did not meet hers.

"Life is crazy," he said.

✳

On Route 41 again, Francesca wiped the tears from her eyes with the back of her hand, and tried to concentrate on the road ahead.

"Shit," she said out loud.

Nick had not given her either an address or a telephone number. She didn't even know the name of the California ranch. She had told him everything about the missing years, and she had seen in his face that he longed to know, and had sucked her dry—but he had told her only part of his own story, had answered direct questions with indirect answers. If Niccolo had been a semi-myth in her mind, Nick was an enigma.

And now she was alone again, and the awful sensation returned that he *had* been a mirage, that she had imagined it all.

And then the longing came back, so violently and startlingly that Francesca was forced to pull over onto the narrow hard shoulder and stop the car. And her smile was rueful.

Was it possible to desire a mirage?

Long before she reached the safety of Mount Vernon Street, Francesca's confusion over Nick had taken second place to a more immediate, and acutely distressing, turmoil.

She could not marry Robert.

She let herself quietly into the apartment, locked the front door, took the phone off the hook, and poured herself a large cognac. It was a warm, still night, but she felt chilled to the bone.

Robert's face bobbed before her eyes. Handsome, intelligent, caring. Francesca swallowed some cognac and shuddered. The catalogue of his kindnesses rolled like a list of cinematic credits through her mind: Robert saving her from deportation—helping her to have her own studio—rescuing her from God only knew how many weeks or months of rotting in a Florentine prison—

And the smaller things, the ones that really counted in everyday life. His humor, his patience, tolerance, respect, passion.

His passion, not hers. She knew that now.

She drank more cognac, welcoming its heat. She was insane, she had to be. A few hours with Nick Dante, a man about whom she knew next to nothing, and she was steeling herself to destroy a secure, contented future with the perfect man. Madness.

And yet that was what she was going to do. Even if nothing came of her and Nick—even if she never saw him again—their reunion had driven all her sensibly suppressed doubts about marrying Robert sharply, painfully into focus. She loved Robert—she always would. But she was not *in* love with him. That was why she'd waited so long before accepting his proposal. Because she'd always known it was the wrong thing to do.

"This is crazy."

He was white with shock and anger. Robert had never been so angry with Francesca before.

"I know it must seem that way—it does to me too."

They were in Robert's office on State Street. Francesca had spent a long, agonizing evening at home, drinking more cognac than she was used to, not answering the telephone, followed by a restless, unhappy night, and first thing this morning, she'd come to see him, knowing that she could not bear to put off the inevitable any longer.

Robert was staring at her, trying to bore into her mind. "You hadn't seen Dante for seventeen years until yesterday—you were both kids."

Francesca didn't speak. She could see that he was trembling, and she longed to put her arms around him, but she knew that it would be wrong and unfair.

"One lunch together. A few hours reminiscing, and you want to throw everything we've shared on the scrap heap."

"No." Francesca shook her head. "God, *no*, Robert—you're just as precious to me now as you've always been. I still love you—"

"But you don't want to marry me." The anger was gone, and he looked suddenly older, worn down. The silver strands in his fair hair shone in the sunlight from the big plate-glass window behind him, and the shadows on his face accentuated the weariness of his eyes and mouth.

"I'm so sorry," Francesca whispered, fighting back tears. She had never hated herself so much in her life, never experienced such self-disgust. "I don't know what else to say to you."

"But are you sure?" Robert saw her misery, and one more desperate flash of hope colored his voice. "Aren't you just overreacting to the bombshell of seeing Niccolo again? Coming face to face with your own history must have been quite a jolt."

He'd always felt, in his heart, that his greatest enemy had been Francesca's past, that luminous, enthralling early life that had so fascinated him the first time they'd met, here, in this same sterile law office, almost four years ago.

"What can I tell you, Robert?" Francesca said helplessly. "That you're the best friend I've ever had? That I would have been so proud to be your wife—*any* woman would."

"I don't want any woman."

She looked at him, desolately. "It isn't just Niccolo, you know—it's me." She was very quiet again. "I can't bear hurting you this way, but I don't know what else to do. Anything else would be a lie, and I owe you much more than that."

Robert's gray-green eyes glinted with tears. "And you see marriage to me as a lie, is that it?"

The self-loathing overwhelmed her.

"Yes," she said.

He swallowed. "Do you think time would help? Maybe even change your mind?"

Francesca had spent the night asking herself that same question, over and over again, and she knew the answer.

"No," she said.

Nick called her one month later. He was back at Sonora, he told her. She invited him to come up to Boston, but he pressed her to return to Connecticut if she could.

It was another glorious day as she drove over the state line, and this time, Francesca was able to look around and to take pleasure from the beauty of the ride. It was too early for fall colors, but there were already small splashes of rosy foliage to be seen, a sure promise of what would soon follow.

They had arranged to meet in Salisbury, at The Saddlery. He was waiting for her outside—seeing him, her breath caught in her throat. He was leaning against a wall, his face upturned to the sunshine, and Francesca thought him the most beautiful person she'd ever seen.

When he saw her, he smiled, and the dark, warm, bitter-chocolate eyes brightened with pleasure, and she saw how white his teeth were against his deep tan, and as he walked toward her car, she noticed the looseness of his limbs and the broad span of his shoulders, and she felt quite weak again, and her heart thudded in her chest.

"I brought a Jeep," he said to her, bending low so that their faces were close together. "If you turn, just behind that gray and white building, you can park."

They drove along Undermountain Road, and on along Route 41 toward the farm. They seemed to drive for miles. At the point where Francesca had taken the right fork on Sonora's main road, Nick turned to the left, and after a while the road became sandier, and rougher.

"Where are we going?" It was hard to speak normally, hard to tear her eyes from his face.

"You'll see." He chuckled, the same bubbling laugh that she had adored as a child.

They stopped at last, on a dirt track, near a small, enclosed paddock. Two glorious golden horses were tethered to the fence.

"What breed are they?" she asked.

"Palominos." Nick turned off the engine. "Coats the color of 'newly minted gold coins' is how they're described." He opened his door. "Leave your purse in the Jeep."

"Are we riding?" Francesca jumped down. "I haven't ridden since Italy." She stared at the horses. "No saddles?"

Nick grinned. "You didn't need a saddle when you rode the *Maremmane*."

"I was a *child*!" she protested, appalled. "And I wasn't much good at it then—I couldn't possibly ride bareback now!"

Gently, but firmly, he took her hand and led her over to the paddock. "These horses are easy to ride—very docile and calm. That one especially."

Francesca looked at the exquisite blond horse with the perfect white mane and tail. "I can't even remember how to mount," she said, panic growing.

"That's easy." With one swift, smooth movement, Nick picked her up in his arms and planted her on the horse's back. The mare shifted a little, but seemed unconcerned.

"Nick, I can't do this!"

He looked suddenly concerned. "I thought you'd enjoy it. You rode well in Italy." He laid a hand on her arm. "Shall I help you down?"

"No." Her fear receded a little. "You used to splash water on my legs to help me grip."

Nick smiled. "I left a bucketful over there." He stroked the mare's velvety head. "Take it easy with this one, *bellezza*," he crooned.

Francesca regained her confidence and control within twenty minutes. Nick had, of course, been right—she hadn't forgotten how to ride —but she had forgotten the wonderful sense of calm and oneness that came with a fine horse and a beautiful day.

They walked, cantered, and finally galloped gleefully, Nick leading the way to a wooded hill, slowing to a trot along an overgrown track, ducking branches and allowing the horses to tread carefully. And then they came to a clearing—

Francesca gasped with delight.

He had laid out a picnic for two, in an idyllic setting, a few yards from a small, sun-soaked, clear-water lake. Francesca saw a crisp, white cloth on green grass, a wicker hamper, a blanket for them to sit on.

"You like it?" he asked softly.

Eagerly, she slipped off the mare's back, tethered her to a tree in the shade, and investigated further, opening the hamper, which revealed a feast.

"Oh, Nick—" She looked wordlessly back at him, her eyes pricking with tears. So much thought and care, to have planned this just for her.

"You like it," he said.

✳

They ate hungrily, fried chicken and fresh-baked bread, and four different salads, and sweet corn, and big, crisp apples, and Nick produced a champagne bottle that he'd hung by its neck in the lake water to keep it cool. Francesca had never felt so relaxed, as they chattered and laughed and sang old Italian love songs. And the champagne and hot sun made them deliciously dizzy, and they strolled, hand in hand, to the water's edge, and took off their sneakers and dangled their bare feet in the cool lake. And again, Francesca gazed at Nick, and all her defenses and doubts had melted away like butter.

"I'm happier," she said to him, blissfully, "than I've ever been in my entire life."

And Nick, in reply, took her face in both his hands and, for the first time, he kissed her on the lips. "I have made love," he said huskily, still holding her face close to his, "to fourteen women in my life—"

"You counted them?" She wanted to laugh and cry at once, and her lips tingled with pleasure and yearning.

"—but every time I closed my eyes, when I was with them, I saw your face—as you were then, so lovely and so alive with joy and fear, and so full of love—as you are now. And I felt guilty as all hell for conjuring you up at those moments, not because of the other girls, God forgive me, but because I think I always felt you were somehow sacred—"

"Me—sacred?" Francesca smiled.

"You were utterly innocent, as I was, and so pure—" His eyes were like hot coals. "But you were also the most beguiling creature I'd ever known—and you still are—"

She felt his breath, warm and sweet with wine, against her cheek, and she quivered with longing.

"And now," Nick went on dreamily, "I want to make love to you more than anything I've ever wanted—and yet at the same time, I'm almost afraid to touch you."

"Nick." Francesca's voice was low and urgent.

"What, my love?"

"If you don't touch me—if you don't kiss me again, I think I may faint."

"*Veramente?*" His face lit up.

"*Assolutamente,*" she whispered.

He kissed her again, her mouth, this time, not just her lips, and there was hunger in the kiss, yet still he took care to be gentle and soft. He touched his lips to her forehead, and to each closed eyelid, and he watched the lashes flutter, and he inclined his head so that he could kiss the tip of her chin and then her neck.

"I don't know which part I love the most," he murmured.

Their feet still dangled in the lake, and Francesca leaned closer, pressing herself against him. "There's more of me," she said, and laughed up into his face.

She wore just a gauzy white blouse with puffed short sleeves, blue denim jeans, and a wide canvas belt that accentuated her tiny waist. Nick drew his feet out of the water and knelt beside her, still studying her.

"Nick?"

He hushed her with one finger. "There's no hurry."

Francesca wriggled her toes, rippling the surface. "I'm burning, Nick," she said, and wondered at her lack of inhibition.

"Good," he said, and began, at last, to unbutton her blouse. "No, don't move—just sit still—"

She shut her eyes.

The gauzy blouse was laid on the bank, and with fingers so gentle that, with her eyes still closed, they might have been a butterfly's wings brushing her, he unhooked her brassiere, and she heard his soft exhalation.

"*Perfetta,*" he whispered, and then he said: "Stand up, Francesca."

She opened her eyes and obeyed him. His voice was as beautiful and compelling as the rest of him, so that she was aware that he had power over her, that however gentle and tender he might be, he could still exert his will upon her. . . .

He unbuckled her belt, and unzipped her jeans, and she thought she would go mad with longing, for he might have been undressing a child for bed, so completely did he avoid touching her skin.

"Now my clothes," he said, and Francesca shivered with delight and anticipation, and as she unbuttoned his shirt, and tugged at the buckle of his leather belt, she felt as if she were unwrapping the most exquisite gift of her life. And when he stepped out of his jeans, and stood before her, completely naked, she heard her own gasp, for his nudity awoke in her appetites she had never known she possessed.

He carried her into the shade, and lay her down on the grass, and her long, straight hair fanned about her head like a dark halo. And then he lay down beside her, and with one finger he traced first the fine line of her remarkable winged eyebrows, and then the aristocratic jawline that Letizia had so resented, and then he ran the same finger down her neck and on down between her breasts, which were round and full, their nipples bursting.

"So white," he smiled, for she had sunbathed at Revere Beach in the summer, wearing a bikini, and the stripes of pale skin aroused him even more than if her entire body had been bronzed.

"Nick, I'm on fire," she moaned softly, beseechingly, and involuntarily her hips strained toward him.

"I know," he said, and Francesca saw that he was hard as rock, and her mind flew ahead of her body and she imagined him inside her, and she felt her own desire trickling over her thighs into the grass—

And at last Nick Dante began to make love to her, and at last he allowed himself his all-consuming hunger, and he kissed her mouth ravenously, and savored the sweet thrust of her tongue—and he let his hands roam freely over her, touching, stroking, caressing every curve, every pucker, every valley. And Francesca, awestruck by her own sexuality, devoured his body with her eyes and hands and mouth, adoring every inch of taut, hard muscle and of softer flesh, and she blew on the hairs of his chest, and kissed his own erect nipples, and she ran the palms of her hands over his tight buttocks, and noticed that he was sunburned even there, and she shut her eyes again for a moment, to imagine him striding naked through a field of corn, and then she took his penis in her hand, and heard him cry out with pleasure—

And when he told her to lie back again, she submitted, quivering violently, and using both his strong hands, he parted her thighs, spread her legs wide, and knowing that neither of them could bear to wait another second, he entered her, and she was wet with lust, and tight and young, and he began to move inside her body, thrusting into her, driving back and forth, and it was impossible to hold back, and Francesca arched her back toward him in a violent spasm, and Nick climaxed into her, and she gave a low scream—and the crickets crescendoed, and the palominos whinnied, and a pair of beautiful, blue-winged birds rose, startled, into the clear sky.

"Am I real?" she murmured against his chest, as they lay, arms around each other, beneath the trees. "Are you real?"

He smiled. "I'm not sure."

"I hope so." She sighed fervently, and rubbed her cheek as his hair tickled her skin. And then, very slowly, she sat up, surveying him. "It's strange," she said.

"What, my love?"

"You're not my Niccolo anymore." She pushed her tangled hair away from her face. "I knew it a month ago, but I think I couldn't bear to let him go."

"And now?"

"Now you're Nick Dante."

He lay still, and his eyes were quite black.

"Yes" was all he said.

They swam together in the lake, playing and cavorting like young seals, without a care in the world—and then they lay again on the grass, side by side, dozing and letting the sun dry their bodies and hair. . . .

And later, when they woke to the sound of the horses whinnying,

Nick got up to let them drink, and as Francesca, too, rose, and came to him, leaning lightly against him, slipping her arms gently about him, Nick picked her up and put her up on the mare's back.

"But I'm naked," Francesca murmured, though her spirit was so light that she felt as if she were filled with golden, intoxicating honey.

"The horse won't mind."

Francesca chuckled with delight as Nick mounted behind her. "Isn't this too much for her?"

"She's strong, and school-trained—she'll put up with almost anything."

He circled her waist with his arms, and gently kicked the palomino to a slow walk, and they rode that way for a while, meandering in and out of the trees, over the narrow, unmade leafy tracks, back and forth, always weaving a path back to the same clearing. And the closeness of their nude bodies, and the rubbing contact with the lovely muscular creature between their thighs and against their loins, and the rhythmic, swaying, rolling motion, all combined in the most sensual, voluptuous sensation either of them had ever experienced—

"You have a scratch on your back," Nick said softly, and first kissing, and then licking, the tiny wound, he felt her shiver, and he raised his hands from her waist and cupped her breasts, and heard her moan—

They were back in the clearing again, in sight of the emptied picnic hamper and the white cloth, its now-rumpled creases being explored for discarded delicacies by ants and flies and droning bees—and with a light pressure of his legs, Nick brought the palomino to a halt, and he buried his face in the sweet black cloud of Francesca's hair.

"Don't move," he told her again when she began, longingly, to try to turn around to face him.

"I want to kiss you."

"Later," he said, and his mouth began to travel over her shoulders, and he rejoiced as Francesca tugged his right hand from her breast and guided it down into the dark, tightly curled hair, moist again—and the mare beneath them shifted a little, still calm and patient, and Nick's fingers found what he sought, and softly, gently, he rubbed and teased, and Francesca groaned and thrust her head back, her neck straining tautly—and then Nick took away his hands and used them to lift her buttocks from the horse's back, and Francesca felt his penis, erect and demanding, and she dug her knees into the animal's sides to raise herself —and when Nick entered her, she felt as if she had been pierced, and as he drew her down, grinding himself into her body, circling, rolling his hips, his eyes clenched tight shut in glorious agony, Francesca cried out again, and the golden palomino mare threw back her great head and tossed her silky white mane and flicked her tail.

And Nick still clung to Francesca, his body aflame, his whole being absorbed in her, and she felt the first tidal waves of her climax beginning to roll through her, and she wanted to scream again. And the horse, at last, gave a great, shrill whinny of protest, and reared violently up on her hind legs—and the lovers crashed to the ground, the breath whistling from their lungs as the palomino bucked and galloped away.

And as soon as Nick could breathe again, he crawled to where Francesca had fallen, and took her in his arms, his face a mask of concern. "Are you hurt?"

"No, my love," she whispered, and though there were tears of shock on her cheeks, she smiled at him radiantly. "Just hold me tight."

And as he drew her close, Francesca saw that he was still erect, and swiftly she reached down and guided him into her, for her body, too, was still aching, still pulsing with need. And now they were face to face, and she kept her eyes open, staring into his face, witnessing his pain and joy and release, her heart contracting fiercely with the most powerful love she had ever known.

The sun had dipped a little in the sky as they packed up the remains of the picnic and rode, silently, back to where they'd left the Jeep. And as Nick drove away from Sonora back onto Route 41, a cool breeze began to blow, and suddenly, as she sat watching him, Francesca felt a great, inexplicable sadness creeping over her.

She had said, on the telephone, that she would like to stay overnight in the area this time, and Nick had reserved a room for her at the White Hart Inn in Salisbury—so she was startled when, after she had checked in, he told her that he had to return to the farm.

"But I thought—" She stopped.

All the ease had gone out of their day, and he looked oddly strained. "I have some work to take care of."

Her hurt made her cool. "Will you be back?"

"Sure." He paused. "Later."

A brief, light kiss, and he'd gone, leaving Francesca alone and bewildered—and when he had telephoned, two hours later, to say that he had been unavoidably detained, and could not see her till morning, she had felt more troubled than ever.

It was as if a blazing fire had been lit inside her, and then roughly, shockingly doused with icy water. For a while, she felt angry and betrayed, and then she began to despise herself—and when that surge had passed, she felt merely desperately sad.

She went down to the restaurant, but found she could not swallow a morsel, and returned to her room and lay down on the bed. The inside of her thighs felt bruised, and while she knew she might have savored the soreness had Nick been with her, now it only made it more impossible to put the afternoon, even temporarily, out of her mind.

A little after eleven o'clock, after Francesca had taken a hot shower and climbed into the bed, knowing that however weary she might feel, she was unlikely to sleep for hours, the telephone rang again.

"Were you asleep?" Nick asked.

"Yes," she lied.

"I have to see you."

She sat up, drawing the bedclothes around her against the night chill. "It's late."

"I know." He sounded strange. "I'm in a booth near the inn."

A furrow marked her brow. "Why didn't you come in?"

"Francesca, please come down—I know it's late, but I have to talk to you now."

Fear tickled her spine. "I'll get dressed."

★

He was waiting for her outside the inn. The Jeep was parked a little way down the street. Francesca looked up at his face, saw pain and a kind of hopelessness in his eyes, and the dread slithered through her body, and lodged itself in a hard ball in her stomach.

Without speaking, they walked to the Jeep. He opened the passenger door, and climbed in on the driver's side.

"Can we have some heat?" Francesca felt icier than ever.

He turned the key. The motor sprang to life, and in a moment, a little warmth began to spread through the car.

Francesca waited.

"I've misled you." Nick's voice was leaden. "There's no way for me to tell you, except to do it quickly." He looked briefly at her fearful, expectant face, and then his eyes veered away again.

"I'm no farm manager," he said. "I'm the owner of a ranch in California, called Sonora. All the stuff about the horses—crossing the Arabians with Morgans—is true. But I bought the farm here just a few months ago. It's mine." He stopped for a moment. His eyes grew darker, more despairing. He looked like a child wanting to run or to cry, but trapped.

A couple walked by, arm in arm. They were both smoking and laughing, and as they passed the Jeep, the man bent down and stared through the window, grinning, as if he expected to see the occupants romping in the backseat.

Francesca felt as if she'd stopped breathing.

"I'm married," Nick said, and the words were stark. "And I have a son, and a daughter."

✳

The heater blew, and the windshield began to steam up, and Francesca sat like a stone while Nick Dante told his story, his voice remote, as if he were reciting a narrative.

The gambling, he told her, had pulled him through the tough early years in America, but it had ultimately led to his downfall, for it was during a marathon poker session with a group of rich and powerful men in New York City that Nick had briefly lost his mind, and everything he owned, to a man named Richard Brass.

Born Riccardo Brazzi, the son of an Italian immigrant, Brass had taken the fine education his father had struggled to provide, and had become a brilliant and ruthless property developer, taking pains to stamp out his name, accent and heritage as swiftly as possible. He had married a suitable wife—a blond, blue-eyed, sophisticated Radcliffe girl—and she had borne him a daughter named Eleanor, a luscious, strong-willed girl with a particular penchant that caused both her parents frequent discomfort—she was irresistibly drawn to dark-eyed, manifestly masculine, preferably Italian, men.

Eleanor's passions, both physical and emotional, were intense, yet she was fickle, with a spoiled, butterfly attitude to everything in her life, including men. She saw, she wanted, she *got*, or there was trouble. Eleanor had met Nick Dante while he was negotiating the first business deal of his career; after working, gambling, and saving hard for five years, he was ready to buy a small riding school at Narragansett, Rhode Island. He had been spending a day with the owner, examining the horses, facilities, and books, when Eleanor Brass, staying with a girlfriend nearby, had come for a ride, taken one look at Nick's dark, dangerous good looks, and known she must have him.

"We dated for two weeks," Nick told Francesca, his voice still dull and strange, "by which time I knew I didn't like her very much. I told her it was over, and I thought she'd accepted it, but she had no intention of accepting it."

Eleanor had wanted him more than ever—not just for sex or for fun, but for *keeps*. And so she had gone to her father, who had never been able to deny her anything. The problem in this case, however, was overcoming Richard Brass's personal, illogical contempt of Italians.

Eleanor had told Richard that she was wildly, irretrievably in love, and that nothing he could say would dissuade her. If she could not have Nick, she wanted to die. Brass had been appalled. Surely, he said, she would get over Dante. Carefully ensuring that she would be found in time, Eleanor had swallowed an overdose of barbiturates. In the emergency room at New York Hospital, Brass had wept and prayed and raged, and had sworn an oath that Nick Dante would marry his daughter or be destroyed.

One week later, Brass had engineered a special poker game in a suite at a Manhattan hotel. Contacts of Nick's were bought, and he was lured to the table like a lamb to the slaughter, unaware that Eleanor's father had fixed the contest. It was a long, grueling night for Nick, for his opponents were experts, not only at cheating but at the arts of inciting and goading a man to his limits and beyond. Nick hardly knew what had hit him, for they operated slowly and thoroughly, letting whiskey, the drunkenness of gambling, and pride assist them in their task of pushing him over the edge and down into the abyss.

Brass was merciless. Nick was not yet an American citizen. The poker game had been as illegal as many of the games that Nick had used to jack up his route to respectability had been. Brass was rich and powerful; if he chose, Nick could be deported, finished. He had one choice. He could marry Eleanor. And on a wet day in November of 1960, he had.

"The irony is that Richard died of a heart attack just a few months later—Eleanor was pregnant by then. It was a lousy marriage from the start, which was as much my fault as hers." For the first time, Nick's voice lost its steadiness. "But we have two children—Kevin is almost ten years old, Alicia is eight—and until a month ago, they were the only people in the world I would have died for."

Francesca had not spoken since he had begun to talk. She *could* not speak, could no longer even look at Nick, just stared straight ahead at the steamed-up windshield.

Once the children had been born, Eleanor had realized that life as Mrs. Nick Dante was a far cry from living as a pampered daughter. She hated Nick for selling their Long Island house and buying ranch land in California, too far from her mother and from Fifth Avenue—and though she'd come to love her visits to Los Angeles, she'd continued to despise her husband. Her father's prejudices and her own frustrations festered in her, making her increasingly vicious. He still attracted her physically, but she developed a predilection to taunting and insulting him, loathing him all the more when he refused to be baited, and embarking on frequent affairs with other men.

He had waited years, for the sake of the children, but as their home life had become increasingly unendurable, and he had come to be sure they would all be happier apart, Nick had asked for a divorce, but Eleanor had threatened suicide.

"Our marriage," he finished bitterly, "is a total sham, glued together by emotional blackmail. But for all her faults, Eleanor's a good mother and the children love her—so how can I risk robbing them of her?"

He had told Francesca everything, right down to the details of the first Sonora, the California ranch, which he had loved with a passion ever since they moved there.

"In a way, I guess I created Sonora East as a refuge, a way to keep from going crazy." Nick paused. "I never really understood, till now, what a coward I was." He went on softly. "And until I walked down Newbury Street in Boston that day in August, and saw Johnny Chase's photograph of you, I'd given up ever finding you again. You were just another dream."

Francesca still sat motionless. She wondered if her blood had ceased flowing through her veins. Her whole body seemed to have stopped functioning.

"I should have told you right away, I know. But I couldn't bear to spoil the magic."

Finally, she spoke. "And today? What kind of magic was today?"

He shook his head. "What happened between us today was like a hurricane—"

"An act of God?" The bitterness came through, at last, like acid. "Or an act of Nick Dante." She paused. "You set it up, Nick, all of it—the picnic, the horses—" Her lips began to tremble, and she stopped, not wanting to weep, not yet.

"If you only knew how I regretted it. Oh, God, not today, but all of it—Eleanor, the marriage—"

"Why regret it?" she asked ironically. "It gave you the land you always dreamed of having—it made you rich."

Nick's jaw tightened. "I worked hard to pay back what I owed Eleanor's father. I earned that ranch and this farm—but though I suppose you won't believe me, I'd give them both up if I could have you."

Francesca stared at him. "How *can* I believe you?" For a moment, Robert came into her mind. Dear, honest Robert, whom she'd hurt so grievously just a month ago. She understood now how he'd felt. She knew.

In sudden despair, Nick clenched his right fist and pounded it against the steering wheel. "Francesca, I can't bear to lose you—we've lost so many years already—" He forced his voice to quieten again. "But I've wrecked any chance we might have had, haven't I?"

The tears began to fall, and a little of the icy coldness melted. "What chance did you imagine we could possibly have?" she asked chokingly. "Nick, I don't blame you for what happened more than ten years ago—it's the fact that you *lied* to me."

"I didn't lie—"

"You didn't tell me the truth—what's the difference? You've proved to me that I don't know you at all. You're not the boy I would have trusted with my heart, with my *life*—"

"Listen to me—"

"I've *listened*!" Francesca was shaking. "I don't want to hear any more!"

"Please, just hear me out! Hear what I have to say, and then tell me to go to hell."

She said nothing.

"I've been trying to get Eleanor to see a psychiatrist, to put an end to her threats. She hasn't agreed, but I'll keep on trying." He spoke rapidly now. "In the meantime, all I can promise you is my time here at Sonora. Eleanor loves California now—her mother bought a beach house to be close to her and the children. She hates New England—"

"Nick—"

"The house at the farm is wonderful—but there's no pool, no solarium, no Jacuzzi, and if Eleanor does come east, she stays in Manhattan."

"What are you suggesting, Nick?"

"I'm not suggesting anything," he said frantically. "I'm just trying to tell you that I love you, Francesca." Again he reached for her hand, and this time he would not let her pull away. "When I was fourteen years old, a Gypsy boy in another world, I saw you for the first time—a skinny, scruffy, terrified ragamuffin with great dark eyes—and I knew that I loved you even then."

"Nick, please—" The tears began again—it was impossible to stop them.

"And you were so remarkable. You had such *courage* in everything you did, I knew I couldn't bear to be parted from you. And when I saw you for the last time on that street in Naples, saw your agonized, lonely face, I swore that one day—no matter what—I would find you again."

"Too late." Francesca felt sobs beginning to shake her. "It's too *late*—"

"No!" He still clutched her hand. "I won't believe that! I'm going to divorce Eleanor—"

"*Stop it!*" she screamed suddenly. "I don't want to hear her name again!"

"—and I'm going to come here, to Sonora, again and again—and I'll wait—and even if you never come, I'll never stop waiting and hoping—"

"*No!*" Violently, Francesca pulled her hand free and fought to open the Jeep's passenger door, her fingers numb, her eyes saturated with the tears that streamed down her cheeks—

"I'll help you." Quickly, though he, too, was trembling badly, Nick opened his own door and strode around to the other side. The door slammed open, striking him on his arm, and he winced in pain, but ignored it. "Francesca, you can't go like this."

Out of the Jeep, she stopped for a moment, and looked up into his eyes, and with one icy, quivering hand, she reached up and, briefly, touched his cheek.

"I wish I had a choice."

And then, without another look, she turned and walked, slowly, back toward the inn.

Chapter 24

THE AMERICAN EDITION of *Zachary Holt* did not enter the *New York Times* best-seller list for four weeks after publication, but once it was in, it remained there for three months, paving the way for a surefire paperback hit. Readers all over the United States warmed to the gentle-hearted detective and his tumultuous adventures and affairs in Paris, a city that almost everyone, everywhere could relate to.

"It's on display all over London too," Kate and Bruno reported, after a few days holiday, while Victor Pillement received checks and negotiated translation agreements with abandon.

"Are you working, *mon ami?*" he would check regularly, telephoning Luciano from Paris.

"Of course I'm working."

"Are you sure? Not spending too much time with *la belle* Claudine?"

"You're out-of-date, Victor," Luciano answered cheerily. "It's Suzette now."

"Either way, my boy, don't forget you have obligations now."

Luciano had no intention of forgetting—and no wish to. Life was, in general, more wonderful than ever. Having made the break he had known was inevitable with Le Rocher, he had bought a sea-facing apartment on the Promenade des Anglais in Nice. It was a superb suite of rooms, with every comfort he could wish for, and though it was modern and a little soulless, he liked it. Houses like Le Rocher, which he still regarded as home, were for families, and in spite of the constant ebb and flow of girlfriends in his life, Luciano was a genuine romantic; he looked forward to the pleasure of seeking such a house someday in the future, with his wife.

Nice was a profound joy. Luciano loved its grace and charm and bustle, its limitless supply of sublime food and wine, its gregarious cafés, bars, and restaurants—its beautiful women. He seldom swam in or sailed on the Mediterranean, but he loved having it at his feet every morning when he woke, savored its sound and its smell and the wonderful light that spun off the Baie des Anges over the town.

Life was grand. Bruno and Kate were a short drive away; Francesca wrote and telephoned regularly and visited when she could; work on the second Zachary Holt novel was going well, and he had plot outlines ready for three more.

Luciano should, therefore, by all accounts, have been blissfully content—but he was not.

He was deeply disturbed.

He was not certain exactly when the random thoughts that had always flitted through his mind had begun to cause him true anxiety. He had always been a daydreamer—and, of course, as a novelist, where would he be if notions did not come to him like unexpected visitors? But the thoughts that had troubled him increasingly over the past year or two had no relation to the young, ingenuous detective of his fiction.

The perplexing ideas that infiltrated his head at all hours of day or night, whether he was dreaming, or lying awake in bed, or making bouillabaisse, or driving his MG convertible on the Grande Corniche, or swimming in the rooftop pool of his building—these ideas were interlopers, more suited to a writer of psychological dramas or, perhaps, of melancholy romance.

He always noted them down as well as he could—for what else could a writer do? But he sometimes worried that a visit to a psychiatrist might be more appropriate, for lately he seemed to be experiencing emotions that simply *could* not have anything to do with either himself or Zachary. Sitting with his uncle and aunt on the terrace at Le Rocher, he would be assailed by a sense of despair and loneliness; in bed with Suzette, even in the throes of lovemaking, he would abruptly feel lonely and rejected; sitting on his balcony, eagerly typing out his latest chapter, he would have to stand up and walk away, so intense and shocking was the wave of bitterness and anger that had overwhelmed him.

Kate, always sensitive to his moods, asked if something was troubling him, but he could not bring himself to talk about it to her. He might have been able to confide in Francesca, but his sister was thousands of miles away. Maybe he ought to stop writing down the thoughts—perhaps he ought to rip them up—destroy the bizarre, confused record of his own instability—but he knew that he would not.

In any case, there was no point, for his *petits démons*, as he had come to think of them, were part of him, taunting, creeping, pervasive.

He could only continue to try to exorcise them by writing them down, setting them aside and then fighting to focus his brain on Zachary Holt.

What would I do without you to occupy me, Zack? he wondered grimly.

He didn't want to know.

Chapter 25

AFTER ELIZABETH'S DEATH, and after the funeral at the cemetery in Dorking where she had been laid to rest beside her beloved Edward, Juliet had returned to Kaikoura for one more night before going back to London.

She had told Hilda Loom to go to her own home, and the house was silent and cold, but Juliet had not lit a fire, nor switched on the central heating that her mother had installed for her during their first winter together. Instead, she had sat down at the kitchen table—the scarred old pine table where they had shared so many happy times, the peaceful normal hours that Juliet had cherished above everything. And there, all alone, she had sat on the straight-backed chair, and had raised her head and howled, like a wounded animal, for her loss. And then she had folded her arms on the table, and buried her face, and wept for a long while, until sleep had rescued her. And early the next morning, she had awoken, stiff and icy and aching, and she had left Kaikoura behind her, unable to stay another moment.

Two years later, however, and she still refused to sell the house. It was her oasis, her shelter, the evidence of her life with Elizabeth.

She had, at last, achieved a measure of success, though it was a far cry from the accomplishments she'd dreamed of in the early days of her career. After the Brayfield scandal, she had seemed, suddenly, to develop a reputation. One minute, she had been a disgraced junior reporter, scolded and tossed aside; the next, she had been an enterprising, cunning muckraker with a nose for vulnerability and the hard core to see a story through to the meatiest possible conclusion. She was no mere hack; she wrote well. If Juliet could track down the stories, the gutter press at home and abroad were willing to print and to pay.

Her refusal to sell Kaikoura had made death duties harder to cope with, but she still had the house as her security, and she was able to afford to rent a handsome flat in Little Venice—yet Juliet still considered herself a failure, both professionally and personally. She had long ago rejected any hope of ever finding a man to love her. Her encounter with Ray Donnelly had affected her so profoundly that she had never allowed any man to take her to bed since that disastrous night.

Until one month after Elizabeth's funeral, when she had found herself at such an unbearably low ebb that her desire for physical release had suddenly overwhelmed her. She'd forgotten the fierce sexual urge that Ray had aroused in her—she'd *forced* herself to obliterate it from her mind—but once the need had surfaced again, she found it impossible to deny.

Juliet acknowledged, at last, that so long as her scars were covered, she was attractive, almost beautiful, and she had begun experimenting in the art of tempting men. She had become an expert tease—until she had come to understand that she was depriving herself more than the men.

She made a calculated decision. Since she could never have love, she would have affairs—she'd even settle for one-night stands. But no man would ever have the opportunity to be repulsed by her scars again, for no man would ever see them. She remembered, the previous year, having seen, in a magazine, a seamless, Lurex body stocking designed by Mary Quant. An idea simmered tantalizingly in Juliet's mind; what she required, she realized, would have to be specially made for her. She began with four—four tailor-made, crotchless body stockings in silky, tactile fabrics that fitted her like a second, perfect skin.

The first time she made love to a man—for that was how it was to be; *she* would initiate her affairs, she would make the rules and, in that way, keep control—Juliet understood what she had been missing. She remembered Ray telling her that she was made for sex, that she was a natural, and now the notion gratified her. She took satisfaction from the act, and she bestowed it with largesse. Sex became her hobby, her favorite pastime, and she became increasingly greedy for it; the more men she had, the more she wanted. But no matter what she and her partner did, no matter how aroused she became, or how desperately any man implored her, Juliet refused to remove the provocative body stocking. She would do almost anything to them—she drove men to the point of frenzy and beyond—but she would not reveal her body.

Her life repelled her—she hated it all.

She hated herself.

On a Sunday morning in September of 1972, while Juliet was enjoying a leisurely and solitary breakfast, thumbing through the newspapers, her telephone rang.

"Juliet, it's Joe Chapplin."

She yawned widely, and then smiled. Chapplin was a thirty-six-year-old photographer with whom she'd had a brief liaison a few months earlier in Frankfurt, while working with him on a story for one of Germany's trashiest magazines. As she recalled, his performance had been above average.

"Business or pleasure, darling?" she asked.

"It's business," he said. "And it's big." He paused. "Very big."

They met the following evening at Boulestin, Chapplin flanked by two American businessmen who, he had told Juliet, had a proposition to put to her. As the evening progressed she became more and more intrigued. The Americans, charming, but crisp, were in London on behalf of a multinational corporation planning a new venture into the magazine industry.

"If you visualize a glossy *Private Eye*—but more daring, near the knuckle, European and in full color—you'll be on the right track."

When they offered Juliet the position of features editor, she thought she must have misheard.

"So what do you say, Miss Austen?"

She stared blankly at Joe Chapplin, who was smiling.

"Miss Austen?"

Her head spun. "I don't know what to say."

One of the Americans, a large, bluff man, looked intently at her. "We're not asking you to commit yourself now, just to indicate whether or not you might be interested."

Juliet sipped a little Chablis to steady herself. "Why me?"

The second man, gimlet-eyed, with crew-cut hair, produced a portfolio of her work: every article, from the very beginning—the successes, the mediocrities, the disasters.

Juliet's pulses raced. "It still doesn't explain why you've approached me."

"We like your style, Miss Austen." He went on candidly: "And of course, as you realize, though there are many talented people perhaps more qualified than you, not all of them have capital to invest."

Her composure slipped. "I'm sorry?"

The new magazine, they explained further, was perceived as a worker cooperative venture. If the key people had a financial stake, success would be that much more important to them.

"What kind of stake did you have in mind?"

"Thirty thousand pounds would buy you in."

Juliet's cheeks flushed. Angrily, she glanced at Chapplin, then back at the Americans. "I'm afraid you gentlemen have been misled," she said. "I don't have that kind of money."

"Pardon me," the bluff one said, "but aren't you the owner of a substantial unmortgaged property in Surrey?"

Juliet bristled at the mention of Kaikoura. "I don't see that's any of your business."

Joe Chapplin reached across to her and touched her arm. "They're just suggesting you get a loan, honey. There's nothing banks like more than giving out money for solid business deals, when there's security involved."

She shook her head, confused. "I don't know."

"As we said, Miss Austen," the crew-cut American said calmly, "we're not looking for an immediate commitment—just your initial response."

In the taxi they shared on the way back to Little Venice, Joe Chapplin told her that he'd been approached a month earlier with his own offer.

"You're looking at the associate art director."

"You've accepted?"

He shrugged. "Let's say I've done my deal, more or less." If Juliet did decide in favor, she would be invited to a meeting of investors in Geneva in a month's time.

"But why us?" Juliet was still disbelieving. "You're pretty good, Joe, but weren't you surprised?"

"Perhaps I don't sell myself as short as you," Chapplin grinned. "This isn't Condé Nast we're talking about, and it's not *Cosmo,* and it's certainly not *Woman's Own.* This is glossy trash, scandal-mongering made halfway respectable—it's what you *do,* for Christ's sake."

"I suppose so," she said wryly.

"These people know about mass-market appeal, honey—and the advertisers are already lining up, which you *know* is what counts."

For the first time, Juliet felt a glow of real excitement surging up inside her. Maybe he was right. Why was it so hard for her to believe that credibility could be offered to her? It happened to other people— why not to her?

When the taxi drew to a halt in her street, Joe kissed her lingeringly, and though Juliet pulled away, her eyes were shining as she jumped out and told the cabbie to drive on.

It was the first time in years that something other than sex had turned her on.

The feeling was too good to waste.

✱

With time to reflect, her sense of jubilation and triumph grew. Joe Chapplin was right—even if it was trash she wrote, she was *good* at it.

She asked herself if it was proper to use Kaikoura in this way—but then, what better way to let the house she so loved work for her, to advance her career. She thought of her mother, always urging her forward when there was a chance, encouraging her to cross new thresholds.

Features editor. Elizabeth would be so proud.

Reluctantly, Juliet went to see Walter Schuster, who had automatically become her lawyer after her mother's death. She guessed that his advice would be cautious. She didn't *want* to be cautious.

She was right. Walter fired off a barrage of questions that Juliet was unequipped to answer, and then shook his gray head.

"You can't invest thirty thousand pounds in a corporation you know nothing about."

Juliet looked him in the eye. "I know this is the right move for me, Walter—I just *know* it."

"And you may be right." He smiled at her. "Just promise me you won't take it any further until I've had a chance to do some checking."

"I promise," she said.

It was a lie. This was her only chance. She was more sure of that than she'd ever been about anything in her life. She didn't want Walter to have time to check—she didn't want to know about the corporation's financial reports for the last ten years. That was history. The new magazine was the future. *Her* future.

She negotiated the loan with a finance company. One week later, she handed over the deeds to Kaikoura, and that evening, in the lounge at the Ritz, over several glasses of champagne, she and Joe Chapplin toasted each other and looked forward to Geneva.

The meeting left her dizzier than ever. She and Chapplin flew first class on Swissair and found themselves in adjoining suites at the Hôtel de la Paix, with all expenses paid. The sense of big-league professionalism continued into the oak-paneled boardroom in the corporate offices on Rue Rousseau. Apart from the two Americans she'd met in London,

Juliet recognized no one at the long table, and could not establish who, out of the dozen other people present, were investors, prospective employees or officers of the corporation, but most of those present exuded power and confidence. Her new colleagues. Juliet rejoiced.

She handed over her check, and signed five copies of her contract. She still knew little more than that the magazine's head office would be based in Mayfair, London, and that she could expect to start work on the first day of 1973. All other details, including the magazine's name, would be kept under wraps until all the prime movers were ready and in place.

That was the way in the big league.

Still aglow, Juliet flew home to wait.

The fear began with the series of messages left by Walter Schuster on her answering machine, asking her, urgently, to call. She did not want to speak to him, but it was difficult to ignore the stark wording of his letter, telling her that on no account should she contemplate going ahead with her investment in the proposed magazine.

Juliet telephoned Joe Chapplin. A recorded message informed her that the photographer had flown to the Middle East on a commission. He would be away for several months.

The fear mounted to panic. She rang the contact numbers she had been given in Geneva, but two lines were unobtainable, and the others belonged to Swiss citizens unconnected to the corporation.

"But they *must* be listed!" she harangued the directory assistance operator, repeating the corporation's name and address until she was disconnected.

"But I have a *contract!*" she told Walter Schuster, at last, distraught and desperate. "I've been at their offices—I didn't imagine them—they were wood-paneled and there were Persian rugs on the floors, and they had secretaries and a switchboard!"

Schuster was horrified, his craggy face making it quite clear what he felt; how could anyone—let alone a young woman brought up by Elizabeth Austen, with every advantage and a first-class education—have been such a colossal fool?

✳

As the enormity of her folly was brought home to her, Juliet plunged into total blackness. In the dead of night, as she stared dry-eyed into the dark, old disjointed memories came back to haunt her—mental flashbacks to agony and loss—and she sat up, struggling for breath, knowing that this new anguish was of her own making.

She did not know what was more unbearable, the fact that she had thrown away her beloved Kaikoura, her only oasis in a hateful world, her last link with Elizabeth—or the undeniable reality that she was, and would always be, a failure.

For days, she remained, huddled and shivering, in her flat, too guilt-racked to think of going near the house. Hardly eating, weeping herself to total exhaustion, she drowned in her own misery, licking her wounds like some distressed creature.

Walter Schuster called to confirm what they already knew, that her contract was worthless, and that her only course of action would have to be via the law.

"Though, frankly, I don't hold out much hope of tracing any of them—except, perhaps, Chapplin—and it'll be your word against his." The lawyer paused, his voice gentle. "I'll do all I can to help you, Juliet, you know that."

"Yes, Walter," she answered numbly, and thanked him.

There was nothing anyone could do to give her justice. It was her own mistake, her naïveté, *her* greed. It was private.

She returned to her grief and isolation, but one word kept echoing in her brain. *Justice.* That was the one thing that still mattered. And gradually, as the worst of the pain abated, Juliet began to find refuge in the two emotions that had been her salvation before—

Rage. And the desire for revenge.

Joe Chapplin returned to London in early March, and moved to a new, high-rent studio in Pimlico. His name began to appear, with frequency, in trade journals and in the national press. He was the coming thing in photography, the flavor-of-the-month; the big names in theater were lining up for sessions.

Juliet was certain that the upswing in his fortunes, concurring with the downturn in her own, was no coincidence, but she knew, too, that it would be almost impossible to prove his small but pivotal part in the fraud. All her feelings of fury against the invisible corporation were impotent and pointless. There was only one person Juliet could punish.

It was May before she managed to pin him down for a face-to-face confrontation. She had been warm on the telephone—they had both been victims, after all, and though she was, of course, bitter about her own loss, she was encouraged by his recent success.

He opened his front door with a smile and outstretched arms. "Come in, poor baby."

She accepted his hug, feeling the tension in his body. "It's good to see you, Joe." She handed him a bottle.

"Rioja—great." He closed the door and led her by the hand into his living room. "Get comfy while I open this."

Juliet glanced around—everything in sight was black and white. "This is beautiful," she said. "You've really fallen on your feet."

As he gave her a long-stemmed wineglass, she thought he checked her face for signs of hostility.

"I meant it when I said I was glad for you, Joe." Her voice was sincere—she saw him relax.

"It was crazy." He sat beside her on the black sofa, stretching out his long, designer jean–clad legs. "After we got back from Geneva, I had no work on at all—I couldn't *wait* for the New Year."

"But you went to the Middle East. That was a job, wasn't it?" She kept her tone interested and friendly.

"Was it ever." Chapplin drank some wine. "A Spanish film producer I know asked me if I'd do some publicity shots for a movie he was shooting in Egypt, so I cabled our friends in Geneva to tell them where they could contact me—and then I flew out to Cairo and had a ball, which was just as well under the circumstances." He grinned at her ruefully. "Needless to say, they never did get in touch, and when I got home, the roof caved in."

"But you dug yourself out."

Chapplin shrugged. "The movie work, and all the bread-and-butter jobs I'd done over the years, suddenly paid off—" He stopped. "Christ, Juliet, honey, I've felt so lousy about you."

"Why? It wasn't your fault."

"Of course not, but I introduced you to them, for God's sake." He paused. "I presume you lost the house."

"I had to sell it to pay off my loan, naturally."

"Shit," Chapplin said, and poured more wine.

"Quite." Juliet brightened. "But I got a good price, enough for a deposit on a flat of my own. At least I won't have to pay rent anymore."

Chapplin moved an inch closer. "I think you're bloody brave, and generous too. If the tables were turned, and I'd lost almost everything, I'd probably have been fucking furious with you, however unreasonable that was."

Juliet lifted her right hand, and lightly brushed his cheek. "But you didn't lose everything, did you? You've been a lucky bugger, haven't you, Joe."

She began to make him even more comfortable. There were three things that worked with most men she'd known: alcohol, the promise of sex, and an invitation to talk about themselves.

"Let's put all that behind us now," she said, picking up the Rioja bottle and refilling his glass. "I want to hear all about you." She made her voice huskier. "You're a winner, Joe Chapplin, and I love being with winners." She let her hand touch his thigh, briefly. "In case something rubs off."

It was so easy, it was laughable. The more Chapplin bragged about his new career, the more relaxed he became. The more questions Juliet asked, the more wine he drank, the more he preened. It really *was* happening for him, Juliet realized as he reeled off the names of his latest clients; the money that had been poured into that fanfare of publicity and into this prestigious address had been well spent.

"Where is the studio?" she asked as Joe ran his fingers through her hair and leaned languidly back against a white silk cushion.

He nodded his head toward a door to the left of the sofa. "Through there—great studio, wonderful light—best darkroom I've ever had—"

Juliet's eyes were on the bulging crotch of his jeans, and a surge of venomous anticipation throbbed in her veins. "Ever made love in there?" she murmured, and blew in his ear.

"With my gorgeous bedroom?"

It was expensively decorated and furnished, but it was not in the least gorgeous, Juliet thought as she undressed Chapplin and told him to lie on his hand-stitched black and scarlet satin bedspread—an uncanny match for the new body stocking she'd had made especially for the occasion.

"I'm going to give you a massage, darling," she cooed over him, noticing that the flesh on his waist and buttocks, which had still been taut in Geneva, now rippled and sagged from too much good living. "Would you like that?"

"I'd like to fuck you," Chapplin said, rolling over to stare at her. "I'd like to rip that damn thing off you—"

"You know the rules, bad boy." She wagged a finger at him, repelled by the sight of his thrusting erection. Sex was the last thing on her mind. Joe Chapplin was not going to lay a hand on her.

He grinned up at her, and she thought his teeth were wolflike. "You're the greatest, Juliet—I'd almost forgotten how fabulous you were in Germany—"

"Do you have any oil?"

"Mmm," he said. "In the bathroom." He rolled back onto his stomach to wait.

Surrounded by marble and mirrors, Juliet looked at her reflection. Her face was pale and thin, but her blue eyes were bigger than ever, glittering with determination.

She glanced back at the door—saw that it had an old-fashioned lock and key. Good. She found the bottle of mineral oil in the cabinet, tucked the key down between her breasts, and returned to the matter in hand.

It was a pity, she thought, that she had to let him enjoy it so much, but she had no alternative. She had learned about the art of massage as a child, still working to regain full use of her limbs; she remembered times when she had felt restless and eager for a session to end, others when she had been lulled into languorous comfort.

She did not intend either to bore Joe Chapplin or to lull him to sleep. Juliet did not care if he woke tomorrow aching or even bruised— she was intent only on driving him crazy, on bringing him fully under her control.

"Mind the bedspread," he said as she splashed oil onto her palms.

"Don't worry," she said soothingly, and watched the first drips trickling over the satin.

It was hard work, and it was boring. She knew that he was having a good—no, a *great* time—but he kept getting drowsy, giving small, indignant grunts when she tweaked his skin to rouse him.

"Turn over," she ordered, and confirmed what she'd already suspected, that he'd lost his erection. *Too much damned wine,* she thought angrily, and went to work on his feet, rubbing and kneading, and using his ticklish soles to wake him fully before finally—for she didn't know how much more she could endure—starting on his testicles.

Chapplin was awake. Wide-awake.

"Jesus, woman, what are you *doing* to me?" he groaned.

"Don't you like it?"

"Of course I bloody like it—come here, baby—"

She shook her head. His penis felt like a steel rod in her hands—he began to writhe—

"God, Juliet, come *here!*"

"Not yet, darling." She paused. "Joe, where's your kitchen?"

"What?"

She ran there and back, stopping only to yank open the freezer door and to scrape ice from its walls.

"Baby, where did you *go?*" Chapplin, burning with desire, stared up at her as she stood right over him. "Christ, you look like the whore of my dreams. Will you take it off if I beg you?"

Juliet smiled. "Do you really want me to, Joe?"

"You know I do, baby."

She lowered her voice. "And do you want me? Do you want to come inside me?"

Joe Chapplin closed his eyes.

Juliet dumped two handfuls of ice onto his erect organ—

Chapplin screamed. "You fucking bitch!" He scrambled up from the bed, clutching himself. "You bloody *sadist!*"

Juliet began to laugh, and he made a grab for her, but she spun out of his reach.

"I'll get you for this—it's your turn now!"

"If you can catch me—" She darted through the door, and into the bathroom, where she stood, provocatively, against the mirrored wall.

"Gotcha!" Chapplin lunged in after her, but the soles of his feet were still oily, and he slipped on the Italian tiles and fell, with a loud and painful thud, onto his backside.

Juliet walked slowly back to the door, turned, and withdrew the key from her cleavage. "If I were you," she said, "I'd have a bath before you try to get out of the window."

Quietly, she shut and locked the door. Then she walked over to one of Chapplin's black ceramic plant pots, and buried the key deep in the soil.

And then she went into his studio.

The destruction was methodical and calm. She used a fire extinguisher, a pair of shears, four bottles of chemicals, and her own bare hands. All the time, she could hear Chapplin bellowing in the bathroom, but she never hesitated, never paused until she had destroyed everything she could touch or see in the studio and darkroom.

On her way out of the flat, after she had washed her hands in the kitchen sink, and dressed, she stood for a moment outside the bathroom door. Chapplin had stopped raving.

"Can you hear me?" she said loudly.

"I hear you, you bloody lunatic." His voice was hoarse.

"You must have known I'd pay you back," she said, and the first wave of exhaustion overcame her. "It's nothing compared to what you did to me—but I doubt your insurance will cover the damage, and I imagine your newfound clients will have quite a few reservations about your reliability after this."

"What makes you think I won't call the police?" He sounded bitter, but weak, and she imagined him slumped on his precious tiled floor, huddled in a towel.

Juliet shrugged. "If you do," she replied, "you know I'll make sure everyone knows exactly what you are—nothing but a con man."

Chapplin said nothing.

"This way, if you're lucky," she went on, "you'll just be dismissed as the low-life *paparazzo* that you are—a foolish victim—a loser." She paused. "Just like me."

When she got back to Little Venice, the first thing she did was to take every one of the costly, provocative body stockings out of her dresser drawer, and to take them into the living room.

It was a mild evening, but she lit a fire in the hearth—the fireplace had been one of the attractions of the flat for her—and when it was burning brightly, she took the shimmering, seductive items, and threw them, one at a time, onto the flames, until they were gone.

There was only one left, the new one she had ordered for today, and which she still wore. She would keep that one—wrapped in tissue in the bottom drawer. Not to use again—for she would never wear it again—but to serve as a reminder, if she needed one, of the depths to which she had sunk.

Yet still she did not take it off, for the day's work was not yet over—there was one more thing to be done.

Juliet switched on her electric kettle, and made herself a cup of tea.

And then she went into her study, and sat down at her desk, and began to write her article.

She tried several headlines, until she found the one that satisfied her:

CHAPPLIN, "NEW BAILEY," RUINED

It was paltry, compared to the loss of Kaikoura, and Elizabeth's faith. But it was better than nothing.

Chapter 26

Francesca could not keep away.

Knowing that Nick spent every available moment at Sonora Farm, never ceasing to hope that she would come to him, it had become impossible to maintain the rage and hurt she had felt when she first learned of his marriage.

She always knew when he was in Connecticut, because he sent her short notes telling her; not love letters, because she had begged him not to write or call. The notes, therefore, were always brief and succinct: he was there—he wanted, more than anything, to see her—on whatever terms she wished.

The day she returned to Sonora, six months after she'd resolved never to see Nick again, Francesca knew full well that she was committing herself to a life that was much less than she had hoped for. But the moment they were in each other's arms again, Francesca knew there would be no turning back, for their past, and the long, hot, passionate afternoon they had shared the previous September, had shackled her to him forever.

That first evening in the house at Sonora, facing Nick over the dinner he had cooked for her, she found herself remembering how she had felt with Robert, how she had so often felt the need to be alone. And a vivid, undeniable joy swept over her, as she realized how right she had been to come back—for she could not imagine ever wanting to be apart from this man.

While Nick was at the farm, he and Francesca lived as man and wife. Whenever he returned to Sonora West, she went back to her apartment on Mount Vernon Street and the Joy Street studio, and immersed herself in work to try to suppress her loneliness. Her last series of photographs, of people eating, drinking, or just whiling away the time in restaurants, bars, cafés, and diners, had been exhibited at the Institute of Contemporary Art, and Francesca knew she was at a point where she might have carved herself a notable career—but her passion for Nick had diluted her ambition. She still loved her work, but her desire to be with him came before everything.

✱

There was no more likelihood of Eleanor Dante agreeing to divorce Nick now than there had ever been. Persistently, he had tried to convince his wife that her refusal to free them both from unhappiness was unreasonable, and that she needed help with her emotional problems, but Eleanor had only become more hysterical and unbearable to live with. If Nick raised the subject of ending their marriage again, she swore she would take her life.

"One of these days, I'm going to call her bluff," Nick said to Francesca one evening at the farm, as they sat quietly after dinner. "I don't believe she'd do that to the kids."

"But you can't be sure."

"No."

"Then there's nothing to be done," Francesca said softly.

They were sitting close together on the large, comfortable sofa they'd bought together on a trip to Newport. It had been the first time that Francesca had been willing to impose her own taste on Sonora's main house—it was hard for her to accept that it was Nick's property rather than Eleanor's, but as the months passed by, and Nick's wife never came any closer than New York, Francesca had begun to relax in the handsome white and gray house, with its beautiful landscaped private gardens.

"Are you still happy with this?" Nick asked her now.

"This?"

"This part-time marriage."

"We're not married," Francesca said gently. "But yes, I'm still happy —not with our situation, but with you." She looked into his face, and smiled. "I don't have a choice, my love. It's this, or nothing at all."

On the last day of April 1974, Eleanor, abandoned by her latest lover, an Italian fashion designer based in Los Angeles, decided it was time she wrought a little havoc in what she thought of as the cozy New England love nest that Nick and Francesca had shared for two years.

"She's out of control," Nick told Francesca on the telephone from California. "I'm afraid she called us every foul thing under the sun, in front of the kids—it's exactly what she swore she'd never do."

Francesca heard the darkness in his voice. "How have Kevin and Alicia taken it?"

"Badly. They've known about you for a long time, of course, at least that you're my dearest friend—but Eleanor made it sound rotten and dirty."

"What are you going to do?"

"I'd like to fly them across—"

"Here?" Francesca could not mask her alarm.

"They're reasonable human beings, darling," Nick said reassuringly. "I want them to meet you—God knows it should have happened a long time ago—and to see the farm. They have to see the truth for themselves, or they'll never have any peace of mind."

✻

She was pale-faced and apprehensive when she opened the front door to welcome them. She had told Nick she felt it improper for her to be at the house when they arrived, but he'd been adamant that Kevin and Alicia should not feel they were being lied to. Francesca was not a guest at Sonora Farm. So far as Nick was concerned, it was her home, and the purpose of this visit was honesty.

She had not expected to feel such immediate warmth when she met them for the first time—she had assumed they would seem to her like Eleanor's children, not Nick's.

"Come in." She hated the forced brightness that her fear pushed into her voice.

Nick kissed her, and made the introductions. Formally, both children shook her hand. Kevin's handshake was firm, his sister's even firmer.

"I'm very glad to meet you," Francesca said, and knew that she was staring at them, but could not help herself.

Kevin, at twelve, was a fascinating-looking boy. Like Billy Chase, he'd inherited a half share of each parent's physical characteristics; his hair was sleek and golden, naturally highlighted by California sunshine, his skin, though tanned, was much paler than Nick's, but he had his father's brilliant dark eyes and the same straight nose. Alicia presumably looked like Eleanor—her hair was blond and her eyes were blue, yet when she threw a brief, true smile at Nick, Francesca could see his light shining out of her face.

She showed them to their bedrooms, trying to be considerate of their feelings, remembering her own arrival at Palazzo Speroza, and that though, of course, her situation had been far more tragic, any emotional upheaval at their age was traumatic.

"This must be very hard for you," she said to them, quietly, in the corridor outside their rooms. "And I'm not going to impose my feelings on you, just for my sake." She paused, meeting their frank eyes. "So I'll simply say three things, because I have to."

Kevin and Alicia waited silently.

"First, I really *am* glad to meet you—I can't tell you how long I've wanted to know you." She heard her voice quiver slightly. "Second, I love your father more than you can even imagine." She took a shaky breath. "And third, the last thing in the world I want to do is to cause you any more pain."

Dinner went surprisingly well, Francesca's honest goodwill putting Kevin and Alicia at their ease. With Nick, Francesca was loving, but careful not to seem intimate, and with the children she was mindful not to offer any more warmth than she thought they could tolerate from a woman they must—no matter what Nick had told them—regard as a home-wrecker. She had prepared an authentic New England dinner, with corn bread, duck roasted with home-grown peaches, and Indian pudding, and had been anxious in case they were too upset to eat, but thankfully their appetites seemed intact.

They don't hate me, she thought, with tentative gratitude, *or surely they wouldn't want to eat my food.* And yet she knew that the evening was only going along pleasantly because they were making small talk about horses and riding, and the weather in New England, and the Patty Hearst affair. It was only a matter of time, she realized, before someone mentioned Eleanor—and then the children's faces would cloud over, and they would stare at Francesca with cold eyes, and she would know that they believed her their enemy.

"What do you think?" she whispered to Nick as he helped her clear away in the kitchen. "They seem almost to like me, yet I know they must hate me."

Nick put down his dishcloth and touched her cheek with his hand. "I think they were prepared to hate you, but I knew they couldn't once they met you."

"I think they like the house."

"They like the atmosphere," he whispered back, smiling. "They feel the difference."

"It must be tough on them—all the battles."

"It's tough on us all, my darling."

"But worst for Kevin and Alicia." Francesca filled the kettle, and turned back to face him. "I told them that I don't want to hurt them, Nick—and I meant it. If it comes to it, we have to put them first."

Nick took the kettle and put it on the stove. "It won't come to that."

The telephone rang.

✶

Nick took the call in his study. When he returned to the kitchen, his face was ashen.

"Eleanor—" He stopped.

Francesca felt a chill of fear. "What?"

"She said that she's taken pills." He spoke quietly. "An overdose."

"Dear God." She stared at him. "Do you believe her?"

"I don't know." He shook his head. "So many threats, so often—but her voice sounded—"

"How?"

"Strange." He looked into Francesca's eyes. "Drugged."

"You have to go to her!"

"She's thousands of miles away—if it's true, I'd be too late." Conscious of the children in the living room, he still kept his voice low. "I called back again, but there was no reply, so I telephoned Eleanor's mother and told her to get the paramedics right away."

Francesca felt ill. "Now what?"

Nick's eyes were anguished. "We wait."

"Are you going to tell them?"

He shook his head. "Not unless I have to. We can't even get on a flight till morning—"

"I'll call Bradley airport." Francesca was trembling. "You'll have to keep Kevin and Alicia occupied—get them to bed as soon as you can."

Nick put his arms around her. "I'm so sorry, my love." He closed his eyes. "I feel so *helpless*. Eleanor's put us all through so much, and there've been times when I wanted to strangle her—but I don't want her to *die*—"

"Maybe they'll be in time," Francesca said, her voice muffled against his shoulder. "Maybe it isn't even true."

But she knew, already, that it was.

The call from California came four hours later, at two in the morning. Eleanor was in a coma, and was not expected to survive. Nick woke the children a half hour later, and Francesca drove them, in deathly silence, through the dark, empty countryside, to the airport, knowing that they faced hours of limbo in their aircraft seats, before they arrived in Los Angeles.

Francesca could hardly bear to look at Kevin and Alicia as, with uncanny, almost courtly good manners, they thanked her for her hospitality and turned away toward the departure gate.

"I don't know what to say to you." Nick was taut, his self-control perilously close to cracking. He began to embrace Francesca, but she pulled quickly away.

"Not now." The children stood, a dozen feet away, waiting for their father, their faces expressionless. "You have to go," she said. Her voice was brusque.

Nick's face creased with pain. "I wish I didn't have to leave you now, of all times."

"Now, of all times, you have to leave me." Francesca's eyes burned. "Your wife is dying." The words sounded harsh, brutal, but she could not help herself. "The mother of your children."

He flushed darkly. "I'll call as soon as I can." He was close to tears. "Will you stay at the farm?"

"Perhaps."

Anxiously, he searched her face. "Are you all right?"

"Don't worry about me." Still, coldness sharpened each word. "See to your children, Nick."

Agonized, he grasped her hand. "We'll get through this, I swear it."

Francesca longed, then, to relent—to hold him close and reassure him—but the specter of Eleanor, and the Damoclean sword she had held over them since the beginning, prevented her. And still, Kevin and Alicia stood, waiting.

"Go now," she whispered. "Please."

They went.

It was noon in California when they arrived. Eleanor had died two hours earlier.

Nick telephoned Francesca shortly after eight o'clock in the evening. "I couldn't call before—it was impossible."

"Of course you couldn't." She held the receiver so tightly that her fingers were numb. "How are the children holding up?" She shook her head, angry with herself. "Stupid, *stupid* question—I'm sorry."

"You have nothing to be sorry about."

"I wish that were true."

Nick's voice was choked. "I want so much to be with you."

"You can't be." She was much gentler now. Her heart ached for him, and she hated herself for her iciness at the airport. "You have all the arrangements to take care of—and you can't consider leaving the children."

"Not for a while."

"Not for a long time. We have to put them first now, Nick. They're very young—they need stability. They need their father."

"Their father needs you." His misery was palpable.

Francesca summoned all her strength. "When the time is right," she said.

The guilt was overwhelming—it consumed her. All the remorse she had fought to suppress since her love affair with Nick had begun rose up inside her like a powerful wave, battering her, suffocating her—

She had never slept at Sonora without Nick, and though she had felt utterly exhausted, as soon as she lay down in the big, lonely bed, every trace of sleepiness vanished, and each time she shut her eyes, images of Nick and the children flashed in front of her.

She'd never noticed the sounds before. All houses gave off night sounds—creaking, contracting pipes, rattling wooden shutters, moths tapping at the windows—but Francesca had never felt so unnerved by them.

She climbed out of bed again, went downstairs, and poured herself a large cognac. Her hands still shook. The living room reproached her. Yesterday evening, it had been filled with hope—until yesterday evening, it had been filled with love.

And now it was all over.

When the time is right, she had said to Nick.

The time would never be right. They both knew that. Eleanor—poor, malevolent, dead Eleanor—had won her final victory.

There was no sleep for her that night.

✶

She drove back to Boston in the morning, and went straight to Joy Street to see Johnny.

"I'm going to France—to Luciano."

"How long for?"

"I don't know." She looked candidly at her friend. "I just know that I have to get as far away from Nick as I can—and for as long as I can."

Johnny frowned. "Does he know?"

She shook her head.

"Don't you think he should?"

"He'll work it out soon enough." Francesca's face was very white. "He knows that if there ever was any hope for us, it died together with Eleanor."

"That makes no sense."

She stared at him. "Do you imagine that her children will ever forgive me? Nick's children."

Johnny did not answer.

"And when they make him choose—as they will—do you think that Nick will abandon them for me?"

"It may not come to that."

"It will." The trembling, which activity and purpose had kept at bay for a time, began again.

Johnny still persisted. "And what exactly do we tell Nick when he calls us to find out where you are?"

"Tell him what he must already know, even if he hasn't admitted it yet." Francesca's eyes were bleak, and bright with tears. "Tell him that it's over."

Chapter 27

MOST PEOPLE AGREED that May was the loveliest month of all on the Côte d'Azur. The weather was mild, the air redolent with blossom, the streets—apart from the crazy days of the Grand Prix and the Cannes festival—were not overcrowded, and in Nice, there was a sense of camaraderie that would vanish as summer approached, as if the natives accepted that springtime visitors had a real love of the Côte and of their town and, therefore, belonged.

"I picked a good time to visit," Francesca said, two weeks after her arrival, as she and Luciano sat on his terrace, eating cold langouste with salad, and drinking chilled white wine.

"There's no bad time here," Luciano said, "except, perhaps, August, and then I usually hide at Le Rocher. I love it here even in winter; seeing the Mediterranean turning gray and wild and cold, and the people huddling under umbrellas—it makes the place more human somehow."

"I wasn't talking about the place," Francesca said. "I was thinking about you."

"Me?"

"And the fact that you need me." She paused, and looked at him intently. "I'm right, aren't I? You do need to talk to your big sister."

"How do you know?"

"Because I *am* your sister. And I've noticed that the carefree, debonair image that you present to the world isn't quite the whole story. The man who takes me out to lunch and dinner in public is that person"— she hesitated briefly—"but the brother I see first thing in the morning and last thing at night—the brother I've observed, when he hasn't been aware I was watching—is deeply troubled."

Luciano was silent.

"By what, *caro?*" Her face was anxious. "What's wrong? Are you ill?"

"No." Luciano gave a small, wry shrug. "Or not ill in the way that you mean."

"How then?" She waited. "For pity's sake, you have to tell me now, or I'll worry myself sick. What *is* it? Is it your writing? Are you having problems with the new book?" Again, she waited. "I've never known you like this. You're so introverted, and you pretend to be happy, but you're miserable inside."

"It isn't my writing," Luciano said, at last, slowly.

He told her. It took time to unburden himself, for he knew that he was unlocking the part of himself that he had striven to keep absolutely secret. It was hard to explain, even to Francesca, about his *petits démons* —his little demons—hard to account for the fact that the random thoughts and feelings that had been a part of his mental process since early childhood had accelerated so uncontrollably that they had become alarming to him.

"What used to be a trickle," he finished, "has turned into a torrent —what was amusing, if eccentric, has become aberrant and frightening."

"Are the thoughts so awful, then?" Francesca asked gently.

"Sometimes they are—but though they are, of course, the cause of my fear, they aren't what really alarms me." Luciano's blue eyes were somber. "It's the idea that I might be going mad—that possibility is more frightening than anything I could possibly imagine. It stops me from sleeping peacefully, from living normally. Suzette left me because of my unpredictable moods—I can't sustain any worthwhile relationship for long—all because I'm secretly terrified that I'm going insane."

Francesca watched him for a moment. Then she picked up the wine bottle and poured another glass for them both.

"First of all," she said, her voice steady, "you are one of the most stable human beings I know. I can't find an instant explanation for what's going on, and I can't stop you from worrying about your sanity—but I can tell you that I'm not afraid for you."

"You can't pretend that this is normal."

"What is normal? Just because you have unusual experiences does not make you mentally ill. You're a writer, for heaven's sake. Even if these ideas aren't pleasant, the most rational explanation still has to be that they're some sort of deep-rooted inspiration—"

"But I've tried to tell you, they aren't *my* ideas!"

"Why? Because they're unpleasant?"

"Because they're far more than unpleasant—they're the thought processes of a melancholic—of a lonely, bitter human being. They're so foreign to me that I couldn't conceive of using them in a book."

"Not in a Zachary Holt book, of course not." Francesca saw the acuteness of his distress, and sought to find an answer that might calm him. "Luciano, maybe this means you should be writing a different kind of book. Holt is a delightful invention—the books are wonderful entertainment, and they've made you a success, but—"

"But what?" Luciano drank some wine, his voice unusually cynical. "Drop him? Turn away from what I love—from what I'm good at?"

"Darling, stop this." Francesca rose and came to him, putting her arms around him. "You're overreacting, and perhaps I'm underestimating how upset you are." She felt the tension in his body. "I'm just trying to point out that you're a far deeper human being than your detective stories allow for, but the last thing I'm suggesting is that Zachary should be dropped."

"Then what?" Luciano extricated himself from her arms, lit a Gitane, and began to pace the terrace.

Francesca sat in his chair and watched him. "Do you ever think about our childhood?"

"Of course."

"Do you realize how traumatic it was?" She shook her head, impatient with herself. "Of course you do—but you don't seem to allow for its effect upon you."

"The same things, and worse, happened to you." Luciano inhaled from his cigarette deeply. "Yet I don't hear you telling me you're being tormented by crazy thoughts."

"No." Francesca smiled wryly. "Everything in my garden is rosy, Luciano."

He sighed. "I'm sorry. I didn't think."

"I'm caught up in the past too—not in the same way, of course not. Everyone reacts differently, and in any case, I'm not a writer—I can't purge my emotions through a novel." She stood up and walked over to the parapet. "I think you feel guilty because our uncle found Kate, and brought you to this Garden of Eden. I think you've tortured yourself for years, because you were happy and alive, while the others were dead."

Luciano ground out his cigarette underfoot, and joined her at the edge of the terrace.

"How does all that sound to you?" Francesca asked softly. "Like half-baked, amateur psychology?"

Her brother shook his head. "Not really." He stared out over the Baie des Anges. "I suppose it makes sense." He forced a smile. "So tell me what to do."

"Three things." Francesca turned to face him. "First, I think you should keep on writing, no matter what. Write whatever you want—finish the new Holt book, of course, and jot down all your little demons, too, if it feels right to do that."

"Second," Luciano interrupted, "see a psychiatrist."

"Maybe a therapist, or a psychologist. You're not mentally ill—you're not deranged—but perhaps a professional could put your mind at rest—help you to understand what's happening to you."

"And third?"

"Stop bottling up your problems. Stop kidding yourself that Luciano Cesaretti must be happy-go-lucky, just because he lives in one of the loveliest places on earth, and has written four international best sellers.

Call me whenever you want to talk, or write to me—or come to Boston, or tell me to come here."

Luciano glanced at her. "You're not planning to leave yet, are you?"

"No." The sun felt warm on Francesca's face, but the deep, private sadness that had been kept at bay for a short while chilled her bones again. "I shan't go back for some time." She forced a smile. "This is too lovely a hideaway to leave too quickly."

"So far as I'm concerned," Luciano said softly, "you can stay here forever."

"Forever? I don't think so." Francesca sighed. "I've become too used to America—my home is there, and my work, and—" She broke off.

"And Nick."

She looked into her brother's face, and her eyes, abruptly, filled with tears. "I miss him," she whispered. "I know I can't be with him—I know it has to be over, but it hurts so much."

"Won't you speak to him, then?" She had refused every one of Nick's persistent telephone calls since her arrival.

"What for? To prolong the pain?"

"But it seems so cruel to you both—and perhaps even unnecessary. His children may understand—"

"*Never.*" The word was vehement. "It's impossible."

"How can you know?"

"I know."

Nick came at the beginning of June. He looked haggard and unhappy, and Francesca's heart wrenched at the sight of him.

"I told you not to come," she said.

"I couldn't stay away."

"You have no choice. There's no future for us."

Nick looked at her. "Luciano says that you hardly go out of the apartment—that you're just as miserable as I am."

"Of course," she said flatly. "But that doesn't change anything." She turned away. "I wish you'd go."

"The children don't hold you responsible." Nick's voice was quiet but desperate. "They loved Eleanor, but they knew she was hysterical and irrational—"

"They don't blame us for having an affair? For creating a situation where their mother felt so hopeless and betrayed that she took her own life?"

"We can't be sure Eleanor even meant to die," Nick said. "I think she wanted to be saved—she'd done that before, after all, God knows."

"Does that make us any less to blame for her death?"

"You were not to blame!" Nick said passionately. "She had threatened to commit suicide for years before we met again—you *know* that. And the kids know it too."

Francesca shook her head. "It all feels so ugly to me now. I always hated our situation—I loved *you*, but I hated being your mistress—and yet it still felt beautiful, in spite of everything, until—" She stopped, unable to go on.

Luciano had left them alone in the salon. Everything was creamy and pristine, and with the blinds half drawn, there was a strange, hushed, unreal feel to the room.

Nick walked over to her, and tentatively put one arm around her. She stiffened, but did not draw away, her longing to be close to him too strong to deny completely.

"Kevin and Alicia have been remarkable," he told her quietly. "I've tried to be honest with them, and I know it's hard for you to believe, but they don't seem to blame us. It's their mother's instability—the fact that they couldn't help her—that's the toughest part for them, not the fact that I love you."

"That's just because they know it's over." For just an instant, Francesca allowed herself to lean against his shoulder, and then she moved away. "If they were faced with me, Nick, it would all come back to haunt them—and I couldn't bear to face them."

"You're wrong, you know."

She looked back at him, her eyes glittering with tears. "I should never have come back to Sonora after that first time—I should have trusted my instincts, and stayed away. As I hope you'll stay away from me now."

She opened the door, and left the room. A moment later, Nick heard another door quietly closing, and then there was perfect silence.

He knew she would not come back.

✴

One month later, on the first Saturday in July, Francesca returned to the apartment from shopping, her arms full of bags. Luciano opened the front door as she began to insert her key into the lock.

"You have visitors."

"Who?"

"Better come in and see." He took the bags from her. "*A la terrasse,*" he said.

Her stomach lurched. "Is it Nick?"

"No." He went toward the kitchen. "On the terrace," he repeated.

Slowly, she walked through the salon, the heels of her shoes clicking on the marble floor. And then she saw them sitting at her brother's white table, drinking lemonade—

Her heart began to pound, and her legs grew weak, but she continued through the open French doors until, seeing her, they rose from their white-cushioned chairs.

"Alicia," she said, and her voice was faint. "Kevin."

The boy moved first. His cheeks were flushed, and there were shadows under his eyes, but he was just as striking, with his golden hair and dark eyes, as she had remembered. Politely, he extended his hand. "Hi," he said, and his voice was a touch deeper than it had been two months earlier. "I hope you don't mind us turning up like this."

Francesca shook his hand, and then Alicia's. The girl's blue eyes were very bright—she looked nervous.

"This—" Francesca's mouth was very dry. She licked her lips. "This is a surprise." She couldn't help staring at them. "What are you doing here?" She was bewildered. "Are you on vacation?"

"It's the Fourth of July weekend," Kevin said, "but we're not really on vacation."

"We came to see you." Alicia sounded strained.

"Oh." Francesca felt inadequate and foolish, as if she were the child and they the adults. "Who came with you?"

"No one—" Kevin's flush heightened. "That is, we started out on our own, but Dad caught up with us."

"Your father's here?"

"Not exactly," Alicia said.

"I see."

For another moment, the three of them stood, stiff as statues, and then suddenly the enormity of the situation struck Francesca forcibly.

"*Dio,*" she murmured softly, to herself, and then, at last, she moved. "Sit down, please. When did you get here? *How* did you get here? I said 'I see,' but I don't see at all—" She floundered. "Please don't misunderstand me. I'm happy you're here—that is, I don't know why you are, but—"

Like an answer to a prayer, Luciano appeared, carrying a tray of coffee, croissants, and marmalade.

"They've come to talk to you," he said simply.

Francesca stared blankly.

"They arrived here awhile before you got back from shopping, and we had a chance to introduce ourselves." Luciano set down the tray and removed the lemonade jug. "And they explained it all to me." He picked up the coffeepot. "For you, Alicia?"

"What did they explain to you, Luciano?" Francesca waited in an agony of suspense.

"That they hope to change your mind."

Kevin and Alicia had, Francesca heard, decided to take matters into their own hands a few days earlier. Their father was wretched without her, and since they had never seen him more contented and at ease than during those first few hours at the Connecticut farm, they had determined to do whatever they could to persuade her to come back to him.

They had their own passports, and having made reservations using Nick's gold American Express card, Kevin and Alicia had secretly packed a few belongings and taken a cab to Los Angeles airport.

"They'd flown unaccompanied on several occasions," Luciano explained, "so they foresaw no problems, so long as their father didn't find out."

An official at the check-in desk, however, had become suspicious and contacted the ranch. Nick had rushed to the airport, intending to bring them home, but learning their intentions, he'd changed his mind, hopeful that perhaps they might succeed where he had failed.

"So where is your father?" Francesca was overwhelmed.

"At the hotel," Kevin said.

"At the Negresco," Luciano added.

Francesca looked at the children. Her heart was so full, she did not know how to respond to such generosity and candor.

"Your father was right," she said at last. "He told me you are remarkable children—I'm afraid I didn't believe that anyone could be so forgiving."

"It wasn't your fault—what happened—" Alicia's mouth trembled.

"We need Dad to be happy again." Kevin's eyes were fixed upon her face.

"And what about you?" Francesca's eyes were full of tears. "Your needs—your feelings. How do you feel about me? You know I love your father, but I told you that evening at the farm that I didn't want to cause you any more pain." Her voice quivered. "And whether or not I did cause it, you've had nothing but pain ever since." She paused. "Do you honestly think you could bear to live with me?"

No one spoke for a moment.

"I don't know," Alicia said, honestly. "We don't know you—except that we both liked you a lot that evening—and you went to a lot of trouble—"

"You cooked a great dinner," Kevin added.

Francesca smiled for the first time. And then she rose from her chair.

"Going somewhere?" Luciano asked.

"To the Negresco," she said.

✶

The big terrace at Le Rocher had never looked lovelier, or more romantic. Kate had lit candles and placed huge bowls of roses everywhere available, and she, Francesca, and Alicia sipped pink champagne while Kevin took charge of the barbecue, aided by his father, and watched, with admiration, by Bruno and Luciano.

"Californians have always known how to do that better than anyone else," Kate said. "It's the outdoor spirit—goes with camping."

"Do you go camping, Alicia?" Francesca asked.

The girl shook her head. "Mother didn't like the idea too much. She let Kevin go a few times, but I never went." She paused. "I'd like to."

"What would you like to do?" Nick brought a tray of spicy barbecued vegetables to the table.

"We were talking about camping," Kate said.

"Really?" Nick sat down. "You'd like to go, Alicia?"

"Sure."

"It just happens that I've had an idea that would sit very well with that."

"What, Dad?"

"Let's wait till everyone's at the table—then we can take a vote."

Nick wanted to see his brother and the rest of his family, and it would mean a great deal to him, he said, if his children could experience, at first hand, the very different world in which he had spent his formative years.

"I'm a Gypsy," he said softly, his eyes lighting, with love, on Francesca, "yet my children live on a California ranch, and shop on Rodeo Drive."

"You like shopping, Dad," Kevin laughed. "You wear Cerruti suits and designer jeans, and I *know* you love caviar."

"I'm an adaptable man," Nick said easily.

And silently, Francesca rejoiced.

The last letter Nick had received from Emilio had been postmarked from Padova. One week after they had arrived in Nice, he, Francesca, Luciano, and the children flew to Milan, rented a car and drove two hundred kilometers east, only to learn that the *zingari* had moved, just a month earlier, to a site just north of Verona, near the River Adige.

By nightfall, they were ensconced in the camp, and the warmth of Emilio and Antonia Dante's welcome had long since eased any anxiety felt by Kevin and Alicia at their first glimpse of the strange-looking people camped by the river.

"It's unbelievable!" Emilio kept repeating, staring at Francesca and Luciano, and marveling at the twists of destiny that had brought them back to their *vitsa* with Nick and his two beautiful children.

"It's so *romantic*," Alicia whispered to Kevin as they sat around the Dantes' blazing fire that night, eating delicious flame-roasted pork and drinking watered wine, while Francesca took roll after roll of film, avidly reabsorbing what had been the greatest, and happiest, adventure of her childhood.

"This sure beats camp, Dad," Kevin told Nick, who hardly took his eyes off Francesca, as she focused and refocused her Pentax, and chattered animatedly with Antonia and Luciano, returning her gaze to Nick every few moments, as if trying to convince herself that he and this night were real.

They stayed at the camp for five days and six nights. During the days, they explored the region, visited Verona, traveled west to Lake Garda, and rode horses; in the evenings, they sat together around the fire, exchanging stories and eating and drinking—and at night, Francesca and Nick made love, endlessly, under the stars and then, together with Luciano and the children, slept like contented babes in the *tsara* lent to them by Emilio and Antonia.

Late on the last evening, after Kevin and Alicia had gone to sleep, an old Romany woman with a leathery face and bright, birdlike eyes came to Luciano and seized his hand.

"She's a *Drabarna*," Nick explained. "A fortune-teller. She's very old, and very wise."

The woman turned Luciano's hand over and gazed at his palm. For a moment, he stiffened, and then relaxed.

"You can trust her," Nick said. "Every person's palm has lines and special signs which she'll interpret as if she were reading a book—we call it the 'book of destiny.' "

"May I photograph her?" Francesca whispered.

"Not now—let her concentrate. She may just read his palm, or she may use cards. Or she may go into a trance in order to commune with his ancestors."

The old woman looked at Nick, and spoke to him in Romany. Quickly, he rose, indicating to Francesca to do the same.

"She wants us to leave them alone."

Francesca glanced down at Luciano. "Do you mind?"

He smiled. "Why should I?"

They waited, near their *tsara,* watching from a distance. For a time, nothing much could be observed; the *Drabarna's* head was bent low over Luciano's hand, her lips moving, Luciano sitting quietly, listening. Then, abruptly, a change took place. Luciano looked up, and pointed toward Francesca—the fortune-teller shook her head vigorously, and then, closing her eyes, continued to speak, becoming visibly agitated, until at last, Luciano stood up and walked away.

Francesca followed him. "What happened? What did she say?"

Even in the near darkness, Luciano looked ghostly pale. "She kept using the word '*phen*'—over and over. She said that it means 'sister' in Romany."

"That was when you pointed to me."

He nodded. "But she wasn't talking about you. She said that I have another sister."

"And you told her about Giulietta?"

"Of course, but she insisted she was speaking of the living, not the dead."

"Perhaps you misunderstood her. Nick said that they sometimes talk about the dead—even about distant ancestors."

Luciano shook his head. "She was very clear. She said that my sister is alive—that she's surrounded by an aura of darkness and loneliness."

"Do you think she might have picked up on Giulietta's last days?" In spite of the mildness of the night and the heat from the fire, Francesca shivered. "You were twins, *caro*—you were especially close."

"I wish I hadn't let her touch me," Luciano said, quietly but violently. "Giulietta's been dead for almost twenty-three years—she's made me feel as if she's never been at peace."

By morning, though, when they woke to the sounds of children laughing and birds singing, the night's disquiet had already melted into memory. A few hours later, back on the main road to Milan, with Kevin and Alicia singing folk songs, it was not possible to feel morose.

By the time they sat on the jet to New York, fully returned to the twentieth century, the visions of the old Gypsy fortune-teller had been almost completely forgotten.

Their lives were transformed.

By November, Nick had sold the California ranch, and the house at Sonora Farm became a real family home for himself, Francesca, and the children. Kevin and Alicia, it had been mutually agreed, would stay on at school on the West Coast, living with Eleanor's mother at her Laguna Beach house during term time, but coming east for the long vacations.

Francesca had given up her Boston apartment and handed over the Joy Street studio to Johnny, had converted the top floor of the farmhouse into a superbly equipped studio and darkroom, and was concentrating for the time being on her wildlife studies and action portraits of the men and women who worked on Sonora. Nick was developing the small riding school at the farm into an equestrian center and, together with Francesca, had opened an official shelter for ill-treated and abandoned horses.

On New Year's Eve, the freshly decorated house aglow with warmth and joy, Nick and Francesca were married, in the presence of their families and friends, including Emilio, Antonia, and their children. That night, as 1974 drew to a close and the New Year began, Francesca, radiant with love, embraced them all—Bruno and Kate, her brother, the

Chases and dear Robert Stern, long since over her, who had come from Boston with his fiancée—before turning back to face her husband.

Niccolo, the Gypsy. Nick, the enigma. And now—

Her heart contracted with joy.

Only Luciano, in spite of his pleasure at his sister's happiness, was not perfectly content that night, for his demons were troubling him more than ever, dancing in his head and stamping on his joy.

As midnight struck, and everyone linked arms and sang "Auld Lang Syne," he stood, Francesca on his left, Kate on his right, and his lips moved to the words, but there was a deadly hollowness in the pit of his stomach—

And he wondered why, in the midst of such joy, he should feel so utterly, and wretchedly, alone.

Part Three

*

REUNION

*

1975–1978

Chapter 28

A NEW GENERATION was born.

On the last day of September 1975, twins were born to Francesca and Nick. Their daughter, born first, was named Andrea Juliette, for Nick's mother and Giulietta; their son was named Joseph Victor, for Nick's father and Francesca's brother.

They were both dark-haired, with large and beautiful deep brown eyes and fine, pale skin. Kevin and Alicia fell passionately in love with them from the first day, as did every member of the family who assembled, ten days later, for the christening at the Catholic church in Salisbury.

In the early hours of the morning after the service, Nick was gently woken by Francesca. He sat up, instantly alert.

"What's wrong? Are the babies all right?"

"Nothing's wrong." She kissed his hair. "I want you to come with me."

"Where?"

"Just come."

Mystified, he allowed himself to be drawn into the nursery. In the two cribs, side by side, the twins slept peacefully, their tiny downy heads darkly contrasted against the white cotton coverlets.

"They'll wake soon," Francesca said softly, "but I wanted us to share something special before their feed."

She pointed to the linen-covered dresser. On its surface lay two little red caps, four strands of red wool, and a pair of red amulets.

Nick stared. "Where did you get them?"

"From Emilio, on our wedding day." Francesca smiled. "He said that he knew we had left their world behind us, but that he did not want his brother ever to feel cut off from him." She paused. "I remembered you telling me, when we were children, that you had not been born into Gypsy ritual, and that some of the more superstitious members of your father's family believed that it brought you bad luck."

His eyes were very dark. "We've proven them wrong."

"I know that. And I know that I'll never be anything but a *Gadja*—and I know that to be truly lucky, this ritual should have been performed just after the babies were born—but then this is just a symbol." She took his hand. "Of my love for you, and for who and what you are—every part of you." She smiled. "And because I want Andi and Joe to have every last ounce of good luck that's possible in their lives."

They came into each other's arms then, and kissed, lips tender—and they were both weeping, and their tears mingled, and tasted salty on their tongues.

"I thought it should be private," Francesca went on, her voice a whisper. "I didn't want to exclude Kevin and Alicia, but I thought it might be too much—"

Nick stroked her hair. "You were right." He leaned back and looked into her face. "But you—isn't it too much for you?"

"For me?" Francesca's eyes were bright, and fierce, and loving. "*Nothing* is too much."

They took the babies from their cribs then, and they were warm, and sleepy, and nuzzling sweetly against Francesca's neck as she held them both, one in each arm, while Nick took the red caps and placed them gently on their heads.

"Now the wool." He wound the strands, loosely, around their arms, and only then, for the first time, did Joe start to protest. "Almost done," he said, and swiftly and carefully, he slipped the amulets over their heads. Andrea, fully awake now, began to scream.

"All right, *piccolina*," Francesca soothed, and kissed her daughter's cheek. She looked at Nick. "Now what?"

"Now you feed them."

"But shouldn't you—shouldn't we say something? Isn't there more to this ceremony?"

"I don't know." And abruptly, Nick's face was full of laughter. "I'm a horse farmer in Connecticut—"

The twins were both crying vigorously now.

"They don't like the caps," Francesca said, and Nick removed them. "Poor little things—holy water this morning, and Romany rituals in the middle of the night—"

"Maybe they're crying because they know they're *Gadje*, too—only one quarter Gypsy. Maybe they disapprove of heathen rites." Nick unwound the strands of wool and took off the amulets.

"Or because they have crazy parents—" Francesca's eyes sparkled.

"Or because they're getting impatient"—Nick took Joe out of Francesca's left arm, and with his spare hand, unfastened the top of her negligee, exposing her full, milk-heavy breasts—"for this." Gently, he bent, and kissed her right nipple.

Andrea's screams redoubled—perfect features contorted into tiny scarlet fury. Francesca's smile was regretful as she pushed her husband away. The infant mouth grasped greedily, the eyes shut, and she began to suck, even before her mother had sat down in the nursing chair.

"Ready for your son?" Francesca held out her spare arm, and Joe swiftly snuggled close.

"I love watching this," Nick said huskily, "more than anything in the world." Eleanor had been repelled by breast-feeding, and though Nick had understood her antipathy, and recognized that neither Kevin nor Alicia had suffered as a consequence, he gloried in Francesca's instinctive pleasure.

For a while, they sat in companionable silence, Francesca wholly physically absorbed with the twins, but her eyes upon her husband's face.

"Sometimes," she said softly, "I find our life almost impossible to believe. All of it. How we began—the way we are now."

Nick stared at her—at his wife, at the twins. "It's hard," he answered, "not to be superstitious—not to be afraid of losing it." He paused. "Was that a part of your reason for tonight?" He still held the amulets in his right hand. "Do you feel that too?"

"Fear?" Francesca shook her head. "If I even contemplated losing you—losing any of this—I wouldn't be able to bear it. I'd destroy the joy for myself."

Nick did not speak. His eyes were full of tears again.

"Tonight," Francesca went on, "was just what I said before. Love—pure and simple. And a kind of pact, I think, with the past." She paused. "And with the future."

Chapter 29

TIME HAD NOT HEALED Juliet's wounds.

Two years had passed since she had been forced to sell Kaikoura, and though she was comfortably off in the financial sense, and her professional talents were still sought after in the dubious world of gutter journalism, Juliet hated her life, and mistrusted the world. Having grown accustomed to emotional isolation, she had vowed that no one would ever be permitted to come close to her again.

Until she met Kurt.

He pushed the buzzer on her intercom just before seven o'clock one evening in the last week of September.

"Miss Austen?" His voice was accented, and soft.

"Who is it?"

"Dr. Kurt Lindauer."

"Who?"

"An old acquaintance of Elizabeth," he said.

Juliet hesitated.

"You'd better come up."

He was tall and slim, with shoulders that stooped a little. His hair was brown, sprinkled with gray, and he had remarkably beautiful, myopic gray eyes shielded by horn-rimmed spectacles. He was German-born, living and working both in Berlin and in Basel, and he had come to London for a symposium when he had decided, on the spur of the moment, to try to contact Elizabeth Austen. Learning of her death, he had felt the urge to trace her daughter, partly to express his long-belated sympathy, and partly to see again the woman he had last seen as a young patient at Stoke Mandeville Hospital.

"You were there?" Juliet felt a chill at the stirring of long-buried memories.

Lindauer nodded. "I was doing postgraduate work. That was when I first met Dr. Austen, and grew to admire her. I have always remembered her devotion to you, and her determination to adopt you as her daughter."

Juliet gave him a glass of dry sherry. Her hand trembled slightly. She hoped he would not stay long.

"I saw your mother again on a number of occasions—usually at conferences in Europe, and once at Great Ormond Street—but then, alas, we lost touch." He paused. "But I never forgot her—nor you."

It was true. He still recalled the child's injuries and, in particular, her burns. Kurt Lindauer seldom forgot scars, or their effects upon the human psyche. He had never forgotten a single patient of his own, though he had treated many hundreds in more than twenty years as a plastic surgeon.

Juliet did not, of course, remember him, and she disliked instinctively anyone who brought back the distant, painful past, but on the other hand, it was a long time since anyone had wanted to talk about Elizabeth—sometimes it was as if she had never existed, as if she were no more than a figment of Juliet's love-starved imagination.

"Would you like to stay for dinner, Dr. Lindauer?" She rose from her armchair.

"I don't want to put you to any trouble."

"It's no trouble," she said cordially. "I have to eat anyway—I had no lunch today." She tried to memorize the contents of her refrigerator. "Do you eat lamb, Dr. Lindauer?"

"I eat anything." He took off his spectacles for a moment, and looked up at her, and his expression changed oddly. "Won't you please call me Kurt?"

Juliet stood very still, transfixed by his gaze. Those gray, intelligent eyes were staring at her—she felt as if he were looking right through her, almost as if he were reading her mind. Yet they were kind eyes, in spite of their keenness—tender eyes, gentle and surprised.

Stirring herself, she walked into the kitchen.

She laid the table with a lovely, embroidered Swiss cloth that her mother had given her, and she used Elizabeth's silver, and lit a candle, though she was not precisely certain why she did it. Nor why she went quietly to her bedroom, and changed from the jeans and pullover she'd been wearing when he arrived, into her favorite blue suede skirt and cotton chambray blouse.

"I found a melon in the fridge," she said, "so we have a first course." She invited him to come to the table. "Do you prefer red or white wine, Dr. Lindauer?"

"Kurt, please."

"Of course—Kurt."

"Red, if it's all the same with you—I find London cool and very damp, I'm afraid." He sat, where she indicated, facing her. "You have taken a lot of trouble. I feel guilty."

"No need." Juliet poured two glasses of wine. "I just tossed the lamb and some potatoes into the oven—not really cooking."

"And you changed." He was staring at her intently again.

Juliet flushed. "I was a mess."

The eyes, covered again by the glasses, appraised her. "You look very beautiful, if I may say so."

"Thank you." She laid her napkin on her lap, and picked up her spoon. *"Guten Appetit,"* she said.

Lindauer smiled. *"Danke schön."*

✳

Their conversation developed easily, and Juliet found herself more relaxed than she had been for years in the company of any man. But then, she realized, Kurt Lindauer was not *like* any man she had ever met. He was much older than she was; she was twenty-nine, and he, she estimated, was fifteen or even twenty years older. He was also, clearly, a cultured man—a person of quality and, she thought, wisdom.

And he wanted her.

She had seen that right away, when he had looked up at her after their glass of sherry. And though it had unnerved her, it had not troubled her—on the contrary, it had been the spur that had motivated her to change her clothes and light the candlestick.

It was not the wanting, though, that made him different from other men. Despite her self-imposed celibacy of the past two years, Juliet was aware that she had retained a wanton image that many men found irresistible.

But this man *liked* her.

✳

They dined out together for the next three evenings, once at a small Italian restaurant near her flat in Little Venice, the next evening at Le Gavroche, the third in the Grill at the Connaught Hotel, where Kurt was staying.

Their conversations continued effortlessly. They talked with a gentle companionableness, sharing memories of Elizabeth, whose name seemed to hover over them, so Juliet liked to think, like a beacon of approval. Kurt spoke of his life and of his career, and urged Juliet to speak of her own, though that was the one area that silenced her, for she knew that her brand of journalism was tawdry beside his vocation.

"You're entirely wrong," he told her firmly, "to be so self-deprecating. The fact that you have elected, as many writers have to, to make a living from your art does not diminish your talent. When the time is right, you will take a different direction."

Kurt Lindauer had never believed in judging others; during the course of his work in Germany, Britain, and Switzerland, where he owned a private clinic, he had treated accident victims, self-conscious teenagers, middle-aged men and women hankering after lost youth, badly beaten prostitutes and razor-slashed prisoners, all with the same respect.

"I don't understand you," Juliet said softly as their plates were taken away.

"What don't you understand?"

She hesitated. "Why you look at me the way you do."

Kurt smiled his gentle smile. "And which way is that?"

"As if you care."

The sommelier poured more Volnay 1969 for them both, and Juliet felt a rare glowing inside herself. Everything Kurt had arranged in the last few days had been of the highest caliber, but she knew that it was not simply a question of money; a plastic surgeon with his own Swiss clinic was, of course, wealthy and accustomed to the finer things of life—but Juliet sensed that it gave Kurt particular pleasure to please her.

The wine waiter departed.

"I do care," Kurt answered her last question. He paused. "Can you tell me why that should be so difficult for you to comprehend?"

Juliet kept her eyes on his. "I don't want to talk about myself—I'd like to know more about you."

"What can I tell you?"

"You mentioned that you were married once."

Kurt nodded. "When I was twenty-eight. Her name was Marianne, and I loved her very much. She died just three years after our marriage, in a train crash." He paused. "Our little daughter, Elise, was killed with her."

"I'm so sorry," Juliet said softly—and found, to her surprise, that she truly *felt* sorry. It was hard to remember when she had last felt anything for another human being. Not since Elizabeth.

"It happened a long time ago."

"And you've never married again?" She could not disguise her curiosity. "You must meet many beautiful women in the course of your work."

"Many." Kurt smiled. "But I never wanted to marry any of them. I never thought of it." He regarded Juliet's lovely, grave, oval face, with its frame of beautiful straight golden hair, and his gray eyes were keener and more tender than ever.

"Until now," he said.

He took her home.

"Will you stay," Juliet asked at the door, "for a cognac?"

"I'll stay," he said.

She left him in the living room, went to her bedroom, and opened the bottom drawer of her dresser. The scarlet and black crotchless body stocking was still there, wrapped in tissue paper, where she had laid it on the night she'd taken her revenge on Joe Chapplin. She had moved since then—had bought her own flat just around the corner from the one she had rented in those days—but though she had packed all her possessions carefully in suitcases and crates, she had never touched the flimsy package in the bottom drawer.

For a moment, Juliet sat on the edge of her bed.

She wanted Kurt. She had not wanted any man so intensely, so completely, since Ray Donnelly. Every time she looked at Kurt's slender hands, or at the graceful, slightly stooped body encased in its elegant silken suits, she ached to touch him and to be touched by him.

He had told her, when he had first come to her flat, that he had seen her at Stoke Mandeville—that he had not forgotten.

She looked at the open drawer. There was no need to hide from Kurt. He knew—he had seen her.

And yet, a child's pain was poignant and affecting, while a woman's ugliness—

Kurt was gentle and wise, and he might even truly care for her.

But he was still a man.

✱

He was sitting in the chintz-covered armchair beside the gas-log fire. His legs were casually crossed, his tie had been a little loosened, one of Elizabeth's beautiful crystal cognac snifters rested in his right hand.

Juliet watched him for a few moments, from the doorway. He looked, she thought, contented—she wished, with all her heart, that she could be what he hoped for. But she knew that it was impossible.

"Kurt," she said, loving the sound of his name.

Hearing her voice, he rose, his good manners natural, and turned to face her. His eyes, behind the horn-rimmed spectacles, widened.

She walked toward him, catlike, undulating. The body-hugging garment acted upon her as a theatrical costume might have—she had not felt so physically in command since she had last worn it.

Kurt put down his glass on the coffee table, and straightened up again. A series of transparent emotions crossed his face—surprise first, then desire—then disappointment and sadness.

"Juliet," he said.

Her confidence had vanished. The flush began at her neck, and moved up to her cheeks. "I don't want to talk."

"What do you want to do?"

"I want you to kiss me."

He said nothing, just continued to look at her, and Juliet knew that he saw through her.

"Please," she said.

Kurt kissed her, lightly. His lips were narrow and cool, and he drew back after an instant.

Fear made her aggressive. "Not like an uncle." Her voice was like a growl, deep in her throat.

"No," he said softly. "Not like an uncle."

He bent his head again, and Juliet, seeing her reflection mirrored in his spectacles, reached up and removed them. The gray eyes surveyed her gravely. The second kiss was longer, yet still chaste.

"Don't you want me?" Juliet challenged.

"Of course," Kurt answered.

She smiled. "Then come."

She took him by the hand, led him into the bedroom—and lay back, half propped by cushions, on the bedspread. She bent her right knee, sliding her foot up toward her, exposing herself to him so that he would be in no doubt.

Kurt sat on the edge of the bed. His expression did not alter. He looked into her face, away from her open thighs.

Juliet's throat tightened. "Touch me," she whispered.

He did not move.

Her cheeks burned. She let her right foot slide back down the bedspread. She wanted to disappear—to die.

"You said you wanted me."

"I do."

She stared at him.

"Not like this," Kurt said.

"There is no other way."

"Of course there is."

And then, abruptly, he cursed himself. Suddenly, his memory stirred and shifted, and became crystal clear. The child in the hospital bed—the sheet drawn back to reveal the ugly scars on her chest—the little hand that, even then, had tugged the sheet back to cover herself, tears of humiliation springing into her large blue eyes—

He'd thought he had remembered, but twenty years had blurred his recall—and on meeting her again after so many years, he had seen only her beauty and sensuality, had been touched by her intelligence and brightness and sensitivity. He knew that scars such as hers could warp more than flesh, but he had allowed himself to forget. He had looked at Juliet not as a surgeon, but as a man.

"Forgive me," he said. He saw that she was crying. "I'm a clumsy fool." She pulled at his heart, twisted his soul.

She could not speak. The tears spilled silently down her cheeks, and she made no attempt to wipe them away.

Kurt stood up and looked around. A satin dressing gown hung on a hook behind the bedroom door. He took it down and brought it to the bed. "Put it on," he said, gently, and gave her the large white linen handkerchief from his pocket. "Put it on, and be Juliet again. And then we can talk."

"About what?" Her voice was hoarse.

"About whether or not I can help you." He paused. "About whether or not you want my help."

She believed him, finally.

It was hard to analyze what made her feel she could trust him— perhaps it was his link with Elizabeth—perhaps it was her own despair, her knowledge that if she did not allow him at least to look at her, she would lose him—

"All right," she said.

It seemed to take forever, though it was only a matter of minutes.

When he looked at her naked body, his face was that of a surgeon, intent, objective. When he raised his eyes and looked back into her own, his face was that of a lover.

"You are as beautiful as I knew you would be," he said softly.

"I'm ugly." Her voice was flat.

"Your scars are ugly—but they're such a small part of you."

Juliet looked away from him. "Another man once told me the same thing. He didn't mean it."

"Did he love you?"

Her smile was small and wry. "No."

"There's the difference, then." Kurt reached out with his right hand, and gently turned her face back to his. "Juliet, I am a plastic surgeon—I would not dream of underestimating your aversion to your scars—"

"Aversion?" She laughed slightly. "That in itself is an underestimation. I *loathe* my scars—I would take a knife and cut them out of myself if I could."

"Especially those on your left breast."

Juliet shuddered.

"But your right breast is exquisite—full, round, without the slightest sag—and yet you avert your eyes from that also." He looked down at the breast, watched its pale nipple growing involuntarily erect, though he had not touched it.

Burning self-consciousness returned, and Juliet drew her dressing gown about her again. "I am repulsed by my body," she said, and her voice quivered. "As men are."

"How do you know, if you've hidden yourself from them as you tried to with me?" He waited. "Perhaps it's you who have underestimated men?"

Juliet was silent.

"Of course, I may be an exception, since I suppose I've grown accustomed to seeing burn scars—many infinitely worse than yours. But they don't repel me, Juliet."

"They repel *me.*" Her eyes were bright again with tears.

"Then would you like me to help you?" Kurt asked quietly.

"How?"

"It would not be so difficult."

Juliet became very still. "You mean—as a surgeon?"

"Certainly." Kurt smiled. "I gather you have not consulted a specialist for some years."

"Not since I was a child."

"Understandable." He nodded. "Many people who have endured a great deal of hospitalization as children shy away from any suggestion of more treatment—but in doing so, they sometimes overlook developments."

"What kind of developments?"

"Many." Kurt's eyes glittered with enthusiasm. "In the fifties, when you had your accident, there was little that could be done—but we live in a new world. Have you heard of microvascular surgery, Juliet?"

She shook her head.

"It's a remarkable area. In lay terms, we take a piece of healthy tissue, usually from the groin, and we latch the blood vessels to the vessels in the damaged skin. Where successful, it leaves a piece of tissue that will not contract, and will be smooth."

"But how would that help me? My scars are nearly twenty-five years old."

"In your case, you have two problems: though your breast was able, in spite of the scars, to develop, its growth was held back to a degree, and so the shape is a little affected—and the scarring is rough and unsightly." Kurt paused. "I would want to try two things, if you agreed—microvascular surgery, followed by the wearing of a compression garment."

"What's that?" Juliet was suspicious.

Kurt smiled at her. "The newest, and perhaps the finest, development of all, and the simplest. It is just as it sounds—a garment made specially for the patient, that fits tightly over the damaged area, and keeps the skin flat and smooth."

"I see."

"No, you don't." Kurt took her hand and held it. "Your mind is in turmoil. I'm making suggestions that are all very well for me to talk about, since I am only the surgeon—but for you, they conjure up horror and pain and disappointment."

Juliet had begun to weep again. "I'm sorry," she said.

"Why should you be?" he asked. "Do you have to be strong all the time? Are you allowed no human frailty?"

Her laugh was bitter, though the tears continued to fall. "I'm full of frailty, Kurt—if you only knew—"

Kurt still held her hand. "I want to help you, Juliet. I *can* help you, which is more important."

She raised her red eyes. "You think these things would work, even on such old scars?"

"I believe we could achieve a vast improvement." He paused. "I'm not speaking of perfection, you understand—but substantial change for the better."

Juliet took his handkerchief and wiped her nose. "You're right about my mind—I don't know what to think—"

"Not yet, but you will."

"Will I?"

"When you're ready."

✳

She agreed.

Kurt had flown back to Berlin for three days, and on his return, Juliet had been ready with her answer.

"I trust you," was all she had needed to say.

"Are you sure?" Kurt had asked. "Wouldn't you like me to explain it to you again?"

"No—I don't want to hear any more, or talk about it any more—I just want it *done*."

"And you understand there can be no guarantees?"

"But you believe it will work, don't you?"

Kurt had nodded. "I do, yes."

"Then so do I."

✳

Although they were both aware of the deep mutual attraction between them, it was as if they had sworn an unspoken vow to suspend the physical side of their love affair until after the operation. For now, Kurt was her surgeon first and foremost, and Juliet's faith in him was boundless. Kurt made her feel safe—he could perform miracles.

He wanted to admit her to the Lindauer Klinik on the outskirts of Basel, but the memory of her visit to Geneva made her uneasy, and so, one week later, Kurt brought Juliet to the Fodor-Krantz Nursing Home, a private hospital just off the Cromwell Road.

Meticulously, he told her what to expect, though Juliet, suddenly excruciatingly nervous, hardly listened.

"Don't tell me any more," she begged him, "or I may just run away —I just want to get it over with."

Kurt was adamant—she would listen to him, or there would be no surgery.

Juliet listened, but she did not hear.

✳

He sat in her room that night, after she had been measured for her compression garment and checked by the anesthetist, and waited for her to fall asleep before going back to his hotel.

Juliet woke as soon as the door closed, and turned on the overhead light. They had given her a tablet, but she knew she would not sleep that night—she was afraid to sleep, for she knew that she would dream.

"All right, *Liebling*?"

She opened her eyes. They had given her an injection, and a curious, heavy tranquility had overwhelmed her. She looked up, and saw Kurt's gentle, loving face.

"No questions for me?" he asked her again.

"Not one," she said drowsily.

"Then I'll see you when it's over."

She woke, briefly, in the recovery room, where a nurse, clear-voiced and reassuring, asked her to speak to her, and then allowed her to sleep again.

When she next saw Kurt, she was back in her own room, and it was dark, the only light shining in through the propped-open door from the corridor.

"How do you feel, *Liebling*?" he asked softly.

"It hurts."

He stroked her hair from her forehead. "We'll give you something for the pain. Is it very bad?"

"Not so bad."

"Good." He paused. "The operation went well, Juliet." His voice was soothing. "Now we all have to be patient, you most of all."

"I know."

✳

The pain in her groin, from where they had taken the skin for the graft, was worse than the ache in her breast. The agony of uncertainty exceeded all physical pain.

"We won't even look at it for another two days," Kurt told her on the second morning after surgery. "And I shall leave it completely alone for about a week."

"I won't be able to look," Juliet said tautly.

"I don't want you to—not until I tell you to."

"Do I have to stay in hospital?"

"Absolutely. Firstly, the donor site must be looked after carefully—and we don't want to disturb the new graft."

"I hate it here," she said.

"You hate all hospitals." He kissed her cheek gently. "I don't blame you."

The first time he looked at her breast, he asked a nurse to hold a sheet of sterile gauze before her face so that Juliet could not see.

She could hardly speak. "How does it look?"

His head was bowed, beyond the gauze. "Excellent," he said, though his voice was remote. "Quite excellent."

"Truly?"

Kurt laid a fresh, light dressing over the graft, and the nurse removed the protective sheet. "I would never lie to you, Juliet."

Her mouth trembled. "I know."

Every day, he brought her flowers and gifts; perfume, paperback books, for their lightness, a beautiful white silk and lace negligee—and a string of South Sea pearls.

She gasped when she saw them. "Kurt, they're too much—"

"Nothing is too much," he said, and his voice was very deep. "Just let me see you wearing them soon, *Liebling*."

"Can't I wear them now?" she asked eagerly.

He shook his head. "Not now."

On the seventh evening, he brought a tray into the room. "Beluga—and a little champagne," he announced.

"What are we celebrating?"

"Another stage. Tomorrow, the dreaded pressure garment."

"Will it be so awful?"

Kurt laughed. "Not at all. It will feel restrictive, but not painful." He poured Krug champagne into two glasses. "But you will be able to wear your negligee—and the pearl necklace—and that is why I feel festive."

Juliet took her glass from him. She felt suddenly shy. "I know I seemed—I *wanted* to seem confident before the operation—and it's not that I don't have faith in you—but I've been feeling—"

"Terrified," he said.

She nodded. "Yes."

"You think I didn't know that?"

"No." She sipped the champagne. "I'm beginning to think you know everything."

His eyes were suddenly somber.

"If only that were true."

✳

He was due to arrive at nine the next morning, but he did not come —and a few minutes before ten, another doctor entered the room with a nurse.

"Where is Dr. Lindauer?" Juliet asked, alarm gripping her stomach.

"En route to Germany," the doctor told her. "There was an emergency in Berlin."

"But he was supposed to be here."

"I'm afraid you've got me instead." The doctor smiled jovially. He was about thirty, and very handsome. "I'm the resident here, and I understand we're going to fit your compression garment this morning."

"No," she said, flatly.

His smile was patient. "It's definitely today."

"But Dr. Lindauer was going to be here," she said again.

"And I'm sure he would be if he could." He paused. "There's nothing to it, you know, Miss Austen—have you ever worn an elastic bandage?"

"No." She didn't intend to sound so rude, but she was too afraid to care. The fear was churning up inside her.

"It's not much different, though as I'm sure Dr. Lindauer has explained to you, it's an invaluable follow-up to your surgery."

He went ahead, much as Kurt had done, lifting the light dressing gently, and placing it in a basin proffered by the nurse.

"Very nice," he said approvingly.

Juliet had waited for the nurse to slip the protective sheet before her face, and when she had not done so, Juliet had done the next best thing, and closed her eyes.

"Take a look," the resident said.

Juliet kept her eyes tightly shut.

"Go on," he urged. "There's nothing to be afraid of, and it's your last chance before we fit the garment." He paused. "Take a look."

Juliet opened her eyes.

"Here." The nurse put a mirror in her hand.

Juliet looked—

And began to scream.

✷

They had tried to calm her, had told her that what she saw was old blood and stitches, that there was still a long road to travel before the skin would look anything like normal, but Juliet had not heard them.

She had thought that nothing could ever look worse to her than the scars she had borne for two and a half decades—but this mangled, bloody mass was like a monstrous outcrop from her most tormented dreams.

They put aside the compression garment and hurried from the room, to return with a sedative injection, waiting until it took effect.

And in a moment, Juliet stopped screaming, and lay very still.

Kurt had lied to her.

He had known, when he had looked at the graft, that it had gone wrong—that he had caused her greater mutilation. And he had run away, unwilling to witness her horror, afraid to face her.

Kurt Lindauer had promised her salvation—she had put all her faith in him. And he had betrayed her.

He might as well have destroyed her.

When they came back to check on her just over one hour later, the room was empty, the clothes and bag in the wardrobe removed. All that remained were Kurt's gifts to her, the remnants of his perfidy.

Juliet had gone.

Back in Little Venice, she locked the front door, took the telephone receiver off the hook, opened her bathroom cabinet, and swallowed what was left of one bottle of aspirin and another of paracetemol.

Instead of dying, she was violently sick before she crawled into her bed, folded herself into the fetal position, and fell mercifully asleep.

When she awoke, the longing for death had left her. What remained was the greatest, iciest hatred she had ever experienced. Nothing anyone had ever done to her compared to this.

Kurt Lindauer was a dangerous man. He cloaked himself in tenderness and generosity and persuasive mystique—but he had the power to maim—to destroy confidence and shatter hope. He had to be stopped.

She would stop him.

She knew that he would come. Once he learned that she had left the hospital before release, he would have no choice. He would come, and he would use all his wiles to persuade her to return.

But she was ready for him.

Kurt was distraught and furious with himself. He had gone to the emergency in Berlin automatically, as soon as he had been called, knowing that he could fly back to London within a day or two.

He ought to have understood the fragility of Juliet's emotional state. He ought to have realized that the surgery might resurrect long-buried terrors—that it might be like treating a newly traumatized child. He ought to have taken the time, whatever the emergency, to properly instruct the resident at the Fodor-Krantz that she might not be ready to look at the grafted tissue. He ought to have *been* there.

At Heathrow, he pushed to the front of the queue for taxis, and gave the driver an extra twenty pounds for the fastest drive possible to Little Venice.

The staff at the hospital had told him that her telephone was off the hook, and had asked Kurt if he wanted them to go to the flat, but Kurt had taken a gamble and said that he was already on his way.

He was a Lutheran by upbringing, though he was not a religious man, but as his driver forged his way through the clogged London traffic, Kurt prayed that Juliet had not come to harm.

He would never forgive himself.

She sat, erect, on a chair in the hall near the front door. She had been sitting there for hours, but she had not fallen asleep once. The pain had kept her awake.

When the buzzer sounded, she rose, stiffly, and picked up the intercom.

"*Gott sei Dank,*" he said, and his legs trembled with relief.

"Come up," Juliet said.

The bottle was by the chair. Slowly, she picked it up and unscrewed the cap. The smell rose, acrid, in the air.

The bell chimed, and she opened the door.

"Thank God," Kurt said again, and stepped forward to embrace her, crazily thankful when she reached up with her left hand to remove his glasses, before she kissed him on the mouth.

The kiss was long, but her lips were cool. Reluctantly, he released her, and stepped back to look at her.

"You must be in pain," he said.

"Yes," she said softly. "I am."

And bringing up her right hand, sharply, viciously, she hurled the bleach into his face—into his beautiful, deceitful, treacherous eyes.

His screams were terrible—the wailing of the sirens violent in peaceful, leafy Little Venice. The hands on Juliet's arms were rough, the voices of the two police constables advising her of her rights, implacable.

But Juliet heard and felt nothing. There was no release, no satisfaction, nor shame, nor physical pain nor grief.

Nothing.

She might as well have been dead.

Chapter 30

LUCIANO HAD never felt worse.

Autumn was one of his favorite times of year on the French Riviera, but this year its loveliness had failed to break through his gloom. The new Holt book had been published in France, Britain, and the United States, and had won astonishingly fine reviews. Even that had not helped.

He had tried seeing a therapist, had gone once a week for a year to her office in Paris, but no matter how long they talked, no matter how honest he was or how hard he fought to dredge up old buried problems and fears, he never felt he was taking any useful strides forward. Perhaps there simply *was* no solution, he had decided. And so the way he coped with his demons now was not to fight them, but merely to continue, passively, turning abstract feelings into words on paper, to be stored away until the time came—if it ever did come—when he might be able to understand them.

He had come to Sonora in early October, for the christening, hoping that his depression might lift if he was surrounded by the whole family. It had worked for a few weeks, but once Bruno and Kate had returned to Le Rocher, and with Alicia and Kevin back at school in California, he had descended into deeper gloom than ever.

On a quiet afternoon, while the twins were sleeping, he and Francesca sat together on the big, battered sofa in her studio. His folder of
notes lay beside them.

"It's grown worse," he said flatly. Dark shadows circled his eyes. "In
the last week."

"Even here? Away from everything."

"Not away from myself."

Francesca looked at the folder. "May I see?"

"I want you to." His jaw was taut. "I need you to."

She picked up the folder. Over one hundred pages, bound neatly
together and filled with Luciano's handwriting.

"This is so organized," she said, surprised. "I imagined you scrawling
down your feelings as they struck you, but this is an analysis."

"Or an attempt at one," Luciano explained. "Initially, of course, I
scribble them down wherever I can, but quite early on, I began listing
them in columns, so that I might be able to link and interpret them."

"Time-consuming."

"Obsessive, you mean. But worthwhile, perhaps, if it had been effective." He stood up and turned away. "As it is, I've neither exorcized my
demons nor found an explanation."

He left her alone to read, and Francesca scarcely noticed the afternoon slipping by. The notes were intriguing, some no more than single
words, others quite detailed, and with about five individual thoughts on
every page, the lists read like a curious journey through the last nine years
of Luciano's troubled private world.

Francesca read page upon page of ideas, emotions, and painstakingly
described abstract sensations, some of them hallucinatory in character—
often repeated feelings of pain, cold, and damp. Some read like well-
documented visual experiences; Luciano saw mysterious places with uncanny clarity—unknown rooms in unknown houses; unfamiliar streets,
parks, and gardens; a hectic, open-plan office; a hospital room, a restaurant . . .

The descriptions of people were less precise, more in the fuzzy, shadowy nature of dreams; but the entries that captured Francesca's attention the most forcibly were the ones relating to emotions—those that caused her brother the most anguish, those that had begun to rule his life. Thwarted love and yearning—desperate ambition—hatred, bitterness, vindictiveness—loveless sexual desire, crushing misery, defeat.

They were undoubtedly the feelings, characteristics, and even experiences of a single individual. Yet clearly Luciano was right when he said that they were not his. They were alien to him.

A new possibility occurred to Francesca. Perhaps there was another avenue to investigate. Perhaps her brother possessed psychic powers of which he was unaware—maybe he was somehow, unwittingly, tuning in to another person's mind.

The idea appalled him.

"You think I'm prying into some stranger's brain?" He shuddered. "It's a hideous notion—more offensive than the thoughts themselves."

"But not impossible," Francesca said gently. "I wondered if it might be worth contacting someone involved in psychical research—I'm sure they'd be deeply interested."

"I'm sure they would." His face was pale. "And they would want to pick at my brains and to have me perform tricks like a puppy—but I have no wish to stimulate that part of myself. I wish only for it to *end*."

Having come thus far, Francesca found it impossible to forget about it. Aside from Luciano's ongoing distress, there was another element of the situation that nagged at her: if, by chance, she was right, and his problem was one of unconscious thought-transference, then the human being with whom he had, somehow, become entwined had, according to Luciano's notes, developed into a violent personality.

It was the most recent entries—those that her brother had logged in the last few days—that had, literally, raised the hairs on the back of her neck and, also, stirred in her a curious sense of recognition.

The very last page, in particular, recorded one of the most unpleasant manifestations Luciano had described. He had logged it as occurring on October 18—six days before—and it read like a waking nightmare, written out in a type of shorthand: *"Bathed in sweat. Want to scream. Pain—hatred! Must wait—control—"*

The rest was described in the past tense, as if the intensity of the experience had taken him over, rendering him incapable of writing it down until later.

"I was holding a bottle—felt like plastic. A man stood before me. I threw the bottle at him—I heard him scream. There was a smell—strong, pungent, like chlorine—"

And beside the entry, he had written a name.

"According to your—vision," Francesca said later, to Luciano, "this —Curt—was the victim."

Luciano's face was grim. "I don't want to talk about it—I don't want to think about it anymore."

"I know." She paused. "It's just that having read the notes, I begin to understand, at last, what you've been going through. It's terrible, yet it's fascinating at the same time. I want to help you get to the root of it —to the source."

"You won't." His tone was short. "And I don't want you to—that wasn't the reason I let you see the notes. I just wanted to share them with you—that's all." His eyes were intense. "Leave it alone, Francesca."

She could not leave it alone. That last, disturbing entry preyed on her mind, its inexplicable familiarity gnawing at her. She said nothing more to Luciano—she ran the household, looked after Andrea and Joe, helped Aggie Cooper, their housekeeper, and tried to concentrate on formulating a new photographic project—but, in spite of herself, she found she was constantly mentally rerunning that entry, worrying at it like a dog at a bone.

Nick grew concerned. He knew only that Luciano had, at last, shared his deepest emotional problems with her, but because he was an uninquisitive man—not indifferent, but respectful of personal privacy—he had kept silent until now.

"What is it, *amore?*" It was after two in the morning, and Nick was aware that Francesca had been unable to get to sleep. "What's troubling you?"

She turned her face to his. "My brother."

"Can't I help?"

She shook her head. "Not with this."

"You haven't been yourself for days. I don't want you getting sick." He put his arms about her. "I seldom pry," he said, "and I don't want you to betray his confidence, but—"

She smiled into his eyes. "You're my closest friend," she said softly. "I trust you with my life and soul, and Luciano regards you as his brother."

Nick kissed her hair. "Then tell me."

Francesca leaned on her elbow. "It sounds wild—it's probably no more meaningful than any of it—yet I feel, somehow, that this single thing is terribly important."

She told him.

"Poor Luciano," Nick said. "And you believe he may be psychic?"

"It's possible."

"I'm not arguing—I'm a Gypsy, after all." He paused. "Do you remember the *Drabarna,* in the camp near Verona? She was drawn to Luciano—she said that he had an aura."

"I remember."

"And now you feel that this vision is familiar to you."

"Something about it just struck a chord."

"Perhaps it reminded you of a movie—something you saw on TV?"

"Perhaps."

"But you think it's more than that."

She creased her forehead, trying to concentrate. "I think it's something I've read somewhere—"

"A book—novel? Or a news item—an article in a magazine or a newspaper—" He stopped, and looked at her. "That's it, isn't it?"

"I think it might be." Her brow furrowed even more deeply as she struggled to pinpoint the hazy memory. "But what was it—and where did I see it?"

"That's not so hard to find out."

"How?"

Nick pulled her back down under the blankets. "Go to the library."

She had been in the library at Hartford for almost one hour. She had scanned all the October 18 editions of every newspaper she regularly read—the *Boston Globe, The New York Times,* and the *Daily Press*—and had found nothing.

And then she remembered.

She drove back to Sonora, fed the babies, and shut herself into her studio. The newspapers lay in a pile on the window seat—the papers that had arrived the day before she'd read Luciano's notes. French and British newspapers, containing the latest reviews of the new Zachary Holt book. She had read the notices, and left the papers there to remind herself to cut out the items for her files.

Now she picked up the *Daily Express* dated October 19. She knew now that it was the right one—that what she sought was on one of the pages she had flicked through in order to reach the book review page. And she found it.

BLEACH ATTACK ON SURGEON

It reported on a case in London the day before, in which an unnamed mentally disturbed patient had thrown household bleach into the eyes of an eminent German plastic surgeon named Dr. Kurt Lindauer.

Francesca stared in disbelief.

Kurt.

She closed her eyes, remembering Luciano's notes: ". . . *a smell—strong, pungent, like chlorine—*"

And the date was precise.

She asked Luciano to come up to the studio.

"I'm sorry," she said right away. "I know you don't want to think about this, but I have to ask you two questions about the notes."

"Why?" He still looked tired.

"Please, *caro*, be patient with me."

He sat down, listlessly, on the sofa.

"The newspapers." She sat beside him. "The files mentioned newspapers several times—"

"And magazines."

"What language were they printed in?"

He looked irritated. "I don't know."

"Try to think." She paused. "Were they printed in French, or in English, or Italian—?"

"I didn't read the papers, Francesca—I just saw them. Sometimes they were just a blur, other times they—" He stopped. "English. Some were printed in English, I think." He shrugged. "I'm not sure."

"Were they American newspapers, or British?"

He thought. "I don't know."

"All right." Francesca felt a pulse throbbing in her right temple. "Now streets. You sometimes see streets that you're certain you've never seen in real life."

"Often."

"Was the traffic driving on the right, or on the left?"

"Didn't I note it down?"

She shook her head.

Luciano closed his eyes, and Francesca held her breath.

"Left," he said quietly, and opened his eyes, looking startled. "The traffic drove on the left—I'm *sure*. How odd not to have noticed it before." He stared at his sister. "You think that the source is in England?" He paused. "I've only been to London three times—I never felt any sense of recognition there."

"But if they're not your own thoughts, as you've always maintained, why should you? Doesn't this just serve to prove the point?"

"But it doesn't help, does it." Luciano's weariness returned. "It doesn't rid me of them."

"Not yet."

"What do you mean?" He waited. "I've told you, Francesca—*leave* it."

She said nothing.

"There's no need for you to go to England." Nick smiled at her impulsiveness. "My lawyers have offices in London—they can dig up all you want about this case."

"All right. But I don't want Luciano to know."

"I won't tell him."

✳

The first information came through swiftly. The person accused of causing grievous bodily harm to Dr. Kurt Lindauer was one Juliet Austen, a journalist resident in Little Venice, in the west of the capital. They had no further details at hand, but the London-based solicitors stressed their willingness to delve further, if Francesca wished.

Luciano left Sonora on the first of November. The next morning Francesca received, by special delivery, the package she had been expecting, containing a photocopy of every one of the English journalist's published articles, together with an assurance that further details about Ms. Austen would follow under separate cover.

It took longer than she had anticipated to read over the heap of newspaper and magazine articles. The writer had some talent, but most of the items were aimed at the trash market, and bordering on scurrilous. Francesca had begun to think that she had read far too much into a pure coincidence, when she came upon an article that stopped her in her tracks.

Austen had written it for the June 1973 issue of a British photographic journal called *FOCUS*. It was an uncharacteristically dry report of the ruination of a London-based photographer named Joe Chapplin, following the sabotage of his studio and most of his work-in-hand. The writer's implication was that the photographer had been naive and careless in his attitudes to security and insurance, and had brought disaster upon himself.

Francesca had spread the photocopies over her studio floor, and now she sat back on her heels, racking her brains, trying to recall precisely what she'd read in Luciano's notes that had triggered her fresh excitement.

It was the name, of course—*Chaplin* had been one of those listed in the folder. And Francesca was almost certain that the name had been aligned with a particularly vivid collection of disturbing, vengeful emotions.

She telephoned Luciano.

"I need you to look something up in your notes."

"*Merda!*" He did not bother to mask his anger. "I asked you stop this, Francesca. You'll never resolve it, and you certainly don't have the power to stop it, and that's all I care about."

"Just a date, please."

"For God's sake!"

"Please?" She held her breath.

"What is it?" he asked coldly.

"A name—Chaplin. I want to know the date on which you made that entry. It may have been in 1973."

"You'll have to hold on."

It seemed an age before his voice returned.

"It was '73," he said. "May fourteenth."

Francesca said nothing.

"What's going on?"

"I'm not sure."

"Don't you think perhaps I have a right to know the games you're playing with my head?"

"Even if they lead to nothing? Would you still want to know, even if it caused you nothing but more aggravation and distress?"

He paused. "You still believe I am psychic?"

"I believe it's a possibility."

"And you are trying to discover the individual whose innermost thoughts and fears I am stealing."

"I am."

"You will not succeed."

Nick brought the mail to the breakfast table next morning. "One for you from London." He passed an envelope to Francesca, and drank the last of his coffee, standing.

"The solicitors." Francesca put down her toast. The twins had kept them both awake for several hours that night, and she was overtired.

Nick, who had eaten his own breakfast three hours earlier, but who always liked to return to the house when Francesca came down, slipped his arms about her neck. "Open it now or later?"

"Later, I think." She looked up at him. "Do you have to go?"

"More's the pity." He kissed her earlobe. She always came to breakfast in a terry cloth robe or a negligee, her hair piled loosely up on her head. Nick loved his wife first thing—loved her face devoid of makeup, her skin unperfumed—

Aggie entered the kitchen. "They're crying again." The babies seldom cried separately. If Joe began first, Andrea invariably followed suit within seconds. Francesca could remember, vaguely, similar scenes from her early childhood.

"I'll have to leave you to it." Nick brought her back to the present. "If you need me, I'll be at the shelter stables."

"I'll probably join you there in a while." She laid a hand on his arm, and left it there for a moment—she never tired of touching him—

The twins crescendoed.

It was another hour before Francesca was able to open the letter. She sat in the armchair in their bedroom, and slit the envelope.

The English solicitor wrote in a formal, courteous manner; if he was not accustomed to being asked by American horse farmers' wives for the personal details and history of British citizens, he did not let it show.

Juliet Austen, he wrote, had been adopted by Dr. Elizabeth Austen, a distinguished pediatrician, on June 15, 1954. Her date of birth was

June 9, 1946, and her earliest known address was at the Ospedale San Felice di Dio, in Turin, Italy, where she had been treated for burns and injuries sustained in a car accident in which both her parents had died.

Her name, prior to adoption and British naturalization, had been Giulietta Volpi.

✶

The letter continued, but Francesca had stopped reading. She sat motionless, and erect, and the letter slipped from her fingers onto her lap.

From outside, she heard a truck arriving, and the sounds of Aggie taking in a delivery of groceries, joking with the driver. From somewhere inside the house, downstairs, one of the babies was crying again.

But she couldn't move.

✶

It was not possible.
Giulietta. June 9, 1946.
Impossible. Anyway, Volpi—not Cesaretti.
Burns and injuries.
A car accident.

✶

She thought that she was probably in shock. That was why she couldn't move. She felt as if her own breathing had stopped—as if life itself had skidded to a halt.

And then she remembered the *Drabarna*—the fortune-teller at the Gypsy encampment.

Another sister, she had told Luciano. *Surrounded by darkness and loneliness.*

✶

Francesca stood up abruptly, and the paper flew from her lap onto the carpet. She went to the window, and threw it open wide. She began to breathe, deeply, sucking air into her rigid lungs. A leaf blew past her face into the bedroom, but she took no notice. She stared straight ahead into the horizon, breathing—feeling the blood pumping more and more steadily through her veins.

And then she looked down, and saw Aggie, pushing the big double carriage, Joe and Andrea bundled up snugly against the November chill.

Francesca called out: "Aggie!"

Her voice carried, clear as a bell, and the housekeeper looked up and waved.

"I need Nick!"

"I thought he went to the shelter."

"I *need* him, Aggie!"

"What's wrong? Can I help?"

"Just bring the twins back inside the house, and go and find him." She knew she couldn't drive—could barely stand.

Aggie caught the urgency, and turned the carriage around.

"Please," Francesca said, and the intensity of her voice jarred in the fresh, cool air. "Get him back."

Nick ran up the stairs and into the bedroom.

"What happened?" His eyes were frantic with worry. "Are you ill?"

Francesca was sitting again, in the armchair, and her expression was dazed. "We have to go to France," she said. "Right away."

"Luciano?" Nick knelt beside her. "Has something happened to him?" He waited. "Or Bruno?"

She shook her head.

"It's Giulietta," she said, and her voice was quivering.

"Who?"

She looked at him. "Our sister."

And she gave him the letter.

"Luciano mustn't know," she said, later. "We have to speak to Bruno first, without his knowing we're there."

Nick had brought her a glass of cognac. "You know this simply isn't possible, don't you, *amore?*"

"I know."

"And yet you still think it's her?"

"Don't you?" She shook her head slowly. "How much can we put down to coincidence?"

Nick's eyes were very dark. "And who else would Luciano be more mentally attuned to than his twin?"

They had telephoned Kate first, to warn her that they were on their way, and that Luciano must not discover that they were there. Confused, but calm as always, Kate had told them that there was no need for concern, since Luciano had gone to Paris to visit his agent, and was not expected back for at least four days.

If Francesca had suspected, even for an instant, that Bruno might have known anything about Giulietta's possible survival, those suspicions were quickly extinguished when she saw her uncle's disbelieving, shattered expression.

Over and over again, gently but relentlessly, Francesca and Nick pushed the seventy-six-year-old man back into the past, forcing him to dredge up the unhappy Florentine days of 1951.

"We knew that Giulietta was taken to the same hospital as Vittorio after the fire," Francesca reminded him. "But we were never allowed to visit her."

"Her injuries were so terrible." Bruno shook his bald head, while Kate held his hand protectively. "You were all so young—it would have distressed you too deeply to have seen her."

His mind was perfectly clear, the memories he had suppressed for over twenty years quite undimmed. He recalled his grief, and his desire to help his brother's children—and he remembered how torturous the hospital visits had been, and his surprise and gratitude when his wife had taken on the task for him.

"It made no difference to Giulietta," he said anxiously, as if they had accused him of neglect. "She was unconscious—she never knew who was with her. And in a sense, I was more equipped to help the three of you if I did not have to go back and forth to Pisa."

"And when she died?" Nick probed softly. "Were you with her then?"

"No." Bruno paused, his face ineffably sad. "No one was with her then. They telephoned Livia, and she called me home from the store."

"But her body," Nick went on. "Did you see her body?"

Bruno shook his head. "It was all very fast—she was buried the same day."

"That was strange, wasn't it?" Kate asked.

"There were reasons," Bruno said. "The hospital said it was advisable."

"Did they tell you that?" Francesca was ashen.

"They told Livia. She made all the arrangements."

"Which included keeping us from the funeral," Francesca said, old bitterness seeping back into her.

Bruno's hands were trembling, his brown eyes urgent. "But I saw her coffin lowered into the earth—it was small, and it gleamed from polish." His mouth quivered. "I remember I was angry with Livia—I said that her sister and brothers should have been there—I said that she should have been buried with Giulio and Serafina and the baby—"

"And what did Livia reply to that?" Nick asked.

"She said it would have been too much for you all to bear, so soon after your other losses." Bruno stared into Francesca's face. "But you came to the cemetery later, for the memorial service—you saw the grave." His eyes were wet. "And Vittorio is buried beside her."

"Yes," Francesca said.

"So there always was a grave," Kate said.

Francesca felt a strange hollowness in her chest.

"But there is also Juliet Austen, alive, in England."

Bruno opened a cabinet of old files, and Nick thumbed through a sheaf of curling papers until he held Giulietta's death certificate in his hand.

"Can you read the signature?" He gave it to Francesca.

She frowned. *"C. Clemenza."* She showed it to her uncle.

He nodded. "Yes," he said. "It looks like Clemenza."

The hospital in Pisa had closed in the early sixties, but the records held at the *municipio* informed Nick and Francesca that there had been a member of the administrative staff in the fifties named Carlo Clemenza. He had never, incidentally, been authorized to sign death certificates, and in fact he had been dismissed in 1957 for fraud and corruption. There was no trace of any patient file for Giulietta Cesaretti.

They drove to Turin, to the Ospedale San Felice di Dio, turning their attention toward the child named Volpi. Forty-eight hours after their arrival, her file was recovered from the hospital archives. Giulietta Volpi had been admitted on September 19, 1951, an orphan who had remained with them for a little over two years, at which time she had been transferred to England in the care of Dr. Elizabeth Austen.

There was a copy, in the file, of the admission papers. The required signature of the adult registering the patient read: *C. Clemenza.*

Returning to Pisa, they telephoned Kate with the news.

"What next?" she asked, though she already knew.

Francesca held the telephone. "Nick will apply tomorrow for an exhumation order." She paused. "I don't think Bruno should come."

"No," Kate said. "But I must tell him. He'd never forgive me if I kept it from him. But if he wants to fly to Pisa, I'll tie him down if necessary." Her voice, as always, was steady. "What about Luciano? Isn't it time to break this to him?"

"Not until we're sure. I see no harm in waiting a little longer."

"You're sure now, aren't you?"

"Yes," Francesca said.

✱

They had to wait twelve days.

"You don't have to come," Nick said, on the morning that the grave would be exhumed. His face was etched with worry; he was afraid for her.

"I have to."

Every moment of every day was a haunting. Her mind could not rest, she could not drive out the dread, even for a second. Normal life had ceased to matter. They telephoned Sonora each morning and evening, but even if Andi and Joe had not been in happy, thriving health, Francesca wondered if she could have felt real, normal anxiety. The babies and Nick were the center of her world, the core of her—yet she felt marooned inside herself, inside a nightmare, and she knew that only the opening of a twenty-four-year-old coffin could release her from her limbo.

Nick bent and kissed the top of her hair. "Then it's time to go," he said.

The work had begun, in order that the waiting, for the family, would not be too protracted. A priest was present, and two officials from the *municipio*, their faces somber and tight-lipped. Only the two grave-diggers seemed unaffected by the atmosphere; Francesca felt that it was hard for them to keep from idly chattering while they plunged their shovels into the ground, coming closer.

Cool rain was falling, but only the priest held an umbrella over his head. Once, he offered it to Francesca, and she thanked him, but refused it. She wished that the rain were harsher, the wind colder, slapping her face, buffeting her.

"*Finito.*"

The digging was completed. The group moved closer to the side of the open grave, and looked down.

The coffin was intact. Livia had, at least, spared no expense over the quality of the wood. The gravediggers scraped off the last clods of soil with their shovels, and one of them, a large, brawny man, stooped to pick off a fat, wriggling earthworm. Perspiration dripped from the digger's forehead onto the lid, and for an instant they thought he would wipe it away, but then he stopped and straightened up.

Nick felt the rigidity of Francesca's body, felt the icy coldness of her hand.

"Open it, please," he said.

✴

The coffin's latches had to be broken before the lid could be raised. It took less than one minute, but it seemed to those who waited to take an eternity.

The priest made the sign of the cross.

The coffin was opened.

They saw the stones and straw, tightly packed. The straw had moldered, moss clung to the stones.

The priest, shocked yet relieved, murmured a prayer. The two witnesses glanced at one another, and shifted a little, silent and uncomfortable. Nick said nothing, but moved closer to Francesca, giving her time.

Slowly, she turned her eyes from the coffin, and looked toward Vittorio's grave.

"May Livia Cesaretti rot in hell," she said.

"Amen," said Nick.

When they broke the news to Luciano, he took his car, and drove out of Nice up onto the Grande Corniche to Le Belvédère d'Eze. It was one of the finest vantage points of the region, and he went there, from time to time, when he most needed to get away. Usually, he would sit at a table at the Café Belvédère, taking a drink and gazing out over the Tête de Chien, the *Caps* of Ferrat and Antibes, and the infinite blue of the Mediterranean itself.

This time, he did not visit the café. He stood for a long time, looking at the panorama, but not really seeing it, and then, for a while, he sat down, at the side of the road, so that the *patron* of the café, observing him, came out to ask him if he was ill. And Luciano nodded, without speaking, and stood up, and returned to his car, and drove on, up to La

Turbie, where he parked, and went into the church of Saint Michel-l'Archange.

He looked, for a time, at the copy of Raphael's *Saint Michel*, but mostly he just sat, unseeing, in the cool silence, trying to think, trying to feel. But in the end, all he felt was the evening chill. And so, driving slowly, he made his way back to Nice.

They were all there, waiting for him, their faces anxious, his uncle agitated and old.

Francesca hugged him. "Are you all right?" She had been weeping.

"I suppose so," he said. "I don't know. I can't seem to feel anything."

"I know."

Luciano looked into his sister's face. "I think I just can't believe it. I can't believe in her." He shook his head vaguely. "And if I do—what then?"

"Are you afraid?" she asked him.

"Terribly."

"So am I."

They tried to speak about her, to raise her from the dead. Luciano hardly remembered her—only a blurred, unreliable memory of a golden-haired, laughing child, who had been screaming in terror the last time he had seen her.

He remembered her death more than her life.

Francesca told him that they had been inseparable. His twin. The person who should have been closer to him than any other human being on earth. And who somehow, miraculously, had remained locked into his mind despite everything.

They discussed what to do next.

"How do we contact her?" Nick asked. "After all, we've no way of knowing how much, if anything, she remembers about her first five years. If Luciano had not had Francesca and Vittorio as his link with the past, he might have no recollection of Giulietta at all."

"And she isn't Giulietta anymore," Kate said, with an uneasy glance at Bruno, who seemed to have aged ten years since the shock. "She came to Turin with a new surname, and she became Juliet Austen three years after that. She's an Englishwoman—a stranger."

"And she's in trouble," Francesca added. "Perhaps even in prison."

Luciano walked over to the open French doors, and stared out into the night. "So much pain," he said softly. "I felt it, for all those years, and never knew."

Bruno stood up. "I should go to her."

Kate got up too, and put her hand in his. "If you do, then I'm going with you."

"No one's going near her." Luciano's voice was suddenly loud. "The shock would be unbearable—she's too unstable, too shaken up."

They all watched him.

"Do you still feel her?" Nick asked him gently.

"Of course I feel her—almost all the time." Luciano's eyes were agonized. "And more than that, I remember *all* the thoughts and emotions through the years—all the suffering, the bitterness, the defeat—" He broke off, the realization too intolerable to cope with.

"I'll write to her," Francesca said. "If Luciano agrees." She looked at him. "You're too close to her—it's too confusing, too disturbing for you to do."

"What will you write?" Nick asked.

Her slanted eyes were very distant.

"Just the truth," she said.

She waited until Bruno and Kate had gone back to Le Rocher and, leaving Nick with Luciano on the terrace, she went to the guest suite and sat at the writing desk.

She laid a sheet of blank white paper on the blotter.

Dear Giulietta—

She began again.

Dear Juliet—

She crumpled up both sheets, and threw them into the wastebasket at her feet.

My dear sister—
And she continued.

She wrote for more than three hours. Her hand ached, her back had grown stiff, her eyes burned, and still she was not finished.

It was the hardest task she had ever undertaken—for how did one reduce two and a half decades to a few sheets of paper? How did one tell a sister—a stranger—that there had been a grave, for all those years, with a stone bearing her name?

She enclosed photographs—that was an easy thing to do—of the whole family, including Kate and Kevin and Alicia, and even Johnny, Della, and Billy, for they, too, were part of her own story.

And as the night wore on, and as Luciano and Nick waited, patiently, for her to finish, sitting out their vigil with a bottle of Chivas Regal at their side, Francesca's letter drew to a close.

> *There is nothing more I can say—not yet at least. We had all believed you lost forever, and we are grateful to God that you are alive. And we long, above all, to be with you, but we must wait to hear your wishes.*
> *It's painful to let even one more hour—one more minute—go by, for we are your family, and we want to see you, to embrace you, to love you.*
> *But we know we must wait a little longer. God bless you.*
>
> Francesca Cesaretti Dante—
> *Your sister*

Chapter 31

THEY HAD TAKEN Juliet back to the hospital—not to the luxury of the Fodor-Krantz Nursing Home, but to a local National Health Service institution, where she had remained for two more weeks, under police guard, until she had been declared physically fit to be discharged.

She had been a model patient.

She had lain still, never arguing or complaining, had obeyed every order. The grafted tissue on her breast, though prematurely disturbed, had not been damaged, and the compression garment, sent over from the Fodor-Krantz, had proven effective.

On her release, she had been returned to Harrow Road Police Station, formally charged with grievous bodily harm, and taken, first, to court, and then to Holloway Prison, where she had been remanded in custody pending psychiatric evaluation.

She had been a model prisoner.

There was no point in being uncooperative—no point in protesting, for Juliet knew why she was there. She had known, almost immediately, when the worst of her shock had receded, the enormity of her crime against Kurt. She had seen his face, his agony, over and over again, every time she had closed her eyes, and she had wanted to scream, but had not screamed—had longed to die, but had not died.

And then she had given up.

∗

She had reckoned without Kurt.

The bleach she had thrown into his eyes had done no permanent damage, for the surgeon, knowing precisely what to do, had staggered into the kitchen even before Juliet's next-door neighbor had called the police, and had bathed his eyes with water until help had arrived.

Had he been blinded, he might have been incapable of forgiveness. As it was, he blamed himself for professional misjudgment, still felt overwhelmed by guilt for pushing Juliet over the brink. The balance of his beautiful girl's mind had been temporarily disturbed—he had been to blame.

When Kurt Lindauer loved, he loved.

Since he refused to press charges, and spoke convincingly on her behalf to the police, Juliet was freed before a trial date had been set.

It was Kurt who met her outside the prison gates—Kurt who put her gently into the back of a limousine and took her home. It was Kurt who made her soup, and undressed and bathed her—

And made love to her.

✴

"How is it possible?"

"What, *Liebling?*"

"That you are here. That you have forgiven me." Her eyes swam with tears. "That I have not lost you."

"You cannot lose me. You will never lose me."

"But why?"

"*Liebe.*" He spoke the word simply. "Love."

"But I tried to blind you—to *destroy* you. How can you love me after that?"

"You were out of your mind with pain and terror," Kurt said gently. "You forgot to trust me."

"And can you trust me, ever again?"

"You will never do anything to hurt me again."

Juliet stared at him in wonder. "You sound so certain."

"I am."

✷

He took her away with him to Berlin and to Switzerland, knowing that it was too soon to leave her alone. He wanted her to share everything with him, to learn all there was to know about him, to see where she might be happiest making a home with him.

"If you could live anywhere," he asked her, "where would you choose?"

"Anywhere—so long as we're together."

"But you can choose," he persisted. "We can be in my flat in Berlin or here—do you like Basel?"

"It's a lovely city."

"Or we could buy a house in England." He paused. "Your own Kaikoura."

Her heart beat faster. "But your work—"

"I have to travel in any case," he said easily. "I could buy a private jet, even learn to fly it myself—"

"No," she said quickly, fearfully. "You must have a pilot."

Kurt smiled. "If I must."

✷

Their lovemaking was exquisite. By the end of the first week, Juliet's obsessional hatred of her body had begun to abate. When Kurt caressed her, he touched every part of her. If he kissed her right shoulder, he kissed the left just as lingeringly—if he simply gazed at her, as he did often, his eyes rested equally on both breasts, and sometimes he would regard her as a doctor, assessing his craftsmanship, while at other times he would drink in her beauty, purely as a man.

"How is it?" Juliet would ask hesitantly, knowing that the fact that she felt able to put the question was a miracle in itself.

"It's good."

"Will it still improve?"

"It will—a little."

And once, after they had made love, Juliet looked deeply into the eyes she loved, and said, softly:

"I don't even mind anymore."

During the years in which she had indulged her sexuality in the only way she had felt possible, Juliet had treated her body as a mere receptacle. She had learned how to titillate and tantalize, how to drive her partners wild, but now, she felt almost like a naive beginner, a novice at love.

Kurt would not let her use her skills for his own pleasure; he wanted to rehabilitate her with warmth and care, to teach her the joys of peace, as well as physical enjoyment.

"You must learn to accept, *Liebling*—to relax."

Sometimes he would massage her with oils, addressing different parts of her body, as if every millimeter was vital to him, and had its own right to gratification. He taught her simple yoga techniques—lay her down on a quilt by the fire, told her to shut her eyes and to listen to his voice. And Juliet learned to sink into an almost euphoric relaxation, in which the vibrations of Kurt's voice would lull her into a new kind of sensuality, after which he would lie down beside her and make love to her again.

And gradually, Kurt allowed her to rediscover her sensual gifts, and to bestow them—and Juliet took the greatest joy from his body and from his face. She loved all of him—the top of his head, his neat, flat ears, the nape of his neck, the white hairs on his chest—the creases around his waist, his appendectomy scar, the strength of his muscles.

"Will you leave me?" she asked him sometimes, unable to stop herself from asking.

"*Niemals*," he said, always. "Never."

"Truly?"

"Truly." He didn't mind even that—he understood her vulnerability, perhaps even more than she understood it herself. "Not until death."

"I hope I die first," she said passionately.

And each night, when the bedside lamp was switched off, her lips moving silently so that Kurt would not hear her, Juliet prayed that she would.

✳

Francesca's letter was lying on the mat inside Juliet's front door, when they returned, at the end of November. Juliet picked it up gaily, together with the rest of the mail, and tossed it onto the kitchen table.

"Mostly bills," she said. "They can wait."

They went out to dinner to a small Hungarian restaurant in Hampstead, and then they came home, went to bed and made love until they fell asleep.

It was just after three in the morning when Kurt woke, abruptly, and heard the sounds from the kitchen.

"Juliet?"

He found her at the table, the letter before her. Her eyes were open, but she didn't seem to see him. She was rocking back and forth, and keening softly, desolately.

"*Liebling,* what is it?"

She seemed unable to speak—only the awful sounds came from her throat—animal sounds.

He stared at her in consternation. "*Was hast Du?*"

She stopped rocking, and sat very still. Her face turned up to his— her skin was ghastly, her blue eyes were torn wide with shock.

Kurt knelt beside her chair and put his arms about her, but her body was stiff and unyielding, almost like a corpse. "Dear God, Juliet, what's happened to you?"

And then he saw the letter.

There were a number of sheets of white, airmail-weight paper, covered in blue slanted handwriting.

"May I look?" he asked her.

Still she said nothing.

He picked up the first sheet—

My dear sister—

Kurt stared back at Juliet's bleached face. And began to understand.

✳

He carried her back to bed, wrapped her in soft blankets, brought her tea, with a little cognac, and, after a while, gave her a sleeping tablet. She never spoke, and when, at last, she slept, he returned to the kitchen and read the whole letter.

Juliet woke again, two hours later, and was violently sick. She trembled and shivered, and Kurt adjusted the central heating and made her a hot water bottle. She began to perspire, and he removed the blankets and took away the bottle, and gave her a little cool water to sip, but she retched again, so Kurt laid her back against her pillows and sat beside her and stroked her hair until she slept again.

Morning brought sunshine and birdsong, but Juliet begged Kurt to keep the curtains drawn and the windows closed. Beyond that, and a soft complaint that her head ached, she said nothing more. Her temperature was slightly raised, and she was unable to keep food down, but Kurt knew that what ailed her could not be healed with drugs.

In the middle of the afternoon, when the sunshine was less bright, Kurt opened the curtains and windows.

"We must talk," he said, gently, "about the letter."

"No," Juliet said.

"It will not disappear." Kurt took her hand, but it was limp in his. "It must be faced."

She removed her hand. "There is nothing to talk about."

"But you will have to reply to her."

"Never," she said.

She left her bed the next morning, and seemed recovered, brighter even, and loving with Kurt. She went out, toward noon, to buy food and other necessities for the empty flat, and she returned, humming, to replenish the refrigerator and to vacuum and dust.

"I'll cook tonight," she said, lightly. "The butcher had beautiful calves' liver."

"Are you sure you feel up to it?" Kurt asked.

"I feel fine."

"Good," he said. "Then we can talk."

"Of course."

"About the letter."

Her face went blank. "No," she said.

"About Francesca and Luciano—your sister—your twin."

"*No!*" For an instant, her eyes were full of hatred.

Kurt replied to Francesca.

He wrote with great warmth and courtesy and sensitivity, for there had been no doubting the sincerity of Francesca's own words. He told her of his joy, for Juliet, at the miraculous news, and he attempted to explain, with as much kindness as possible, that Juliet had been through too much trauma lately to be able to cope with more.

"I'm sure it will not be too long before she feels able to contact you herself," he wrote. *"It is simply too soon."*

He did not tell Francesca the complete truth, which was that he believed Juliet had emerged from the initial shock with the same two emotions that had ruled and ruined most of her adult life—

Bitterness and hatred.

It erupted, at last, in a short but violent explosion, while Kurt went out to post his letter to America. He returned to the flat to find Juliet sitting huddled on the living room carpet, surrounded by fragments of paper. She had ripped apart Francesca's letter, and torn up the photographs that had been enclosed.

Kurt's heart sank. In a sense, it was a predictable reaction—a desire to shred and destroy an invasive truth—and it might have been a healthy, welcome release of pent-up tension. But the way she sat there, so limp and helpless and remote, her golden hair wild about her face, her skin clammy and pale, stirred new foreboding in him, for she reminded him, for a moment, of the withdrawn patients he had seen in the psychiatric wards of hospitals over the years.

"Liebling," he said tenderly, and brought her back to her feet, held her in his arms, wishing that she would cry, or even scream, do anything to allow him to help her to move forward into a fresh future. But she did nothing more, and said nothing at all. And later on, when she slept, he sat at the kitchen table, and patiently pieced together the fragile paper and the photographs, mending them with sticky tape, as well as he could, before placing them in a sideboard drawer, for a time when she might, after all, want them.

She spoke about it, finally, the next day.

"At first," she began, so softly that Kurt could hardly hear her, "I told myself it was not true. It was impossible—insane. Nothing so monstrous could happen in real life—no human being could be so evil as Livia Cesaretti."

"It's hard to believe," Kurt said, steadily.

"Don't say anything, please. I know how much you want to help me, but don't say anything—not yet."

Kurt was silent.

"I knew, of course, that I was wrong—that it must, after all, *be* the truth, for no one could invent such a story." She paused. "And so I fell apart." She smiled at him, a small, wan smile. "And you nursed me, and looked after me, as you always do, and brought me back to myself—to you."

Kurt touched her cheek with his hand. For an instant, Juliet brought up her own hand to cover his, and then she took it away.

"You've wanted me to talk to you about it—to tell you how I feel, *what* I feel. But I didn't really know, until now." She gave a small, enigmatic nod. "Now I can tell you, if you're sure you want to hear."

"I want to."

"Three things." She shook her head. "So many years, and she wrote so many pages, this woman who says she is my sister. And yet it all comes down to three—facts."

Kurt kept silent.

"They want to tell me—these strangers—that I am not Elizabeth

Austen's daughter." She paused. "I know, better than anyone, that I was adopted. But I also know that Elizabeth was the only mother I ever knew, or wanted." For a moment, the bitterness flared vividly in her face. "I won't allow them to try to change that."

"I don't think they want to change anything about you."

"Please," she said fiercely. "Let me tell you."

"Go on."

"The second fact." She paused, and her voice was brittle. "They abandoned me. Even my twin brother—who claims that he mystically sucked my innermost thoughts from my brain, who says that he actually *felt* my pain—nevertheless did nothing about it for almost twenty-five years."

"He believed you dead, Juliet."

"The third truth." Her mouth twisted. "They buried me. Or at least, they buried a little girl called Giulietta Cesaretti." Ice replaced bitterness in her blue eyes. "I don't remember ever *being* that little girl—I don't remember them. And I don't want to remember."

"Not now, perhaps, but—"

"Not now. Not ever." She softened again. "You saved me, Kurt. You've brought the greatest happiness I've ever known—except perhaps with Elizabeth. I love you—I want to live my life with you."

Kurt was filled with sadness. "But surely that needn't preclude—"

She raised a finger to his lips, stopping him.

"My name is Juliet Austen," she said, slowly and clearly. "I do not want to be anyone else."

Kurt's letter arrived at Sonora on the fifth of December. Francesca opened it at the breakfast table, with nerveless fingers and a pounding heart.

Nick watched her, willing the letter to bring her joy. "Well?" he asked, gently. "What does she say?"

"It's from him—the surgeon, Lindauer." Francesca tried, but failed, to keep the grievous disappointment out of her voice. "She doesn't want to know us." Her mouth trembled.

"He says that?"

"Not exactly." She passed him the letter.

Nick's jaw tightened as he scanned the courteous, tactfully worded rejection. "He says she needs time." He looked back at his wife, and his heart wrenched for her.

"It's understandable, I suppose," Francesca said quietly, her face very white. "A shock as great as that."

"Do you want to go to her?"

"I'm not sure." She looked at him helplessly. "I don't know what to think." Her voice was choked. "I thought it would make her happy, Nick. I thought she would want us as much as we want her."

"There'd be no point in confronting her now," Luciano said, after Francesca had read the letter to him over the telephone. He was depressed and drained, yet not unprepared. "I knew how she was feeling— how she feels now."

"Lindauer says that it's just too soon."

"He's lying," Luciano said.

"What do you mean?" Francesca's stomach clenched with foreboding.

"She hates us. Lindauer may not write that—he may be too kind a man, or he may not even know it, but our sister hates us with all her heart."

"That can't be true," Francesca said fiercely. "And if it is, we can make her change her mind. We'll go to London, and she'll see how we feel about her, and she'll understand."

"Perhaps." Luciano's voice was dull.

"It seems so terrible to waste another minute—we've all waited so long."

"I think we have to respect her wishes," Luciano said.

"How long for?"

"As long as we can bear it."

A week before Christmas, Francesca, Nick, and Luciano flew to London, and took a taxi to Little Venice. Kurt had warned them that it might prove pointless, but nonetheless, they came.

It was a cold, wet day, and an icy northeast wind lashed their cheeks as they stood on the front step of the white Victorian house, listening to Kurt's voice over the intercom speaker.

"I'm sorry," he said, in his gently accented voice. "I'll have to come down."

The door opened.

"Come into the hall at least." He ushered them in. They all shook hands. The atmosphere in the long, polished hallway was hushed and awkward.

"She won't see us?" Francesca asked.

"I'm afraid not." Kurt looked strained and unhappy.

"Even though we've come so far." Nick knew that he sounded judgmental, but couldn't help himself.

"May we not even come up?" Luciano asked.

"To be truthful," Kurt said, "if you do come into the flat, I'm afraid of the consequences."

"Is she so unstable?" Francesca was tired and drawn.

"She's calm," Kurt replied. "Too calm. She appears quite normal— we're very happy together, she and I. But she refuses to discuss your existence, let alone the possibility of a meeting."

"But surely, if we confront her—" Nick had never believed in suppressing deep emotion. "Surely if she meets her brother and sister face to face—"

"I don't think that's advisable," Kurt said steadily, though his eyes showed his distress. "I tried to explain it to you, on the telephone, to tell you that it would be better to keep up the correspondence for the time being—"

"But we *couldn't* wait any longer." Luciano's frustration was almost unbearable.

"I know."

"Shall we go somewhere—have lunch, perhaps?" Francesca asked, feeling pity for Kurt, liking him enormously for his obvious sensitivity.

"I seldom leave her for long." Kurt was apologetic. "When I travel, for my work, Juliet accompanies me—we do most things together. If I go out with you, at this moment—" He shrugged helplessly.

"This is crazy." Nick felt Francesca's pain.

"Does she hate us so much?" Luciano was near to tears.

"I think that hatred is her shield against the pain that you represent," Kurt admitted. "She holds you responsible for your aunt's crime against her."

"But that's irrational," Nick said hotly.

"Juliet is irrational."

"You said that we represent pain to her." Francesca was more distressed than ever. "And we want only to love her."

"I know that." Kurt glanced anxiously up at the staircase. "But in order for Juliet to believe that, she must first come to terms with the past, with all that buried pain." He paused, his gray eyes intent. "The greatest miracle of her life was her transformation from a disabled, scarred Italian orphan into Elizabeth Austen's cherished daughter. She's terrified of losing that precious identity."

"But nothing can take that from her." Francesca appealed to him. "We don't want to change her—just to get to know her again, to spend time with her."

"I'm sorry," Kurt said again. "It's too soon." He sighed. "Write to her, please—as often as you can. Perhaps that may help her to reconcile herself to you. I give you my word that I will do whatever I can for my part."

"I'm sure you will." Impulsively, Francesca reached up and kissed his cheek. "Thank you," she said, "for everything."

"I only wish I could do more."

"At least you're helping her," Luciano said dully.

They walked out, together, through the front door, down the steps, and along the path to the gate. The rain was falling even more heavily, but none of them cared.

"What did you think might have happened," Nick asked, a little curiously, "if you'd invited us into the apartment? What exactly are you afraid of?"

"I am afraid," Kurt answered, "for her sanity. There is always a limit. A brink. I do not intend to push Juliet beyond it."

Nick and Kurt shook hands, and Francesca kissed Kurt again. "I hope you know how much we—" She stopped, looking around for Luciano.

He was standing a little way off, staring up at the old white house, at one of the upper-floor windows. He could see a figure standing there, half hidden by a flimsy net curtain.

It was a woman, slender and dressed in black. Slowly, she lifted the curtain to one side. She had long blond hair, and a pale, expressionless face.

She was watching them.

Giulietta. His twin sister. A stranger, whose thoughts and feelings he had unwittingly shared for twenty-four years.

Until this moment.

Now, when he most yearned to know what was in her mind, and to have her know what was in his heart, there was no contact at all.

Nothing.

Chapter 32

FRANCESCA AND LUCIANO continued to write to Juliet. They told her whatever they could, in order to try to make her feel a part of the family. They shared their joys and sadnesses. When Luciano won an Edgar award, he wrote to tell Juliet. When Joe and Andrea both cut their first teeth in the same week, Francesca wrote, and sent photographs. When Bruno died, during his siesta on a lovely July afternoon, Kate wrote to tell Juliet how deeply affected he had been by her survival, and how intensely he had hoped for her happiness, and Francesca described to her the arrival, at Le Rocher, for the funeral, of Fabio and Letizia. They had come, without their respective families, had hardly spoken to Kate and not at all to Luciano or Francesca, had stayed until the reading of Bruno's will before returning, incensed, to Italy, for their father had included Juliet in his estate.

They told her everything. Juliet told them nothing.

Not of her marriage to Kurt that February, nor of their handsome new house on the border of Hampstead Heath, nor of the Learjet Kurt had bought, keeping his word to her, converted for the movement of patients, and to make commuting to Berlin and Basel less irksome and time-consuming.

In many ways, Juliet was a new woman, thriving on Kurt's love and

care, and on her new, prosperous life-style. She had discovered the pleasures of extravagance and shopping. Presents for Kurt, new items for the
house, clothes for herself, particularly shoes and handbags—when she
was in London, Knightsbridge and Bond Street became her regular
haunts, and she became a favored customer at Harvey Nichols, Harrods,
and Gucci. Juliet knew that she would never need to write another
scandalous article, never have to humiliate herself again with men she
despised. She was Mrs. Kurt Lindauer now, the wife of an internationally
feted surgeon—and she had the home, and trappings and the credit
cards, to prove it.

The letters poured, in a generous flood, from Francesca and Luciano,
including invitations to all family events, and frequently updated photographs of the babies—but no matter how often Kurt urged her to relent,
Juliet always laid them aside, unacknowledged. Her husband wrote back
regularly, but Juliet pretended to herself that they did not exist. She told
them nothing.

Not even about her pregnancy.

Their daughter was born in early December of 1976. They named
her Elizabeth. She had gray eyes, like her father's—like the first Elizabeth's—and golden hair, like Juliet's. From the first day, she was easygoing, placid and good. Kurt was in seventh heaven, idolizing the en-
chanting baby, vastly grateful for his second chance at marriage and
fatherhood. Juliet was overwhelmed with emotion at the time of the
birth and euphoric for the first five days of Elizabeth's life. But then
everything changed.

It began with sharply changing mood swings; one minute she felt
acutely happy, aglow with the joy of motherhood, and the next she
became moody, irritable and tearful.

Kurt reassured her. "It's just the baby blues," he said comfortingly.
"Most mothers suffer from them for a little while—it's perfectly natural,
just a resettling of the hormones after pregnancy."

"But I feel so out of control," Juliet told him. "I've been depressed before—we both know that—but I've never felt anything like this before."

"You've never been a mother before."

She was in the nursery, powdering Elizabeth's bottom, when it began in earnest. A dark, creeping misery that swirled around her like fog. All her nerve endings seemed to prickle menacing warnings to her suddenly muddied mind. She looked down at the baby, wriggling on the white terry towel that was spread on the changing table—her daughter, the most precious human being she had ever known. And abruptly, the twenty-or-so inches of sheer, silken perfection seemed transmuted into an infinitely burdensome, terrifyingly flimsy, blob of helpless humanity.

Juliet stared down at her, totally unable to complete the simple task of changing the diaper. She felt panic-stricken and exhausted at the same time—her limbs were leaden, she thought she might suffocate. And then, bizarrely, she remembered what Francesca Dante had written, about her own grave in Pisa—and she shut her eyes, and experienced the sensation that she was lying in the earth, with spadefuls of soil cascading down onto her body, covering her face, filling her nose and mouth—

Elizabeth began to cry.

Juliet began to scream.

Kurt, deeply worried, confided, by telephone, in Francesca.

"Serafina," she said. "Our mother. Uncle Bruno told us, years ago, that she suffered crippling postpartum depressions after each of us."

"Did you suffer, after your twins?"

"No." Guilt clouded her voice. "I sailed right through. I got tired, of course, but I've never been so happy." She paused, filled with frustration. "I'm so sorry, Kurt," she said. "I just wish we could help."

Kurt, naturally, ensured that his wife had the finest care, the latest drugs, and as much practical help as possible, but, aware that she would instinctively reject professional counseling, he battled to draw her out of her black cloud with every other means at his disposal. An understanding nanny was employed to see that Elizabeth lacked nothing; a masseuse came to the house every morning, armed with tiny vials of aromatic oils, to soothe and to stimulate; each afternoon, in the marble-surrounded swimming pool in their basement, Kurt encouraged Juliet to swim beside him, allowed her to float passively, then provoked her to violently splashing outbursts of crawl, knowing that occasional eruptions of anger directed at him were far more therapeutic than the deadly lethargy in which she might otherwise have drowned.

Juliet felt tormented—by his kindness, by his bullying, but most of all, by her own inadequacy. Sometimes, she thought she would explode, and then she paced, like a caged animal, up and down the long corridors of their house; but most of the time, she felt listless, useless and ashamed. She was not worthy of Kurt, nor of their daughter. She wanted to die.

Kurt would not let her give in. His love was relentless, his patience inexhaustible. He feared, uncharacteristically, that Serafina's ghost was with them. That unfortunate woman had given Juliet life, had died in a state of emotional agony, had almost totally wrecked the lives of her whole family. Yet Kurt suspected now that she had also, inadvertently, caused even more of Juliet's lifelong unhappiness than anyone could have guessed.

But Serafina Cesaretti had lived in a place and time where no one had understood enough to help her—and she had been destroyed.

Kurt would not let that happen to Juliet.

She emerged from the darkness, vulnerable and tentative, but alive again. Elizabeth was almost four months old, soft and plump and healthy. Juliet felt shy with her, apprehensive lest the baby should reject her, preferring the nanny she'd grown used to, but her daughter was as pliable and sweet-natured as she had been from birth. It seemed to Juliet that she had been granted another miracle.

Life began to move forward again.

"We must take a holiday," Kurt said at the end of April.

"Not without Elizabeth," Juliet said quickly.

"Of course not, if you want her to come."

"I do—" Her face was urgent. "I don't ever want to be parted from her again—we've missed too much time together as it is."

"I'll arrange it, *Liebling.*"

Juliet felt a pang of pleasure. "Where shall we go?"

"I have a few ideas." Kurt smiled secretively. "Will you trust me?"

"Always."

Kurt knew that what he intended was far more than a mere holiday. This was to be a carefully orchestrated, tenderly arranged journey into the past, that he hoped, with all his heart, might do something to soften her resistance to her family.

He planned meticulously, and then brought home a tentative itinerary, presenting it to Juliet with bated breath. Venice to begin with—the Gritti Palace, the Grand Canal, Santa Maria della Salute, and the Piazza San Marco. Then Rome, Florence, and Milan for culture, shopping, and some of the most romantic restaurants in all the world.

And then a few days of gentle, tranquil driving through Chianti, Umbria, and Lucchesia.

Juliet said: "I see what you've done."

"What, *Liebling?*"

"The stirring of old, suppressed memories." She smiled.

Kurt looked at her, startled. "You don't mind?"

"Why should I?" She paused. "It won't touch me, my darling—it can't hurt me." Her voice was lighthearted. "I was five years old—even if I wanted to remember, I couldn't." She embraced him. "It will be a glorious trip for two lovers. That's all that matters to me."

It was perfect. They went in May, while the air was fresh enough for the baby, and they took the nanny, and Kurt cut himself off from the clinics and the real world. Wherever they went, they took large suites, with a separate bedroom and bathroom for the nanny and Elizabeth— and they rested, and ate and drank, and went to the opera, and Juliet bought meters of silks, suits and ties for Kurt, exquisite clothes for their daughter, and a dozen pairs of shoes for herself. And their suites were filled with red roses, and the baby kicked and gurgled on the fine linen sheets put down for her on the hotel carpets, and Juliet and Kurt made love every morning and every evening.

And then Kurt risked everything.

They left the baby with the nanny at their hotel, and he drove her to the *cimitero* near Pisa.

"No," she said, when he stopped the car.

"Please," he said. "For me."

They found Vittorio's grave, easily. The space beside it had been planted over with the wild flowers of Tuscany—red poppies, pink gladioli and ragged robins, blue iris, primroses and cornflowers, anemones and columbines.

"That was your grave, Juliet," Kurt said softly, holding her arm tightly. "They laid your brother beside you, instead of burying him with your parents, so that you would not be alone." He paused. "And when they learned that you were alive, they had the stone that had marked your grave smashed into fragments, and they arranged that no one else should ever be buried in that spot, and that flowers should grow there instead."

Juliet was very white, her face stiff.

"Flowers," Kurt repeated. "For life." He put both his arms about her. "Giulietta did not die, *Liebling*. She is alive, and even if you don't remember her, she is inside you—a part of Juliet Austen Lindauer, my wife."

And when Juliet began to weep, quietly, against his shoulder, Kurt felt that they had, at last, broken through the barrier, and he was immeasurably thankful.

It was one of the greatest miscalculations of his life. For instead of pushing Juliet gently forward, as he had hoped, into the safety of the future, he had, unwittingly but irrevocably, driven her back, into the dangerous past.

Francesca's latest letter awaited them on their return to London. Juliet and Kurt immersed themselves in the pleasures of Elizabeth's bath time, and Juliet fed her and tucked her into her crib before coming down to the drawing room, where Kurt was at their baby grand piano, playing and singing Lehár in his sweet tenor voice.

Juliet came to him, and draped her arms about his neck.

He went on playing, softly. "I put your post over there." He nodded toward the secretaire.

"Her letter, you mean." Her tone was cool.

"And others," he said mildly. He closed the piano. "Would you like a drink, *Liebling?*"

She gave a small sigh, and straightened up. "I'll read it now," she said. "Until I do, it will stand between us, like a reproach."

It was another invitation. Nick, Francesca wrote, was on the verge of fulfilling his lifelong ambition to participate in the Palio of Siena. He had found a horse, a beautiful mare named Tosca, ideally suited for *palio* racing.

> *His mother's family still live in Siena, and Nick*
> *has persuaded his cousin, who holds an important*
> *position in his* contrada—*that's a ward of Siena,*
> *of which there are seventeen—that Tosca should*
> *be presented for possible selection in the Palio*
> *this August.*

They would not know whether or not Tosca would be chosen until three days before the race, but Nick had already transported her to Italy for preparation. In early August, he and Francesca, who had been commissioned to photograph the event for *Newsweek,* would travel with the twins to Tuscany, where Nick had rented a villa for the whole family just outside the city.

There would be plenty of room in the villa. It would be an exciting and memorable time, and they all—she and Luciano, most of all—hoped, with all their hearts, that Juliet, with Kurt and their little Elizabeth, might, at last, agree to meet them.

Juliet read the letter twice, before passing it, silently, to Kurt, and leaving the room to go upstairs, to the nursery.

Elizabeth lay sleeping peacefully in her crib, making tiny, nuzzling sounds. Pale pink elephants flew on the walls—a heap of amiable teddy bears watched her from the corner.

She sat for more than a half hour, and then she left the nursery and went back downstairs.

Kurt had poured himself a whisky, and sat, waiting.

"Would you like to go to Siena?" she asked.

"Yes," he said. "I would. Though I think we could not take Elizabeth with us this time—it will be too crowded, too hot."

"No," she said. "We could not take Elizabeth."

She sat on the sofa, near him. For several minutes, she gazed into the empty fireplace, silent and immobile. And then, at last, she raised her head and looked back at Kurt.

"Yes," she said, and her face was quite composed. "We'll go to Siena."

Kurt had furnished a study for his wife, a large desk and two walls of bookshelves, all in polished walnut, hoping to tempt her back to work, but Juliet had not written a word since meeting him. Now Kurt suggested to her that the Palio might be just the catalyst to stir her dormant creativity. It was much more than a horse race—it was a vital part of the everyday lives of most Sienese, and utterly unique.

"I shall have to spend a great deal of time in Berlin and at the clinic before August," he told her. "Perhaps you might do a little research? It might make an interesting project."

"Perhaps."

Juliet had already begun to read about the bareback gallop around the Piazza del Campo, and the festivals and rituals that surrounded it. The more she read, the more she found herself being drawn into its web. She spent increasing periods of time in her study, reading, allowing Elizabeth's nanny to take over many duties that previously she had insisted on doing herself.

She read about festive dinners, about the time-honored enmity between competing districts, about whips made of the dried, stretched phalluses of virgin calves, about the nineteenth-century mounted *carabinieri* who rode around the track before the race, their swords drawn—and about the race itself, when the massive crowds roared with unbearable passion, screaming and fainting as horses and riders rounded the Campo three times, making for the finish—

And Juliet's imagination had indeed been stirred, and she felt almost as if her brain were aflame, for when she read about the grand dinner, she thought about poison and agony—and when she read about the *carabinieri* and their swords, she saw blood spurting—and when she read about the frantically galloping horses, she imagined a body lying crushed beneath the stamping, trampling hooves. . . .

Francesca's photographs lay on her desk, propped up against her books, together with a letter from Luciano, joyfully written, telling her about the strangeness of the destiny that was, finally, to reunite them; for Nick's family *contrada*, Lupa, represented the she-wolf that had suckled Romulus and Remus, and the founding of Siena had always been especially associated with twins.

And Juliet stared at the photographs, torn by her and mended by Kurt, of those happy, loving strangers, and she knew that she despised them more than ever.

And she gazed at Luciano, at the smiling, handsome face of her twin brother. And at Francesca, so beautiful, so self-assured and contented. And her heart and mind contracted with the old, familiar hatred and vengefulness she had felt for so much of her life. Never accurately directed—

Until now.

Chapter 33

LUCIANO HAD REACHED a turning point in his career.

Liberated from the fears of madness that had haunted him for so long, and that had made him determined to keep both feet planted firmly in the good, sane soil of his Zachary Holt stories, he had taken the plunge, and had embarked upon an entirely new genre of novel. Normally, he worked with precision, following well-defined plot outlines; for his new project, however, he intended to draw from his own experiences and emotions, to write about a pair of twins—fiction, still, but founded in the strange reality that he now felt compelled to transmit to the printed page.

Their lives had been distorted, twenty-five years before, their fate smashed by one act of insanity, and another of evil—and yet all through the years, Giulietta had held him, unknowingly, in her thrall, had bound him inextricably to her, against all odds, all logic, all rationality. She had remained, and would always be a part of himself, and Luciano planned to dedicate his new novel to her.

He had not experienced a single instance of psychic contact with her since that moment in December 1975, when he had looked up and had seen Juliet, fleetingly, at her window, but though his overriding reaction had been relief, he had nevertheless sometimes felt conscious of missing something essential to himself. When, at the beginning of July, however, the phantom thoughts began to occur again, Luciano found himself wishing, fervently, that they had not.

In the past, they had varied in intensity and in nature. Now they were more impossible than ever to ignore, all equally potent and demanding, and all of the same strident, undeniable timbre—of alarming violence.

For weeks, he struggled against them in fresh despair. He felt unable to tell anyone—not even Francesca—for now that he knew that they were Juliet's emotions, it would seem like a betrayal. He lay awake each night, wondering what to do—whether, perhaps, he might attempt to write to Juliet, to express his concern. But he knew that was impossible.

He could not tell a virtual stranger that he knew what was in her mind—at least its gist, its essence—and that he knew that it was terrible, and that it appalled him.

And that he begged her to stop.

Chapter 34

FRANCESCA HAD NEVER felt so apprehensive.

The Villa Bel Canto was square, and pink and peaceful. It stood in a perfect position, symmetrically framed by cypress trees, with an ilex grove to the east, and stone pines to the west.

They had come with great optimism—she and Nick, Alicia and Kevin and the babies—on the first day of August. Nick was energized with the culmination of boyhood ambition, not caring whether Tosca won or not, only caring that they were here, at last—that it had all come to him, all that he had yearned for so many years ago. And his ebullience had transmitted itself to his wife and children, and for the first few days, while Nick and Kevin had immersed themselves in *contrada* affairs, Francesca and Alicia had busied themselves with making the villa as warmly welcoming as possible.

Luciano had arrived on the eighth, one week before the Palio. He had come alone, for Kate had lately been unwell, and had felt unable to face the August climate. Francesca had known immediately, by his strained expression, that it had begun again.

They walked, together, in the terraced gardens. The day had been stiflingly hot, but the worst of the heat was receding as they sat down on a stone seat, facing the ivy-covered back of the villa. It was a gentle garden, its formality muted by its pastel colors, all shades of pink and beige and soft greens, even down to the mosses that had crept from between the old paving stones, and the fungi around the terra-cotta sculptures.

"I thought it was over," Francesca said.

"It was, until about a month ago. It felt quite strange, living without the demons—as if I'd found her and lost her at the same time. Perhaps she was at peace for all those months."

"Kurt said she was very depressed for a while."

Luciano shook his head. "I have no explanation."

"And how is it now?"

"I think she's close to the edge—it's like the bad old times, but much worse." He paused. "When will they arrive?"

"Tomorrow. Kurt is flying them to Perugia—they'll be with us just after lunch."

"How do you feel?"

Francesca took her brother's hand, and squeezed it. "Very nervous. And guilty for feeling that way." A bee hovered near her face, and she brushed it away. "Kurt says that she seems to be looking forward to it—that she's quite calm."

Luciano's face was bleak. "I don't believe that."

They came out through the tall, arched entrance gate, to await them in the dusty quadrangle. The twins, almost two years old, wore pink and blue matching shorts and T-shirts, and tugged at their mother's hands, keen to escape back into the cooler freedom of the garden. Kevin and Alicia, now nearly sixteen and fourteen, looked Californian and fit in tennis whites, and were bursting with curiosity to see their stepmother's mysterious sister.

"We look like a receiving line," Francesca said anxiously to Nick. "It might be too much for her."

Nick reached down for Andrea's hot little hand. "We look like a family, wanting to welcome her. Stop worrying."

Francesca glanced at Luciano. "All right?"

His face was drawn. "I'll wait inside," he said, and walked quickly back into the villa.

It was, as they had known it would be, strained and disappointing, the emotions of all involved held tightly in check. There was none of the ecstatic warmth and relief that Francesca and Luciano had experienced after their years apart, nor the explosive joy that Francesca and Nick had felt. This reunion was entirely different.

"Welcome to Villa Bel Canto," Nick said, shaking Kurt's hand and then, gently, kissing Juliet's cheek.

Francesca stepped forward and embraced her sister. "Welcome to your family, Juliet," she said, and her voice shook.

Juliet stood very still. She wore a sleeveless black linen dress with a white belt, and her hair was swept away from her oval face in a French twist. She looked cool and calm—almost detached.

"Thank you," she said.

Kurt's eyes, behind his spectacles, were on his wife's face. "A special moment," he said, quietly.

"For us all." Francesca smiled, and knew that her cheeks were very flushed. "Forgive me for staring at you, Juliet—I can't help it."

"I understand."

Kevin and Alicia were introduced, and Nick picked up Andrea, and grabbed Joe's plump arm, just before he toddled away toward the garden. "These are the twins—Andi and Joe."

"Go in garden!" Joe beamed.

Nick grinned. "What a pity Elizabeth can't be here."

"She's used to the English climate," Kurt said, trying to help. "We thought the heat would be too much."

Juliet raised her face, briefly, to the sun. "It seems we were right." She turned to Francesca. "Where is Luciano?"

"He's waiting for you inside." Francesca hesitated. "I think he wanted to meet you alone. He's terribly excited—and rather nervous, I'm afraid."

"I think we're all pretty nervous," Nick said easily. "It'll pass soon enough."

"I've been longing to meet you." Alicia seldom had trouble with new relationships. "You're a journalist, aren't you?"

"That's right."

"I'm thinking of studying journalism at school—maybe you could give me some advice?"

"Avoid it." Juliet looked into the eager, open young face. "It's a hard world. That's the best advice I can offer." She touched Kurt's arm. "Can we go inside?"

"Go in house," Andrea echoed.

The main hall was vaulted, white and blissfully dim after the relentless August sunshine. Nick and Kurt took the suitcases up the circular stone staircase, and Alicia and Kevin went through the frescoed *salotto* out onto the terrace.

Francesca and Juliet remained in the hall.

"Luciano's in the library," Francesca said. She wanted to say more, to be more physically demonstrative, but Juliet's stiff deportment forbade it. "Just through that door," she told her gently.

Nick showed Kurt their room, with its *en suite* bathroom and black marble bath. "She seems very calm," he said. "Is she, or is it a front?"

"Of course she isn't calm." Kurt took off his spectacles, and rubbed his eyes. "It was a difficult decision for her, you know that."

"Yes."

"But the right decision, of that I have no doubt." Kurt lightly massaged the bridge of his nose, before putting back the spectacles. "She's been working—for the first time since we met."

Nick smiled. "That must be a good sign."

Kurt nodded. "I'm sure it is."

She walked into the library, her high-heeled Ferragamo shoes clicking on the polished stone floor. The room was carved out of dark marble, its shelves filled with ancient, musty books. A majestic gold clock, twisted and ornate, ticked loudly.

Luciano and Juliet stood face to face.

"Are you really my twin?" she asked.

"You know I am." His throat was tight.

"Only because you tell me." She paused. "I don't know you at all." Her voice had a touch of dreaminess, its Englishness cool, like rain. "I wondered if there might be something, some old, suppressed recognition, perhaps." She shook her head. "But there's nothing."

"Not yet."

"No." She smiled slightly. "Can you really read my mind?" she asked curiously.

"Sometimes."

"Can you read it now?"

"No," he said. "Not now."

Again she smiled, without warmth. "I'm glad."

He could not. Just as they had stopped in London when he had seen her at the window, now the dreadful, clairvoyant thoughts had ceased again.

But there was no relief. For in their place was something infinitely harder to cope with, because he could share it with no one, and it filled him with shame.

He was afraid of her.

"I've never felt so disillusioned," he told Francesca later as they tucked the twins into their cots. "So let down."

"I suppose it was bound to be a great anticlimax. We knew it couldn't really be any other way, yet we all still hoped it might be."

"She isn't exactly hostile," Luciano said. "But she's so cold."

"Not with Kurt, or Elizabeth. At least we know, from him, that she's capable of warmth." Francesca sighed. "There's no reason for her to care for us. Not before she even knows us."

"More patience," Luciano said wanly.

"I think we have no choice."

Kurt watched Juliet changing for dinner. He loved to watch her dressing, or putting on her makeup, or brushing her teeth or even shaving her legs. It was those small things, he always felt, that stressed their intimacy.

He hesitated before speaking.

"Couldn't you be a little kinder, *Liebling?* They're all trying so hard."

"I know." She drew her stockings carefully up over her long legs.

"It's a great strain for you, I realize that more than anyone—but you seemed so cold, so remote."

"I feel remote." One of her polished fingernails pierced her right stocking, and she tugged it off again and tossed it into the wastebasket. "Kurt, please—I'm simply being myself."

"That's not true. My Juliet is a warm, responsive woman."

"Because of you. I am your Juliet—not theirs. They want something else—someone else. Someone I am not."

"You're wrong, *Liebling.* They want you."

Nick and Francesca lay in the great, soft-mattressed four-poster bed, close, but not touching. It was three in the morning.

"Are you all right?" he asked.

"I don't know."

"We knew it would be difficult."

"But not *this* difficult." In the darkness, Francesca brushed tears from her lashes. "She looks so like Luciano, but it might as well be a mask—hair exactly the same color and texture, the same lovely blue eyes. But I can see through his eyes, into his soul. With Juliet, I can't see anything—not even hatred."

"It's only the first night."

"I heard Alicia and Kevin talking. He said that he thinks she's 'really weird'—they stopped when they saw me."

"They didn't want to hurt your feelings."

"But that's just it—" Francesca screwed up the corner of the sheet into a ball. "I don't seem to *have* any genuine feelings for her. I was so sure I would—" She broke off.

Nick moved closer. Their bodies, naked, touched from their shoulders to toes, comfortingly. "Guilt," he said. "Piled on, through the years. When you were children, because she was dead—when you grew up, because you were happy—when you found she was alive, because you hadn't known." He paused. "And now, because you can't feel for her."

Francesca clung to him. "I do feel," she tried to explain, "but as I would for anyone who'd been through all she has—not as I should for my own sister."

"Give it time, *amore.*" Nick stroked her back. "Give her time."

Luciano began to get headaches.

Wherever they were—by the pool, on the terrace, sitting in the *salotto* beneath the sparkling chandelier, while Kurt tried to play Mozart on the harpsichord—Luciano was assaulted by sudden, violent pains in his head whenever he and Juliet came physically close together.

Francesca became concerned. "More aspirin? Perhaps you should ask Kurt."

"He's a plastic surgeon, not a general practitioner," he said, swallowing another pill with *acqua minerale.* "Anyway, it's just a headache. Probably the heat."

"You have heat in Nice—you don't get headaches there, do you?"

"Because of the sea," he said.

"Maybe," Francesca agreed.

The aspirin ceased to work.

And his fear magnified.

Chapter 35

YELLOW EARTH had been laid on the Campo, and each evening the Sienese came, as they had for centuries, to touch it. The wooden fencing around the center of the piazza had been erected; the benches were in place, and the judges' stand had been built. Thick mattresses had been placed at San Martino and Casato, the two most perilous corners of the track, where the jockeys were most likely to fall.

It was time for the *tratta*.

Three days before the Palio, in the morning, Nick, together with the other horse owners, brought Tosca, his chestnut mare, to the Cortile del Podestà to be considered. First, the veterinarian examined the horses, then the *capitani* of the ten participating *contrade* evaluated and voted on the animals, most of which they had already seen in action, some at the secret night trials held over the last few days.

Tosca was chosen. The next step was for the horses to be assigned to the *contrade*. By sheer chance—for it was fate, above all, that controlled the outcome of the Palio—Nick's mare was assigned to his family's ward. The Lupaioli cheered wildly, for Tosca was believed to be a promising *palio* horse—the members of Istrice, their archenemies, groaned, for even if they, too, drew a fine mount, their enemy had a good chance.

✳

That same evening, the first of the *prove*, the six trial-races, was held in the piazza, Tosca finishing in fourth place. After every trial, each horse was led back to its well-guarded stable, surrounded by singing, cheering *contradaioli*, in an informal parade that often passed, with deliberate provocation, through "enemy" territory. With each successive *prova*, the Sienese grew more frenetic, and fights between rival districts added to the seething atmosphere.

"This is really far out," Kevin enthused to Alicia as they followed Tosca from the Campo to her stable after the third trial-race. "It's half festival, half war—some of these people are almost crazed."

Near the top of the Via de Vallerozzi, there was a sudden commotion, as Tosca, upset by something, bucked without warning, struck a stone wall with a hind leg, and scattered the crowd.

"What happened!" Alicia craned her head, trying to see Nick. "Is Tosca all right?"

"I think it was a cat!" In spite of the heavy surge of people, Kevin managed to stay by his sister's side, holding her arm. "Dad told us she gets spooked by them."

Nick fought his way back to them. "I think it's time to get out of here—they've started throwing punches up in front!" His voice was raised above the growing roar of the crowd.

"Kevin saw a cat, Dad!" Alicia shouted.

"That's what caused the fight—some fool on our side accused Istrice of deliberately putting the cat in Tosca's path to scare her."

"Any ill effects?" Francesca asked Nick the following morning, after he had returned from a dawn visit to Tosca's stable. The whole family were assembled on the terrace for breakfast.

"A slightly bruised fetlock, but she'll be fine."

"Do you think someone did try to wreck it for Lupa?" Kevin asked his father.

"I doubt it," Nick said. "Siena's full of cats."

"I love the intrigue." Alicia grinned. "How many people knew about Tosca's phobia?"

Nick shrugged. "Her *barbaresco*—that's her groom—the jockey, the *capitano*—and us."

"Was anyone injured?" Kurt asked.

"The groom has a handsome black eye."

It was then that Francesca noticed that Luciano, his eyes furtive, was looking at Juliet, who stood at the serving table, helping herself to peaches and plums. The morning was already very warm, and Juliet had rolled up the long sleeves of her white, peasant-style blouse. Her left forearm bore a number of fine, red scratches.

They looked, to Francesca, like claw marks.

"Who's coming to the Mangia Tower?" Francesca asked, one hour after lunch the same day. "I'm going to shoot a few rolls of film up there."

"I'll carry your camera," Nick offered.

"What about the twins?" she said.

"We could stay with them," Kurt volunteered.

Juliet looked put out. "I'd like to go."

"All right, *Liebling,*" Kurt said lightly. "I'm happy to stay here on my own—I have to make some phone calls in any case."

"How high is the tower?" Alicia asked Francesca.

"Five hundred and three steps high."

"In this heat?" Alicia looked at Kevin. "How about a swim and a game of tennis?"

They knew they'd made a mistake before they reached the summit —it seemed as if at least half of Siena's population were trying to stimulate their appetites for the festive dinner that each competing district would hold that night.

"Why weren't we as bright as our children?" Francesca blew out her cheeks, her face scarlet with effort. It was impossible to stop for more than a moment, without creating a logjam of tourists on the steps.

"Not much farther," Nick encouraged her.

Francesca glanced back over her shoulder. "Any sign of the other two?" Juliet and Luciano had begun the ascent at the same time, but a group of energetic Swiss tourists had come between them.

"Forget them," Nick panted. "Save your breath."

"I'll never take any decent shots with all these people," she groaned. "My legs are killing me—"

"It'll be worth it for the view."

It was, once they were able to squeeze over to the parapet. The whole of Siena, its glorious red stone toasting in the hot afternoon sun, shimmered far below, and as they walked slowly around, the hazy green Tuscan countryside rolled out toward the horizon.

"Which way is Monte Amiata?" asked Nick. "I want to take a look."

"The other side, I think—I'll stay here." She held up her exposure meter. "I'll have to come back up one evening," she muttered to herself, and then, leaning over the parapet, she squinted through her camera at the piazza nearly ninety meters below the platform.

There were people all around her, their bodies brushing her, arms grazing, breath against her ear.

She felt a hand, on the small of her back.

Francesca began to turn. One second, the hand was there, seeming to position, to centralize itself—the next, it was pushing her, *shoving* her forward—

She stumbled, off balance. Propelled by the unseen hand, she tipped toward space—

"*Nick!*" she shrieked, clutching at the hot air—

He grasped her around the waist, grabbed at her hair, at her arm, dragging her back. "Dear God," he gasped, his lips white, "what were you *doing?*" He clutched her to his chest. "You could have been killed."

Francesca turned her face up to his, and her eyes were torn wide with shock and fright—

"There was a hand, Nick," she whispered, urgently.

"You're okay now." He held her close, protectively, but she pulled away—

"Someone pushed me," she said.

The tourists who had seen the incident cleared a path for them back to the steps, and Nick, making sure that Francesca was sufficiently recovered to climb down, went ahead of her.

Reaching the bottom, they walked wearily through into the Podestà courtyard, and saw Luciano, sitting on the ground.

They quickened their steps.

"What's wrong?" Francesca knelt by her brother. "Your head?"

He nodded, his forehead creased with pain. "It got really bad halfway up, so I turned back." With an effort, Luciano sat up straighter. "It's better now. Too much heat and too many people."

"Where's Juliet?" Francesca asked.

"I think she went to the top."

"We didn't see her."

Nick helped Luciano to his feet. "You really should ask Kurt about these headaches."

"My brother's too stubborn," Francesca said. "He prefers to suffer."

"I'll talk to him—he'll tell me to take aspirin, and not to climb high towers in the heat."

Francesca looked at her brother's strained face, and closed her eyes, feeling again the pressure of the hand against her back. Then she opened them, and looked toward the mass of tourists descending from the tower and milling around the Chapel of the Square.

There was no sign of Juliet.

✳

Back in the cool of the Villa Bel Canto, Kurt told them that Juliet had returned some time before, drained by the heat, and had gone to lie down.

"I think we'll miss the *contrada* dinner tonight," he told Nick. "We want to save all our energies for the Palio."

"That's a pity," Nick said. "For many people, tonight is the most enjoyable part of the ritual—the best night of the whole year."

"I know," Kurt smiled. "Singing, dancing, speeches—too much food and wine. All good reasons to stay here and relax—tomorrow is too important to be spoiled by a hangover. And besides, we can baby-sit for you."

"Francesca's already arranged a sitter."

"Then you can cancel the arrangement. We'll enjoy it, I assure you."

"Missing Elizabeth?" Nick said.

"Dreadfully."

Later, in the kitchen, Francesca found Juliet taking cold meats and cheeses out of the refrigerator.

"Everything okay?" Francesca asked.

"Perfectly." Juliet laid the cheeses on a board. "We'll eat early, on the terrace—we'll be able to hear the little ones if they cry."

"That's great—thank you." Francesca bent and sniffed at the slab of *pecorino.* "This always brings back memories," she said. "It was one of the things we stole from the larder at Palazzo Speroza when we ran away —it kept us going for a whole week." She smiled. "We were so hungry, your brothers and I."

"Just as well I wasn't there too."

Francesca looked into her sister's face. It was the first time Juliet had spoken, voluntarily, of the past. "You'll never know how much we wanted to have you with us," she said softly.

"I believe you." Juliet took a sharp knife, and cut paper-thin slices of Parma ham onto a plate, before returning it to the refrigerator. "Still," she said, and smiled, "a buried corpse was probably far less trouble."

Francesca and Nick bathed the twins together. Andrea and Joe sat happily in the lukewarm water, dark hair slicked back off their round, rosy-cheeked faces, little hands slapping up and down, splashing and making miniature waves.

"I don't think we should have canceled the sitter," Francesca said. "I'm not happy about leaving them."

"Leaving them at all, or leaving them with Juliet?"

"She was like ice, Nick. She intended to cause me pain." Francesca tipped a little shampoo onto her palm and rubbed it into her son's hair. Joe chortled with pleasure—neither he nor his sister had ever objected to water on their faces. "They're both strange, don't you think?" she asked uneasily. "Not wanting to come to the dinner. That wasn't just Juliet—Kurt seemed to prefer the idea of staying here too. They're a very tight couple."

"So are we." Nick finished rinsing Andrea's hair.

"Daddy ducks!" she demanded.

Francesca dive-bombed two plastic ducks into the water. "But we're tight—close—even when we're with other people. We've never excluded others from our lives. I get the impression that Juliet and Kurt could cloister themselves with Elizabeth, never needing another soul."

"He must see scores of people most days."

"But I'm not sure he'd mind if he didn't."

"Maybe you're right," Nick said. "We should stay here."

"But the dinner—it's so important."

"Not as important as your peace of mind, *amore*." Nick pulled out the bath plug, and Joe grasped it.

Francesca looked at him. Tonight, she knew, was the zenith of celebration, when everyone could still dream of winning. Nick had waited all his life for the Palio—she knew he would not go to the dinner without her.

"You think I'm worrying unnecessarily, don't you?"

Nick plucked Andrea out of the bath, and wrapped her snugly in a big white towel against his chest. "If Kurt weren't here, to be honest, I wouldn't dream of leaving your sister alone with these two, but—" He stopped short.

Francesca made up her mind. "We'll go." She forced herself to brighten. "I was overreacting."

"Are you sure?" Nick waited.

"Mommy go!" Joe said.

✶

Kurt and Juliet sat, an hour later, eating their supper on the terrace. They were very quiet.

"You could have gone with them," Juliet said. "I wouldn't have minded."

"I'd rather be with you, *Liebling,* you know that."

"Nick's very excited about the race."

"The culmination of a lifelong ambition—and the Palio excites many people." Kurt drank some wine. "I imagine that tomorrow will be a little like the ancient Coliseum—almost a struggle to the death—all those passions."

"He's a strange man. A Gypsy, an American rancher—and now a Sienese."

"I think he's always wanted this for his mother's sake. I believe she had a great influence on him." Kurt looked at Juliet. "As your mother had on you."

A dark shadow crossed her face.

"Which one?" she asked.

She left the table shortly afterward, saying that she would check on the twins, and then take a long, relaxing bath. She kissed him, and pressed her cheek against his. And left.

In the bedroom, she undressed and stood, naked, before one of the long antique mirrors. Despite her greater ease with her scars, she had never become able to look at her nude body without rekindling the old sense of shame and self-disgust. Two years were not long enough to unlearn a lifetime habit of averting her eyes from her own reflection— and it was, after all, not necessary, so long as Kurt could watch her with admiration—with love.

Now she forced herself to look.

The scars were still ugly. Improved by the operation, but ugly nevertheless. The difference was that they did not matter anymore. That, perhaps, had been Kurt's greatest gift to her.

She turned away, and sat on the edge of the bed. The pain in her mind, in her soul, was growing worse with every passing minute.

"*Which one?*"

That, in a sense, was what was tormenting her. That was what had changed everything, destroyed everything. It had begun with Francesca's letter—and ended with the visit to the cemetery—to the grave.

Kurt had helped her to survive the letter—yet he, with his limitless love and care, had been the one to finish it. To finish her. He had taken away, irretrievably, her ability to pretend that she was Juliet Austen Lindauer—the identity that had made her life tolerable. And he had not even realized what he had done.

She could not tell him. That was the saddest thing of all, for their mutual honesty and trust had always been precious to her. But now that, too, like everything good in her life, had been tainted—ruined.

She hated them so *much*. Her sister, so complacent in her marriage, her perfect life. Her brother—her parasite—who feared her more than he loved her—she could see it in his eyes. The hatred was so strong that she could taste it, like hot, bitter blood, in her mouth. Every moment she had spent with them, swallowing it down, had been nauseating, torturous. She had only borne it with the knowledge that she would, at last, be able to punish them. That was why she had come to Siena.

Small things, until now. The cat, to spoil their familial pleasure. The push, on the Mangia Tower, to frighten them.

And now, the child.

She went into the bathroom, and ran water into the great black marble bath, and then she dressed herself again, put on a plain white linen shift, and white canvas espadrille shoes, and wiped away her makeup, and brushed her hair, long and straight and simple. And then she walked, quietly, into the nursery.

They were fast asleep, lying on their backs on top of the sheets, their arms flung above their heads. Fraternal twins, like Luciano and herself, yet so very alike.

She looked at the little girl. Andrea Juliette—her namesake. When she picked her up, the boy stirred in his sleep, but did not wake. And when Andrea opened her eyes and looked into Juliet's face, but did not cry, Joe opened his eyes too, but was silent.

The child was heavy and sleepy in her arms, and her skin was soft and silky, and her scent was of talc and soap. And Juliet thought about Elizabeth, her exquisite golden baby, and the tears seeped from between her lashes and sprinkled onto her niece's dark head.

Swiftly, and noiselessly, Juliet carried Andrea out of the nursery and down the circular staircase, and out through the front door, and into the night.

In the *salotto*, Kurt played a Chopin nocturne on the harpsichord. In the bathroom, the water began to flow over the sides of the black marble bath.

And in the nursery, Joe began, at last, to cry.

Nick and Francesca and Kevin and Alicia were singing along with the rest of the Lupa *contradaioli*, as they sat at one of the long, cloth-covered tables set up in the street beneath fairy lights and flags—boisterous, provocative, partisan songs—when Luciano stood up, suddenly.

"Giulietta," he said, his voice hoarse.

Francesca stopped singing. "Luciano?" The chill, driven out by wine and atmosphere, was back in her belly.

"We have to go." His blue eyes were urgent.

"What's wrong?" Nick looked at his brother-in-law's face, and his skin crawled.

"The babies—" Luciano looked sick.

"Oh, my God." Francesca jolted to her feet. "I knew it—oh, dear God—"

"What's up?" Alicia asked, confused and unable to hear in the tumult.

"Something's happened—I think we're leaving," Kevin shouted.

The singing crescendoed.

Nick knocked over his chair and gripped his wife's hand.

"*Now!*" he commanded.

✳

No one spoke a word as Nick drove the rented Mercedes with violent, barely controlled speed out of the ancient walled city, back toward Villa Bel Canto. The moon was high and full, the stars massed and glittering, the tips of the cypress trees gleaming silver, the yellow stone houses turned white, the red-tiled roofs pale rose.

Kurt was standing in the quadrangle, near the arched gate, waiting for them. Francesca opened the door and jumped out, racing across to him. "What's happened?"

"They've gone." His face was chalky. "Juliet and Andi."

Francesca clutched at his arm as the car doors banged and the others ran over. "Gone? What do you mean *gone*?"

"Not Joe," Kurt said softly. "She left Joe."

Francesca gave a choking cry, and flew into the house, Alicia behind her.

"What happened?" Nick felt as if his bones had frozen. "God damn it, Kurt, tell me *exactly* what happened."

"I'm so sorry." Kurt shook his head, his distress acute. "I wanted to give her a little time to herself—a little peace for her bath, that's all—"

"How long?"

"I heard the pipes creaking—as they do when the taps are turned on —but they didn't stop, and when I—"

"How *long*?" Nick grasped his arm violently.

"About an hour—maybe a little more—"

"Dad, take it easy," Kevin said, and Nick dropped his hand to his side.

"Have you called the police?" Luciano asked. His heart pounded crazily, his headache was piercing.

"Half an hour ago. I waited a while—I thought she might come back, but—"

Francesca came running back out, her hair flying, her eyes wild. "Joe's all right."

Nick embraced her briefly. "It'll be okay. We'll find them." He looked at Luciano. "You and Kurt take one car." He looked at Francesca. "Do you want to stay here?"

"*No!*" She fought against tears. "Alicia said she'll look after Joe."

Kevin had already opened the doors of the Mercedes. "Come on," he said. "Let's go."

They went in opposite directions, their headlights on full beam whenever possible, driving slowly through the dark country roads, windows wound down so that they might hear any uncommon sound—a woman's voice, a child's weeping—

And later, they parked their cars and walked, separately, into the city, quiet now while most Sienese slept off the wine they had drunk during the evening. They stared into black alleys, peered at every woman they saw, and into every bar, every doorway, every church, before they returned to the villa to drink black coffee, check with the police, and then start the search again.

But though they looked all night, and right through the glory of the soft Tuscan sunrise, there was no sign of them; and when the Archbishop of Siena held mass at the foot of the Mangia Tower—and when the final *prova* was held in the Campo, the Dantes and Luciano and Kurt raked the seething crowds with weary, desperate eyes, but still they did not see either Juliet or her little niece.

"The police have their photographs," Kevin tried to reassure Francesca. "They'll find them."

"How can they *hope* to find them with tens of thousands of strangers filling the city!" Francesca burst out, violently distraught. "They won't find them—unless Juliet wants to be found."

Kevin could not argue with her, for Nick had told him the same thing. Of all the days of the year, this one was the most trying for the police, the most frenzied, the most unpredictable.

The ritual continued.

In the early afternoon, Tosca was taken to the church of San Rocco to be blessed, before being escorted by a group of Lupaioli in magnificent costume through the city to the Cortile della Prefettura, where all the groups and horses would assemble before the parade.

The Sunto, the bell of the Mangia Tower, began to ring, calling all *contrade* into the square. Flags waved, drums were beaten, and, as if by magic, the streets of Siena were drained of life, the city's heart and soul sucked into the pulsating, steaming Campo.

At five o'clock, they all reassembled in the *salotto* at the villa. The atmosphere crackled with tension and strain and fear.

"She's dangerous." Francesca held Joe on her lap, aware that he wanted to get down, but not letting him move. She spoke in a harsh whisper. "I knew it—Luciano felt it. We should never have left them with her."

"I should have listened to you." Nick's voice was agonized.

Kurt rose from his chair, his eyes unreadable behind his spectacles. "Juliet won't hurt Andi," he said.

"How can you be sure?" Alicia asked, and blushed hotly, seeing his pain.

"He can't," Francesca said dully.

Abruptly, Nick looked at his watch. "I think we should go. I know it sounds crazy, but I think we should go to the Palio."

Francesca stared at him in disbelief.

"Not for the race," Nick went on. "We have seats on the *piano nobile*—with binoculars, we'll be in the best possible place to see the whole square."

"Dad's right," Kevin said gently. "If Aunt Juliet is still in Siena, the Campo's got to be the place she's most likely to be."

"What do you think, Kurt?" Nick asked.

Kurt nodded. "It's possible."

"Get *down!*" Joe protested, and began to cry.

Francesca released him. She was looking at Luciano, who had said nothing for several minutes. "What about you, Luciano?" She paused. "You knew at the dinner that something was wrong. Don't you know where she is now?" Her voice was brittle with tension. "Can't you *feel* her?"

"No." Luciano was very white beneath his tan. "I can't feel her at all." His eyes were full of tears. "I'm sorry," he said, and turned away.

The pressure in his head was worse than ever.

Chapter 36

IT WAS TWILIGHT.

The Campo was full to bursting. Every window and balcony overlooking the piazza was packed with spectators—even the rooftops were perilously crowded. After more than two hours, the parade was at an end, and the devoted *contradaioli* were peering up at the weathervane on the summit of the Mangia Tower, to see at which *contrada* it was pointing, for it was believed that this would be the victorious district.

The *mortaretto* was fired for the first time, to clear the track—startled pigeons soared into the sky, and once again, the superstitious checked their direction for an omen. Siena was at fever pitch.

In the Cortile del Podestà, the jockeys and horses waited nervously. The *fantini* had removed their ceremonial costumes, and now wore the riding habits of their respective *contrade*—they splashed water on the insides of their trousers to help them grip the bare backs of their horses more effectively.

"*A cavallo!*" came the order. They mounted.

The *mortaretto* was fired again. The ten *fantini* began to ride toward the track—each was presented with a *nerbo*, their special *palio* whip, by the same two policemen who, moments earlier, had frisked them for concealed weapons.

They approached the starting enclosure.

✳

"There's Tosca." Kevin spotted her first, as the mare, coat gleaming, her special Palio head ornament in place, was ridden to the starting rope.

No one else spoke. Francesca, Nick, Luciano, and Kurt sat rigid in their seats, their binoculars clamped to their eyes, scanning the crowd from north to south, east to west. Their eyes burned with strain, their lips were taut, perspiration ran down their straight, aching backs.

Kevin looked at Alicia, who sat right at the back of the balcony, under the shade, playing with Joe. Nick had wanted them to stay at the villa, but Francesca had refused to be parted from her son. Alicia met Kevin's eyes and smiled tensely.

"See horses," Joe said.

"Later, darling," Alicia replied.

All of Siena was focused on the starting rope. Nick, Luciano, and Kurt were still scanning the crowd below.

Francesca lowered her binoculars, and turned her head.

Suddenly, she was watching Luciano.

✷.

Down in the Campo, adrift in an ocean of people, deaf to the tumult, blind to the flags and to the vibrant colors and to the open, shrieking mouths, she stood, not far from the fence that divided spectators from the track. Her fate, unlike that of the ten jockeys, was already sealed.

She stared up at the *piano nobile,* saw the rich, red velvet banners, saw her family. She could not see their faces or their expressions, but she knew that they were willing her to return to them.

But she could not.

It had all turned upon herself—all the hatred, the revenge, the malice. The child had brought her to her senses, had shown her what she had to do. So innocent, so blameless, as she must have been at that age. She had realized then that she could not hurt the child—had known, with a dull certainty, that when, months ago, in their peaceful house in Hampstead, she had read about the Palio, and had imagined a body lying crushed beneath the trampling hooves, it had not been her sister, nor her brother, nor the small, sweet child—

She could never go back. For she no longer knew who she was.

I am not Giulietta. The thought rolled around, like a hard, heavy marble, in her mind. *And if I ever was, you buried me, in a lonely grave. Abandoned me. Buried me.*

She half pushed, half slithered between the roaring men and women, getting closer—

I wanted no part of you. I am the daughter of an English doctor, the wife of Kurt Lindauer, the mother of Elizabeth. I could have been happy, at last, but you wouldn't let me.

There was no one to stop her now—no one even to see, until it was too late.

You buried me, but you wouldn't let me rest. Even Kurt, poor, loving Kurt, had to show me the truth. Or the lie.

Her hands were on the wooden boards. Bodies squeezed against her, hot, sweating flesh stuck to her. The air steamed, her blood pounded in her head. She could see the jockeys at the start, their faces alive with tension—she could see Tosca, foaming at the mouth—

If I was Giulietta, then I am rotting in a grave near Pisa—

The tenth horse had begun to gallop toward the rest. The starter dropped the rope.

It was a good start.

The crowd bellowed.

Istrice, Bruco, and Aquila fell at Casato, the horses whinnying in panic, their jockeys crashing against the mattresses. The others thundered on.

She saw them coming closer, for the second time.

So if I am Giulietta, how can I live?

Tosca and her jockey had fallen at San Martino. Kevin was out of his seat, caught up, for just one moment, in the fever of Palio, while Nick and Kurt still searched, in grim, silent concentration, through their glasses.

But Francesca, again, was staring at Luciano, mesmerized by him, unable to move, to breathe—

And then, without warning, he began to scream, and the binoculars crashed to the floor, and his eyes were torn open wide in anguish, his arms outstretched in despairing, demented appeal—

"*Giulietta!*"

And Francesca came to life.

"Is Andi with her?" She clamped her own glasses to her eyes, but saw nothing. "Can you see *Andi?*" she shrieked at her brother.

"There!" Nick grasped her arm, dragged her to the parapet, stabbed his finger down, toward the track.

And only the people watching from above, or those closest to the red earth, witnessed the full horror, saw the woman's crushed body, and the spurting blood, and the snorting, maddened horses and the bleached, terrified faces of the jockeys—

Francesca clung to Nick, and her binoculars fell heavily against her breasts, and the tears poured from her eyes—and she heard her own wailing, and saw Luciano's possessed, haggard expression, and she turned, for a moment, to Kurt—

But he had already gone.

And in his place stood a policeman, holding a small girl in his arms. She had dark curly hair, and wore a pale lemon nightgown.

Francesca was beyond words. Nick, ashen and openly weeping, moved first, taking Andrea from the policeman. She was dusty and sleepy, but completely unharmed. For a moment, Nick held his daughter very close, felt her heartbeat against his own, the returning pressure of her strong little arms—and then he gently pushed Francesca down onto a seat, and placed Andrea onto her lap.

"*Amore,*" he said, softly.

They had found her, the policeman said, after the city had emptied into the Piazza del Campo, at the top of the steps of the Duomo—at the foot of the single column bearing a sculpture of the she-wolf with Romulus and Remus.

There had been no sign of her aunt, but Andrea had held on to a scrap of paper, a note—

> *May she be like Romulus, the more*
> *fortunate twin.*
>
> *Giulietta*

And Luciano knew, now, when it was too late, how wrong he had been—how falsely he had read her thoughts—knew that even he, who had believed he could see into her mind, had never truly understood her.

He had been so afraid of his sister, near the end. But he should, above everything, have been afraid *for* her. For if he had only realized that one thing, he might have saved her.

And now it was too late.

They held two services for her.

The first was in a tranquil English churchyard. The sky was gray, the trees rich summer green, and a pair of magpies watched from a nearby chestnut tree as the coffin of Juliet Austen Lindauer was lowered into the earth beside her mother's grave.

The second was in a hot Italian cemetery not far from Pisa, where quiet words were spoken, and tears were shed over a bank of wild Tuscan flowers, in memory of a child long since departed—named Giulietta.

Chapter 37

KURT HAD DONE it for her, out of love.

He had seen her eyes, pleading, burning blue out of the bloody ruins of her face, and even before she had been able to whisper to him, he had understood what she had wanted him to do for her. And although it had been unthinkable, an affront to everything he had ever believed in or practiced, he had known that he, better than anyone, had the power to help her.

He had told the doctors, when they reached the *ospedale,* that he would take over her case, that he would transfer her to his own clinic, that he would take full responsibility. And by the time Francesca and Nick and Luciano had stumbled into the hospital in Siena, he and Juliet were already in a private ambulance on the road to Perugia.

And he had flown her, in the Learjet, to the Lindauer Klinik, and he had operated on her, for the first time, one hour later. And he had telephoned Francesca late the same night, had told her that he had been unable to save Juliet, and that they should not come—that she had begged him, before she had died, not to let them see her as she was—she wanted them to remember her as she had been.

He had flown to London, a few days later, with the sealed coffin. And after the funeral, and the memorial service, he had closed the house in Hampstead, and had taken Elizabeth, and brought her back to Switzerland.

He had shut off the whole west wing of the clinic for her, and only his closest colleagues were allowed to enter, while the operations continued.

And they had repaired her shattered bones and torn flesh. And Kurt had given her a new name, and slowly, painfully, a new face, and the promise of a new life, safe from the past.

And she was responding, almost as she had as a child, with silent stoicism against the agony, and with the dull torpor of drug-induced calm. And Kurt did not know if her soul would ever recover. Or if she would forgive him.

But he would make her body whole again. And he would protect her, and take care of her, and of their daughter, for the rest of his life, no matter what.

Livia had done it out of hate.

This was different.

Chapter 38

On the last day of 1977, New Year's Eve and the third anniversary of Nick and Francesca's marriage, family and close friends, except for Kurt and little Elizabeth, gathered at Sonora for a quiet celebration—for if there was anything they had all learned from the tragedy, it was that, more than ever, they needed to be together whenever possible.

Very late that night, in the early hours of 1978, when the others had gone to their beds, Francesca asked Nick to come out of the house with her.

"Where are we going?" he asked.

"Wait and see."

And she drove him, bemused and icy cold, in an open-topped Jeep, along silent, frosty Sonora lanes, past barns and stables and water towers and outbuildings, until they came to a patch of forest. And then she turned off the motor, and took a flashlight from the glove compartment, and tugged him by the hand through the dark trees until they came to a clearing—

"I don't believe it," Nick said.

For it was the same clearing in which he had prepared that precious, fateful picnic lunch back in the summer of 1971—where he had seduced her, knowing that he was wrong to do so, yet hoping beyond hope that he was right.

And instead of sunshine, they had starlight, and Francesca had planted a circle of flaming torches to light and warm them—but in every other detail, it was as it had been then, from the crisp white cloth on the grass, to the hamper and the fried chicken, and the Cristal champagne—

And after a while, Francesca disappeared for a few moments into the dark, and when she returned, she was leading a horse by a neck rein.

And Nick saw that it was the same palomino mare of that long-ago, idyllic summer afternoon, and then he saw the glitter in his wife's beautiful dark eyes—

"It's winter," he said. "It's the middle of the night—we'll freeze to death—"

"No, we won't." She pulled him to his feet.

"We're parents now," he protested.

But Francesca just smiled, and kissed him on the mouth.

In his guest room, back at the house, Luciano stood at the window, as the Jeep returned from the forest. And he saw Nick help Francesca down, saw their arms twined about each other, saw her lean her head on his shoulder. And Luciano's eyes pricked with tears of longing and despair.

The crumpled, scratched-out pages of the new novel sat on the desk at the other side of the room, abandoned after yet another abortive attempt.

He needed so badly to do that one thing for her. But he could not work on this manuscript, or on any other.

He had thought that they would stop after she was dead.

But they had not. They had continued, on and on, and now they were louder, more clamorous than ever. And it was almost like starting all over again, from the beginning—the agony, the fear, the despair and isolation. She was in his head, in his brain, invading his soul even from the grave. And Luciano knew now that he would never be free of them.

And he did not know if he could bear it.